BRAIN DAMAGED

by

David Owain Hughes

A HellBound Books Publishing LLC Book
Houston TX

David Owain Hughes

**A HellBound Books LLC
Publication**

Printed in the United States of America

Other David Owain Hughes Titles
<u>Novels, Novellas and Short Story Collections:</u>
All-Wound Up
Wind-Up Toy
Wind-Up Toy: Broken Plaything
Wind-Up Toy: Chaos Rising
White Walls and Straitjackets
Escapees and Fevered Minds
Choice Cuts
Walled In
Man-Eating Fucks
Man-Eating Fuckers
The Rack & Cue
Collision Course
Granville
Home Improvements
Psychological Breakdown
Brain Damage
Puckered
<u>Anthologies:</u>
Shadows and Teeth Vol.3
Trapped Within
Hell of a Guy
Unleashing the Voices
Rejected for Content Vol. 4, 5 & 6
Crossroads in the Dark Vol.1 & 2
Fifty Shades of Slay
How to Cook a Baby
Madame Movora's Tales of Terror
Big Book of Bootleg Horror Vol. 1, 2 & 3
Shopping List
Depraved Desires
Easter Eggs and Bunny Boilers
Bah! Humbug!
Slashing Through the Snow
VS Vol. 1 & 2
Black Candy
Into the Abyss
<u>Compiled & Edited Anthologies:</u>
What Goes Around
Man Behind the Mask
Fuck the Rules

Foreword

Brain damage [brān dăm'ĭj] n. When your penis hurts after a vigorous blowjob.

Oops. That's the Urban Dictionary definition. My bad. Let's try this again.

Brain damage [brān dăm'ĭj] n. Injury to the brain that impairs its function, especially permanently.

Brain damage is, in a nutshell, the degeneration or destruction of brain cells. If you've ever read any of David's work before, you might be inclined to believe he indeed suffers from brain damage based on that definition. However, I assure you he does not. I mean, would a man ailing from such affliction wave at you while he's standing in the bushes outside your living room with his pants around his ankles, free arm moving frantically near his crotch?

No—that's just good manners.

That's David Owain Hughes.

Would some dude with an impaired noggin bring you Man-Eating Fucks (and Fuckers), Wind-Up Toy(s), White Walls and Straight Jackets, Escapees and Fevered Minds, plus a slew of more dark novels, novellas, short stories, and even drabbles? Would he gather together yet *more* stories featuring everything ranging from one-titted roller-girl zombies and hot, tatted creatures of the night to confused serial killers, Hellish ghosts, and more Man-Eating Fucks, call it Brain Damaged, and put it up for sale?

Would he purposely elicit hard-ons or wet panties with simple words in a story?

Wait—what? He would?

Well, yeah, David is prone to bouts of irritability, increased aggressiveness, impatience, hysteria, and lunacy. And he must have suffered lack of oxygen to his gray matter at some point—his apparent penchant for autoerotic asphyxiation is pretty obvious, really. He chuckles when we squirm while reading his unapologetic brand of horror containing bucketloads of filth, smut, dark humor, gore . . .

Well, shit. That certainly fits the definition.

David Owain Hughes is brain-damaged.

For our sake—and the sake of the horror community at large—let's hope he stays that way.

Jonathan Edward Ondrashek – The Human-Undead War Trilogy

BRAIN DAMAGED

Contents:

Brief Encounter

Why have those beers? James thought, smashing his hand against the steering wheel. He clenched his jaw until it clicked. Tears threatened. *I'll never make it to Mark and Lilly now, not with how the fucking traffic is.* He hammered the dash.

"And why, *why* did I have to get caught sleeping in my office by Derek and his limp-wristed goon, Chris? *Damn.* Bastards will never let me live it down." He shook the steering wheel, his neck turning red and his eyes bulging. "Oh, we thought you'd already left, James," he mimicked Derek's voice. "*Fag.*"

Turning to look out his passenger window, James saw a man in a car moving towards him from the opposite direction, on the other side of the road. He was staring, smiling and shaking his head.

"*Hey*! What are you smiling at, pal?" James gesticulated, the veins in his neck protruding. "I'll punch your lights out and kick your teeth down your throat." James raised his middle finger, but the man was talking on his mobile phone and seemed disinterested, looking away as he passed.

Good thing you're moving, mate, or I would have flattened your beak.

James swivelled his head and scanned the sea of metal before him, which disappeared around a corner, out of sight.

Like a metal snake…

He blew his horn. "Come on, some of us have children at home on Halloween waiting for their dads to get home." James saw his flushed face in the rear-view mirror and his children's fancy-dress costumes lying on the parcel shelf.

"I want to be a pumpkin princess, Daddy!" Lilly, three, had squealed when asked what she'd like to wear for trick or treat adventures with James and her older brother, Mark.

"There are no such things, dipshit!" Mark, five, had interjected.

Mark and Lilly's mother, Millie, had jumped down her son's throat for using such language in front of her and his sister. James had heard the background conversation over the phone as he spoke to his daughter, all the while imagining how cute Millie used to look with a black eye.

The thought aroused him.

Wouldn't mind giving her—

"Mark's in trouble again, *Daddy."*

This brought a smile to James' face. *You're always one for stating the obvious, chicken.*

His gaze shifted from the pumpkin costume to Mark's Jason Voorhees outfit.

"He's a badass, Dad," Mark had whispered down the phone, letting James know Millie was still close by – she liked to hear what the children said to him when in her company.

"She thinks you poison our minds, Dad – whatever that means," Mark had confided one Saturday when the lad was in his care.

Bitch. If I don't get there in time to pick them up, she'll use it against me and won't let me see them for weeks. Maybe months, he thought.

"Just let her try." His grip tightened on the wheel. "She'll be nursing more than a broken jaw." James' eyes narrowed.

The traffic was unmoving, doing little for his temper.

"Sorry, Lilly. Sorry, Mark – doesn't look like Daddy's making it home for Halloween. Crap."

Like his children, James loved the spooky holiday which had helped get him into the game-designing industry. He'd never forget playing such classics on the holiday as *Resident Evil*, *House of the Dead* and *Silent Hill*, to name a few.

Before Millie had fallen pregnant, James had planned to move to Japan so he could get a job with Nintendo, or one of the other big game companies. He had good references, a solid work history in the business, and awards to his name.

But then Mark came along, setting James' plans back.

"It'll be easier when he's a little older, James," Millie had argued.

"The schools there are great, and it'll be easier for him to learn the language whilst he's a baby," he protested.

Millie had none of it. She put her foot down and took control of the situation, much like she had with the relationship in the early years.

Like the gutless wimp I'd been, I took it on the chin and let her crush my dreams under her heels. My balls belonged to her, he thought.

When Lilly made her appearance, James knew his plans were well and truly scuppered – there was no way Millie would leave. Not only that, but Millie's parents didn't want her moving halfway around the world with *their* grandchildren.

"You can make as much money here, James, if not more. Hell, with your achievements, you could sign your own ticket," Millie told him.

He hadn't bothered wasting his breath trying to explain the opportunities Japan, their companies and workers could offer him – it wasn't about money. Well, not all of it. And, even though he was exceptional at his job, he wasn't getting any younger, with no overseas training, which was something influential businesses were looking for in candidates.

James found himself stuck in the company he'd joined upon leaving University, which he took as failure. With this came misery, and soon the once-gifted employee who'd had it all found himself deflated, the hunger, desire and passion burned from him.

He became a mediocre worker. When various openings presented themselves within his corporation, James didn't bother engaging. His big chance in life had been snatched away, and it hadn't taken long for cold, hard bitterness and resentment to grow within him.

Still, he never took his frustration out on the children. He loved them and would do anything for them.

Millie was always his target, and when he got upset or frustrated at work, she'd get a smack, and he loved it. However, she only took his abuse for a couple of years, even though he thought he'd hit the tough bitch out of her and broken her.

When she found the courage to stand up, walk away, and take him to court, James knew his life would never be the same.

Barely kept my job when it all came out, he thought, his face flushing.

A restraining order was put in place, but Millie didn't stop or want to keep him from seeing the children, even though she felt he deserved it.

Calm down. There's no point thinking about the past. Since she's been out of my life, I've been a different person.

He turned on the radio.

"Happy Halloween!" screamed a rock DJ. "Time for some Alice Cooper on this, the most frightful night of the year, kids. Aaaaoooooowww!" he howled like a wolf.

"Ha-ha!" James laughed. "Howling Henry never fails to raise a smile."

Music kicked in, and Cooper was off singing about a haunted house.

James' rage died as he looked out his windshield, his head resting against his window. His fingers drummed the steering column and he sang along to the slow, sombre, creepy tune.

A mass of brake lights glared in the cold, blustery autumn evening with the setting sun as a backdrop; it tainted the clouds with a pink-orange hue, reminding him of summer peaches, ripe for picking. Crisp leaves had gathered on the bonnet of his stationary vehicle as the first spots of fat raindrops hit his windshield. The wipers kicked in automatically, sweeping aside the gathered foliage.

Gazing to his left, James spied a lone, limp scarecrow in a large, unkempt field – an unkindness of ravens had settled on the battle-torn Scarer of Black Birds. Tufts of hay jutted from the thing's tatty, outsized and hanging clothes.

Not something you see every day – an anorexic scarecrow, he thought, a smile parting his lips. A laugh escaped him.

Rotted pumpkins were dotted here and there, with a ramshackle farmhouse looming in the backdrop. Most of the slate was missing from the roof, the windows smashed, the doors amiss and one of the chimney-stacks had toppled most of its bricks.

In that instant, James thought he saw a large silhouette standing beyond the building's front door-frame. He squinted, positive something or someone was moving around inside what he assumed to be an abandoned house.

The rain started falling heavier, reducing his vision.

"Bloody imagination. Guess that's what you get when you design scary games for a living," he muttered, reaching a hand over to the passenger seat and resting it on the CD there. "You're going to love this, Mark."

That's if I ever get home.

James loosened his tie and rolled down the passenger window. When he did so, he noticed the cars on the opposite side slow until they came to a grinding halt, forming a neat line. Horns blared.

"Yeah, now you know how I feel," he said, staring out his window. He couldn't help but cackle like a witch when he saw drivers explode with anger: some were shouting, and others were waving their arms and hitting their dashboards as they ranted at their passengers. "Welcome to my world."

He turned the radio up and relaxed into his seat.

No point stress—

A teeth-rattling blast rocked James' car – the windows vibrated and a crack appeared in his windscreen, jarring the wipers to a mid-swipe stop.

"What the—?" James studied the rear-view mirror as a second explosion tore the early evening asunder. A ball of flame and smoke mushroom-clouded into the air a few hundred yards behind – the heat and smell carried on the wind and worked their way into his car via the open window and vents.

Black smoke engulfed him, along with tiny particles of ash.

Sweat broke across his brow and trickled down his face.

"*Ugh*!" James retched, pressing a button on the door to control the window. "Jesus! The hell happened back there?"

The drivers around him didn't seem to notice. Or care.

"People are cold machines these days, man," James muttered, reaching for his mobile phone, which he always kept in the small compartment by the gear-stick. But it wasn't there. "Where—damn it, I've left it at the office. Great. Just great. I can't ring emergency services, let alone Millie to inform her of my lateness. Not that I would, anyway."

"Always thinking about yourself, James, you selfish son-of-a-bitch," he heard her say.

"It's that mouth of yours that gets you in trouble, whore," he regularly told her in front of their children.

"What example are you setting for your son?"

She'd had the salt to say that to him only once, for he'd broken her jaw with a fierce hook and a wind-stealing jab to the guts. When she was doubled over, James had yanked her head back by her hair and jabbed his finger in her nose as he spoke.

"Say that again and I'll rip your goddamn lungs out!"

He let her go. Sniffling, with blood spilling from her nose and mouth, Millie got to her knees to retrieve her smashed teeth, which reminded James of broken Tic Tacs. When she stuck out her hand, James stepped on her fingers, breaking three.

"Argh!!"

"Like dry kindling, Millie."

"Crap. Fancy leaving my phone at work? Derek and the other jokers will mess with it. Bastards rang a shit-ton of sex lines and takeaways the last time they—"

A glow from behind made him turn in his seat. Brow furrowed, his eyes narrowed as he looked out the back window. The blaze-like light was coming from a half a mile or so up the road but he couldn't see its source.

"I wonder if that tanker that passed me earlier hit something. Why isn't anyone doing anything, like getting out of their vehicles to investigate, or call the police?" When he observed the drivers opposite, they appeared to be motionless. Robots. They sat rigor-mortis still, their faces front and centre.

They were angry a moment ago.

As if they'd read his mind, they turned to glare at him, one by one: men, women and children. A coldness like he'd never felt before inched its way down his body. Chills nestled in his guts and scrotum, feeling as though he had ice-snakes writhing inside him.

His scalp itched, and his hands were sweaty.

"What's going on?" At that moment, he was thankful for the rain on his windows, for their view, like his, distorted, and he couldn't see their eyes. "Why—" He thought better of speaking again and turned to look out his windscreen.

They'll lose interest…

"…And here's another classic for you crazy—*aaaaoooooowww*—kids on this special night," Howling Henry barked, breaking James' train of thought.

As "The Monster Mash" kicked in, James turned his head so he could eyeball the people opposite him, but couldn't tell if they were still gawking his way.

What am I, a fish in a bowl?

Before James could fully investigate, a horn from behind stole his attention. It was alerting him to the fact that their lane was moving, and so he put his car in gear and drove. After a few hundred feet, he came to a stop and engaged the handbrake.

Howling Henry continued to DJ – the news nor traffic report interrupted.

"Can't have been an accident," he said, turning in his seat to peer through the back window again. Nothing, apart from the same red glow – smoke still hung in the air. "Odd." He checked both wing and rear-view mirrors in case he'd missed something.

He faced front and resumed tapping his fingers on the wheel.

No more memory lane bull or thinking the other drivers are staring at me in unison. It was coincidence.

"Huh, the rain's stopped. When did that happen?" James rolled both front windows down but was tempted to do them back up when smoke entered. "Ooh, the cool air is nice, man. Goddamn stuffy in here."

All around, horns honked, headlights flashed and people yelled obscenities and threats of violence from their vehicles, as their tolerance grew thinner by the minute.

James' car clock read seven-thirty.

"*Two* hours I've been sat here like a lemon." He grabbed the game from off the seat beside him and looked at it – *Hell Beasts at Nightmare Beach*. This was James' baby, and was still in pre-production. He'd planned to play the game to the end with Mark tonight to see if there were any kinks. James was also hoping his son would make suggestions on what to remove, make better or ramp up (gore-wise).

He tossed the game back onto the seat.

"That's not going to happen now."

Before leaving for work that morning, James had trimmed his house of Halloween silliness in readiness for the children, knowing they would love it, especially the fake blood he'd plastered all over the house and massive plastic cobwebs with giant spiders attached to them in the hallway.

James had also lined up a few guests to come over – friends of his and their children – along with games such as bobbing and swinging apples, Blind Man's Bluff and musical chairs with eerie music.

"People are probably wondering where I am – I'll have hundreds of missed calls on my phone come Monday. And the food. *Shit*. It'll all be as hard as a rock by the time I get home."

"Hey, handsome," came a voice. "Been stuck here long?"

"*Huh?*" James turned and saw a woman parked opposite him. A scream lodged in his throat when he saw her disfigured face: the left side appeared to have been eaten away by an alligator or half-starved cannibal, the eyeball gone. Dried blood graced her chin, cheeks and the chest area of her top. Her smile was lopsided.

"See a ghost?" She laughed. "Happy Halloween."

He then realised it was make-up, and huffed out a laugh. "Jesus, you scared the living hell out of me."

"We're all entitled to one good scare on Halloween."

"I guess so. Two hours, in answer to your question."

"Oh, not too bad. I've been here *years*."

"It's starting to feel the same for me, Miss…?"

"Croft. Miss Silvia Croft, at your service, er…"

"James. James Foster. Going anywhere special?" He indicated her make-up and attire.

"*Hm*? Oh!" She looked down at herself. "I was meant to be going to a Halloween dance with my boyfriend—"

"Boyfriend?"

Shit, I hope I didn't sound disappointed. Going to think I'm a loser. She didn't seem to notice, as she stared over his shoulder into space. Her mouth moved, but her eyes were unflinching. The ice-snakes returned to his belly. *She looks robotic.*

"Yeah, boyfriend. I'll never see him again, not now."

At that, James expected tears to burst from her good eye.

"Bit drastic, don't you think? It's only a traffic jam. I'm sure—maybe…we could hook up for a drink?" He smiled, giving her a cheeky wink.

"Drastic? Traffic jam? How long did you say you—?"

Another explosion.

James ducked in his seat, covering his head with his hands. "*Fuck*?!" He looked out the rear window, spotting plumes of smoke and orange-red glow and, if he wasn't mistaken, the tips of flames.

Another accident? Impossible…

"I would love to have had a drink with you, though. You're handsome." When she smiled, blood trickled from her eye, nose and mouth. "We'll never get that opportunity. Sad. Say, why don't you come over here and hug me, James? I'm cold. So very, very cold."

"You're *bleeding*, Silvia. Or is that some kind of Halloween effect you've got going on with your costume?"

"Please. Hold me. I need to feel the embrace of a man once more before I swim His Lake of Fire. I've been on this road so long, James, waiting my turn." Her teeth chattered, a worm wriggled out of her ear and a spider scurried across her face.

She got out of her seat and leaned through her window, her arms reaching, gnarled fingers with their broken, chipped nails seeking him out. "I'm cold." Her breath was visible. Her chest was ravaged, and when her midriff appeared, her guts spilt out and splashed to the floor – blood sprayed up and landed on James' passenger seat. "So cold." Her dirty digits latched onto his door. "Kiss me, James." Her tongue came at him like a writhing snake, zigzagging from her mouth at an impossible length.

"Holy shit!" James reached for the control switches on his door and pressed the button that operated the passenger window. It whined and smoked as it tried to lift out of its slit – Silvia held it down.

"You can't escape your fate, James. You might as well accept it and be with me before our final moment."

"I don't know what you're talking about."

"Do you know how long I've waited for a man, James?" The tip of her tongue caressed his cheek, making him squeal and bat it away. "Fifty years. Fifty years I've been on this road—"

"And here's one from Chris Rea, kids –, the King of Rock. *Aaaaoooooowww!*"

James smashed his fist against the radio, killing it, before reaching for the gear stick and putting it in first.

"Where do you think you're going, James?" Silvia was now half in, half out of his and her car. She put a bloody handprint on his glove compartment and dashboard. "There's no escape."

Before James knew it, Silvia was sat next to him, her entrails coiled around the handbrake, tongue buried in his ear. "Don't you find me sexy? I was Miss UK sixty years ago, before I was killed and gutted by a psycho, that is. You don't age on this road, James – you stay the same as you were when you got here."

With that, Silvia angled the rear-view so she could view herself. "I see a beautiful woman with lush hair, a tight body and a fantastic rack."

James closed his eyes, gripped the wheel and tried holding his bladder and bowels together. "Please. I don't know what's going—don't hurt me."

"Oh, James, silly – I'm not going to hurt you – unless you like that kind of thing? I just want a last encounter with a man, no matter how brief."

"I don't know what you mean—" His voice pitched high when her bony fingers slipped between his thighs and grabbed his crotch.

"Don't be coy."

"I want to go home to my children." His chin wobbled, and tears slid down his cheeks. When he turned and looked out the window, he noticed he was parked opposite the tumbledown farmhouse with the dingle-dangle scarecrow. "No! I passed that ages ago."

And then he *did* see something move in the swaying field: a large, looming, black shape with a curved, bladed implement slung over its shoulder. The figure didn't seem to walk but rather floated.

"He has worker bees, you know?"

"Who?" James whispered, allowing her hand and tongue to continue their molestation.

"Death." Another boom burst to life from behind, followed by a second, third and fourth. "Do you know what that noise is?" She nibbled his earlobe.

James shook his head.

"That's Death's master feeding us naughty little boys and girls to His Lake of Fire, James."

"But—but—"

"You're dead, hunny. Don't you get it? I hate to break it to you and that pretty face of yours. What was it, car crash? That's what I'd guess, with your smashed-in chest and crushed head. Die on impact?"

"I—" James grabbed the rear-view and looked in it. He saw a man in his late thirties, reasonably good-looking but slightly haggard. And then he *felt* his face, finding it deformed; his chest and stomach, too. "*Argh!*" He yanked his hand back. "What? Where? How?" he panted and spluttered. "Silvia—"

"*Shh*," she soothed, putting her fleshless index finger to his lips. "There's no need to be scared. I'm here with you, and we'll ride the waves together. Now, hold me."

"*I thought you'd already left?*" he heard Derek's words reverberate inside his head.

"Had I?" James said. "Had I left and not fallen? Was I dead, not sleeping in my office?" His jaw sagged. "I'm—*dead*? Gone? *Forever*? Lilly, Mark…" Tears slipped down his face.

"I'm afraid so."

"Wait, if I'm on a road to—"

"Yes, it means you did some terrible things."

"I was"—James lowered his head, his chin touching his dented chest—"a wife-beater." He started bawling. "I lost my way and became a man I swore I'd never turn into, Silvia. I became my dad."

"Crying won't save you, baby."

"Wh—what did you do?"

"Huh," she sighed. "I murdered seven men."

"What?" He sat bolt upright, pushing her hands away. "You said *you* were killed."

She nibbled her lower lip, which was pierced. "I was. The last guy I stalked turned out to be a murderer. Shelby. I've seen him on this road, too. How's that for karma, friend?" When she smiled, more blood poured out of her and dribbled onto James. "I guess you're a saint compared to me." Her hand reached between his legs, her fingers wrapping around his privates.

"Get off!" The tightness in his underwear sickened him.

"I think you're enjoying it," she said, licking his lobe.

"If we are where I think we are, then why are we travelling in different directions?"

"Because you're in a queue, silly boy. When you get around that bend up ahead, it leads to a roundabout that brings you back this way."

"Then why am I seeing that farmhouse again? What is it?"

"This place has a way of playing tricks on you."

"What is the building's significance?"

"A portal to the world you once knew. You, like the rest of us, came in that way."

"Then why don't I see anyone dropping in? And why does this road look like the one I take to work every day?"

"Questions, questions, James. Like I said, this place messes with your mind. Now, sit back, relax and enjoy your last ride." She unzipped his fly and lowered her head to his lap.

"Don't—" He wanted to shove her disgusting, bleeding head away, but the warmth of her mouth was too pleasing, and it had been a long time since he'd had such an experience.

His car started moving by itself, and before he knew it, he'd rounded the roundabout and was heading back the way he'd come, but on the opposite side of the road. Mountains which ran with molten lava loomed before him, as large as countries. Thick, cloying black smoke rose to the death-grey skies.

James felt as though he was inside a cooking pot, its lid secured.

His breath became tight.

"I'm scared," he managed to say.

Silvia raised her head, her lips wet with blood and saliva. "There's no need to be. Relax. Enjoy." She winked, lowering her head again.

"That feels so nice." His lips pulled back, revealing gums and teeth. "Don't stop, Silvia."

Her pace picked up; his car's, too.

When her mouth left him again, he felt loss. "My time is close. I can feel it, James. Thanks for this final chance."

"I should—*ooh*, that's so nice—be thanking you!" He almost laughed at the absurdity of the situation, his orgasm building.

"The pleasure's all mine, believe me. It's been an age since I've been able to kill. Well, you won't die. You're already dead."

"What do you mean?" He smiled, about to throw his head back when his car rounded another corner. He saw in the near distance a massive expanse of choppy, broiling water, with people being pushed in left, right and centre. Imps danced.

"I didn't tell you?"

"Tell me what?"

"How I used to murder my victims?"

"No…"

"The papers labelled me the Black Widow. I liked to hump and dump, quite literally."

Tightness enclosed around James' penis as Silvia's teeth bit down, through his flesh and veins. Sucking, slurping sounds ensued, as he felt a part of him detach.

His legs kicked; his body convulsed.

"Ugh-*argh*!" he whimpered, feeling his orgasm fill her destructive mouth.

Before passing out, he saw her rise out of his lap, her skin burning, peeling and fluttering into the sky. "Happy Halloween, and thanks for the brief encounter, James," she screamed. "See you around."

Butter Wouldn't Melt

Sat on the stairs and looking between the banister's spindles, Poppy watched her mother writhe and scream in agony. Her midwife sat poolside, whispering words of support and encouragement in her ear as she rubbed the back of her hand.

"Almost there now, Ann," she said.

Dad sat the other side of the birthing pool, and held his wife's other hand. He was in a worse state than Poppy's mother, as he sobbed and blubbered words of support.

"Fucking pathetic!" Poppy said, not taking her eyes off the scene before her. In her hand she held a small voodoo doll she'd purchased in a witchcraft shop called *Bone Shakers* in town. It sold all manner of weird trinkets like shrunken heads, potions, spell-casting books, incense, die and tarot cards.

Even the woman behind the counter, Mary, had all the hallmarks of a witch, complete with a black cat and a bulbous wart at the end of her beak. The sudden thought of that hairy mole caused eleven-year-old Poppy to judder – her pigtails wobbled like puppets on strings.

So far, the Hessian doll had proved useless, as expected.

There's no such thing as black magic! She told the *toy*, shaking it violently and poking her tongue out at it. To her, it looked silly, with its stitched smile and odd buttons making up its eyes and nose.

It had come with a handbook containing spells on how to inflict pain on people. Once the hex had been spoken, the holder of the doll could then stick pins in it or twist the arms and legs, or even slam it against walls and floors to hurt the person it was aimed at.

Sadly, it hadn't worked, along with all the other spells and incantations she'd tried. *I don't need a fucking voodoo doll to be bad*! She thought, throwing the thing aside. *I've done plenty of evil things over the last four years, and nobody suspected a thing.*

'Aw, she's so cute. Like butter wouldn't melt in her mouth,' old man Lewis would always say when seeing Poppy and her mother out shopping.

And he'd always pinch my fucking cheek – I'm sure he got a stiff dick over touching me and stroking my pigtails, she thought. *Makes it worse that he lives next door*! *Well, used to…*

Last summer, Poppy had killed him.

She'd been out in the garden, playing in her Wendy House, when Mr. Lewis had innocently popped his head over the fence and invited her to his house for a cool glass of lemonade.

After pouring a drink for both of them, the old man had pinched her cheek once more, pushing Poppy over the edge. When he hadn't been looking, she'd dumped a killer concoction of various pills in his lemonade.

She'd giggled and pointed as Mr. Lewis had choked, struggled, gasped and screamed in his last living moments. His death had been an open and shut case, with the police deeming it a suicide via a lethal cocktail of drugs.

Mr. Lewis was Poppy's only human kill to date, but not through lack of trying. Oh, no. She'd found fun in other things over the years, such as torturing and killing the pets on her street, lying, general mischief and getting people in serious trouble.

Poppy couldn't recall when the evil streak had started, or how old she'd been, but she did remember her first true act of wickedness. It happened just after her sixth birthday, when she accused Mr. Atkins of *touching* her.

She'd seen things on the news and had heard older children and adults talking about such things.

Poppy wasn't stupid; she knew a lot for her age, and her giant lollipops, sweet smiles and pigtails kept everybody fooled. She was also a good, helpful student. So, after Mr. Atkins had kept her after class one day to scold her for talking over others, she set out to bring him down by telling her parents the teacher had fondled her 'no-no place'.

Of course, they'd believed her.

So had everyone else.

After all, butter wouldn't melt in young Poppy's mouth.

The police had taken the teacher in to custody, before the lynch mob could string him up from a lamppost by his bollocks. Her testimony via video link from the court's backrooms was so impressive it drove the women of the jury to sobs and dry heaves.

My tears and description of what that pervert had done to me were priceless.

So horrific had been her account of Mr. Atkins' actions, the judge had sentenced him to serve no less than ten years, with no appeal.

'You strike me a very cold and calculated individual, Mr. Atkins – if I had the power, I'd recommend castration!' Poppy recalled the old man in a fun wig saying, before bringing his gavel crashing down several times.

When Mr. Atkins was condemned and hauled off to the holding cells below, the people of the court erupted into gasps, with some of the men shouting and jeering. Order could not be restored, and so, Poppy and her family were ushered away and into an awaiting police car with protective escort.

A couple of weeks later, it was reported that Mr. Atkins had hung himself in his cell. This act of cowardice only helped to strengthen Poppy's diabolical lie and odious crime; the media whipped up a storm, with one report stating *'Atkins' guilt clearly got the better of him – that's one less paedophile to worry about!'*

"Breathe!" The midwife said to Poppy's mother, dragging her out of her thought. "That's it, Ann, nice and easy. Let Mother Nature do her thing…"

Ugh, it's fucking disgusting! To think, I was pushed out of that hole of hers – her 'honey trap', as dad likes to call it. Sick, she thought.

Looking over at them, Poppy could see the water inside the birthing pool had turned into a vile-looking soup of sorts: faeces, piss, amniotic fluid, blood and God knows what else. It reminded Poppy of a fish tank or pond that hadn't been cleaned in months.

All the scum has risen to the top!

At first, Poppy had been against her mother having another child when she'd overheard her parents discussing it. She didn't want a '*Little baby brother or sister,*' as people kept saying once her mother had fallen pregnant.

Poppy found the idea insufferable.

After hearing their conversation, she'd flown into a temper and tore the heads, arms and legs off her dolls and teddies. Once she'd managed to regain control over herself, she'd sat and formulated plans on how to try and stop it from happening.

Her immediate thoughts were violence against either her mother or father, but that was the rage talking. Poppy's sadistic thinking led her to bodily damage – *Maybe I can cut his dick off, or pour glue down inside it! Or damage his balls by blunt force trauma. What about her? Sew her shut?* When her fury subsided, her thinking became clearer. *I could chemical castrate him or destroy her reproductive system with drugs.*

Poppy had learned how to use a computer in school. Plus, her parents had encouraged her technological learning by buying her a laptop for her bedroom. They had no idea that she was good at exploring the dark depths of the internet and excellent at extensive research.

She'd even learned how to bounce things around online to hide her IP address.

Being evil is fun.

Why use brute force, when you can be a sneaky little shit?

With her laptop, Poppy had firstly checked on different drugs that could be used on her father. The most interesting tablet she'd found was Cyproterone Acetate or Cyprostat, as it was also know – a drug commonly used to fight prostate cancer, she'd read.

It wasn't what the drug could do to *help* men Poppy was interested in. Oh, no. It was what its side effects were capable of, especially the sexual ones. Not only did the drug cause erectile dysfunction, but a loss in libido.

Perfect. I could lace his meals or drinks no problem. Mum lets me help in the kitchen, so it would be easy-peasy.

With a note made on that drug, Poppy had researched many Chemotherapy drugs that helped destroy women's reproductive systems.

Same goes for mum – drugging her would be easy, too.

Getting the drugs were not a problem for her, either. She had money saved up in her piggy bank from her paper round, baby sitting and grass cutting jobs that she did on the weekends. If she ever wanted to buy something online, she would ask to borrow her mother's card and give her the money.

What about the delivery of the drugs? Simple, I can have them sent next door, to Mr. Lewis. His home is still empty, and I can access the inside by using the cat flap. Either that, or have the drugs sent to Aunt Janet. What with her Alzheimer's, that poor bitch doesn't know whether she's coming or going. Then again, her coming days are well over!

Her naughty little mind worked wonders.

However, by the time the drugs had arrived from somewhere in Asia, it was too late. Poppy had discovered her mother was pregnant. Even though this had annoyed her, she still knew she had time.

After all, the baby still had to grow, and she had been determined it would die inside her mother before it had the chance to see the light of day. *This way could also be much easier*, she'd thought. *At least I don't have to sneak around with illegal drugs and try to spike meals. And, if caught, that would be the end of me and my fun and games. No, it makes much more sense this way. This way, I can make the death of the baby look like an accident. I could put something on the stairs for her to trip over, or make the laminate flooring in the kitchen slippery. The possibilities are endless.*

However, after numerous attempts at trying to terminate the baby in her mother's womb, in a multitude of different ways that included the voodoo doll, Poppy had given up. She'd resigned herself to the fact that maybe it was meant to be. That maybe she was meant to have a little follower.

After all, I came out evil. Maybe you can't kill true wickedness? she'd thought.

"Ugh! I think the baby is coming!" Ann screeched.

Her husband mopped her brow, whilst the midwife tried to calm her.

"Just breathe, that's it. One, two, three…"

Poppy's mother breathed in and out of pursed lips, her face twisted into a red, angry image of pain and discomfort.

"Do you feel the need to push?"

"Uh-huh!" Ann grunted. "It hurts!"

"Try and relax…"

Standing, Poppy looked over the banister and stayed as quiet as she could – her parents had banished her to her bedroom for this occasion, and had told her not to come out, no matter what she heard.

'*You may hear mammy screaming in pain, but that's only because of the baby coming into this world*', her father had cooed.

Looking at him now, Poppy thought it was he who needed to be taken by the hand and held like a six-year-old, as he blubbered over his wife's startling screams.

Never had she heard her mother swear in her life, which thrilled her, on top of all the hurt she was going through.

Women can still die during childbirth, she thought, then silently prayed for her mother's end. *If you can, spare the child, Lord. I've grown quite attached to the idea of moulding a baby brother or sister into an evil minion. But the bitch? No, she can go.*

"Push, Ann! That's a good girl. One more. And, relax."

"I'm in so much pain! Is there anything…" another wave of contractions overcame her, causing her to scream. Her father yelped as Ann squeezed his hand as hard as she could.

All the while, Poppy watched on and smiled. She had to fight to stop herself from giggling.

"Please honey, try and calm down," her dad said. "It won't be long now, and it will be all over."

"Yes, baby is on the way," the midwife reassured. "Are you ready to start pushing again?"

"Mm-hmm!" Ann said with a moan. Her lips were pressed together so tight that they were turning bright red. Her face trembled. Her arms and shoulders shook as she pushed once more.

"Breathe, Ann. Breathe," the midwife instructed.

Poppy continued to watch the scene unfold.

Her mother took in a few large gulps of air, and then resumed pushing and grunting. Her breathing became a sharp, hissing sound.

She's like a demented snake! Poppy thought.

Disappointed at how long it was taking her sibling to put in an appearance, Poppy went back to thinking about some of the other fun things she had done, such as drowning a litter of kittens belonging to a blind girl down the street, desecrating headstones, stealing from the old, bullying, drenching letters inside a post box with piss, vandalising property, and setting fire to the local church.

Her list was inexhaustible, and she got away with it every time. Poppy only had to flutter her eyelashes.

'*My little princess*,' her father would say.

Raising the church to the ground was fun, she thought. A smile spread across her face at the memories. *It's just a shame I missed Sunday service. That congregation came within minutes of becoming barbecue. You can't beat the smell of burning bibles in the morning.*

Two weeks ago, Poppy had visited an old people's home with her school, where the children sang Christian songs for the residents. After slipping out of the room undetected, she had wandered the halls to cause mischief.

Firstly, she'd gone from room to room and swapped all their pills around before stealing hearing aids and glasses, which she'd taken outside and thrown in the river behind the building.

Her spree hadn't stopped there, however. She'd flattened wheelchair tyres, disabled vital life support equipment, hid crutches, and pocketed personal possessions and promptly placed them on eBay when she got home.

I've made a pretty penny over the years!

"*Arrgh!*" Ann screamed, pulling Poppy to the here and now. "Something's not right! You have to help me. It burns!"

"Ann, you have to try and…"

"Stop telling me to *fucking relax!* There's something seriously wrong! My…*Argh!*" she bellowed. "My privates are on fire!"

"It's…"

The water around her mother started to bubble and pop, as though someone had lit a fire underneath it. Poppy immediately thought of a caldron coming to boil. *All that's missing is a pig turning on a spit! But then again, my mother could be classed as the oinker!*

Thick steam started rising off the water's surface, as Ann continued to scream and thrash her arms around. Poppy could also see her mother's legs kicking beneath the cloudy water.

"What's going on, Samantha?!" Her father screamed at the midwife

"I have no idea. We better get her out of there, now," she said, going for Ann's arms. "She's red hot! Help me!"

Her mother's eyes fluttered and her body went limp. Samantha and her father tried pulling the dead weight of Ann out of the pool. Their hands slid off wet skin, which started to peel away from the arms due to the heat.

"She's being roasted!" he said. "Ann! Stand up!"

But she could hear no longer. Blood started seeping from her eyes, nose and ears.

"God, I have to try and save the baby…"

Ann's head burst into flames. Her eyeballs popped and blew fluids into her husband's face and mouth. He gagged, spluttered and coughed as he fell backwards and tripped over the coffee table. He crashed through its glass and tore his face and arms to shreds.

Poppy got to her feet and clapped feverishly. *This is awesome*, she thought, looking down at her voodoo doll. "You came through for me!" Picking it up, Poppy hugged the Hessian plaything. "When I asked for an evil spawn, I didn't think this would happen," she admitted, looking at the carnage before her.

What was left of her mother slipped under the water – her charred skin rose to the surface and mixed with the rest of the scuzz. Ten seconds later, the pool erupted with an almighty explosion.

Piss, shit and blood splashed up the walls, and glued fragments of rubber to them. The water rushed in all directions, and washed the armchairs into the couch, so powerful was the current.

Samantha was blown off her feet and thrown against a sideboard. She cried in agony when her back connected with its solid wooden frame. A snapped rib protruded through her side.

With her voodoo dolly, Poppy walked downstairs and stood in the contaminated water. The carpet made disgusting squishing sounds as she walked up to the burned remains of her mother.

"Get out, Poppy!" her dad screamed from where he lay. "Go and get help – I can't move. My ankle's broken."

She giggled as she looked at him. "You have a piece of glass stuck in your willy, daddy," she said, pointing at a large shard sticking out of his crotch. Blood had spread, making a mess of the beige-coloured trousers he wore.

Stepping to him, she put a fingertip to the glass and started wiggling it.

"*Argh!*" he screeched.

"That'll teach you for sticking that thing where it doesn't belong!" she said, pushing the glass deeper into the soft area.

Sniggering, she turned and looked at her mother.

A horrible sound like bed sheets ripping assaulted her ears. Covering them, she saw a split race up her mother's body, which ripped her in half from her privates to her sternum.

Blood exploded into the air, making it look like some kind of morbid fireworks display.

"Cool!" Poppy said, stroking her doll.

Out of the mucus slid a subhuman baby. Its top half consisted of a large head, with one, bloodshot eye. Its ears and nose were deformed, and its mouth was filled with miniscule, piranha-like teeth. A tuft of dark hair clung to the back of its head; beneath it, a horn could be seen in its early stages of formation.

When its bottom half slithered out of the overdone cocoon, Poppy could see it had no legs – they were melded together, making a flipper of sorts. Pulsating veins were visible beneath its translucent skin.

It screeched as it hurried towards Samantha.

The midwife shrieked and crawled away as the thing made a beeline for her and got under her skirt. Poppy could hear the thing bite, rip and chew exposed flesh. It smacked its lips together in a happy, gratifying fashion.

It burrowed its way through her genitals and burst from her stomach like something from the film, *Alien*. The thing then skittered across the floor and dined on her father. As it did, Poppy went into the kitchen and grabbed the collar and lead off the back of the door.

It had belonged to their old dog, Nippy, before she'd poisoned his food a few months back.

Resizing the collar, she looked at it.

"Yes, this will do nicely," she said.

She returned to the living room in time to see her new pet devour her father's tongue and lick its malformed lips clean.

"Come here, Odd. Come on, boy," she coaxed. The thing slinked towards its new master, and purr-growled at her feet. "That's a good boy, Odd. We're going to be best friends for ever and ever!" she said, slipping the collar over the thing's head.

"Let's go outside and play with the other children…"

Camp Lovejoy

'*Camp* Lovejoy*?! Good God! Sounds like a retreat for pedos – a place where they can go to gargle ten-year-olds' balls in private, Andrew. Are you mad? It'll ruin your moral path,*' Lovejoy's father, John, had said.

'*Dad, that's no way for a man of the cloth to talk,*' Lovejoy replied, smiling.

'*Calling it as I see it, boy – the Lord doesn't like that kind of cavorting, which your pet project's name suggests.*'

'*It's only a—*'

'*Signifying is as bad, lad, and you don't want to end up like all 'em dirty little fecks who wear the collar and touch the altar boys, now do you? They'll all burn on the horned one's toasting fork like marshmallows!*'

There was no talking to the fire-and-brimstone-eating John after he'd consumed a few slugs of Mother's Ruin. However, the retired, forward-thinking minister had been wrong: Camp Lovejoy, a summer home for wayward boys and girls of ages eight to fifteen, was on the cusp of celebrating its fifth year in business this weekend.

"A shame you're not here to see it, Dad," Andrew muttered. He took a drag on the last of his cigarette (his only vice nowadays), tears threatening. "Glad you got the chance to see me transform, though. God bless you." He looked toward the heavens, making the sign of the cross.

Andrew's righteous course started when he was released from prison after serving six to ten for the attempted armed robbery, whilst naked, of a strip joint called Jugs Jugglers. He'd done this with a hard-on and a sawed-off shotgun; he'd also strived to take one of the showgirls, Silver Dollar Sandy, hostage, but she kicked him in the balls and saved the day.

Pole Cat Pounces, a newspaper headline had read the following day.

'*I was off my tits on alcohol and cocaine, your Lordship. I didn't know where my cock was, let alone what the fuck I was doing,*' Andrew had slurred whilst on his hands and knees in court, drugged to the eyeballs and giving the lady taking the minutes come-to-bed eyes. '*Good tits, gal,*' he said with a wink, his lawyer trying to yank him to his feet.

They'd thrown the book at him.

'*Your conduct in my court of law is a disgrace, young man,*' the judge condemned, pointing his gavel at the giggling Lovejoy, who was in the process of dropping his trousers. *'Bailiffs! Take this specimen downstairs.'*

Andrew's dad, who'd been sat in the public gallery, shook his head, prayed for his son's soul and vowed to alter Andrew's ways when he was released and under his care.

After four years, Andrew was out on good behaviour.

'I found Jesus inside, Dad. I've seen the errors of my ways, and I want to help others.'

'Good, boy, and if you've let him into your heart as claimed, then it'll make your transformation easier.'

'I'm clean, too. I've kicked the drugs and booze.'

After John drove his son home, Andrew went to his room to clean and renovate it of evil, turning it into a sanctuary where he could pray to his god with peace of mind. From his walls, cupboards, doors and mirror, he removed his heavy metal and screamo band posters, some of which depicted the crew members raping nuns, beating people with baseball bats or other bone-busting implements, slaughtering goats and drinking blood.

Crosses and portraits of his Lord and Saviour replaced the filth once the black and red walls had been turned cream and his unchristian duvet and sheets tossed.

When the offensive material was black-bagged and thrown, Andrew had binned his nudie-girl pictures and a stack of skin magazines. This was followed by the boxing up of his horror comics, graphic novels and titles on such rubbish as Satanism, the occult and UFOs. Once achieved, Andrew placed his "angry CDs" and "devil-worshipping DVDs", as his late mother had called them, into a container alongside the books.

They were taken to charity shops. So, too, were his unholy t-shirts.

'*Into a crusher, they should go,*' John argued.

'*Waste not, want not, Daddy.*'

Andrew didn't stop there.

He disposed of his jewellery and everything that bore the devil's mark: finger, nipple, nose, dick and earrings; plugs, necklaces, pendants, insignias, patches, eyeliner, nail polish; and sex toys (cock bracelets, anal douches, beads, gags, whips, chains, spanking canes). Not even his prized possession, a gimp suit complete with zippered mask and male chastity belt, survived the cull.

Standing before the bathroom mirror feeling cleansed (but not fully), the hulking, six-three Andrew, whose body was covered in tattoos, had still looked his former self. The ink, which John told him was his curse, would never be removed. However, the rest could.

Andrew took clippers to his beard and handlebar moustache.

'*That's better. Now will you accept me as one of your flock, Father?*' he'd whispered, closing his eyes, clasping his hands and kissing them. He silently prayed before heading to his refuge. '*Tomorrow will be a big day, as I set out on a new adventure.*'

All this shot through Andrew's mind as he finished off his cigarette and crushed it beneath his shoe. He pushed off the tree he was leant against, shaded his eyes with a hand, and peered down the dirt track that led to his bible camp.

Nothing.

He looked at his watch. Almost midday.

They should have been here by now, he thought.

Shrugging, he lit another cigarette and propped himself against the tree, letting his mind wander.

I really did start my venture the next day, didn't I? Took all the money I'd saved from my tattooing days and bought this little campsite in the middle of nowhere, God's country.

Andrew looked over his shoulder and spied the six cabins and barn he'd renovated with his own two hands.

'You should employ helpers, son,' John suggested.
'No, Dad – I have all the help I need in Jesus.'

The half-dozen cabins served different purposes: sleeping quarters each for the boy campers and male staff, another two for the girl campers and female staff (not that Andrew had anyone work with him up until this year), one that held sports and play equipment, two shower blocks (male/female) and a cabin used as a staff room where they could sit and watch TV, drink tea or coffee, or relax and do their own thing. Andrew had even fitted a pinball machine and jukebox filled with heavenly songs.

The barn had been transformed into a church where Andrew delivered daily sermons over the summer. It was also where Andrew slept, read scripture and prayed furiously to his Lord, Father and Saviour six times a day.

The arduous labour of refurbishing the busted-down camp had taken Andrew the better part of eleven months to complete, leaving him ready to open for that year's summer. He hadn't been expecting many parents to send their wayward children to him, a Christian camp, in that first year, and he'd been surprised when a bus full of thirty youngsters descended upon him.

That first bunch had been wild. They'd departed their ride all attitude and bubblegum, with their heavy metal t-shirts and bad eighties hairdos. Still, Andrew had not let the task at hand dissuade him, nor had he let the daunting situation rattle or make him question his ability.

He met the youngsters with a misspent youth head-on, bull-charging the circumstances to get an early advantage. Ruling with an iron hand, a kind ear and a loving heart was the only way to beat the devil from them. This would be his first major learning curve – something that would hold him in good stead for years to come at Camp Lovejoy.

Or so Andrew had hoped.

Might not make it past this first summer, he'd thought.

But he need not have worried, as he could relate to the boys and girls who harboured Satan, rage, and hatred toward their parents. Some of them were merely naughty – skipping school, sniffing glue, petty robbery, destructive behaviour, temper tantrums, and the like – whereby some of the older ones had been arrested for drunk driving, assault, underage sex, possession of hard narcotics, etc.

Andrew's first summer had gone without a hitch, and every single one of the children went home happier, calmer, and with Jesus in their hearts.

Over the years, Andrew's numbers grew steadily from word-of-mouth: 35, 39, 42, 46, and so on. The previous year, over 60 children had attended. None returned home the way they arrived. And, out of the five summers he'd played God's servant, Andrew had only failed one.

"Gordon Phibs," he muttered, blowing smoke from his nostrils. He scrunched his face as the name rolled off his tongue. "A bad seed indeed. One far beyond professional help."

The brute had been part of the campers who came to Andrew four summers ago. He'd been big for fourteen – pushing six-two and fourteen stone of pure muscles.

When the boy wasn't doing the devil's duties, he'd worked on his father's farm with his daddy and three older brothers. Gordon's dad, thinking it best to pull his errant son from full-time education, had kept an eye on Gordon.

However, the man was no better himself. He beat his wife, got drunk, and ruled his family with an iron fist and leather belt. But the man's reign was cut short when Gordon pushed him into a spreader headfirst, spraying his remains over a field as though he were shedding fertiliser.

Or so Gordon's mother had told Andrew in confidence.

'I told the police it was an accident, Father Lovejoy. I couldn't see my son go to prison. We're taught to protect our flock, right? I just want to see him set straight,' she'd said.

Looking the mother in the face, Andrew had spotted fading bruises around her eyes, nose and mouth. Her lip had been split. When he'd asked her about it, she'd unloaded onto him what Gordon's dad had been like.

'I'm not saying he deserved it, but he was a bad man. Forgive me, Father.'

'Shh, child.' Andrew stroked the woman's hair, her head bent, her chin touching her chest. *'I'll help Gordon the best I can, but you need to set things straight with the police. You don't want your soul to burn in hell, Mrs Phibs! The boy needs punishing.'*

'When Gordon comes home, I will.'

For six whole weeks, Andrew had spent as much time with Gordon as possible, without neglecting the others. He preached, spoke with, and prayed with the oversized boy until he was blue in the face, thinking he'd broken through in the final week of summer.

'Thank you for trying to help me, Father Lovejoy, but I don't believe in your imaginary sky fairy.'

Gordon slapped Andrew, laughed and got on the bus to leave.

A few weeks later, Gordon's mother sent a letter to inform Andrew that her son had become increasingly worse over the weeks he'd been home. He'd even threatened to kill her and his brothers and burn the farm down.

'He told me you touched him, Father, but I don't believe a word of it.'

Outraged, Andrew had responded, telling the mother she needed to go to the police as promised, or he would, and that Gordon had the devil's look in his eyes.

When Andrew didn't hear from Mrs Phibs after a fortnight, he informed the police, who told him the matter would be investigated. Andrew, at the time, felt bad about betraying the woman's trust, but knew, deep down, the right thing had been done.

The poor woman's life could be in danger, Father, he'd prayed.

A couple of days later, a Detective Jennings called to inform Andrew that Mrs Phibs, along with all three of Gordon's brothers, had died.

'Murdered by Gordon, Mr Lovejoy,' Jennings said.

After the call, Andrew never heard about the Phibs again, and didn't know what had become of Gordon.

"Tragic," Andrew said, dropping his cigarette and crushing it. He heard the faint sound of a laden vehicle approaching from the distance. Dust rose above the tree line from off the dirt track, kicked up by tyres. "Almost time to tend a new flock."

"That them, then?" a voice squeaked behind Andrew.

"Yes, Linnea. Those are the children. Are Brinke and yourself ready for this?" he asked, turning to look at the older sister.

She snapped her gum, drew it back into her mouth, smiled and nodded. "Sure. If I can handle two snot-nosed younger brothers, I can cope with a bunch of mischievous ten-year-olds."

"Some of them will be difficult," he muttered, turning from the red-headed, pint-sized girl.

"S'cuse me, Father?"

"Nothing, dear. Call Brinke. I'd like you both by my side when I greet the children."

"Got it. Just a sec."

He heard Linnea walk off to retrieve her sister as he watched the bus round the bend, getting closer by the second. When it came to a squealing halt feet from him, Linnea returned with Brinke.

"Should be a big group this year, ladies."

When the bus doors sprang open and a dozen children lumbered out – seven boys, five girls – Andrew was taken aback.

"No more?" he questioned the driver, scratching his chin.

The driver shook his head, causing ash to fall off the fag dangling from his mouth and flake across his thighs. He snapped the door shut, turned the bus around and left, leaving Andrew bewildered in a cloud of smoke.

Odd, he thought.

"Welcome to Camp Gay!" one of the boys yelled, provoking shrieks of laughter from the other children.

"That's right, children. You're about to have a gay ol' time," Brinke said. "Nothing but fun, fun, fun and happiness here," she continued, handing bibles to each of the youths.

"I don't think he meant *that* kind of gay, sis," Linnea said.

Andrew put a hand on his face, shaking his head. *This is going to be a long summer.*

****

He watched from the bushes.

His large, dirt-covered hands with overgrown fingernails parted the foliage before him. Gordon's view was spectacular. Not only could he perv on the fine, golden legs and tanned midriffs on display thanks to the two lovelies helping Lovejoy, but he could also see the disappointment etched on the Father's face due to the poor attendance of children.

An unhinged smile stretched across Gordon's face. He laughed inwardly, making his body shake and the branches he was holding quiver. Leaves scattered about his feet.

When he spoke, he sounded inhuman. "I'm fine with killing kiddies." One hand pulled from the foliage and rested atop the eight-inch buck knife sheathed at his hip. "I tried to warn them off. The blood will be on *their* hands."

Gordon, whilst planning his revenge attack the past three years, had tried tarnishing the good Father's name and Godly deeds by spreading stories about him all over the internet, tales about Andrew's errant ways before becoming a man of the cloth.

"I'll butcher them all and make it look as though he went berserk. I'll cut off his fingers and slice out his tongue so he can't tell the truth. It'll be a credit to the oath you took, Father. Andrew. Lovejoy." The words were spat; spittle plastered the leaves.

Gordon watched as Andrew, Linnea and Brinke rounded up the children, none looking older than twelve, and herded them towards the cabins.

"Time to unpack, settle in, and *die*!" With his targets now further away, Gordon laughed and sent birds squawking from the trees around him. "Oh, how I'm going to enjoy myself." His hand shifted from the blade to the bow and quiver of arrows on his back. "Yes, indeed." A machete lay buried under leaves at his booted feet.

When he stood, his movements caused the hatchet that dangled from his utility belt to pendulum. He lifted the balaclava off his face and wiped the sweat from around his eyes, nose, and forehead. His moustache and beard glistened. Before lowering the face cover, Gordon changed location, as his prey was out of sight.

"Peek-a-boo, I see you!" He grinned, poking his head from behind a large oak tree. The boys were being ushered inside their cabin by one of Andrew's helpers, whilst the Father and his second aide escorted the girls to their log structure. "I wouldn't get too comfortable if I were you, oh wee ones. Daddy Gordon and Uncle Buck Knife here are planning on making your stay *dead* dire."

He laughed at his pathetic excuse for a joke.

"You'll be phoning your travel agencies for a refund after this one."

Once the girls were taken into their cabin, Gordon watched as Andrew, Linnea and Brinke met outside it and spoke amongst themselves. "Wish I could hear what they are saying, damn it."

I could move closer? No, I might give myself away. Andrew was gesticulating as he spoke. *The boring fuck is probably running over itinerary and gospel shit.*

The aides laughed.

Goin' to make them bitches scream, and not with my knife alone...

Gordon looked at his watch. Almost two p.m.

He saw the three split up and head in different directions. The women, leaving together, headed to their cabin, whilst Andrew seemed to be walking towards the barn.

Gordon licked his cracked lips when he saw the ladies slip inside their dwelling.

"Excellent."

Making sure the coast was clear, he moved from his spot with stealth, repositioning himself beneath an open window to the cabin the women had entered.

"You have to admit, he's pretty hot, sis. You saw the photos of him online when he was younger, right? *Phwoar*!"

"Yeah, but he's not like that now, Linnea. He's a God-botherer, hun, and spends his time swallowing the Lord's words."

"A bit like you and cock, eh?"

"Cheeky bitch."

Both girls laughed.

"Pillow fight!"

"No. We're supposed to be grabbing our shower— *ugh*! You cold-cocking little witch. Now you're going to get it."

I need to see this, Gordon thought, peeping inside to see the semi-naked sisters embroiled in a fully-fledged slumber party fight.

Thump.
"Oomph!"
Poof.
Feathers fluttered.
Hair bounced.

The girls shrieked as they jumped on and over beds whilst chasing one another from one end of the cabin to the other. Breathless, they collapsed onto a bed close to the window Gordon was hid by, laughing until they were holding their sides.

He watched their braless breasts heave beneath their t-shirts; their nipples jutted through the thin fabric.

"I think I won that fight fair and square, Linnea."

"Uh-uh, no way. I had you well beat, madam."

"I guess we'll need a rematch after lights out."

I might spare them until after *I see that!* Gordon thought.

"You're on. Come on, we need to grab a shower if we're going to be ready by three," Brinke said.

"Reckon I can convert him?"

"Who, Father Lovejoy?"

Linnea nodded.

"Not a chance, hun. He's devoted. His old ways are long behind him."

"*Le* sigh. Love with a woman isn't cool for him?"

"Okay, *Pepé Le* Douchebag. Knock that shit off and get your stinky arse in the shower, *le* pronto."

Both girls cracked up, grabbed their toiletry bags, fresh knickers, and towels and then headed out the door.

Gordon crept around the cabin and stuck to the shadows as the women passed, too engrossed in chatter and laughter to notice a thing. When they were beyond him, he stepped from his hiding place and walked behind them, confident nobody would see.

When they reached the shower cabin, he stepped inside with them and hid in an empty stall. He listened as they spoke of Andrew, the summer ahead, and what they thought it was going to be like looking after awkward children.

After their shower, Gordon peeked from behind the curtain and spied on Linnea and Brinke as they stood before two mirrors, their towels wrapped around their waists, their tits exposed and their red hair wet and clinging to their backs.

He groaned.

I could take them right now, have my fun, and then slit their throats.

No, it'll be more pleasurable when it's just them left to deal with.

His eyes fixed on Linnea's small, firm tits. The areolas were neon pink.

He licked his lips as eagerness grew between his legs. Gordon envisioned latching onto them with his mouth and hands. So lost was he in his perversion, he failed to spot the girls finishing up and leaving.

Trance over, he didn't waste time returning to their cabin. Instead, he snuck to the barn and slunk inside, going undetected by Father Lovejoy, who was inside somewhere.

Taking a chance, he hid behind a pile of stacked hay.

I've been looking forward to one of your sermons, Father.

Not.

Twenty minutes later, the barn started to fill with the children, and Linnea and Brinke put in their appearance. A further five minutes later, Andrew took to the makeshift pulpit with bible in hand.

"Come on then, fag. Tell us how we're all going to burn in a lake of fire," said the same outspoken boy from earlier. "Get a load of this jackarse," he continued.

"Sit. Down," commanded Andrew, his tone fierce. "This is the Lord's house, young man, and we will not have you blaspheming."

"Whatever, dick—"

"*Sit!*" Andrew's voice bounded off the walls. The children took a collective sigh.

"Y—you—"

"Be seated, or I shall lock you in this barn and have you reading scripture from now until the end of summer."

"But—"

"I can't do it? Look around, you ungodly heathen – you're all alone. You belong to us," he said, holding up his hands, "and if I so wish, I can spank your bottom until it shines like a welcome home beacon."

Laughter erupted from the children.

The youth sat, his face turning scarlet.

"You shall, indeed, swim naked in a lake of fire if you don't alter your ways."

For the next two hours, Andrew delivered a powerful sermon with gusto, hardly stopping for a breath, let alone a sip of water from the glassful he'd provided. By the end of it, the girls were crying, and a couple of the boys were, too.

Motherfucker's good, I'll give him that, Gordon thought, peeking from behind the hay. *He's broken most of them on the first day. A shame he won't be around to finish what he's started.*

"Dismissed. Go now, back to your respective cabins and get some rest. The remainder of today will be spent reflecting on what's been said. Tomorrow, if I see signs of improvement, we will have fun with sports activities."

"Sir," a girl of eight said, raising her hand.

"Father, child," he corrected.

"Father, when do we eat?" She lowered her head as if ashamed for asking such a thing.

"Dinner will be served at six in your cabins. Lights out at eight. After food, start reading your bibles because there'll be a quiz on the first ten pages tomorrow afternoon."

The children shuffled out in silence, dazed by the bombardment.

Gordon enjoyed beholding the look of confusion and fright in their eyes.

Couple of bedwetters in that bunch of fucking pussies, he thought as the last of the children exited the building and closed the door with a soft click.

"I don't think we'll have many problems with these kids, ladies," Andrew said.

"Seemed tame," Linnea added.

"An easy first summer to break us in, Father," Brinke chirped.

"We shall see. I've had this before. They start out sheepish but turn. Nevertheless, we're off to a good start."

"Would you like us to begin prepping food, Father?" Linnea asked.

"Yes, my child. If you need me, I'll be in my room praying and reading. I shall see you both at six."

The sisters nodded, turned, and left, leaving Andrew alone at the pulpit.

"Huh," Andrew sighed. "Forgive me, Lord."

Gordon peeked from behind the hay as Andrew walked towards the back of the barn and through a door.

Hmm. Now what? Go for Andrew? The girls? The children?

No, let's wait for lights out. It'll be more fun that way.

Gordon left the barn, finding a new hiding spot beneath a tree opposite the cabins that held the boys and girls.

Soon.

****

At precisely six o'clock, Linnea and Brinke, with no sign of Andrew, began serving the children their food—veggie burgers and salad, with a side order of carrot sticks and a carton of prune juice—before retiring to the staff cabin.

They'd hoped to find their temporary employer there, but no.

"Think we should check on him? See if he's okay?" Brinke suggested.

"We could take him a plate of food," Linnea added.

"Good thinking. I get the impression he's always too wrapped up in his work to look after himself."

"Yeah. And it could definitely do with a woman's touch around here." Linnea ran her finger over a kitchen unit that was covered in dust. "Going to be a busy summer."

Brinke nodded as she dished up Andrew's dinner. "Come on, let's get this to him."

Outside, they were shocked to find it had turned almost pitch dark in the space of an hour and a half. And, with only the odd spotlight here and there lighting the camp, the girls found they had to take their time in case they tripped or slipped.

As they passed the girls' cabin, Linnea popped her head through the door and called lights out.

"But it's only a quarter to eight!" one of the girls protested, slamming her bible onto the bed. "It's not fair." She poked her tongue out.

"You don't want me to tell Father Lovejoy of your disobedience, do you?"

On that note, the girls placed their bibles aside and snuggled in their beds.

Linnea hit the lights.

The same rigmarole was played out at the boys' hut before the aides continued their journey to Andrew.

"Bloody odd we haven't seen him, though." Linnea picked up her pace. "No man can be that caught up in his work to ignore the grumble of his belly, surely?"

"I'm sure he's fine."

"Well, his back light is on." Linnea pointed.

"Grab the door for me, chick?" Brinke asked.

"Sure." The pint-sized girl inched the creaky door open enough to get her head around and look from left to right. All the candles were lit. *A fire hazard if you ask me,* she thought, spying a heap of hay with a pitchfork standing in it. "Father?"

"Come on, babe – I'm freezing my titties off out here," Brinke complained.

Linnea threw the door wide, stepping inside. Brinke followed. "The man's a workaholic, Brinke."

"He might have fallen asleep…"

"Meh, true." Linnea edged forward. "Father?"

Nearing Andrew's back rooms, they heard a commotion.

"Oh God, *no,*" Andrew was saying repeatedly. "Please, please Lord. Help. Help me!"

"He's in pain, Brinke. Quick."

"Oh, Jesus." Brinke let the plate drop from her hand and rushed after her sister.

They went through the back door and were met by another, which was where Andrew's pleas were coming from.

"It's everywhere. I can't stop—*argh*!" the Father screamed as the girls burst in on him.

"Oh, shit!" Linnea laughed, raising her hands to her mouth.

Brinke could only stare agog at the sight of the naked Andrew, who was holding his hard, jism-trickling cock in one hand and a couple of Polaroid snaps in the other. More pictures graced his bed, beside puddles of spunk and crusty-looking underwear.

"*Ladies*!" he blurted. When he removed his hand from his dick, strings of come trailed after it, reminding Linnea of saliva.

"What a naughty, *naughty* boy," Brinke said, picking up some of the photos from off the bed. They were of her and Linnea – close-ups of their tits, legs and arse, taken from various angles. "He spied on us skinny-dipping, babe." She placed a hand on her hip.

"*Andrew*!" Linnea stamped her foot. "I thought you were a decent man."

He and his cock shrunk. "I—I—"

"I think he needs to be taught a lesson, Brinke."

"Shall we tell on him? What a pervo."

"No. Ladies, please—I can explain." Sweat dribbled down his forehead and dripped off his nose.

"Yeah, but before we do, I have an idea. Close the door," Linnea said, giggling.

"I'm begging you. I've never done anything like this—"

"Pretty sure I saw some rope in the barn," Brinke said with a smile.

"Please!"

The women laughed.

****

Gordon watched and listened to Linnea and Brinke from the darkness as they rushed back and forth between the cabins serving the children their dinner.

Once the task had been completed, and the camp workers had retreated to their staff cabin, Gordon had stalked around the boys' and girls' units with glee.

It'll be lights out soon, ya little fucks, he thought as they ate and then returned to their reading.

Twenty minutes later, Linnea and Brinke walked his way.

"*Shit*," Gordon said, ducking out of sight.

"Might as well turn their light out whilst we're at it," one of them said.

"Agreed."

Gordon smiled and drew his knife, feeling every inch slide from its leather pouch. The machete still lay where he'd left it under a pile of leaves. *I'll use that on Andrew…*

One by one, the bulbs winked out in the girls' cabin.

And then the boys'.

Gordon, shrouded in blackness, watched as Linnea and Brinke became blurred shapes in the distance; the volume of their voices dropped by the second.

The low hubbub of chatter and sniggers coming from inside both cabins died off within ten minutes, replaced by soft snores.

Gordon gave it another quarter of an hour before unclipping his flashlight, which was purposely fit with a low-watt bulb, and proceeded to the girls' unit.

The door didn't so much as squeak when he pushed it open.

His boots made a hollow sound as he walked across the wood floor to the first bed that held a sleeping girl of eight or nine years old. She clutched a dolly to her chest.

"Cute," he muttered, clamping her mouth with one hand whilst starting to saw through her throat with his knife. Blood bubbled from her mouth and covered his palm. Its warmth stirred butterflies in his stomach. "Mmm…"

The buck came away from the brittle neck with a slurpy, sucky sound. A squirt of blood raced up Gordon's face. Before moving on to the next bunk, he illuminated the body with his torch and laughed when he saw the sheets by the young girl's crotch were soaked through.

I knew there were bedwetters among you wee fucks. Smiling, Gordon clonked his way over to the next bed and slit that girl's throat, and then a third. *This is easier than I thought.*

By the time he'd killed the last child, the cabin's floor was awash with running blood and he could hear it drip off the beds and splash into puddles. Before leaving, he cut locks of hair from each of the girls and pocketed them.

Time for the boys to get theirs.

The first lad he came across was the loudmouth who'd lipped-off to Andrew twice since arriving.

"Such a set of balls on you, kiddo."

The boy's eyes shot open as the knife was shoved into his skull. His muffled screams excited Gordon beyond words but didn't hamper his work.

When the boy stopped moving, Gordon carved the initials AJ into the child's belly, which he would do with all of them.

"Oh, Andrew. How could you? They were mere children." He stifled a laugh, going to the next bed and clamping a hand over the sleeping boy's mouth before ripping his knife up through the boy's stomach and pulling the guts out.

Gordon tore, hacked, cut, slashed, stabbed and carved his way through the boys' cabin. By the end, he had to sit on a bunk and catch his breath. Five minutes later, re-energised, he collected hair trophies from the boys, sheathed his knife and collected the machete.

Gordon made his way over to the barn.

"It'll be nice to catch up, Father." Gordon clenched his teeth.

He pulled the barn door open and stopped in his tracks. The loud sounds coming from the back room startled him.

Fuck. I forgot about Linnea and Brinke. Have they not left here yet? Shit. I might have to erase them first. Damn.

"Ha-ha! Look how red he's gone, Brinke."

"Something tells me he's enjoying it, hunny."

"What the—?" Gordon mouthed, moving closer to the back and picking up on a faint buzzing sound. *Is someone crying in there?* His forehead furrowed.

"Maybe we should stop? He's starting to bleed."

"Nah, let's keep going. He deserves it."

Gordon stepped through the first door and saw a second, just ahead of him, standing open. The cries and muffled screams intensified. *What's going on?*

As he got closer, his heart slammed against his chest and a breath hitched in his throat. He chanced a peep around the doorframe and almost laughed at the spectacle before him.

The ladies had the Father on his side with his arms and legs tied at the wrist and ankles with rope. The runoffs were fastened to the bedpost. A large, bright purple dildo jutted from Andrew's arse, its base covered in blood. His cock stood on end and leaked come.

Linnea worked the dildo in and out with a glove-covered hand. "Bet you're glad I brought my toys, Brinke."

"Uh-huh," the sister said, pinching Andrew's nipples with clamps.

With the girls and the Father too preoccupied to notice, Gordon removed his phone from his pocket and snapped off a dozen or more photos of the unfolding scene. Then he immediately uploaded the images to the internet.

So this is why you killed your helpers, is it, Andrew? They told the children, tried to get them out of here, and threatened to expose you to the world. Excellent.

He withdrew from the back room, hid behind the hay and let the girls finish.

Three hours later, Linnea and Brinke emerged from the rear room in hysterics.

"Take it out! It's too big to go up there, do you hear me? *Too* big—*argh*," one of the girls mimicked.

The other erupted in laughter. "He's a right little squirter, isn't he, babe?"

"Yeah – of blood."

More laughter, which turned to shrieks of terror as Linnea was speared through the left eye with an arrow, pinning her to the barn door. Blood splashed down Brinke's legs, face and t-shirt, plastering the thin fabric to her chest. Her nipples jutted.

"Cold, dear?" Gordon asked, drawing another arrow and placing it in the bow.

"*Argh!*" Brinke cried, holding her hands skyward, her fingers bent and gnarled-looking.

The homemade arrow, decorated with feathers, slammed into her guts and knocked her off her feet.

She tried to crawl away, but Gordon straddled her back and drew his knife. "I was hoping we could be friends. I wanted to play with you ladies, badly, but plans changed. You can blame yourselves for that."

"Wait—"

Gordon's blade sawed through her scalp in a slow, meticulous fashion. Blood spewed. When the steel got so far, Gordon replaced his knife and ripped the woman's hair off with a vicious tug, before snapping her neck like a chicken bone.

Standing, Gordon looked at both women and grinned.

Time to get yours, Father.

"What's going on out there?" Andrew shouted from the other room. "Enough is enough, ladies. Please untie me."

Perfect.

"I won't tell if you don't, okay? Come on, you've scared me enough. I'm sorry. Please."

"Hello, Andrew. We meet again," Gordon announced.

"Who—?"

"Don't you remember your old pal, Gordon?"

"Gordon. Gordon *Phibs*?"

"You catch on fast."

"You look nothing like him. Who—oh, God… No, it can't be. But why?"

Gordon smiled. "You took everything from me, Andrew. My life, my family."

"But—but—"

Gordon moved closer to the bed, wielding his knife. "You were the one who told me to inform the police, that it was the right thing to do, and everything would turn out roses. Remember?"

He leaned in closer to the Father.

"It—it—*was* the right thing to do, Mrs Phibs."

"Gordon," he corrected, tapping the tip of his knife against the Father's chin.

"G—G—Gordon."

"That's better."

"What happened to you? You were reported dead. Your sons, too, apart from… Gordon."

The fake beard pulled away from Mrs Phibs' face, but she pressed it back into place. "Do you know why my dad was the way he was with us, Andrew?"

"But you're Gor—"

"Concentrate, Andrew." He reminded him of the knife.

"N-no, I don't."

"Because my fucking whore of a mother was a rug-muncher – a dirty lesbian who liked licking mat. She gave him little attention or sexual release, turning him into a raging lunatic. He beat us out of frustration."

"Why didn't he leave her?"

"He loved her, but I couldn't stand the sight of him beating her."

"So you killed him."

Gordon nodded. "When my cunt of a mother went to the police, I went crazy and killed the rest of my family. My neighbour, Miss Brunt, too."

"So that explains the female found in the fire… But, what happened to the *real* Gordon?"

For the briefest of moments, Mrs Phibs' voice rang true. "I had to kill my Gordon. He came at me, and I defended myself. I didn't burn his body with the rest of 'em, see. No, I buried him close to home."

"Why didn't you turn yourself in? It would have been self-defence."

Mrs Phibs shook her head. "No. I preferred them to think I was dead and that Gordon was on the loose."

"Covering your tracks to come here and—what have you *done*?"

"Nothing for you to concern yourself about, Father."

"Oh, Christ – you plan to pin it all on me, don't you?"

"Yes, but it won't matter."

He was almost too scared to ask. "Why?"

"Because you won't be around, Father."

"But they'll find me here, mutilated. You won't be able to—"

"I plan to make it look as though you ran, Father. It's all in the note I've written."

"Don't do this, Mrs—*Gordon*. I beg you. Argh, help. *Police*! She's killing—"

Gordon snatched at the Father's tongue and sliced it from inside his mouth in one swift movement.

"Argh-*ugh*," he cried, tears spilling down his face.

"Kiss 'em goodbye." Gordon smiled, cutting through Andrew's testicles and penis. Before inserting the detached privates up Andrew's widened anal canal, thanks to the dildo, he removed the sex toy and threw it to one side. "Think I'll keep that as a souvenir. I'm sure I'll have fun licking it clean."

Gordon proceeded to cut Andrew's restraints and roll him onto his back.

He was dying, his body bucking and twitching.

Gordon removed the hatchet from his belt with one hand and picked up the machete from off the floor with the other. He then hacked away at Andrew until there was nothing left but a bloody, pulpy mess.

It took Gordon less than thirty minutes to bag Andrew's corpse and bury it in a deep hole behind the shower blocks. With that done, he dragged the bodies of Linnea and Brinke out into the open, propped Andrew's confession note on the table in the staff cabin, and set the barn ablaze.

By the time the final toasted beams of support timber hit the deck, Gordon was long gone.

Twin Jesters, Bridgend

I can hear their harsh, raspy breathing and low snarls mocking me from the shadows as they give chase. They're not racing after me, although it feels like it. They're teasing me, much like a cat does with a mouse.

I dare not stop, not even to wipe the stinging sweat from my eyes. My only hope is to push forward and make it back beyond the border of Twin Jesters.

They may not wander that far from their town…

My mind is a scrambled mess.

The sound of rushing blood pounds the inside of my ears. I cough, stumble and stagger over a small stone bridge with parapets lined with flowers. On the opposite side of the humpbacked structure, I spot a warm glow spilling from a large edifice looming in the darkness. A low hubbub of chatter and laughter floats on the air.

"Goin' to rip your gutssss out, ssssnoop…" a snake-like voice says from just behind.

"Argh-*ugh*!" I cry, holding a hand out towards the pub.

Tears threaten.

I stumble again but stay upright.

My laptop carry case and camera bag slap my back as I continue at a jog. I take a fleeting glance over my shoulder, spotting their red eyes that stand out in the darkness like burning match heads, and trip over my feet. I don't go down. Instead, I rush headlong, down the other side of the bridge and slam into the pub's side wall. I bounce off it with force and flop to the ground.

More hissing from the shadows gets me moving.

I don't see them advancing.

I thought they'd stay—

I get on my feet, and a rock sails from out of nowhere, missing me by centimetres. The projectile ricochets off the floor and rattles out of sight. I don't have time to think about it, as a shower of stones rains down on me. I cover my face with my arms but it's no use—the rocks strike my head, arms and shoulders. One cuts my cheek, another hits me in the eye, a third splits my bottom lip.

Yelling, I run for the pub's main entrance. Rocks continue to pelt against the wooden tables and chairs, walls and ground as I enter.

I crash through the door and slam it closed, then collapse against it.

My actions bring the roaring pub to a graveyard silence. People cease talking and laughing, men playing pool look up and stare, mouths open, whilst darts miss the dartboard and the landlord stops drawing a pint.

"Jesus!" I manage between sharp intakes of breath. My eyes are running. *Don't—* I shake my head, unable to finish my sentence. *Keep quiet. I don't want to be carted off to a mental hospital.*

"Brandy," I tell the owner. "Make it a double-double, Rodney."

"You not been out there chasing 'em big, wild cats of yours again, Owen?" he asks, drawing a hearty laugh from the barflies and the men playing darts.

A laugh hitches in my throat as I wipe my face clean with the sleeve of my coat. Blood mixed with snot smears the fabric down to the cuff. "Something… like that…" I manage, my breathing coming back under control.

Pool balls begin clacking, darts thump at their black, red, and green beds.

"You okay, matey?" a man at the bar asks, turning on his stool to look at me.

I nod. "Fine, thanks. I took a tumble on my way here."

My hand is shaking, and it takes both to grab my drink from Rodney. The ice cubes clatter against the tumbler's rim, bringing to mind ships caught in a storm. The fiery liquid is in danger of sloshing over.

"You positive you're okay, Owen?" Rodney asks.

"A little shaken," I reassure him. "I went down pretty hard, banging my knees and elbow." I wince, making it look as convincing as possible. I even grimace as I hobble to a corner table, out of sight, out of mind. "A couple of hits of your finest Eight Bells and I'll be as right as rain. You'll see."

Rodney shrugs, goes back to serving his punters.

The chatter and laughter have hit their zenith by the time I've sat down and got myself comfortable. My camera bag, laptop case and weatherproof jacket lie by my side.

Before reaching for my laptop, I drain the glass of half its contents and set the brandy to one side. I gasp, sigh and wipe my mouth. On the table is a glass tube housing a candle which is burnt down to a stump. It offers little light. A faint smell of jasmine rises from it.

The wallpaper is drab and uninspiring; and in the spots where it has peeled off to reveal the bare wall, damp has taken hold. Still, the place is warm—a safe haven—and Rodney is someone I have known for years. If need be, I could spend the night, no questions asked.

I guzzle the last of the brandy and order another.

"Run me a tab, Rod, please."

"Sure thing, Owen."

I take my drink back to my table, hands no longer shaking, and sit down. Placing my glass on a coaster, I take my laptop case and unzip it. I remove my mobile PC, open it and switch it on.

The battery is full.

Good, it'll need it.

With my laptop set up, I turn to the carry case and dig out a pile of handwritten notes, files, a pad and pen. I also remove the memory card from my camera, and pause when my gaze crosses the backs of my hands. The skin has been torn off both sets of knuckles. Dried blood has crusted over the cuts. Ignoring this for now, I slip the small plastic card into a port at the PC's side.

I may as well send the images. I don't think this can wait. Besides, if something should happen to me after I leave here, it'll be good to know my information has been passed on to Jim and Sam.

I open a fresh Word document and take a large gulp of brandy, inhaling deep and exhaling noisily.

Where, and with whom, do I start? What about Twin Jesters itself? The people have a right to know about the town, about its chequered past... But is the violence and bloodshed relevant? Of course; it shows how cursed the place is. In that case, I'll start with Sam Enrich.

"Sam Enrich." I say aloud, making me think about the conversation I had with the private eye a week ago.

* * *

"Hello, this is Owen Figs, Bridgend News Post. How can I—*Sam*?" I smile into the phone.

"I need your help, Owen."

"Okay, if I can. What's on your mind? You don't sound yourself. Is everything—?"

"Dandy, mate," Sam cuts me off. "I'm looking for information to help me with a job I'm on."

I slide my legs off my desktop, sit up and huddle closer to the phone. "This wouldn't have anything to do with Twin Jesters, would it?" I whisper into the receiver.

"How—?" Sam stammers. "Doesn't matter. Yes, possibly. They've put you on it?"

"Yes, I'm looking into it. Strange, don't you think?"

"Very. Do you believe the grapevine?"

"And what would that be, Sam?" My grin must be infectious. Sam laughs.

"Look, you scratch my back and I'll scratch yours. Deal?"

"Depends…"

"What will it take to get you up off your arse and out there with your camera??"

"You think I'm crazy enough to go there?" I reply, my voice pitched. "The police have the town sealed off. It's a no-go area. I'd be arrested on sight."

"Then what the hell have you been doing? You're supposed to be a ball-busting journo."

"Sure—talking to eyewitnesses, the police…"

"Oh, really? I suppose you know the army is planning to bomb Twin Jesters?"

"What?" I sit bolt upright. My colleagues turn to look at me; the hubbub in the office dies.

"You heard," Sam grunts. "In the next week or so, they're sending in a team of soldiers to try and eradicate the problem. If not, bombs away."

"Don't be crazy, man."

"You're talking to the best damn snoop there is, friend. I have contacts everywhere, and I paid good money for this information. Now I need some from you."

My hands are shaking. "What?" I choke out, my voice barely audible.

"I need you to get into the town and confirm the problem's existence, Owen. With photographic proof."

"Why?"

Sam hesitates a long string of moments before responding. "Because I believe the problem has spread to another town close by. Like I told you, I'm working a case, and I think it coincides with Twin Jesters. My client seems to think there's something strange going on at a pub by the name of The Lamb and Flag. I've confirmed it. If this truly does connect with Twin Jesters, then we could be sitting on something huge."

I chew my lower lip in trepidation. "Okay, you've got my attention. Tell me more."

"Remember the incidents in Bridgend many years ago, the ones involving the cannibals?"

I almost laugh. "No!"

"Then I suggest you look it up, connect the dots, Owen."

"But—"

"We've wasted enough time talking. Research Bridgend's history and seek out the murderers they used to call the 'Man-Eating Fucks'. When you do, get back to me *after* you've been to Twin Jesters."

"I—"

The line cuts to a dial tone. Grimacing, I drop the phone back on the hook.

* * *

A day after the call with Sam I had a meeting with Jim Hengroth, my boss and head editor at the Bridgend News Post. I needed his advice.

After I'd told him in confidence what the P.I. had said, Jim answers, "You're my top reporter, Owen. I'd hate to see you go out there on a whim. Nobody knows for sure what's going on inside Twin Jesters. Do you really want to risk your career—hell, your life!—for hearsay?"

"Isn't that what we do?" I smile.

"I suppose, but this is different. This is outright dangerous."

"If I don't live for the scoop, then what's the point of living?"

He chuckles. "I guess you're right, and I won't stop you. You know that. After all, I have a business to run." He claps me on the left shoulder with a huge, weatherworn and scuffed hand.

That's what happens when you spend your summers as a child, teen and young adult pitching hay on your daddy's farm, he'd explained one drunken evening. *Hard to cry it down, mind—the seasonal work helped pay me through five years of University.*

No amount of Neutrogena is going to soften those babies, I'd ribbed.

But that's where the joking ended with Jim. He was a good man and a blessing to work for, the hands-on sort of boss who wouldn't expect anything of anyone that he wouldn't do himself.

"Thanks, Jim. I'll be careful, promise."

* * *

I take another swig of brandy.

"You're going to be one ecstatic snoop when you receive my email, Sam. You too, Jim," I think aloud as I swirl the remainder of the drink in my glass, then finish it off and shout for another. The warm-bodied drink helps deaden the pain in my face, body and hands—especially my hands, which are hard at work typing an email to the private eye.

* * *

Dear Sam,

You were right. Merciful God, were you right! It's true. All of it—every last blood-soaked detail from the past to present regarding the Man-Eating Fucks. But there's more, much more, and only you, the government and I know exactly what's going on at Twin Jesters. However, we'll change that. I have the proof you need attached to this email.

Upon escaping Twin Jesters I was followed to the town's borders by the Fuckers, as they've been so grossly named. They almost got me, but I managed to make it to safety, to a pub I know. Still, I fear they are lurking outside, waiting to tear the flesh from my bones and the organs from my body.

I may wait it out here until daylight. The landlord is a friend.

This danger is also the reason why I've decided to email you from my current position. I don't want to die without someone else knowing the truth. After I've sent this, I plan to communicate with my editor, whose contact details can be found at the bottom of this correspondence.

You may want to speak with Jim should something happen to me.

Before I go into what happened at Twin Jesters, I need to tell you what I know about the Man-Eating Fucks and the town itself, for Twin Jesters is steeped in a bloody, violent past.

First, the name: Twin Jesters is an odd name for a town, isn't it? There's a reason for that. And the place is hardly a town—before the evacuations, some 452 people lived there; and now less than half remain. It's said that fifty or sixty of the escapees are in critical condition and won't last the week. But I digress. Let's get to the history of the place.

The town didn't exist until after the Roman garrison departed the isle in 410. At the time, Wales was divided into a number of separate kingdoms, the largest being <u>Gwynedd</u> in northwest Wales, and <u>Powys</u> in the east. Glywysing, or Glamorgan (Morgannwg) as we know it today, was a much smaller kingdom in modern <u>Gloucester</u>, ruled over by King Glywys.

According to twelfth century sources, after King Glywys died, his kingdom was divided into seven *cantrefs*, and each of his sons received one. These were a form of medieval Welsh land divisions, often ruled jointly by the head of the family or sometimes treated as appenage subkingdoms.

This is where it gets really intriguing, Sam. I never knew so much about Welsh history until I started digging.

Pawl, son of Glywys, settled in the cantref named after him (Penychen), and built a castle there. The land held great economic potential, and Pawl sought to develop it into a market and farming town. Construction was finished in the year 510. He named the new settlement after his twin jesters—Ddu and Coch, which translates to Black and Red. I can only assume their names were derived from the colours they wore.

This pair didn't look like your typical clowns of the day. Most jesters of that era wore brightly-coloured costumes comprising of bells, tassels and three-pointed cloth hats. They looked gaudy and told jokes. Not these two. In the scant records that mention them, they are depicted as looking sinister. Even though it was the medieval period and everything was ghastly and frightful, this pair took the biscuit.

Their black and red costumes were meant to evoke terror and blood. They both wore half-masks similar to the one made famous in *The Phantom of the Opera*, and the halves were said to interconnect when the two were placed together. On the exposed sides of their faces, black daubs of make-up shrouded their eyes, and white make-up was applied over their lips to give the impression their mouths were full of razor-sharp teeth.

Their make-up is worth commenting upon. With modern cosmetics, their look can be achieved with ease, but in the year 510, it was quite a feat.

The two men were said to be brutally strong. When they weren't in costume, they went about bare-chested, exposing tattoos that snaked around their torsos. And instead of a marotte with a carved, smiling head on it, they carried shrunken human heads impaled on a spike.

There is nothing funny at all about the jesters. They looked more like executioners than clowns.

* * *

I stop typing and pull away from my laptop.

My brandy sits untouched. I pick it up and take a small sip, starting to feel light-headed. Replacing the glass on the coaster, I sort through the files at my side and fish out the blown-up image of Ddu and Coch.

A fresh shiver rips a path down my back.

I resume typing.

* * *

There's hardly any information to be found on the jesters. I don't even know if they were real twins. All I do seem to know, which I've taken from history books and the local mythos, is how they came into Pawl's care, what they did, and their fate.

By all accounts, Pawl was a generous and sympathetic ruler. He is said to have found the twins in the wilds just outside the settlement that would become Twin Jesters. At the time, Ddu and Coch were youths, and Pawl, thinking them to be orphans, took them in and raised them as his own.

Then, one night, for reasons which have since been lost to history, the twins are believed to have gone on a killing spree. In the span of three nights, the pair is said to have slaughtered half the town's population. Among their victims was Pawl himself. Grisly as the murders were, the killings had been conducted in such a way that conclusive evidence could not be raised against the twins. Furthermore, a desire among the ruling class to "sweep things under the rug" helped ensure the twins would not be brought to justice.

Clwyd, Pawl's cousin, was next to rule over Penychen, which meant that the youths fell to his care. There was peace over the next ten years, though the town never fully recovered from the massacre. A curse had descended upon Twin Jesters.

Crops fared worse from season to season until eventually the yields were not enough to support the population. Each generation of calf was thinner than the previous, until at last the livestock failed to produce live births. Calves emerged stillborn from their mothers' wombs.

Eventually, the town came to be shunned. People wouldn't go near the place for fear of the curse attaching to them.

It was not long before trouble struck again.

Over the course of a week, there had been a rash of house fires that had resulted in several deaths. The guilty parties were never identified. This was going on in the midst of mysterious infant deaths—children as young as the newly-born were found murdered in their baskets where they slept, their throats cut. The terrified villagers demanded justice, which came swiftly enough. Just as tensions were approaching a boil, Ddu and Coch were caught in the act of starting a barn fire. In the minds of the townspeople, evidence of the twins' recent crime was enough to make them responsible for the previous arson attacks as well. In addition, the depravity of their offenses made it a foregone conclusion that they must also have been responsible for the infant murders.

With the evidence stacked against them, the twins were summarily declared guilty of their crimes. Clwyd ordered their deaths by hanging in the town square. Their bodies hung from the gallows for a week, at which point they were cut down and their heads were impaled on pikes with a message nailed to their foreheads:

Dyma beth sy'n digwydd i lofruddiaethwyr
(This is what happens to murderers)

Their heads remained on the spikes until their flesh, eyes and tongues had been pecked away by carrion birds, until at last the bone weathered, cracked and fell apart.

But even in death, the village would not be free of the jesters' curse.

Almost as soon as the twins' rotted remains hit the earth, the town was beset by all manner of disasters: swarms of rats, floods, disease, famine—death. Not even Clwyd, who had ordered the jesters' executions, was safe from the curse. Within months, he was found dead, his severed head impaled on a pike.

The string of disasters proved to be too much for the townsfolk to bear, and the village of Twin Jesters was ultimately abandoned. It remained that way until the tenth century, when Gruffydd ap Llywelyn used the ghost town as a garrison during his conquests against the English, and later, his home. Legend has it that he chose to settle here after a vision in which he beheld a pair of jesters who persuaded him that the town would be the site of a great victory.

He saw it as a blessing, Sam.

A fucking charm, of sorts.

Gruffydd ap Llywelyn had thought he'd been touched by God.

Goddamn idiot!

When I looked into Gruffydd's life, I turned up some interesting information you won't find in most history books. The official story is that Gruffydd allied himself with Ælfgar, son of Leofric, Earl of Mercia, who had been deprived of his earldom of East Anglia by Harold

<u>Godwinson</u> and his brothers. They marched to <u>Hereford</u> and did battle against a force led by the Earl of Hereford, <u>Ralph the Timid</u>. Gruffydd destroyed them, then sacked the city and crushed its <u>motte-and-bailey castle</u>. Shortly afterwards Ælfgar was restored to his earldom and a peace treaty was concluded.

What the historians won't tell you, however, is that two jesters were often seen on the battlefields, helping Gruffydd and his army defeat the opposition. Wherever the jesters were spotted, the battlegrounds were always a scene of great bloodshed, even by medieval standards.

By 1056, Gruffydd had seized full control over <u>Morgannwg</u> and <u>Gwent</u>, along with extensive territories along the border with England. After another victory at Glasbury, the English finally recognized his sovereignty as the King of Wales. Gruffydd then returned to Twin Jesters to rule over his newly-acquired dominions.

By this time, though, Gruffydd was a changed man. The town—or perhaps the influence of its jesters—was turning him into an overconfident warmonger. All he could see was power. Gruffydd was blinded by it, and through his victories, he'd started believing his own hype.

Some five years after establishing his rule, Gruffydd received another vision from the jesters. Following their advice, he reached an agreement with <u>Edward the Confessor</u>, but the death of his ally Ælfgar in 1062 left Gruffydd vulnerable once again. In late 1062, <u>Harold Godwinson</u> obtained the king's approval for a surprise attack on Gruffydd's court at Rhuddlan. The general consensus is that Gruffydd was warned of the attack in time and escaped out to sea before he could be captured, but that's a lie. Gruffydd was slain at Twin Jesters during Harold's surprise attack, his head impaled on a pike in the town square. With his death, the land of Wales fell and was annexed into England.

The rest is history, as the kids say.

People will believe what's been recorded in books, of course, but local Welsh historians will tell you otherwise. And, from what I've witnessed tonight in Twin Jesters, I believe the rumors, Sam. I'm not easily spooked, but I'm positive on this one and I hope I can convince you.

Others, too.

There's darkness at work, here. Twin Jesters is cursed by Ddu and Coch, who still roam, their reign of terror unending after Gruffydd's death.

Harold Godwinson, who orchestrated the attack on Gruffydd, died in Pawl's castle at Twin Jesters. He was murdered, his body mutilated nearly beyond recognition.

The town was destroyed in a massive fire one hundred years after Harold Godwinson's conquests. It lay in ruins for two centuries, then was rebuilt by a businessman who sought to exploit the surrounding natural resources. The atrocities started back up again: murders, rapes, plagues, deaths… the jesters' doings? I think so. There are reams of blood-drenched stories about the place the historians all disregard as local myths.

You're probably wondering why I'm telling you all this. Tonight, with my own two eyes, I saw the fools of yesteryear, and I believe they've brought the threat you spoke of to Twin Jesters, a town that's seen peace, bar for the odd incident here and there, for the past five hundred years.

Why has it started again? While I can only guess, here goes.

This year, 2010, marks the town's fifteen-hundredth anniversary. The townspeople have begun celebrating with street parties, fun and games. Even the local brewers got in on the action by brewing a new beer for the festivity: Weeping Fools.

Plus, the restoration of Pawl's castle has been completed.

When two jesters turned up for a party, one wearing black, the other red, nobody suspected a thing—that is, until the killing started.

A few days ago, I spoke to one of the survivors, a Mr. James Gogwin, who's currently laid up in the hospital with minor injuries. He told me the week leading up to the festival, which had been planned to span from late Friday evening through to Monday afternoon, was "pleasant and peaceful. Nothing seemed out of the ordinary."

"It was your average working week," he continued. "When Friday rolled around, and the party kicked off, everything ran smoothly. And then, on Saturday afternoon, as people took to the streets to continue enjoying their town's activities, a pair of fools strolled into Twin Jesters with a bunch of naked people caked in mud and leaves. They looked like feral cave-dwellers."

I didn't have to push Mr. Gogwin for answers.

"At first, we stood about, laughing and joking, thinking the jesters had been hired by someone from within the community. We didn't think anything of it, you know? The nakedness was inappropriate because there were small children present, but I thought it was part of some strange act. Besides, you couldn't really see their privates—the filth and greenery hid their modesty. They were led by these clowns, who were juggling flamin' daggers whilst riding unicycles. When they themselves got closer—and I don't mind telling you this—I almost soiled myself."

Before I could ask why, Mr. Gogwin continued.
"They were—dead—behind the eyes, I mean. There was no colour to their faces, even though they wore make-up. The laughter all around me turned to gasps. The children started sobbing, screaming and pointing, as the jesters snarled and snapped their teeth, which looked like needles; hundreds upon thousands of needles, all stained red. Then they started throwing their burning blades. Mrs. Salls, who was standing next to me holding her granddaughter to her chest, caught two daggers in her eyeballs, which exploded like water balloons. A third, fourth, fifth and sixth, thunked into Olivia, the child, pinning her to her grandmother as she wailed, bled and burned. Pandemonium ensued. A stampede erupted, as burning bodies hit the ground one after another: men, women, children… When the jesters ran out of knives, they unleashed the cave-dwellers, who started attacking people by—eating—them. Flesh, tongues and eyes were torn from p-people. Their skin… devoured—"

Here, Mr. Gogwin broke down, refusing to speak further. I had to find others willing to open up, thinking it would be easy, but most refused, except a young widow, a Ms. Peterson, who'd come face-to-face with the "cave-dwellers."

"I wouldn't call them cave-dwellers," she told me. "They looked more like cannibalistic freaks to me— things that live deep in the woods or underground. They snatched my Lilly from my hands—"

I discovered Lilly was Ms. Peterson's six-year-old daughter.

"They tore the flesh from her face. One of them ripped her leg off—it took me days to—wash—her blood from my—my hair."

I didn't want to push her, but she continued once she'd composed herself and stopped crying.

"There were loads of them; fifty or sixty. Maybe a hundred. I don't really know. The streets became chaos, and I found myself ankle-deep in bloody water that had body parts, organs and party food floating on it. It was like something out of a horror film. When I got to the town's border, I saw the police arriving—they had a helicopter in the sky. I was told by others that the army would eventually turn up, but I'm not sure."

After getting all I could from Ms. Peterson, I went to the police station for more information, but didn't turn up much—they were tight-lipped about the whole thing. They also denied the army's involvement, even as they escorted me off the premises. I was lucky to escape their clutches with my camera, notepad and laptop.

* * *

I stop typing, my fingers aching. As I sip my drink, which will be my last, I read through my email, making sure all information is present and correct.

"Another, Owen?" Rodney yells over.

I look up, startled, and shake my head. "I'm feeling dizzy."

This rouses a few titters from the men propping up the bar.

I ignore them and go back to my PC.

* * *

These "cave-dwellers" are your "Man-Eating Fucks," Sam. I found pictures of them in old newspaper clippings at the library. Do you think the jesters brought the tribe back to life? What if they can't be stopped? Are there more? Maybe the jesters conjured up a new clan of Man-Eating Fucks based on the history they know about Bridgend?

Whichever may be the case, you were right about us sitting on something huge!

Don't bother returning my email, Sam, as I want to speak with you face-to-face. I need to get everything straight and down on tape if I'm going to write about it in the paper; I might leave out the part about seeing ghosts.

Having said that, I could mention them and say that someone could be masquerading as Ddu and Coch—that a couple of local nutters want people to believe the history. Then again, do I want a straitjacket as an early Christmas present? Leaving the jesters out is for the best.

Anyhow, I need to tell you about what happened at Twin Jesters tonight.

* * *

Again, I stop typing.

Maybe I'll have that brandy after all, Rodney, I think to myself.

I get the barman's attention and ask for a double.

"A double-double?" he calls back.

"Please, Rodney." My voice wavers, and I fail to see the rotund landlord walk over to me and clamp a meaty hand to my shoulder.

"Are you fine there, lad?" Rodney asks.

"Ye—"

"I've never seen you this…"

"This what?" My guts knot and I fear they'll fall out of my anus if I don't clench.

"Like—like you've seen a ghost. You're as white as a sheet, Owen."

"It's nothing—"

"You never put brandy away as you're doing this evening. Is something troubling you? Is *someone* giving you trouble?"

I shake my head, take my drink and swig a mouthful. "I promise you, everything's okay."

"Well, if there *is* anything I can help with, yell. You've been a loyal customer over the years, and I'd hate to see anything bad happen to you."

I give a half-hearted smile, even though I'm genuinely pleased by Rodney's concern. "Trust me, please."

The man nods and lumbers to the bar. As I watch him go, I notice some of the barflies looking in my direction. They're smirking.

Nosy fuckers.

I give them an aloof, distasteful look, before shaking my head and dropping it back to my laptop. My eyes travel along the last few lines I've written. I take a small hit of brandy and place it to one side.

The shakes have subsided.

The ice-vipers that were nestled in my guts have melted and burned away.

I take a deep, shaky breath.

* * *

I have to admit, I wasn't going to go tonight, Sam. I saw it as a wild goose chase. Not only that, I was worried I'd get myself into a heap of shit. But hell, how could I not? I'm a journalist. A "hard-nosed" one at that, remember?   In my twenty or so years of covering news stories for various papers, never, ever have I seen or heard of anything like I have tonight. Hell, I've never taken such a risk before.

I've wished for excitement, even thinking about moving to a large city—

Ah, I've gone off on a tangent…

I went to Twin Jesters with an open mind, putting the eyewitness reports down to some sort of mass delirium or madness that had been contracted from a gas leak or virus that had wormed its way into the town. I even swept aside what you'd told me, Sam.

How wrong I was! I'm also glad I decided to pick up my reporting equipment and head out there—even if it ends up costing me my life.

The army are out there.

Or were, rather.

My first thought was to walk to Twin Jesters, but I decided against it last minute, thinking I might need a fast get-away. I'd almost laughed at that. The smile was soon wiped from my face when I was met by armed soldiers blocking the town's main entrance.

"This is a government zone now, sir—you'll have to turn around and go back," I was told. Normally I would have pushed, tried worming my way in with a silver-tongued response, but I felt threatened by the G.I. Joe wannabe, who had three others with him.

They loomed over me, Sam, and the one who'd spoken to me kept his hand on his holstered handgun the entire time. I didn't utter another word. Instead, I left and searched for another way in, but was met by the same resistance.

I had one option left: I ditched the car and used the night as camouflage. When someone wants to gain access to somewhere badly enough, they'll find a way. And so I crawled through a sewage pipe like a rat, popping up in the middle of Twin Jesters.

The lengths we go to...

* * *

A genuine laugh escapes me. It feels good, even though it attracts the attention of Rodney and the bar bozos. I gulp some brandy and avoid eye contact.

* * *

Even though the stench of shit was overpowering, I could still smell the charring of flesh, which is unmistakable to me as I worked four summers at my dad's crematorium when I was younger.

It was all around me, filling my nostrils.

Tears stung my eyes.

The heat within Twin Jesters was staggering.

Within seconds, my shirt matted itself to me, my forehead was like a burst dam from the sweat.

I shot to my feet, unloaded my camera, and started sneaking around. It didn't take long for me to locate bodies that had been burned by the army. Some were still alight, others were burned-out husks.

I feel sick thinking about it.

I'm not ashamed to say that I vomited all over a flaming corpse.

Hell, when I was being chased, I wet myself, and that's a hell of a thing for a grown man to admit. But I think anyone would have, had they come face-to-face with what I did.

After following a trail of scorched remains, I ran across the soldiers doing the burning. They were kitted out in suits that made them look as though they belonged on a space programme, with flamethrowers in their hands and petrol tanks on their backs.

It was crazy.

There were five of them in total, and they were guarded by three soldiers brandishing automatic weapons.

Sound like something out of a film, doesn't it?

Believe me, it's not. I was there, and I probably still smell to high heavens of human waste and smoked barbeque.

That's probably why I'm getting such strange looks here at the pub.

Twin Jesters looked war-torn. Cars and buildings were riddled with bullet holes. I even saw a tank stalking the streets. Craziness.

Had I been caught, I fear I would have been shot on sight. Hell, if we go public with these pictures and stories, I could end up in jail. I'm not sure what scares me more—the fate of Bridgend as a whole, me dying or being incarcerated for treason. They'll probably throw me in a deep, dark hole beneath London to rot.

If you don't hear from me in a day or so, make sure you get all this out there—don't let me die in vain.

Once I'd captured enough images of the soldiers participating in body burning, I moved around the town as stealthily as possible. Where no soldiers roamed, the place was a ghost town—hollowed-out buildings and empty houses with smashed windows and missing doors. Some structures had even collapsed, spilling their bricks and mortar into the streets.

A cloying, thick-as-soup dust hung in the air and the multiple fires cast searing, wavering and bottomless shadows. I heard their snarls; the Man-Eating Fucks'. I was terrified, Sam, but nothing could prepare me for the sight I was about to witness.

Towards the back of Twin Jesters where the land runs out and a river cuts through, soldiers were digging a mass grave. Bulldozers were ploughing dead and burned bodies into it; there must have been fifty or sixty being dozed.

I've also included those photos.

Before the soldiers could finish burying the townspeople's remains, the Man-Eating Fucks attacked. They came out of the darkness all shadows and teeth—

and tore through the military before they could react, let alone get a shot off.

In minutes, the bulldozer and digger sat idling, their drivers devoured. And when they were finished…

* * *

I grab my brandy and drink the remainder greedily. Some of it spills out of my mouth and splashes into my lap.

* * *

…they were led into the heart of the town by Ddu and Coch.

I swear. I saw them.

It wasn't a trick of light or anything such, Sam. They were there, with God as my witness, and they led the charge like a pair of demented dragoons minus their horses. I even took photos.

Ddu and Coch saw me, too, even though they were stood at an impossible distance, when you consider I was shrouded in blackness. They pointed their fingers and let out a deafening cry, wail, screech—no human has ever produced a noise like that—which I took as a battle cry.

Blood trickled out of my ears and nose, the shout was that powerful.

And as I retreated, taking as many snaps as I could, I saw more and more Man-Eating Fucks spill out of the foliage at the backs of those advancing. It was as spectacular to watch as it was terrorizing.

I ran, screaming, with piss trickling down the legs of my jeans.

When I bumped into soldiers, they tried stopping me, which, by then, I was gibbering, crying wreck, trying to warn them.

They soon lost interest in me as shots rang out from behind.

Somewhere in Twin Jesters, a siren began to wail.

"Here they come!" someone bellowed.

More gunfire.

The reek of cordite was choking.

Before making a dash for the bridge at the town's edge, I stopped and looked back. The carnage was horrendous. The Man-Eating Fucks, which I could then see plainly, were hideously disfigured—monsters. There's no other word for them, and seeing them in full fight, with blood, guts and gore decorating their chops and chests, was far-fetched, but I was witnessing it.

Flesh was torn away, along with privates and eyeballs.

And the screaming, Sam; God, the screaming—it'll haunt me forever.

When the remaining soldiers were torn up and torn through, the jesters and Man-Eating Fucks set their sights on me, and that's when I fled to this pub.

They didn't follow.

I had a gut feeling they wouldn't, but why? Are the jesters trapped there? If so, why did the Man-Eating Fucks stop? After all, you've seen them elsewhere, which brings me back to an earlier point—did the jesters reanimate the Man-Eating Fucks of yesteryear? The ones killed in the articles you told me to read? If that's the case, then we're dealing with spirits. There's food for thought!

How do we explain that if nothing's found in Twin Jesters tomorrow morning? Will the bodies of the soldiers have disappeared? Will the government then level the place with bombs and explain it away as a gas leak or some such tripe?

Before I sent this email to you, I read through it and realised I waffled far too much, but I needed to tell someone all this. I was worried I'd take the knowledge to my grave.

Anyway, I'll be in contact soon.

Best,

Owen.

* * *

I pack away my laptop and camera, suck the dregs out of my glass and return it to the bar to settle my bill.

The barflies give me a fleeting look.

Outside, I glance at the bridge. My nut sack shrivels and I pull my coat's collar around my neck that bit tighter.

I hear their hisses and cat-calls from beyond the darkness.

"Going to pull your tongue out through your arssse, sssnoop!"

The icy threat cuts me to the marrow. I turn from the pub and make my way towards home.

* * *

Sam Enrich rolls over in his bed, the morning light coming through his window blinds having grown too strong to be ignored. Groaning, he plods to the folding table where he'd left his laptop powered on. Wiggling the mouse to kick the PC out of low-power standby mode nets him a view to his desktop and its cluster of icons. A new email sits in his inbox. He opens it, already knowing who'd sent it without stopping to read the addressee line. A grin crosses his lips—he knew he could trust Owen with this job. The newsman's snooping has paid off in spades.

He sits, hunched over his laptop's tiny screen, devouring Owen's message word for word. Minutes later, at the stroke of eight in the morning, his PC goes into a fit of stuttering chirps as new emails flood his inbox. He ignores them, as he knows these are from the various newspapers to which he's subscribed—information is a P.I.'s stock in trade, after all, and newspapers were often good for leads.

Eventually, he can ignore them no longer. The insistent notification beeps and alert boxes piling up along the right side of his screen demand his attention. He turns his gaze to the headlines, and his jaw drops in the sort of awe and terror that can clench a man's guts to the size of a tangerine.

"Twin Jesters Destroyed by Fire." —*South Wales Media.*

"Town Detonated by Terrorists." —*The News Corner.*

"Mysterious Murders & Mayhem:What Are *You* Hiding?!" —*Herald.*

"Award-Winning Journalist Found Dead in River." —*Bridgend Mail.*

Crazy Horse

Leanne pulled into a parking space, applied the car's handbrake, killed the engine and plucked the keys from the ignition. She yawned, relaxed back in her seat and looked up at the jade-coloured neon sign of the new shopping market called Crazy Horse.

It was too bright – the blazing green sickly – for her burning, sleep-laden eyes. She looked at the clock on her vehicle's dash which alerted her it was eleven thirty p.m.

I don't know if I can do this tonight, she thought. And then her new home came to mind – her new *empty* home. *No, I need to get this shopping done especially knowing I have tomorrow off. When will I do it otherwise? I can't go another night without a kettle!*

"*Ugh!*" She forced air through her flaring nostrils, placed her keys in her handbag and got out. She slammed the car door. "Let's go spend money I *don't* have."

Before moving to the roughest part of the city for the only job she could land, a nursing assistant in a care home, Leanne had had it all: fiancé, well-paid medical job for a private hospital, fabulous house and car to be proud of. Not that she was materialistic, but, no matter how much she tried to convince herself otherwise, she did like the finer things in life. What girl didn't?

Her fairy-tale lifestyle (*if* you could call it that, being as she was a working stiff) had come crashing down around her when she walked in on her white knight being sucked off. When Leanne strolled through their bedroom door in their castle, the Rapunzle-wannabe from down the street, with her arse-length blonde hair, had had six inches of her man's seven down the back of her throat, her face already covered in a money shot.

Leanne exploded like TNT capable of levelling three blocks of buildings with fancy glass, grabbed Rapunzle by her sweat-soaked hair and threw her down the stairs.

She'd rolled like tumbleweed, smashing through most of the spindles supporting the banister.

Leanne's knight, spurting pre-come, had tried to get to his feet to stop her from giving chase.

"I'll *kill* you!" The veins in her neck had protruded, with one throbbing at her temple. Her eye twitched. She'd raced downstairs, her knight behind her, his limp dick bouncing.

"Are you *insane*, Lee?!"

Rapunzle had been gathering her naked form off the floor when Leanne reached her, kicking out with a booted foot and snapping one of the woman's ribs. Before Leanne could inflict more pain and damage, her knight reached her, picking her up and dragging her off into the living room.

"Get out of here, Sheila! I'll call you later." He proceeded to pin Leanne to the sofa, and she went at him with her teeth and tried to claw his face with her hands.

Call her he did, after telling Leanne he no longer wanted to be with her even though she'd been willing to forgive him. In hindsight, she'd only wanted to retain the lifestyle she'd grown accustomed to.

Plus, he was an incredible fuck.

Even his cock, tongue and technique in the sack were perfect, she thought, gathering her belongings, packing and leaving.

Within the week, news reached Leanne that her knight had moved his Rapunzle in.

She'd been crushed, broke and had to take the first house and job she could find, having no family to rely on, her parents dead.

She walked towards the supermarket and the glaring image of Crazy Horse loomed over her, as though the brave chief was gunning for her on his trusted steed. She could almost hear the thunderous noise of galloping hooves and the war leader's battle cry, could taste the dry Nebraska dust thrown by the beast's charge.

We're getting more like America every day! Isn't it bad enough their fast-food chains, Halloween and cinema made it here, without their shops too?

Leanne swallowed her frustration when she thought of Penny, the young nurse she worked with.

"It's real cheap there, Lee, and they stock *everything* from food to toys, clothes to cars. Once you start, you won't be able to stop."

When she got closer to the entrance, with Crazy Horse now behind her, Leanne saw the massive, open-air car showroom to her left.

"This place must have cost a small fortune to build," she muttered, grabbing a trolley and pushing it towards the automatic doors.

The car park alone boasted more than two thousand bays, not counting the spaces for surrounding shops such as McDonald's, KFC, an Army and Navy store, a sex vendor, cinema and countless others – the retail park stretched as far as the eye could see.

"You can probably spot its glow from Mars!" Leanne entered the superstore, the security guard giving her the once-over as though he could detect how poverty-stricken she was.

Come on, I'm not that *broke... Hardly rolling in it, either.*

As if on cue, the guard unclasped his radio and spoke into it. Leanne couldn't hear what he was saying, but figured he was informing the eye in the sky of her presence.

When their gazes fused, she looked down at her feet and pushed her trolley away at a hearty pace.

If he didn't think I looked shady before, he probably does now. She chanced a look back and wished she hadn't, for he was staring at her. *Jesus, paranoid much, pal?*

She gambled on another glance, blushing, to find the guard had gone.

Her heartrate slowed.

My silly, overactive imagination. She expelled air through her nose and laughed. "Right, what do I need?" she muttered, plucking her shopping list out of her back pocket. "Ah, yes – let's start with the electrical goods. A girl needs her coffee of a morning."

Thirty minutes into her shopping, with the clock ticking past midnight, Leanne felt confident she was almost done.

"I should be home by one." She grunted, directing the laden trolley towards a new aisle. "Coffee, coffee…" she muttered, scanning the shelves. She spotted what she was looking for at the end of the row. "Sod it." Opting to leave her basket on wheels where it stood, Leanne walked to get her goods. As she scanned the brands, she also picked up a bag of sugar and a box of tea bags.

When she returned to her cart, she saw an envelope resting on top of her mound of cheap commodities. There was a single word on it, marring the otherwise pristine and starch white wrapper with big bold lettering:

LEANNE

Her heart hitched and her breathing became erratic.

The jar of coffee she clutched almost slipped from her loosening, clammy grip.

She turned, on the spot.

The aisle behind her was deserted; before her, too.

The hell…

Silence grew around Leanne, and she blocked out the soft, instrumental muzak that played overhead and all about, as her vision became tunnel-like. She couldn't remove her gaze from the chunky word and its thick black lines.

Tentatively, she reached a hand out and snatched the envelope off the trolley. Before ripping it open, she checked once again to make sure there was nobody standing close by.

Leanne tore at a corner, creating a hole big enough for her pinkie, then slowly ran her finger across the top, tearing the package open in a careful manner. Inside she saw a piece of paper, and, with caution, plucked it free between her thumb and forefinger, holding it away from her like a revolting sports sock.

After placing the envelope aside, she unfolded the lined, three-hole paper, and something fluttered to the floor. When she looked, she gasped, for it was a fifty-pound note that lay at her feet.

She gasped. "*Jesus!*"

Wanting to snatch it up, Leanne unfolded the paper and read aloud:

"Dear Leanne, come and play with me. For further instructions, go to the bread aisle, my wholesome angel. You'll be glad you did. Warmest Regards, SOG (Student of Games)."

"*Student* of Games?!" Had she not been rattled, Leanne would have laughed. However, it did help lessen her anxiety. "At least it's not my crazy ex with a threat, or something worse. No, why would he – I've not heard anything from him in weeks."

Leanne shook her head. *This is something else...* As she retrieved the note, she looked about her again to make sure there was nobody watching, and then pocketed the money. *If someone wants to give me free cash, who am I to turn my nose up at it? Not like I'm breaking a law...*

Leanne grabbed her trolley and pushed it towards the bakery.

What the hell am I doing? There isn't going to be more money, you know. This is someone's idea of a sick—

Her heart sank when she saw the colossal size of the bread area: loaves, bagels, treats, savouries. The bakery itself was in darkness, with no staff to be seen. Apart from the muzak, the whole place seemed still. Quiet.

It brought with it a sense of unease.

Leanne turned, thinking she felt an unwanted approach, but there was nobody there.

It's the note and money. Got me all jumpy.

Steeling herself and leaving her trolley behind, Leanne strolled along the rows of bread, searching. She had no idea what she was looking for.

My wholesome angel. Wholesome. Wholesome bread?

Leanne scanned those types, all brands, and was tempted to swipe them off the shelves as she went, but she didn't need to.

"Ah-ha!" Her outburst caused her to wince. She hunched her shoulder and scrunched her eyes closed, hoping nobody had heard her.

On a shelf level with her midriff, Leanne saw the corner of an envelope protruding from a wholesome loaf. The brand: Angel. With the rapidity of a striking snake, she grasped it from under the bread, toppling a few others as she did so.

Like the last one, it was addressed to her. She tore it open and removed the note from inside, spying something coloured in the folded paper.

God, more *money!*

Before she got too enthusiastic, Leanne unfolded it, her breath catching in her throat. Two fifty-pound notes lay in the crease.

Fuck. No, this must be some kind of—

"Dear Leanne, *congratulations*!" she read aloud. "You've taken your first minor step on the road to fun and riches. More awaits. Do you have the courage to proceed? I do hope so. At one a.m., take five with the Tribe. You'll be glad you did. Yours, SOG."

She forgot the clue for the time being and felt the money. Smelled it.

Am I involved in some kind of 'lucky shopper' type of thing? Leanne looked for signs indicating such an affair, but there weren't any.

Not knowing what was going on scared her the most, more than the free money and 'game', but there seemed to be nothing she could do about it.

"Why the hell am I complaining? I have a hundred and fifty quid in my arse pocket. For doing nothing…"

But then other thoughts dawned on her: Who was this person, and what was his end goal? Did he wish her harm?

To kill her?

Rape her?

Capture her?

Torture her?

What kind of madman plays childish games and makes a nobody like me rich? A madman, *that's who!*

Leanne took sneaky glances this way and that, spotting nobody. It made her think that she was the only person inside the massive, ghost-like ship of a supermarket.

She looked at her watch and noted it was twelve thirty, which gave her less than half an hour to figure out the clue and get to the next one.

"If there was fifty in the first, and a hundred in the second, will the next one contain two hundred?"

At that point, she thought her heart was going to stop.

Her mouth became dry.

Take five with the Tribe? What does it mean…?

For the next ten minutes, Leanne walked up, down and around the shop, trying to spot something, *anything*, that pertained to the clue found in her last letter.

She stopped in the middle of the shop and thumped the trolley's push bar. "*Fuck*! I can't work this out at all." Leanne raked her stiffened fingers through her hair and expelled air through her mouth. "Damn. I was doing so well. Maybe this is a blessing?"

At the point of thinking about giving up, paying for her goods and heading home, Leanne spotted the supermarket's inner coffee shop in the distance: The Tribe's Tepee.

Her heartbeat increased in speed as she pushed the trolley in the café's direction.

Yes!

As she continued along her path, Leanne failed to notice the unmanned tills, empty aisle and complete lack of staff and customers.

The coffee shop was vacant. However, the scene before her suggested it hadn't been that way for long. Plates of food and full mugs of hot drinks with steam rising from them sat on the tables.

"What the…" Thinking she saw a flash of movement to her left, Leanne looked. There was nobody there. Behind the counter was empty. A ceiling fan squeaked as it turned. "Hello?"

Leaving her trolley, she ambled deeper into the space.

"Is there anyone here?"

Only the fan answered.

Her feet squealed on the freshly mopped tiles.

"Is there—?" Her eyes latched onto the coffee machine in front of her. There was an envelope taped to it with LEANNE written on it. She crossed to it and pulled it free, not taking a moment to open it. "Fill the provided mug and have five – you'll be glad you did. SOG."

There was a mug under one of the pipes connected to the hot drink machine.

Leanne pushed the button directly above, which dispensed water over the tea bag within it.

How thoughtful!

Taking her tea, Leanne went and sat at a table. She read the note again.

No clues. What am I supposed...?

She looked up and saw a huge clock adorning the wall behind the counter.

Take five. Five minutes. Time—is that the clue? Excitement coursed through her. On shaking legs, she stood and walked to the till. From there, she could see behind the clock – which wasn't flush to the wall – and saw a piece of paper hanging there.

"Holy shit!" The sound of her voice in the deserted room startled her, and she looked around. *Where the hell is everyone?* The thought was a fleeting one, her eyes drawn back to the note.

Pound signs danced.

Probably two hundred in there – think I'll need a chair to reach it. She bit her lower lip.

Leanne leaned over the counter and saw a stool close to the till.

"That'll do nicely."

After grabbing the seat and positioning it beneath the clock, Leanne kneeled on it, reached up and plucked the envelope free. It felt thicker. A smile grew on her face. Without getting off the stool, she tore the note open and sought the money out first.

As suspected – she clutched four fifty-pound notes.

"That's three hundred and fifty quid so far for doing *nothing*, and there could be a lot more to come!"

With purpose, she unfolded the note and read, "My dearest Leanne, if you haven't already finished your refreshment, please do. You have something to consider: do you want to continue with the game? If not, you may opt out now and keep what you have already won; things will get riskier from here on out… If you wish to continue, leave your trolley here in the Tepee, venture outside to the back of the shop and seek where the trolls hang out. You'll be happy you did. PS: I suggest taking something hard and heavy with you from the sporting goods section. My love, SOG."

Trolls? "Got to be a bridge!" She giggled, the clue hitting home. "Hang on. He said things will get riskier, and suggested a weapon…" It then dawned on her that it wasn't the shop playing some sort of 'lucky shopper' game with her – there was a weirdo fucking with her.

Does it matter? she thought, looking at the money. *He's not hurting me, and the next envelope will probably contain four hundred pounds!*

"Think what I could do with that. My woes would be over."

Is it worth the danger? a small voice at the back of her mind asked.

"Fuck this!" She swallowed the remainder of her tea, stuffed the cash in her back pocket, and headed out of the coffee shop.

Leanne found the sports section and got herself a baseball bat.

"I can't remember the last time I had so much fun." She swung the bat, relishing the sound it made cutting through the air.

The front doors had been locked, the gates lowered.

The guard was nowhere to be found.

"They've shut me in!" Panic fluttered in her guts. *No, it's all part of the game,* she thought, trying to soothe her nagging mind. Fear nipped at her subconscious. *The back door?*

Definite movement to her side made her jump. Something fell.

Leanne turned in the direction of the clatter.

Nobody.

On the floor, a stray can rolled towards her.

"Who's there?" She gripped the bat tighter.

One by one, the lights in the store winked out—*oh shit*—until she was standing in darkness.

She yelped.

A whimper developed in her throat.

When the back-up generator kicked in, it gave the inside of the shop a haunting, azure glow.

Leanne forced her thighs together.

Silence, bar her whine, engulfed her.

Someone was standing by that stack of cans. Watching…

The urge to piss weighed on her, and perspiration broke across her brow and upper lip.

Holding herself together, Leanne, almost jogging, made her way to the back of the supermarket, finding a door that led to the warehouse. Once there, she searched for an exit and found one behind a couple of forklifts.

Leanne pressed the push bar down, thinking this door would also be locked, but it opened, and she almost fell through it in surprise.

And that's when the voice came over the Tannoy.

"You have twenty minutes to retrieve the money and return inside. If you fail, the game will end."

"*Fuck!*" Leanne gathered herself and ran across the grassy patch in front of her until she reached the mesh fence that encircled the supermarket. Beyond it, she could hear the trickle of water. *How…?* She looked up, finding the top of the structure some fifteen feet in the air. "I'll never get over it!"

Not wanting to waste too much time debating it, Leanne started her climb, slipping a dozen times before making it up and swinging her body over the other side.

She looked at her watch after dropping to the floor.

That ate up six minutes!

Her nursing home-issued trousers had been torn, a gash adorned her elbow, and blood trickled down her forearm.

It's a scratch.

There wasn't a second to spare.

Leanne dashed from the fence, towards trees and foliage, pushing her way through low-hanging branches. When she popped out the other side, she saw an old stone bridge.

Who's that trip-trapping over my bridge…?

She heard laughter and chatter coming from under the structure.

Smoke billowed – a hint of weed clung to the air.

Leanne tried to swallow her fear and calm her heart. Her hands felt slippery on the bat.

Any shit, and I'll bash their teeth out!

"Fuck me harder, Steven!" she heard.

More laughter.

Thanks to the moonlight, she could see that colourful graffiti decorated the brickwork; crude images and words jumped out at her. Her cheeks flushed, but there was little time for bashfulness.

She went under the bridge and found three people. Two were fucking, and the other was recording the act on his phone. The woman, who was naked, tits bouncing, had her face pressed against the wall whilst the man screwed her arse. They were drenched in sweat.

"Grab her tits, man!" Camera Boy said. He had a stupid, shit-eating grin on his face that reminded Leanne of a dopey cartoon character.

Over his shoulder, stuck to the opposite end of the wall, she saw an envelope – its starch whiteness stood against the black-grey light.

"I-I—oh, God—I'm coming, Steve. I'm *coming*!"

Leanne wanted to look away but couldn't. There was something about the woman's orgasm face that amused her, and, against her will, she laughed. It was loud and braying – a roar – and it bounded off the walls.

Fucker immediately stopped, pulled out, yanked his trousers up and looked at her, as did the other two. As soon as the woman knew there was an outsider present, she ran off, leaving her belongings behind.

"Sorry to disturb your play, fellas, but I need something from—"

"Who the *fuck* are you?" Camera Boy asked, producing a flick knife. The blade made a sickening click as it snapped into place.

Fucker produced chains. "This is *our* turf, *bitch*!" He spat at her feet, his limp prick swinging like a club.

For the first time, Leanne noticed the men had matching tattoos.

"MeatHooks," she muttered, reading the ink on their upper arms.

"Yeah, that's us, Holmes."

Leanne laughed at that one. "Sorry."

Fucker got in her face. "You think this shit's funny?"

"Out of my way, little boy – you have something I need."

"You've—*ooph*!" he cried, doubling over as her knee smashed into his balls. He fell sideways, crashing into the murky water.

"The *fuck*?!" Camera Boy's mouth hung open, and he was too slow in reacting to the swinging bat, which caught him in the face. His nose crunched. Blood flew. "*Ugh!*" He was propelled backwards, his feet tangling with one another, and he too flopped into the water.

Leanne raced for the envelope, snatching it off the wall and doubling back to the fence. When she got there, she scaled it as fast as possible.

As soon as she was on the other side, she glanced in the direction she had come from, and saw two forms rushing out of the darkness.

Shit. She ran for the supermarket's back door, pleased to see it still open, and flew inside, slamming it closed behind her. Leanne collapsed against it and caught her breath.

"Jesus!" she panted, holding her heaving chest. "I'm out of shape."

That could have gone so wrong... The nagging voice was back.

But it didn't.

With her breathing under control, Leanne looked at the crumpled envelope and ripped it open.

Four hundred pounds graced the interior, along with a note.

Seven hundred and fifty pounds! She jumped up and down and squealed.

"My dearest Leanne, I hope the MeatHooks didn't give you too much bother? In my humble opinion, those boys need the love of a good mother." Leanne stopped reading, laughed, and imagined SOG saying such a thing to her face. "Now, back to the more serious matters at hand, my dear. You've proven yourself quite capable, a fundamental player in my game, but how far are you really willing to go? Remember, there's no backing out at this point... I'd hate to see you lose *everything*."

Leanne didn't like that sound of that. *A threat?* She continued. "Find the security guard, give him a blow job, and collect your reward at the Tepee, where you can take another rest. Warmest, SOG."

"A fucking blow job?! No. Fucking. Way. Not a chance! Are you listening to me?" She stamped her foot, crumpled the note, and threw it to one side. "*Shit!*" Heat rose up her neck, colouring her face. "*Argh!*" The veins in her neck protruded. "I'm not, not, *not* doing it! No. *Way.*" Tears threatened as she thrashed her body.

"Pouting like a four-year-old child won't get you anywhere, dear," a voice boomed over the Tannoy. "You have thirty seconds to make up your mind..."

"You—you *bastard*!" There was no reply. "I'm not doing it." She shook her head, her hair flying.

You'll double *your money. For what? A few minutes of awkwardness... Yeah, and lose my morals and everything else along with it. Nope.*

Eight hundred pounds for a suck job.

A grand total of fifteen hundred and fifty pounds.

"That's a lot of bills," she uttered. "Shit."

"Fifteen seconds…" the voice taunted.

I could pay off a fair bit of my debt with that kind of cash. And there might be more. Loads more!

"Ten…"

But sucking a dude's dick? I never did it that much for—

"…Nine…"

"Okay! You win. I'll do it."

What the hell was she saying? Was she really prepared to blow a man, especially a bloke she didn't even know?

Have I entered the Twilight Zone? Her head started spinning. Leanne grabbed a wrapped pallet of goods in front of her and steadied herself. Vomit burned in her throat, and tears once again stung her eyes. *I can't believe I'm thinking of doing it. Thinking? You've agreed!*

"I suggest you get moving, my dear," the voice came again. "Don't make me count you down."

"Fuck you, SOG, if that's who you are."

No reply.

Leanne swallowed the bile, righted herself and walked towards the door that would lead her to the shop floor.

All the lights came on, along with the soft muzak.

I can't do this...

And then her situation hit home. Reality came back into focus: she wasn't just in a low-paying job with long, soul-destroying hours, but under the weight of life-changing credit card and catalogue debt, and now on her own, paying for an over-priced house in a part of the city she was sure was run by hoods and corrupt politicians. But what choice did she have? It was the only affordable place within strolling distance of her job.

The walks home at night are no picnic, either.

On a few occasions, Leanne had been approached by winos, drunks and druggies. The rape alarm and mace she carried had come to her rescue each time.

What I'm about to do goes against every fibre of my being, but it's for a greater good. Right?

She felt drunk, her legs made of rubber bands.

Leanne steadied herself once more and put a hand to her mouth, fearing spew would jettison out, but it didn't.

"Bing-bong," a voice said over the Tannoy. "This is a customer announcement. Would the debt-riddled princess please report to aisle four? Thank you."

She wanted to scream, to beat her chest and pull her hair, but she shoved her rage aside and prepared herself.

Think of the money. A better standard of living.

Before she knew it, Leanne was standing at the entrance to aisle four. At the far end, a man dressed in a gimp suit stared back at her. He had one hand on his crotch.

A breath caught in her throat.

The man wore a security guard jacket and hat.

He's stroking it through the leather?

Her mouth dropped open.

He was bigger than the guard she'd seen earlier, standing at over six-and-a-half feet tall and weighing a good hundred pounds more.

Neither of them moved.

Time seemed to stop. Her heartrate galloped, and she feared it would punch a hole in her chest and race away into the night.

When he took a step forward, she whimpered. Her bladder pinched.

She thought to move backwards but held herself together.

As he drew closer, Leanne was surprised she hadn't bolted.

"You hardly ever want to screw, Lee," had been White Knight's words on a constant occasion. "Why can't you let go and be dirty with me at times? I want a woman, not a little prudish girl." His needling had hurt, but she'd not paid much attention – she'd had everything she wanted, and would have allowed him to keep his fuck-puppet from down the street. But he hadn't wanted her.

A tear slid down her cheek.

I'll show you prudish, fuck-face.

When the gimp stood towering before her, Leanne took a deep breath, smiled, and brushed her hair over her shoulder. "Is that for me, big boy?" She flicked her tongue and pointed at his crotch.

He nodded, slowly, and unzipped his mask.

His lips were coated with purple lipstick.

She reached out and removed his hand from the erection visible through his suit. Leanne put her fingers to his hardness and stroked.

Water filled her mouth, but she ignored it.

"Want to take your clothes off for me?"

He nodded, turned and indicated the zip at the base of his neck.

Leanne grabbed and lowered it, trying to make it as sensual as possible. When his smutty garb gathered at his ankles, he turned around, his dick pointing at her, his bell-end glistening. His breathing was raspy.

Wow! He seems pretty excited. This shouldn't take—

"Bing-bong," the voice came over the Tannoy again. "This is a customer announcement. You may want to consider swallowing his load for an eight-hundred-pound bonus. Thank you."

Leanne's fingernails dug into her thighs, but she kept smiling.

He knows exactly what the hell he's doing. Bastard!

She cleared her mind and drank in the man before her. He was heavyset with muscles; his chest rippled and his arms bulged.

I bet he could pop my head like a grape with those thighs.

His legs were trembling, his shoulders hitching as his breaths came in ragged rips.

Leanne hated to admit it, but she found him and the situation a smidge of a turn-on.

It would seem flirting with danger is a kick in disguise.

Gently, she wrapped her hand around his dick and eased his foreskin back.

He groaned, his knees buckling.

"You want me to put it in my mouth, don't you?"

He nodded.

Leanne lowered herself and, before she could give it too much thought, engulfed his hot cock with her mouth and swallowed as much of the prick as she could. Pre-cum hit the back of her throat. She gagged, but it didn't stop her from polishing his bell-end and teasing the pisshole with her tongue.

A large, rough hand planted itself on the top of her head. His fingers curled, bunching a tuft of her hair in his fist.

Leanne scrunched her eyes closed, fearing he would yank her head back and forth, aiding her in mouth-fucking him, but he didn't.

"*Ooh*!" he gasped. "Don't stop."

From the way he spoke, she could tell his teeth were clamped together, his lips pulled back.

After a few more minutes, he started thrusting in and out of her.

He's getting close.

Before she had time to consider the bonus, a hot, sticky spray flooded her mouth and filled her throat. Leanne pulled away, coughing and spluttering, with strings of saliva mixed with jism going with her.

Most of his muck had been swallowed.

"*Ugh*!" he cried, sagging to one side, grabbing a hold of a shelf to keep himself upright.

Another small jet of semen splashed across the shop floor.

"*Shit*!" Leanne said. "That's not fair," she pleaded. "I swallowed his mess."

Turning, Leanne walked away from the juddering muscleman and headed back to the Tepee.

"Your efforts will be taken into consideration," the voice over the speakers said, rubbing salt into her wounds.

The first thing she noticed when she returned to the café was that her trolley was missing.

"My things!"

Leanne stormed over to the table where her trolley had been and peered down at the envelope that lay on one of the padded seats. She was furious and wanted nothing more than to tear the package up, but knew she wouldn't, or couldn't. She was hooked, and she was pretty sure she would be willing to jump through any hoop SOG provided.

How far am *I prepared to go? Hurt someone? You've already done that... No, they were punks, and deserved it. They would have done worse to me. Would I...*kill *someone for the right price?*

Leanne grabbed an empty chair and sat with a thump. Between the thought of Muscleman's spunk wriggling around inside her guts and what SOG had in mind for her, her world spun.

This time, she did throw up.

I hope that won't disqualify me! Wiping her lip, she grabbed the envelope and ripped it open. There was four hundred and fifty inside, along with a note. *That's two grand in total.*

"My dearest, you continue to amuse and surprise me, and I'm pleased to grant you most of the bonus." Leanne stopped reading and counted the money. There was twelve hundred and fifty present, which gave her a grand total of two thousand pound thus far. "Now, let's see if you can take the next step, shall we? Same rules as before. If you don't comply, you will lose everything. And I do mean *everything*. At three a.m., you and Pinkie should dice with the slicer. Your reward will be waiting for you here. Warmest, SOG."

Leanne knew what the clue was driving at, and so she looked up at the clock. It was a lick after two thirty. She stayed in her seat, the fight and energy taken out of her. After a long, fourteen-hour shift, this had been the last thing she wanted, but there was no stopping now.

I have to see it through to the end.

Yet she wanted nothing more than to rest her head on the table and drift off to sleep. She yawned and spied the coffee machine.

On her feet, she walked over to the hot drink dispenser, ordered herself a black coffee and loaded it with sugar until she was pretty sure a spoon could stand upright in it unaided.

Her eyes felt red-raw and gritty. She rubbed them, yawned again, and took a hearty swallow of the liquid, which was tepid at best. Even though she made a face at the taste, she drank the rest and tapped the bottom of the cardboard cup to make sure she got all the sugar out.

At exactly ten to three, Leanne gathered up the note, pocketed the money and binned her empty cup as she left the Tepee.

Leanne made a beeline for the deli counter.

Her mind was already made up.

The only problem she had was whether she would have the nerve to carry out the task when the time came.

She looked down at her hand—it was shaking—and zoned in on her pinkie.

I can get it reattached, she repeated, on the verge of bursting into tears and pissing her knickers at the thought of what lay ahead.

As she passed the numerous aisles on her way, Leanne spotted the pharmacy counter and made a stop. She walked around the till and entered the back puff of the department where the drugs were kept.

She spent a few minutes rooting through drawers, picking out various pain killers, pads, gauze and other bits she thought she might need.

It doesn't say anything about me not being able to treat myself after the incident...

Once Leanne had everything she needed, she left the area and continued towards the delicatessen, which came into sight.

A breath caught in her throat when her gaze fell on the slicer. Her mouth became dry.

She closed her eyes and drew in a long, shaky breath, which she held before blowing it out her nose.

It'll be over soon. Think about the money – a better life.

Behind the counter she ambled towards the slicer. A jolt of pain shot through her arm.

I'm crazier than SOG!

A bottle of sanitizer stood by the machine, which was on and ready for use, the blade dripping with soapy water.

Leanne pushed the activation button and the cutter came to life with a whirring sound that iced her guts. Her skin crawled, and so she let go of the button.

Do it now, before you lose the nerve! It'll be just like ripping a plaster off.

Before she could give it another moment's thought, Leanne put her little finger by the blade and started the machine. It whined when bone met steel – a puff of smoke was emitted.

A squirt of blood powered its way up her face and into her hair.

She gasped, yelped and pulled her hand back.

The top portion of her digit rolled onto the floor. She retrieved it and put it into the ice behind her.

Her world spun. Black dots danced before her.

"*Ugh!*" she cried, keeping herself on her feet.

Blood pumped down her hand, even though she choked her wrist as tight as possible. "Fuck, fuck, fuck! I should have—"

Her eyes fell on the mini handheld blowtorch beside the slicer.

How caring!

Leanne let go of her hand, blood jettisoning, and grabbed the implement. After lighting it, she put the blue flame to her stump and screamed until her lungs were fit to burst and tears streamed from her eyes.

With the wound cauterised, she dressed it, dry-swallowed a few pain killers and sat in a puddle of her blood on the floor.

She felt faint, the colour draining from her lips and face.

"I-I need a drink," she gasped. "I'm spitting feathers here."

However, she couldn't move. Her legs were pillars of trembling jelly, and her backside felt like it weighed a ton.

"Bing-bong! This is a customer announcement. Would the lady with the nine-and-a-half fingers report to the Tepee as soon as possible, please? Thank you."

"Urgh-*argh!*" Leanne stamped her feet and pounded her thigh with her good fist. "I can't take much more of this! You mother*fucker!*" Her spittle flew.

Leanne tried to get up, but between light-headedness and weariness she slipped in her blood and sat back down. Hard. Ruby red droplets splashed up her face, and the bones of her arse ached.

Again, she attempted to stand, putting her good hand flat to the floor to bolster the support of her weight. She grunted. Her neck and cheeks flushed a deep scarlet-plum.

"*Fuck*!" Her hand slipped and her legs went in opposite directions, taking her into the splits. "No, no, no!" Before it became painfully too late, Leanne managed to shove herself to one side, clearing the blood and landing on a clean part of the floor. "I'm too old and tired for this shit."

She stumbled to her feet, propelled forward, and staggered from behind the deli counter. Once she had her bearings, Leanne headed for the end aisle, walked down it and grabbed the first bottle of whisky she could lay her hand on. She ripped the seal off with her teeth, stuck the bottle under her arm, and unscrewed the cap. After tossing the lid aside, she took a massive gulp.

"*Ugh*!" She coughed, spitting firewater residue. "Disgusting."

The liquid burned in her chest and drove a tingling sensation down her body and into her guts.

Her hurt numbed, but she knew it was just her mind denying its existence.

Leanne took a few more swallows before placing the glass container on another section of shelf and shuffling away.

The Tepee came into sight, and she thought she saw flickers of movement from within.

SOG!

She moved as fast as she could, but her legs and feet wouldn't cooperate, and by the time she got to the café, it was empty.

"Show yourself, you cowardly son of a bitch. Scared to meet a lady one on one, huh? Pussy."

Spotting the next note, Leanne pushed herself forward and flopped into a seat at the table where the envelope lay. It looked thick. She licked her lips. She put her trembling hand out, grabbed the package and squeezed it.

My, God... This can't be happening? It has to be some kind of—

She tore it open, the envelope coming apart at the seams and sending money fluttering to the floor.

Leanne took time to count it.

Four thousand pounds.

That made six in total.

If this pattern continues, the next task will be worth eight. Surely not? Who has this kind of money to throw away? Why me? What's going on? Is this illegal in some way? Am I being watched?

Her own grilling rattled her.

She removed the letter and read it.

"My dearest Leanne, I invite you to play just once more, if you wish. This will be one for the road, shall we say?" She pulled herself out of the note, thinking she could hear laughter. "Find the Golden Cherokee out front and set it free. You'll be glad you did. SOG."

Leanne lowered the paper and mulled it over. She had no idea what it meant.

Is there an Indian running around out there? A gold one?

As if to reassure herself there wasn't, because it had been a strange old night, she went to a window and looked out into the car park. It was deserted, bar a car or two.

"Wait a minute... Does he mean a four by four, as in the Jeep Cherokee?" Leanne pressed her face to the glass again and looked towards the supermarket's outdoor car lot. She couldn't make anything out. "Damn."

She was hesitant about going outside, in case the MeatHooks were still hanging around.

They could be waiting in the shadows to pummel my arse. A sudden throb of pain shot through her hand, and she winced. *I need another slug of booze, especially if I'm going outside.*

In the reflection in the window, Leanne saw a huge figure standing behind her. She turned on her heel, gasping, and pressed herself flat to the glass. The gimp security guard stood over her holding a bunch of keys in his hand.

"For me?" she asked, pointing at her chest.

He shook his head, his mouth zippered.

"Shall I, you know…?" Her hand went to his mask.

He nodded.

Leanne grabbed a hold of the zip and pulled, opening the mouthpiece.

"I'm here to let you out," he said. His tone didn't match his appearance and build.

Speaks like a child, she thought, *but looks as though he could eat bayonets for breakfast.*

"Oh, okay."

"Follow me, please."

He turned and walked towards the front door. When they got there, he slipped the appropriate key into the lock and turned it until the bolts clacked.

"You're free to go, and congratulations on your success thus far, Leanne."

The mention of her name startled her, but she didn't question it. She inched her way out through the door, her eyes on the giant in case he should try and grab her or take the money off her.

"I do hope you will keep playing with my master. You're on the road to wealth."

The door closed in her face, and the locks engaged.

"Who is your master? How do you know me? *Why me?*" She had dozens of questions she wanted to ask, but she knew she wouldn't get that opportunity. Not yet, at least.

Outside, the early morning was cold, biting, and she wrapped her arms around her chest to try and warm herself.

"Jesus. Let's try and make this quick." Her teeth chattered.

She headed in the direction of the outside car showroom, a little shocked that the sky had started to lighten.

"How long have I been here?" And then all thoughts were lost when she realised her car was missing from the bay she had parked it in. "Where…? Oh, *no!*"

Leanne rushed over to the empty space and looked about. Her vehicle was nowhere in sight.

She wanted to fall to her knees and cry, but then she remembered the huge chunk of change she had in her back pocket.

I can buy something new. Better.

With the briefest of mournings behind her, Leanne continued towards her destination, finding the gate in the chain-link fence that surrounded the open-air showroom ajar.

Must be my lucky night. She smiled, slipping through the entrance. There, before her like a beacon in the night, sat a gold-coloured Jeep Cherokee. There was an envelope taped to the inside of the windshield. *It can't be this easy, no way…*

Leanne glanced about. There was nobody there.

When she stepped up to the vehicle's bonnet, she saw a pearl-handled dagger resting on it.

She scrunched her eyes in confusion.

For me? Picking it up, she turned it this way and that – it was stained red, the handle tacky. "I don't get—"

Something thumped against the windshield.

Intense growling filled her ears.

"What the?!" She jumped, dropping the knife. The front of the Jeep was filled by the biggest Rottweiler she'd ever seen. "Holy fuck!" Leanne took several steps backwards.

The dog's maw was squashed against the glass, its breath fogging it.

"That fucking thing could eat a bear."

The Jeep rocked, and the hound snarled and snapped its jaws. Spittle flew.

A light glinted off the knife's blade, calling for her attention.

Leanne shook her head. "No. I-I couldn't."

Eight thousand pounds says you can…

Leanne edged closer to the blade, knelt and picked it up.

When she looked at the mutt, she noticed its eyes were rolled back in its head, its body shoving against the widow, trying to break it.

Spiderweb-like cracks appeared in it.

"Shit. If I don't run now, there might not be time in a few more seconds."

The glass cracked further; particles of it slipped down the bonnet and tinkled on the floor close to her feet.

Run. Now*! For the love of God.*

The hound's mouth shoved through a hole it had made, which grew and grew as its shoulders weighed against the windshield.

She clutched the knife for all she was worth, her knuckles turning white.

The flesh around the dog's face ripped and blood squirted as it thrust itself through the opening. And then the whole window exploded, catapulting the mutt towards her.

Leanne had time to yelp before the heavy beast fell on her, flattening her to the floor.

The dog whined.

Hot liquid trickled down Leanne's hands, and she couldn't stop screaming.

It's going to rip my throat out.

And then the dog was still.

She opened her eyes to find it dead.

Leanne managed to roll it off her, and found the steel sticking out of its throat.

She put her hands to her mouth. Tears threatened.

By using her hands and arse, she pushed herself backwards, away from the fast-spreading pool of blood. Her gasp lodged in her throat. When her back met the fence, which rattled and startled her anew, she got to her feet and ambled towards the Jeep with a sway.

She felt high.

Her world was slanted, focus skewed.

Putting a hand to the driver's-side door handle, Leanne tried it, and it opened.

A huff escaped her. She didn't know whether to laugh or cry.

It would have killed you, remember that. Torn your throat out and drank your blood. It was it, or me, she reasoned.

Leanne got behind the wheel and closed the door. When she looked in the rear-view mirror, she saw shopping bags lining the back seat.

My stuff.

A smile played across her face.

"What a fucking night." She took the envelope off the glass, opened it and read, "My dearest Leanne, if you are reading this, then congratulations are in order – you've made it to the end of my game! Or have you…? Only you can decide. For now, head home, heal, rest up and enjoy your new 'wheels', as the kids would say. If you wish to continue playing, then head to your local cemetery tomorrow night at midnight. *Sharp*. There will be instructions awaiting you on the door to the caretaker's house. Thanks for playing, and I do hope you come and have some fun tomorrow. Warmest, SOG."

After counting her money, all fourteen thousand pounds of it, Leanne put the Jeep in gear and drove out of the compound by smashing through the chain-link fence.

Sleep was needed.

A big decision was to be made.

Would she go and play in the dark with SOG, or take her winnings so far and run?

Doorknob Davey and the Window Watchers

e gave the door another hard thump with his fist, causing the small brass knocker to rattle. He looked up at the glass in the top of the door and saw the hallway light burst to life.

"Thank fuck for that!" he muttered, huddling as close to the door as he could, trying to get out of the wind and rain.

"You're late, Geoff!" his sister said, when she opened the door to greet him. "And you reek of whisky!"

"Well, gee, Gina – it's so nice to see you, too. I'm doing you a favour here, not the other way around."

"Yeah, great. Thanks," she said, rolling her eyes.

"Besides, you know how much those fucking brats of yours love their uncle Geoff!" he said, hiccupping a few times.

She stood there in her bra and panties and stared at him.

"Are you going to invite me in, or are you going to let me freeze my fucking titties off?!" he snapped. Geoff could feel rain water trickle off the end of his nose.

"You're a drunken cunt who shouldn't be allowed near children…"

"And you're a dirty whore who shouldn't be allowed to bear children! You should have had your reproductive bits ripped out of you at birth, slut!"

She went to slap him, but he caught her arm and shoved her backwards. He loomed over her. Rain water dripped off him and splashed against her cleavage. "One of these days, I'm going to break your neck like a fucking chicken's, Gina. *Snap*, just like that." He whispered, and then looked down at her tits. "Dancing or whoring tonight? It's got to be one or the other!" he smiled at her, and then belched.

She snatched her arm back and spat in his face. "It's work, either way, you bastard!"

"Whatever helps you sleep at night! Now, where are those little shits of yours?!"

"You're an insufferable piece of shit," she screeched, giving him another crack across his whiskery face before turning her back on him and marching upstairs. "If I had someone else to call to look after the girls, I would."

He pushed himself off the wall and staggered into the living room where his nieces were playing – Rosie, twelve and Stephanie, ten. Geoff scoffed as he watched the girls play Monopoly and dropped himself into a nearby chair. He then removed his flask from the inside pocket of his old leather coat, which creaked and squeaked as he moved.

The girls giggled.

Geoff removed his cigarettes, took one out of the box, and popped it into his mouth.

Before he could light it, Gina was screaming from upstairs.

"You better not be fucking smoking down there!"

He smiled, and then lit his Marlboro. "Fuck you, bitch."

The girls stopped giggling and went back to their game.

"Is that slaggy, no-good-sister of yours still doing the phone sex gig?!" Rosie and Stephanie looked at him, with the latter poking her tongue out at him. Geoff laughed. "You're a little cunt, just like your mother!" he told Stephanie, who smiled at him.

"Yes, Geoff," Rosie said. "Susan is still…talking on the phone with men."

"A family of sluts!" he uttered to himself, then tutted. "You pair should have been drowned at birth," he giggled. He took a large swallow from his flask, followed by a drag on his cig.

"And you should have your balls cut off!" Rosie said, scrunching her face up at him.

"Ha! You tiny pricks. Where is Susan?!"

"She's in her room," Rosie said.

"Just above me, right?"

"Uh-huh," she said.

"Mmm," he grunted, and then grabbed his cock. *For a sixteen-year-old, she's one mighty fine piece of meat!*

He thought. *I've had a thing for her for a while now, and she's at the right age for plucking...*

"I don't know why mum doesn't just ask Susie to look after us!" Stephanie whispered to Rosie.

"What did you say?!" Geoff said, giving Stephanie a slap on her cheek."

"Ow, you bastard! I'm telling my mother."

"What's going on down there?!" Gina screamed. "I can't leave you fuckers alone for five minutes."

Geoff laughed, drank and smoked.

The girls continued to play.

"One of these days, Doorknob Davey and the Window Watchers are going to come for you pair, your sister and your mother. Davey and his posse just love dirty, naughty little bitches like you lot. And when they do come, I'll let them rip you up and take away what's left!" he sneered, before draining the last of his flask and taking another drag on his Marlboro.

"Doorknob Davey and the Window Watchers?!" Rosie said, erupting in laughter which caused Stephanie to do the same. "You're a loser and a drunk, Geoff!"

"Oh, am I really?! Well, you don't know as much as you think you do, child," he pulled his lips back with a scornful look, exposing his yellow, smoke-stained teeth. A few were chipped and broken, others were wonky.

"Loser, loser, loser!" Rosie taunted.

"In that case, you don't want to hear about Davey and his gang then? About what you should do if he ever comes rattling your doorknob at the dead of night...!"

Rosie gasped.

"I do..." Stephanie said. Slowly, she turned her head towards Geoff. "Will you tell us?"

He took one final drag on his cigarette, licked his palm, and then stubbed it. Before enlightening the girls, he withdrew another Marlboro and lit it.

"So, you want to know about the legend that is Doorknob Davey and the Window Watchers?!"

Stephanie nodded.

Rosie scoffed. "We're not in the mood for some child's story!"

"I am!" Stephanie said, smiling. Her pigtails bobbed.

"Come on then, let's hear your stupid, made up bullshit!" Rosie said.

Geoff glared at her and then settled back into his chair. "Doorknob Davey and the Window Watchers were a metal band who performed back in the eighties. They formed in the late seventies and could have been megastars. They could have gone the distance, but they were cut down in their prime. You see, Davey, who was the lead singer and the one who put the band together, drove himself and the rest of his band member's crazy, after a heavy night of drinking and playing LPs backwards…"

Rosie laughed, "Are you fucking kidding us?!"

"It's true! Certain LPs had subliminal messages when played backwards. It's said that this was the reason the band gave up their musical talent and hit the road."

"Oo, scary! What did they do, play a bunch of gigs out on the motorways!" Rosie said, poking her tongue out at Geoff.

Stephanie laughed.

"Actually, no! They went on a five-year killing spree, which hwas brought to an end when the band were captured and placed in a high-security nuthouse.

"Get lost!" Rosie yelled. "You're full of shit, just like mum says."

"Okay, if you don't believe me, but they were held right here, in this town."

Rosie's mouth flapped.

Stephanie looked away.

"Not so fucking brave now, are you!" Geoff said. "That's right, they were a Welsh metal band, and were put away in Castell Hirwaun."

"No," Rosie said, her voice shaky.

"Oh, yes. And they would still be there now, had they not escaped some four or five years ago. Some people say the group live wild in the hills and, every now and then, someone hears the screech of a guitar or the crash of a drum in the still of the night…"

"You're lying!" Stephanie said.

"I'm so not. The streets run red with the blood they have spilled, girls, and there's nothing more they like than the blood of dirty, filthy little whores like that of the ones who live in this house!" he yelled, and then laughed like a madman.

"Shut up!" Rosie said.

"There's four of them in the band. You have Davey, the ringleader and vocalist; Jon, Needle Sticks, Ondrashek – the drummer; Peter, Skull-fuck, Wonder – the bassist: and Dawn, The Texan Torturer, Cano on six-string. Remember the band Kiss? Well, Davey and his crew also used to wear black and white make up, but not like Gene Simmons and his boys. Oh, no. The Doorknob and the Watchers' make-up made their faces look like they were skeletons."

"Stop it! You're starting to scare Stephanie!" Rosie said.

"No, he isn't – you're the one pissing in your panties," Stephanie said. "Why was the drummer called Needle Sticks?" she asked him.

He smiled. "That's a good question, and it's one I'm only too happy to answer. You see, old Needle Sticks liked to file the end of his drumsticks down to sharp points, until they resembled stakes. He used to do this before he and the rest of the band turned loopy. But, once he'd lost his marbles he used to take those pointy drumsticks of his and poke the eyes out of small children. Yeah, he'd dig them out and eat them. Just chew them up like they were balls of chewing gum…Every seen an eyeball pop? It's disgusting. All yellow, yoke-like fluid bursts out."

"Oh, God…I think I'm going to be sick!" Rosie said.

"When the eyes were gone, Skull-Fuck would come along and deposit a hot load of love muck into the cavities. They didn't call him Skull Fuck for nothing!"

"He would do it to…*children*?!"

"Yes. He'd also do it to men, women and family pets. He didn't give a fuck!"

"That's enough!" Rosie said.

"What about the woman…?"

"*Phew*, the Texan Torturer? I'm not sure you want to know about…"

"Tell me!" Stephanie pushed.

"The Texan, being the lead guitarist, would use the strings of her B.C Rich to torture her victims. She would wrap it around the dicks of her male captives and slowly, but painfully, emasculate them. It's said that she wore a necklace of chopped cocks!" he said, laughing.

"Mum!" Rosie yelled. "Mum!"

"Shut up!" Geoff said. "You said you didn't believe a word…"

"You're sick!"

"You know what else the Texan Torturer would do?!"

"*What*?!" Stephanie gasped.

Geoff smiled. "She likes to wrap her strings around the nipples and tits of women, and then cut them off. Yeah, the Torturer likes to hear her prey scream and beg for their lives. She also likes to watch them bleed out or choke on their tongues!"

"They sound pretty awesome!"

"I'm not sure you would think that, little lady, if they turned up at your door."

"My God, don't get dragged into his bull, Steph! If there had ever been people like that, we would have known about them. Especially if they were on the run…"

"But that's the thing, the government covered up their escape, Rosie. Castell Hirwaun is on its last legs as we speak, due to escapes in the past – it doesn't need any fresh headaches. If the place does incur any more trouble, then the government will be forced to close it down and I'm sure the private owner wouldn't want that!" Geoff said, smiling and blowing smoke in the girls' faces.

A thump from above caused him to look up at the ceiling. As the girls spoke among themselves at his feet, Geoff tuned them out. He pricked his ears and squinted. Faintly, he heard Susan's voice – she was on the phone.

"Would you like to know what I'm wearing…"

What a dirty, disgusting little whore! he thought, smiling. *It would be much better if she was down here where I could hear her better. But if that was the case, she would be free to look after her sister, and I wouldn't be here to hear her at all…*

"I'm wearing a negligee, with no panties or bra…"

Oh, God…I wonder if that's true? She's probably lying around in old joggers and a jumper…

"My pussy is completely…"

"Geoff, Geoff!" Rosie yelled in his face. "Tell her you're making that shit up. She'll have nightmares otherwise. Come on, she's only ten!"

"Get out of my space, bitch!" he said, startled and dropping his cigarette onto his lap. "Ah, shit…" he screamed, slapping his hands against the ash and crushing the glowing end of the Marlboro. "Christ, girl. I could have gone up in flames."

"Yeah, or burnt down the only tree in your fores…" Stephanie muttered, then giggled.

Rosie laughed.

"And no, it's not a lie. It's all true."

More thumps from above.

He looked up.

God, what I wouldn't give…

"But it can't be true!"

"Look, you little shit, I told you it is! You want proof. Here," he said, reaching into the inside pocket of his coat and pulling out his wallet. When he opened it, he withdrew a ticket stub. "August '84 – I saw them live in Cardiff."

"Let me see!" Stephanie said, snatching the ticket from her uncle's hand.

"You can't read," Rosie said, taking it from her. "Okay, this proves nothing."

"It shows the band exists! Not only that, it was an all access area ticket – I met the band backstage."

"Oh, *wow*!" Stephanie said.

"*Pft*, please. I ain't falling for this mumbo-jumbo," Rosie said.

"Well, you looked pretty scared earlier," Geoff said.

"Yeah, well…"

Geoff smiled, pulled another Marlboro from his box and lit it. "Go and play for a bit. It won't be long before your mother goes. Scram!"

When the girls returned to their game of Monopoly once again, Geoff went back to listening and daydreaming. Looking up, he blocked out the noise around him and homed in on Susan's voice.

He failed to spot Rosie pick up her iPad.

The floors and walls are so thin…

"Bet you'd like to be here right now, wouldn't you? Touching me. Kissing me…*fucking* me!" he heard Susan say.

*Oh, God…*he groaned internally, then instinctively grabbed his stiffy.

"I'm touching my tits for you."

He'd seen her tits. They were magnificent for her sixteen years – they were small, pert and tight. *The nipples were so pink…How badly I'd wanted to suck one into my mouth.*

Geoff felt pre-come drizzle into his pants.

A shiver slithered down his back.

Maybe she's not wearing joggers. Maybe she has her little orange shorts on – the ones she likes to wear to the gym; the ones that show the under curves of her arse.

He put his fist into his mouth and bit down.

"I've found them!" Rosie screamed, jumping to her feet. This brought Geoff out of his dream-like trance. "It says here that they were a band, but they disappeared some ten years ago. That they were feared dead!"

"I knew you were talking shit!" Stephanie said.

"Okay, okay! So I lied."

"Arsehole!" Rosie said.

"Hey, I only lied about them still being out there. Or did I…?!" he said, grinning.

"How can they be – they were 'feared dead' a decade ago!"

"*Pft*, that's just a cover up."

"Whatever!" Rosie said.

Then he heard footsteps on the stairs – his heart caught in his throat.

Susan...

"You brats make sure you listen to your bum of an uncle!" Gina said as she reached the bottom step.

Geoff got off the couch and made his way into the kitchen. There, he opened the fridge and pulled out a beer. After popping the top off, he went back into the living room and clapped eyes on his sister.

She was wearing next to nothing.

He drank her in.

She wore suede fuck me boots, which were bright pink, matching her lipstick.

The dress she wore barely covered her arse and snatch, with the front exposing her cleavage. Her make-up was thick. Her hair long, black and curly – it flanked her pretty face.

"Off shagging, then?!" Geoff said, laughing.

"In front of the kids?!" she asked. "Really? You fucking dickhead!"

"Like you're one to talk!" he said, taking a swig of beer. "Susan going to be on the phone all night?!" he asked, wiggling his eyebrows.

Gina slowly turned to him. "Yes!"

"Pity."

Gina walked up to him and slapped him across the face. "You stay away from her, you hear? I've seen how you look at her…"

"Slap me again and they're going to find your body in a gravel pit!" he told her, getting close to her face. His spittle plastered her chin and forehead.

"You're disgusting!" Turning her back on him, Gina bent over and gave her girls a kiss goodbye. "Remember, no later than ten to bed!" she told them whilst pointing a threatening finger in their direction. "I'll see you both in the morning…"

Her words derailed as she turned to face Geoff.

"What?" he asked. "You know I always drink out of the bottle!"

"I'm not looking at you, Geoff. I was wondering what the hell that noise was?!"

"What noise?!"

"That fucking noise!"

Geoff listened with intent. At that moment, he heard Susan panting and groaning.

"Well, that would be your dirty whore of a sixteen-year-old talking filth and having an orgasm over the phone to strange men!"

"I'm not talking about Susan, you bastard! I'm talking about *that* noise!"

As he opened his mouth to talk, Geoff heard it. It sounded like scratching.

"Fingernails on glass?!" he uttered, scrunching his eyes.

"Girls, turn the TV off," Gina instructed.

The four of them stood there and listened, waiting for the sound to come again. It did.

"It does sound like someone is scraping the front window!" Geoff said.

"It's probably a branch," Gina said. "Right, girls, I'm off." And with that, Gina headed out and down the passageway to the front door.

Geoff followed close behind and watched as Gina disengaged the locks.

"Don't go out there…!" he whispered.

"I don't have time for your games," Gina snapped. "Take good care of my girls." Opening the door, she pulled it back. Geoff could see the rain coming down in sheets – the streetlights appeared to be out. It was like looking into a black hole

"Close the fucking door!" he snapped.

"Fuck off, Geoff. I have to go to…"

They both heard it then, and peered out into the rain-soaked night. It was a faint whistle, followed by the sound of someone singing. The heavy rain drowned the words out.

Until the music-maker came closer.

Then closer still, until they could hear the person's heavy breathing and matching footfalls, and not just the words they sang.

"Who's that tapping at the window? Who's that knocking at the door? I am tapping at the window. I am knocking at the door…" the person sank in a cheery tone.

"Lock the fucking door!" Geoff said.

"Mum, what's going on?!" Rosie asked, stepping into the passageway.

"Get back in there!" Geoff yelled. "Shut the…"

But it was too late – the person's voice was now booming, as they came out of the rain and twisted, nightly shadows.

"Who…the fuck are you?!" Gina's voice warbled.

The strange man who stood before her was over six-feet tall – he wore a Stetson. His hair hung long and his face was painted like that of a skeleton. He sported a large black beard with a smattering of grey.

"Boo!" he said to Gina, bending over and getting close to her face.

She jumped back and straightened. "Look, dickhead, you're a little late for Halloween!"

The wind picked up and blew his long trench coat open and far behind him. Geoff could see that a Welsh flag had been sewn into the lining.

"Davey…" he uttered.

"Howdy, Geoff!" the painted man said, taking his acoustic guitar off his back. He then grabbed it by the neck, swing it over his shoulder like a golf club, and appeared to bring it forward with all the force he could.

The edge of the acoustic connected with Gina's jaw, snapping her mouth shut. The instrument let out a long *boooonnng* sound, and one of its strings came free. Teeth fragments pinged off the walls, floor and ceiling, as she was thrown backward.

"*Ugh!*" Gina groaned, hitting the deck. Blood spurt out of her mouth and nose.

"Nap time!" guitar man said, braying with laughter.

"Oh, fuck!" Geoff said.

"Mum? *Mum!*" Rosie screamed.

"Get back!" Geoff told the youngster. A deafening crash from upstairs, followed by a scream, caused him to snap his head in the direction. "*Susan!*"

"Still touching the kiddies, Geoff boy?!" guitar man said, before violently stamping on Gina's head until it was crushed – her right eyeball popped like a burst water balloon. Blood spurted up his black jeans.

"Mum!" Rosie cried. As she attempted to run to her mother's side, Geoff stopped her.

"No! Get in the living room with your sister. Now!"

She didn't need telling twice.

"I think I'll wait until she's gone cold before I fuck her in the arse!" guitar man said, as he advanced on Geoff. "She's your sister, right? I remember her. I'm surprised she even lets you near her children, Geoff boy. Didn't she know about your reputation?!"

Geoff said nothing, just looked at Davey in surprise. From behind, he heard Susan screaming and crying. "Get off me!"

"*Wooo-hooo*…We're going to have some fun with you, girly!"

"Davey, don't do this!" Geoff pleaded. "I thought you were dead! Had I known, I would never have double-crossed you. You have to believe me!"

"Yeah, we thought you'd be pissing in your pants right about now," Davey said. "Bring her down, lads!"

Geoff looked over his shoulder and saw Needle Sticks and Skull-Fuck. His stomach somersaulted. "Please…Don't."

Davey smiled. "Go on, cry. You know how much that shit makes me hard. We've had a hard time tracking you down, Geoff. You've stayed in the shadows, ain't ya?!"

Geoff nodded.

"Chicken shit knew we were gunning for him!" Needle Sticks said from behind, who hurled Susan down the remaining stairs. She slid along the floor before slamming into her dead mother. "That one has an innocent smelling cunt!"

Susan screamed.

Geoff looked down at her.

So she was wearing the shorts…he thought. His dick hung lifeless in his pants.

Needle Sticks clapped his hand on Geoff's shoulder and twirled him around. "Hi! Pleased to see your old band buddies?!"

Over Needle Stick's shoulders, Geoff could see Skull-Fuck making his way downstairs. When he averted his eyes, he saw Needle Sticks drumsticks holstered at his hip. The points were blood encrusted. Like Davey, he too wore a long trench coat. Unlike the vocalist, the drummer had a bald head, but his face was painted the same.

So too was Skull-Fuck's, who donned a patched denim jacket, complete with spiked pads on the shoulders. His hair was cut short – a goatee graced his face.

"Yeah, Geoff. Pleased to see us, old mate?!"

Geoff swallowed, hard. "I'll get you the money…"

"Oh, we're beyond the money, you so-called manager," Davey said. "We're going to fuck your shit right up! Take him in the living room, boys," he ordered Needle Sticks and Skull-Fuck. "Where's the Torturer?!"

"Getting her wires ready for big boy here!" Skull-Fuck said. He slammed his palm against the small of Geoff's back. "Into the living room, fuck-face!"

The front door was thrown shut, as all four men lurched into the other room. Needle Sticks, who had grabbed a hold of Susan by her hair, dragged her behind him.

"Torture!" Geoff said, when he clapped eyes on the fourth band member. Her long, black hair was caveman-wild – she wore spurred boots and leather chaps over blue jeans.

Her hands were covered in thick, work gloves. Six-string wire hung from her left grasp.

"You're looking at me like you want to fuck me, Geoff!" she said, walking up to him. She put her hands around his neck and kneed him in the balls. The air gushed out of him as he buckled and went to ground. "Well, you're going to need a harder piece of wood than that, cowboy!" she told him.

"Their skulls are mine!" Skull-Fuck said, pointing at Rosie and Stephanie.

"Yeah, but their eyeballs belong to me!" Needle sticks said, withdrawing his tools of the trade and twirling them.

"Have 'em, boys!" The Torturer said, pulling the wire tight between her hands. "This douchebag and his balls belong to me!" she said, looking down at Geoff.

"Please…" he gasped, holding his bollocks. "Let the girls go."

"Not a fucking chance, sunshine!" Davey said, putting his foot on Geoff's chest, pinning him to the floor. "You're going to watch."

The girls screamed as they were pulled apart and held down. They all watched as Needle Sticks raised his drumsticks overhead, with the points facing downwards.

"*Argh*!" Steph screamed, "I thought Doorknob Davey and his gang…"

Her words were cut short, as the drumsticks were shoved through her eyeballs and into her brain.

As her small body bucked, Needle Sticks got off her and straddled Rosie, who lay in a pool of her own piss.

"Alright, the little one is still bucking!" Skull-Fuck said, lowering his zip and removing his cock which he inserted into Stephanie's ruptured eye socket. "Aw, yeah – it's all warm and gooey!" he said, starting to thrust in and out.

The slurping-sucking sounds made Geoff gag. Vomit raced up his throat but he couldn't do anything. He felt dizzy.

"I'm fucking coming!" Skull-Fuck yelled, ramming himself against Stephanie's skull for the last time. His body trembled as his jism blast out of him. When he was spent, he let go of her small head.

His white, sticky goo could be seen trickling out of her left eye socket.

"Fuck me, that load was just busting to get out of me!" he said, gasping for air. As Skull-Fuck was about to move over to Rosie, the family's cat tried to rush through his legs, but he caught it by the tail, causing the feline to hiss and try to scratch his eyeballs out. "What a vicious fucking thing!" he said, howling with laughter. He then started to swing the cat around in circles above his head, before he brought it down hard onto the hearth. The all witnessed the cat's head explode.

"Wow!" Needle Sticks cried out. "Look at that moggy go!"

Davey had now removed his foot from Geoff's chest and was currently kicking Susan around the room. The Torturer now stood over Geoff. "Offie with the trousers!" she said, unbuttoning them and lowering his zip.

He didn't have the strength to fight her off – his body ached.

As he felt her guitar wires wrap around his manhood, and then he saw Needle Sticks stab out Rosie's eyes with perverted glee. It was the last thing he would ever see, as the Torture pulled the strings tight around his package, severing his cock and nut sack…A scream lodged in his throat. His world turned dark.

Elicit

At least once a week Kenny *had* to spy on her, no questions asked.

The urge had become too intense to ignore. To brush under the carpet. When the thought of spying on her crossed his mind, he'd get out-of-control horny. So unbalanced was the feeling, that he'd shake with excitement and almost lose his load in his pants.

Sometimes, when the impulse to peep on Kitty came on and set a fire ablaze in his trousers, he would sate his desire by masturbating over voyeuristic porn or finding another *young* thing to satisfy his observing ways.

They had to be young, though – he yearned for barely legal flesh. The milky, soft smoothness of it; the virginity of youthful skin drove him wild. Kenny knew it was sick, but he couldn't help it. It was built into his sexual kinks, and that was that.

It's not like I rape or touch them, he thought, looking through the spy hole he had created in the floor that looked into her bedroom. Before coming here, he always made sure the teenager was alone.

He feared being caught a lot, but, in the ten years he'd been peeping, no one had seen him at it or suspected a thing. Kenny planned on keeping it that way, too.

After seeing the girl's mother leave that day, Kenny had got himself into position to spy and wank. When the girl thought she was alone, she'd stripped, taken a shower and now lingered in the nude, much to Kenny's absolute pleasure, on her bed.

The old houses on his street had no partition between the attics, so he was able to move freely between houses, getting his jollies all day long.

But Kitty was his favourite.

When she turns eighteen, I'll have my way with her, whether she likes it or not! I don't care if it'll mean prison time. It'll be worth it...

His hardness pressed against the floorboards – pre-cum leaked out of his cock as he watched her roll around on her bed bare-arsed, her phone in hand, her loud music camouflaging his creaky movements from above.

"Are you coming over or what?" he heard her ask. "Come on, you said you would, remember?"

I wonder if she's talking to...

"Thanks, Jenny! We can go swimming from here; bring your costume. You can change and get ready here."

...Jenny... Kenny didn't think it was possible, but his dick grew harder at the mere mention and sound of Kitty's friend's name...*I'll shortly have two of them to peep on!*

Even though Kitty was definitely his favourite, Jenny Smithers was quite the girl for her sixteen years, and was a few days younger than her friend. For one thing, she'd had an early spurt of growth – her tits had developed from bulbs into melons overnight, and she had the smallest, tightest arse Kenny had ever seen.

She also liked to jog, as well as swim, which kept her frame that extra bit compact. Kenny had seen her out running before school on many a morning, whilst he did his milk round.

*Oh, those tight jogging trousers she likes to wear, along with taut sports bras that seem to enhance her already impressive jugs…*He drove the thought away, before the first waves of orgasm sprung themselves upon him. *Concentrate on the lovely Kitty – that's who we're here for…boy, does she look amazing.*

He traced her legs from ankle to hip, but briefly stopped at her puppy-fat thighs for a better look. Raising his vision further, he licked his dry, cracking lips at the sight of her bald patch.

If there's not grass on the pitch….

She flipped over on her bed, as though she could read his mind.

…Turn them over and play in the mud…

The sight of the dimples in her arse cheeks caused him to roll over, unbuckle his belt, pop the button on his jeans, and slide them down his fat, hairless legs. His short, fat cock barely poked out of the button-less fly to his boxers. Tearing his underwear off, he grabbed his hardness.

Moving onto his side, he continued to look through the hole. Kitty had turned onto her back again, revealing to him her tiny breasts with bright pink nipples.

From where he lay, he could see her recent birthday cards – the number sixteen was spelt out on some, with others donning the number.

*Scarcely legal...What I wouldn't give to get my mouth around those...*he thought, gliding his hand slowly up and down the length of his short shaft. His orgasm was close. Kenny didn't want to pop his glue-like load just yet – he wanted to tease himself into hysteria.

Suddenly, as if his mind was searching for a way to help him pull on the reins, the image of his wife popped into his head. His face reddened. His hardness wavered.

Sharon would be very disappointed in him.

When they'd first met twenty years ago, she'd blown him away with her amazing body, pretty face and off-the-wall personality – she hadn't just become his girlfriend, his fiancée and then his wife, but also his best friend. His clichéd rock.

Once Sharon had come onto the scene, Kenny had been able to kick his sick, voyeuristic fetish for youthful bodies to one side – sex with Sharon had been amazing.

In fact, it was like fucking an underage girl, as she was so very petite…

But then swollen bellies and babies had come along.

Long, sleepless nights turned into weeks – months even – of no intimacy. His sex life became stagnant. Non-existent. She began to bore and disgust him, and soon Kenny found he was back doing his perverted watching at a terrific rate; when they did make love, he faked his orgasm every time, due to an inability to climax.

Stop thinking about that bitch! he thought, increasing the speed of his strokes. Whilst lost in thought, his hardness had fully left him. *Fuck, got to start all over again. Never mind, at least thinking about Sharon has killed my urge to spurt.*

"Well, stop talking to me, and get over here, you little bitch!" he heard Kitty say, bringing him out of his daydreaming trance.

Leaving his cock alone, he lay flat on his stomach and got his eye as close to the hole as possible.

Her arse was once again in plain sight.

Just then, a board beneath him creaked in between one song on her CD player finishing and another starting.

A breath caught in his throat as she stopped talking – was she looking up and directly at his peephole? *Can she see it, even?! No, she can't suspect a thing…*

When the next song started, she began talking again.

"No, it's okay – I thought I heard something…"

Fuck, that was too close.

Shifting to his left as gently as possible, Kenny distanced himself from the troublesome board. *That should do.*

"Well, I'm not going to talk anymore – I'm going now, Jenny. Hurry up and get over here. The pool will be closed by the time we get there…Ha! I know, right? Maybe that fit lifeguard will be there again…?"

The dirty little thing. She shouldn't be thinking about boys at her age!

"…And that bulge in his shorts. *Phwoar!*"

Filthy bitches!

It drove him wild. The veins in his cock protruded with the throbbing stiffness.

As he furiously masturbated, he continued to listen to her nasty talk about the lifeguard, until she finally said goodbye to Jenny and disconnected the call.

When he was at the point of no return, he let his prick go. He felt his semen slink back down his tubes and splash into his nutsack. His whole body trembled with sexual excitement. His bell-end tingled.

Oh, God! He shivered – his teeth chattered, as he lay on his back once again. He took a few deep gulps of air. *Breathe*, he told himself. *Breathe.*

He hadn't realised how long he'd been lying there, panting and quaking, until he heard Kitty's music go low and a few hard knocks at the front door assaulted his ears.

"*Coming!*" Kitty called.

Rolling onto his stomach, he was in time to see her heading out her bedroom – she had a skimpy towel wrapped around her dainty frame.

What I wouldn't give to be able to rip that towel off her!

Below him, the room was empty. As he looked through the hole, the innocence inside the bedroom almost got the better of him – but his depraved nature fought against his guilt. The pink, fluffy bunny toys, posters of boy bands and glittery diary did nothing to shoo him off.

It's not like I'm hurting anyone! he argued with his sick self. *I'm hardly a paedophile. It just turns me on, that's all…I can't help the urges. The fantasies. Nobody can help what fetish they get drawn with in life. It's just the way it goes, right?*

"You brought your stuff then, Jenny?"

"Duh, of course!"

Both girls crashed through the bedroom door, causing Kenny to shrink away once again. Slowly and silently, he put his head back to the hole. Both girls were directly below.

"Want to take a shower?" Kitty asked.

"Yeah, I think I will. I jogged over here. I buzz of sweat. Smell!" Jenny said, thrusting one of her armpits close to Kitty's nose.

"Ew, you're gross! Get away from me, Stinky McGee!"

The girls crashed into each other and Kitty lost her towel. Jenny's impressive breasts jiggled.

Shit, that's so fucking hot!

"Ha! Oops, I can see your boobies!" Jenny said, as Kitty hastily pulled her towel back up. "No need to be shy, I have them too."

"Yeah, but you have cantaloupes!"

"Ha-ha!"

"Not funny. Best get in the shower, so we can get out of here. I'm going to get into my bathing costume whilst I wait for you."

"Put some tunes on, then!" Jenny said, heading out the door.

"Yes, sir!" Kitty called after her.

As Kitty busied herself with the music, Kenny eased himself along the floor to a second spy hole in the attic. This hole overlooked the shower in Kitty's house. He was in time to see Jenny close and lock the bathroom door.

He smiled as she rattled the door to test its lock.

You may think you're alone, pretty girl…

Satisfied, Jenny started to slip her skin-tight jogging trousers down her shapely thighs, revealing a pink thong with kittens on them – her pure innocence made his cock twitch in the dusty room.

Once out of them, she removed her body-hugging sports bra. When her tits flopped out, he gasped. This was the first time he had seen Jenny's breasts, even though she had called on Kitty many times in the past.

"Fabulous!" he whispered.

As though she'd heard him, Jenny stopped moving and looked around the bathroom, before glancing up.

After a few seconds, she stepped into the shower and started the water.

He watched closely as she soaped herself, and hoped she would touch herself, but she didn't.

In fact, her shower was brief.

Bloody Kitty – what's the big rush?

Jenny wrapped a towel around her wet body and picked her clothes up. Kenny particularly liked the fact that the girl stopped to sniff her knickers before leaving the bathroom.

Rancid!

With the room below empty, Kenny shimmied across the attic floor commando-style. Once he was above the bedroom again, he could see both girls chatting as they prepared to leave the house.

If I'm going to get my toss in, I best do it now – doesn't look as though I have much time left.

As he continued to watch the giggling girlies, a groan from behind caused him to look.

His heart quickened. He squinted.

Nothing appeared to move in the gloom beyond his position.

Bloody rats – there must be hundreds of them up here. Best I make sure they don't nibble the end of my Johnson, and try to get to the cheese!

Ignoring the space around him, Kenny focused on his young prey – he was pleased to see Kitty in her bright pink all-in-one swimsuit.

Mmm, look how it makes her buds poke out…

Another creak from behind him.

"*Huh?*" He gasped, a breath hitching in his throat. "Anyone there?" he whispered.

Old man Jefferson had come up to the attic a few times whilst Kenny had been there in the past, but he'd never spotted him. He'd hid in the shadows. Behind boxes.

I'm too smart to be caught out by a fucking coffin-dodger!

Again, Kenny peered into the darkness, but he couldn't see anything. Just then, a rat brushed his arm. He bit down on a shriek and covered his mouth, just in case.

He felt a bit of piss squirt out his cock.

The huge, black rodent sniffed his thigh, then urine, before losing interest and scurrying off into the blackness.

Sighing, Kenny let out a held breath.

I can't believe I pissed myself – what an infant! Well, it was a slight shock, having that huge thing brush me.

Momentarily lost in fright and thought, the sound of the girls laughing grounded him once again – looking down, he saw they were now play fighting with pillows.

How the hell did that happen? And why are they naked? They were getting dressed a moment ago.

Then they stopped and gazed into each other's eyes.

Holy shit!

Before he could grab his cock to shuffle it, Kitty's and Jenny's lips locked. Their inexperienced hands roamed each other's bodies – nipples were tweaked, buttocks slapped.

Am I fucking dreaming?

Kitty groaned.

Jenny 'Oo'ed.

A cold shiver of delight passed through Kenny's body as though he'd been struck by lightning.

His semen raced up his dick's pipe – he couldn't hold it back any longer, as he wanked with a ferocious desire. His breathing came in ragged rips as he pounded away. Without noticing, his elbow kept clipping the floor below him as his arm raced up and down, working hard to pump his shaft.

Got to get it out...

Sweat burst across his brow like a dam with a broken bank. His face reddened. He pushed his eye as close to the hole as humanly possible – had its circumference been bigger, he would have fallen through it.

I wonder if my eye can be seen bulging through, like some cartoon character!

The comedic thought washed over him, and had he not been on the cusp of orgasm, he would have laughed.

Then, just like that, the rules of the game changed by the utterance of one simple word...

..."Dad..?"

Memories of her as a baby came flooding back to him – bath time. Story time. Bedtime. Her first word (Hiccup). Her first few steps. The faces she would pull when chuckling...

A tear escaped him.

"My baby," he sobbed.

Instantly, his cock retreated and resembled that of a peanut. The pain in his throat from trapped air was excruciating – Kenny felt as though he was being strangled by a man who had hands the size of elephants.

No, it can't be...

Kenny tried to force himself backwards, away from his sin, but couldn't.

Don't open your eyes!

The music below switched off.

"It's okay, Mr. Samuels. We know you're up there," Jenny said.

Oh, my fuck! Not possible...How? he thought. His fears were confirmed as his eyes shot open – his daughter and friend were both looking up at the hole.

"Mum found out what you were up to weeks ago – we've just been waiting for the perfect opportunity to…get you!"

Get me? If I keep quiet, I might still be able to get out of this…

Kitty, his daughter, beckoned him with a finger. "Why don't you come down. You know you want to!" she said, giggling. This caused Jenny to join in.

What's going…?

"You made a fatal error – you let yourself get detected by Mr. Jefferson from next door. This pricked mum's curiosity as to what you were up to, making regular trips to the attic. Then, she found your hole."

"You're a pretty sick man, Mr. Samuels," Jenny said.

He wanted to speak, to protest, but he knew the jig was up. Scrabbling backwards, with blood rushing in his ears, he failed to hear the violent creak of boards behind him until it was too late.

"*Argh!*" he cried on feeling a sharp pain rush the length of his left shoulder blade.

Turning, he saw the face of his wife lunge out of the gloom.

"Sharon!" he squealed, falling onto his arse and out of the way of her knife, which she slashed at his chest. "Baby! Please, I can explain!" he whimpered, crawling away. His jeans were now around his ankles.

He could feel splinters inserting themselves into his buttocks and anus.

"Explain what, that you're a paedo bastard? That you've been spying on our little girl? That you've probably been doing it for years? How could you? Our child, you sick motherfucker!" she screamed, crisscrossing the blade across his face in severe swift movements.

Blood squirted up her bare legs and dress and mixed with the dust and cobwebs in the attic.

"*Ugh*!" he screamed like a four-year-old. "You're killing me!"

"That's the plan, you fucking monster!"

"Go on, Mrs. Samuels!"

"Yeah, Mum – cut his dangler off!"

His heart leapt into his throat on hearing the way the teens were talking, causing his prick to stir.

"Please, Sharon…I'll get help! Anything…I…"

As his mouth flapped, she rammed the seven-inch steel into his mouth – the sound of steel on ivory was horrendous. The tip of the knife caught his tongue in mid-flap and speared it to the back of his throat.

Blood pissed from the orifice.

Tears spilled down his cheeks.

As she pushed on the haft of the butcher knife, he was forced to his feet, allowing her to grab his balls and pull them away from his body – the skin taut. With one violent yank, the steel was free of his mouth; blood and bits of teeth jettisoned out of his gob.

In one fluent movement, she began sawing through his scrotum, causing his body to spasm. As he choked on his own blood, he felt his balls slip out of his ruptured scrotum and plop onto the floor one at a time.

He flopped onto his stomach to try to crawl away, but he was stopped by his wife.

"Now for that thing!" she said, trying her best to grab and stretch his pathetic manhood so she could slice it off.

As she carved away at him, he could see through the hole. His blood had seeped through the ceiling, covering the girls, who rubbed it into each other in a playful way.

Bitches...he thought, feeling himself slip into unconsciousness, his eyes closing. Then, nothing…

…The elicit behaviour had come to a painful end.

Experiment of an Ancient Breed

Elizabeth, who was named after her great-great-grandmother, had been the sole manager and proprietor of the Lamb and Flag pub for the past nine years. When she'd first acquired the establishment fifteen years ago, she'd been the joint owner, along with her brother. He died six years into running the place, forcing Elizabeth, who preferred to go by Liz, to take on full responsibility.

Paul, Liz's brother, had been taken ill unexpectedly.

"I'm sorry for your loss, Elizabeth. It seems Paul had a rare, and certainly unusual, blood disease that we've not seen or treated in this hospital," had been the doctor's cold, unforgiving words. "We'd like to keep your brother's body for a couple of weeks, run some tests and see if we can prepare for the next case we have involving the extraordinary illness."

She'd found his frankness astonishing. Had she not been emotionally drained at the time, Liz would have taken more than a few strips off him, but then he added, "It would be a good cause towards medical science . . ." swaying her judgment somewhat.

Her mind had reeled. *What if it's in me? What about Jason? The babies!*

"By all means, come in for a check-up," the doctor had said after she'd told him her concerns.

Six weeks later, Paul's body had been retuned, and the green light to bury him had been lit.

Liz hadn't had time to mourn. She had a business to look after along with her family: her baby twin girls, four-year-old nephew and younger brother, Jason, who all lived at the pub with her.

The first four years without Paul had been tough. A slog. Not just physically, but mentally, too. Had Liz not had Jason to help mind the children whilst she worked every hour God sent, then it would have been an impossibility to keep everything going no matter how good she was at spinning plates.

When Jason turned sixteen, Liz put him to work behind the bar – not that she had to do much arm-twisting. He'd been chomping at the bit to get involved ever since Paul had passed.

"It's not fair to take all the work on yourself, sis," had been his words after they'd buried their brother. "Let me at least do some bar work for you."

"No," had been her stern reply. "You can help me out by looking after the little ones – keep them entertained, warm, and their bellies full for me. That would be a massive help."

Jason coming of age had been a welcomed relief, taking away much of the strain that had been building and threatening to cave her in. When Liz realised how much of a good thing it was, she'd suddenly become scared, knowing that if her baby brother had been slightly younger, meaning there wouldn't have been aid for another year or two, then she would have gone under.

Stress would have killed her.

And if the stress hadn't, then giving up the pub would have. That act would have been like the hammer called Life slamming down on the one bullet in her revolver's chamber.

The Lamb and Flag was her lifeforce.

Not only that, but the place had been in the family for two decades – it had been passed down from father to son, mother to daughter, brother to sister, and so forth. And, with no immediate relations around her except for her nephew, brother and children, who were all too young to take the pub on, then it would have been sold to a stranger and lost to her blood forever.

Besides, working the Flag gave her a sense of purpose in life. It filled her with pride and get-go whenever she thought about how hard she'd worked to build the place up – to get back a lot of the trade and punters it had lost when it had been in the hands of her parents.

Her mother had placed blame for the pub's decline and descent into near rack and ruin squarely at her father's feet. "He's become a no-good lush and womaniser," she'd said. Whereby he had drained the profits dry, she had chased off the female customers by accusing them of fucking her husband.

When it looked as though the pub was going to close down, a miracle happened – her mother died and her father fell ill within weeks of her going. The doctors had labelled his sudden deterioration into an early grave as a 'broken heart'.

"Yeah, you see it all the time," the undertaker had told Liz and her brother. "When one dies, the other normally follows pretty rapidly. They start pining, see. A sad thing, the human heart."

He'd said it in almost a cheery way.

Liz could have sworn she'd detected a wry smile on the bone collector's face.

Not that she cared. She was glad to see the back of them, knowing her and Paul could start their new venture together and breathe new life into the battered, bruised business.

All it's going to take is a bit of elbow grease and some honest sweat and toil, she'd thought, standing before the pub with her brother.

They'd gutted the place, all four floors, getting rid of the olde-worlde décor, fixtures and fittings that had been there since their parents had taken over the pub forty years prior.

"This joint probably hasn't seen an update since it was built, sis!" Paul had commented. "Let alone a lick of paint or a splash of colour."

"You know how Mum and Dad were . . ."

"Frugal?"

They'd both laughed at that one.

All the booths, sofas, tables, chairs and the bar were also ripped out so they could modernise completely. They'd decided that they wanted to make the place hip and chic, so it would attract the attention of the younger crowd – they even put in stylish and expensive drinks, along with craft ale and a pool table.

When they were fully up and running, they decided to upgrade the rear of the pub and install an elegant kitchen so they could start providing meals.

"You don't go to a pub for food," their father had always argued. "The only grub that should be served is nuts and pork scratchings."

He's such a short-sighted fool, Liz had thought when her dad had responded with that after their mother suggested a chef be brought in. Even as a child she'd had good business acumen. Her mother had clearly had it too, because she was forward-thinking: serving food to bring in a healthy profit/income in an ale house around the time was uncommon.

But with him gone (her mother too, God rest her soul), they'd been free to turn their business into a booming success – something she knew their mother would have been proud of.

Things had been going swimmingly.

The place ran like clockwork, and there was hardly ever any violence or the need for the police to be called, unlike when their parents had run it. Liz could recall many occasions when there was trouble at their door late at night, which had been scary. Still, nothing ever came of it.

Liz had used to look forward to getting up in the morning and heading downstairs to the bar to get an early start. Life was good. Great, in fact. She had her brothers, nephew, baby girls and her own business. *What more could a girl ask for*? she'd thought.

But it had all crashed down around her ears after her brother died, and it had taken all her strength to keep the place from slipping under.

"You should get some staff in to help you," a drunk, loyal punter had once suggested.

But Liz hadn't wanted that – she wasn't particularly keen on the cook being there, but knew it was necessary. So she'd struggled on until Jason was able to fully help take control. As soon as he'd become of age, she'd made him a legal partner, too. She'd showed him all the ropes, from locking up and setting the alarms, to filling in orders and keeping the books.

"I want you to know all this stuff in case something ever happens to me," she'd told him.

And so she'd soldiered on with Jason, who helped her iron out all the creases that had occurred after losing Paul. It took them less than a year to get the place back on track, with the punters and money flowing in once more.

Since then, things had been peachy.

They were living the dream.

It's been a rocky road, she thought now, looking across the bar at Jason, who was serving someone with a pint of beer. *But I – no, we – have managed to pull through it. And look at us now!* "And to think I almost lost my dream job . . ." she muttered, looking about her.

"Any chance of some service here, *bitch*?!"

Ugh! Liz inwardly groaned. *But sometimes, just sometimes, the arseholes on a Friday night have a knack for getting you down,* she thought, turning to the man who had so rudely interrupted her chain of thought.

"Give me a fucking beer!" the guy demanded again, belching. His eyeballs resembled marbles: they were glassed over and rolled around in his skull. Liz couldn't tell if he was looking at her, or through her.

She wondered if he'd been eating tuna, and had a hard time in not pinching her nose closed. He didn't so much as stand there, but swayed, as though manipulated by a breeze. Liz couldn't understand how he hadn't collapsed or fallen backwards onto a table.

His face didn't look familiar, either.

He didn't fit.

"*Sir*," she said in a calm yet firm tone, "I think you may have had enough to drink. I can't, and won't, serve you another—"

He slammed his fists down on the bar. The knuckles on both his hands were scuffed and bloody. "No fucking bitch is going to tell me when I've had enough!" he screamed, his voice breaking.

A hush fell over the crowd in the pub – only the jukebox could be heard.

Her tone took on an edge. "Don't make me have to call the police, sir!" Whilst he mumbled and drooled, she glanced over at Jason and saw he had his hand on the phone. All it would take was a nod off her, and Jason would speed-dial the police – they'd be here in minutes.

She shook her head and turned back to face the drunk.

"Call the fucking army or the prime minister, *whore*! See if I care!" He slammed his hands on the bar like a spoiled brat.

Whore? How dare he! She saw red, walked around the bar and grabbed the man by his ear. She twisted it and escorted him to the front door. He tried to protest and wrestle free, but he was no match for her sober superiority. "And stay out! You're barred."

She went to the window. The man hung around outside, and then slipped down the alley connected to the pub. Inside, after a few people commended Liz on how she'd handled the situation, the place became raucous once more.

****

He eyed her from a barstool located at the counter. He was lost among the drunken barflies who sat all around him; his face was invisible, his person unknown and nameless. He knew her but she didn't know him, and that's the way he intended to keep it, right up until the point when he killed her.

Then he would tell her who he is.

He wanted to hear her scream his name; to see her cry, bleed and plea for her life.

He picked up his glass, put it to his lips and sipped at the whiskey. All the while he kept his eyes on her from over the rim of his tumbler. The scotch was sour and fiery, just the way he liked it and his women. It caused him to pull his lips, exposing his well-polished teeth and healthy gums.

"That's a damn good drink," he muttered, nobody hearing him due to the thumping music and the hubbub of laughter and chatter.

His stare remained on her.

He watched her every move, like he had done for the last six years; he'd stalked her, crept in her shadows. He knew when she ate, slept, shit and drank – he knew all there was to know about her.

Liz, he thought. The name sounded poisonous. *That's because it is fucking poison. Her whole fucking family is toxic.*

As he continued to glare, he rolled the glass between his palms. He enjoyed playing this game of cat and mouse. *Soon it will be cat eat mouse*, he thought. *Liz thinks she's so clever – thinks nobody knows about her and her lot. Well, I know. I made it my business to know.*

Most people around the city didn't pay much attention to the killings and the missing people, but he had. Especially after his son had been murdered, his body dumped and discovered in woods roughly ten miles away.

The police had called it an accident. They had said the lad, who turned eighteen on the night he went missing, had stumbled through the woods drunk and fallen. His head had been caved in. The authorities had also reported that the wildlife had picked the body clean – foxes and other wood-dwelling animals had ravaged his face and shredded his carcass.

There hadn't been much of his lad on the slab to identify. Had it not been for the tattoo on his left shoulder blade, he wouldn't have been able to I.D. his own flesh and blood.

The man sitting on the stool, burning a hole through Liz as he nursed his whiskey, went by the name of Tokyo. He didn't even want the drunks knowing his real name.

If someone should come asking questions, he thought, *it wouldn't take the cops much to put two and two together*.

Up to now, he was fairly confident his tracks had been well and truly covered - nobody had suspected a thing. Nobody had come knocking. And, since he'd killed three members of her family over two decades, he was certain he was safe.

She has no idea that I've been slowly tearing her family apart. He laughed into his whiskey as he raised the glass to take another few sips.

At first, he'd been happy with the police report. Like a man, he'd accepted it, and reminded himself that life can sometimes throw you a curveball, and that the senseless accident that had happened to his son occurred the world through on a daily basis.

Life, sadly, is fragile.

Not only that, the youngster had been drinking copious amounts. After all, it had been his eighteenth birthday.

But then word reached him that two of his son's friends had also disappeared that night – their bodies were never discovered. And, when he'd looked further into the matter, he found that a series of people had been going missing around the same time, and were still doing so.

Soon his son's case, the missing friends, and scores of others hooked him. Consumed him. It took over his life, forcing him to give up his job as he played private dick. In the process, he lost his home and wife as well – his life came away at the seams.

You've cost me more than you will ever know, you fucking cunt! he thought, glaring at the pub owner. If he could have killed her there and then, along with her other brother, he would have. *Going to keep biding my time. Soon. I just need to see the rest of her family before I make my final move. Then again, killing babies won't fucking bother me. They've all got to die.*

At the start of his investigation, he'd retraced his son's footsteps on the night he'd been killed. By now, he was convinced his son had been murdered and his body moved to the woods. His search was narrowed down after the police divulged to him the approximate time of his son's death – this meant he was able to eliminate some of the pubs he knew his boy had called at.

The Lamb and Flag had been last on his list, and after an uneventful quest for justice up to the point of visiting this final ale house, he had started feeling despondent.

Like in all the other pubs he'd been to, he'd shown Liz's parents a photo of his son and asked a series of questions. When he'd asked about viewing their CCTV tapes from the night in question, they'd agreed, but something about their vibe, body language and facial expressions told him something different. They'd also bumbled their way through some of his questions.

The husband had gone off in search of the tape.

"Surely you mark your tapes?" Tokyo had said to the mother.

She'd given him a forced smile.

As he'd expected, the husband had come back empty-handed. "I appear to have misplaced *that* tape, along with a few others. Would you like to call back in a few days?"

A smile briefly flickered across Tokyo's face. "Sure, why not?" he'd said, turning to leave. As he did, he could almost feel the weight of relief and panic lifting off them. After he walked out the door, he took a sneaky look through one of the windows and saw the pair arguing.

He knew then that something was up, and that they knew more than they were letting on.

The jig's up, kiddos! he'd thought, walking away and not returning to ask about the 'missing' CCTV tape.

Instead, he'd started looking into the couple – he did background checks and asked about them around the city. Not only that, but he watched them and held stakeouts outside the pub.

This went on for months, with nothing strange occurring. Also, he'd drawn blanks on finding out about them – who they really were, where they came from and if they had more family in the area. It got to such a point of boredom and frustration that he thought he had the wrong place and people; that they lived a quiet, peaceful life, and didn't want trouble. At that point of breakdown, he'd thought himself a stupid old bastard – he'd thrown his life away playing detective.

But then a few things happened. Two more people went missing – they'd been reported as being last seen at the Lamb and Flag pub. When he saw photos of the teen girls, he remembered seeing them enter the pub, but not leave.

Secondly, an old friend he'd asked to dig up details on the pub owners had finally found something. The information had been relayed to him on his answer phone whilst he'd been on a stakeout.

Beep: *"Looks like your friends at the pub there are hiding a huge secret, Tokyo. I'm not sure if you're old enough to remember the incident in Bridgend some sixty or seventy years ago, when a pack of cannibals living in the woods attacked some concert that was being held there? It was massive news at the time. Anyway, I won't go into it over a robot – if you want to meet for coffee, get back to me. Also, if you check the library archives, you'll find plenty of information."* Beep.

Tokyo had set up a luncheon with his friend at a café around the corner from where he lived.

"Your message more than intrigued me, Sam. Tell me the rest."

"Did you go to the library?"

"I did, but I couldn't find much – a lot of information was missing from the archived documents."

"Yes, I should have told you: the authorities tried to cover it up, but they did a poor job. I know the full story, and I'll probably have the answers to all your questions."

"But?"

"It's going to cost you."

"I'll give you five hundred for everything you have," Tokyo said.

"Make it a plump thousand and I'll also give you my services – you might need my help in what you're dealing with, friend."

The revelation had startled Tokyo. What was he getting into? How deep did the river of shit go? Who exactly were the people at the Flag?

His mind had swum.

"Deal," Tokyo had said, offering his hand. "Shall we go back to mine for more privacy? I have a bottle of Hennessey with ten years worth of dust on it."

Sam unfurled an age-old story before his brandy-glazed eyes, once Tokyo had slid his lifesavings across the table and into the small, bespectacled fella's greasy mitt.

"The tribe that came out of the woods were old – hundreds of years old, Tokyo. They attacked a concert and snatched the daughter of a police officer. The father went looking, along with a few other men. They thought they'd killed all the 'Man-Eating Fucks', which is what the trashy tabloids labelled them as. But they came back a couple of years after and went for the father and his daughter once more, succeeding in doing plenty of damage."

"But the wood-dwellers were all killed off. What does this have to do with the Lamb and Flag?"

Sam was visibly shaking. "No," he whispered. "Between us, we've managed to unearth something quite extraordinary, my friend."

Tokyo had felt his patience wearing. "Right, but what does it have to do with my dilemma?"

"The tribespeople were killed off the second time, yes, but what people didn't know, and still don't, is that a woman had been snatched at some point in the two years the cannibals laid low. Also, one of the cannibals that survived the first attack had babies. When the cannibals made the second attempt on the police officer, or so I can gather – the story is rather sketchy, but it's all true – the woman was left behind with the offspring. She was also pregnant with the tribe leader's child."

"Are you trying to tell me this woman stayed in the woods and raised them?"

"No, but you're not far off the money."

"Then what are you—"

"She stayed in the woods for a number of years, allowing the babies she'd adopted to grow to teenagers and mate with each other. She then moved her 'clan' out of the woods and integrated them into society. She taught them to count, read and everything else a growing mind would need in the real world. The disfigured children were kept out of sight – they stayed at home with their mum and helped out. As the tribe grew, she shipped them out into the world to fend for themselves. I've heard that some have gone as far afield as the States, but I've yet to confirm this. Most of her children and grandchildren stayed here and continued to grow the tribe. Yes, Tokyo – they walk among us!"

"How do you know all this?"

"When I started digging, I had to go to other sources – people who are up on local legends, history and various other fields. Most of this has been dispelled, but I believe it's true, and the couple living at the Lamb are direct descendants. I also have a contact who was once close to the tribe, but I will never divulge his details."

"But…but, they're normal!"

"To look at, yes. But they still have the urges. It's built into them – it's something their 'normal' breeding will never stamp out."

"Jesus . . . If this is all true, then we're dealing with real-life monsters."

"We are indeed, sir. And I think it's our duty to rid the world of as many as we can, starting with the nest in the Lamb."

"But some of them are children!"

"Who will grow up to kill and devour our fellow man, Tokyo."

He nodded. "I certainly want vengeance for my son."

"And you will have it. So, will you help me destroy as many as we can, starting with that lot?"

Tokyo picked his glass up, reclined, and thought about it for a couple of minutes. He eyed Sam as he took delicate sips from his tumbler. "Yes, I will."

After hatching a plan together, Sam and Tokyo had visited the Lamb and Flag – because Tokyo had already exposed himself to the owners of the pub, he'd gone in disguise.

Their idea had been simple: poison.

They'd gone equipped with a couple of vials of untraceable killers: wolfsbane and cyanide. The former of the two was slower-acting than the latter, which they'd decided to give the father.

After biding their time within the establishment, they'd taken their opportunity after seeing the couple with drinks in their hands at separate periods in the evening. Once the cyanide had been dumped into the mother's coffee, they stayed to watch her die, which wasn't the spectacle they had been hoping for. In one way, it was a good thing.

A few minutes after taking a gulp of her drink, the woman collapsed, never to move again. The husband had been paralysed with grief. When they knew she was dead, Sam and Tokyo had left.

Within weeks of her dying, the father was reported to have lost his life, too.

Their plan had worked but it took Tokyo a few more years to claim his next cannibalistic offspring, as Sam passed away unexpectedly, leaving him in disarray.

At first, Tokyo had taken Sam's death as a huge blow. Luckily, the man had told him everything he would need to know, especially where all the other cannibals were across the country.

He never did find out if a few had made it to the States.

Well, they're not our concern! Tokyo had thought at the time.

After a few weeks of reflecting on Sam's passing, he'd started to see it as a blessing. Did he really want to kill the parents' children? And, more importantly, the children's children? He didn't think he could do it. Had Sam been here, then he probably would have felt obliged to.

Tokyo became dormant.

The way he saw it, he'd had his vengeance – his thirst for revenge had been slaked.

And then people started to go missing again, forcing him to take action.

Sam told me they'd kill. I should have listened to him. Had I, then lives would have been saved.

Before others were murdered, Tokyo took immediate action. He went back to the pub but didn't bother with a disguise. Along with him, he took the slow-acting poison and slipped some into the brother's drink when he wasn't looking.

The result had been perfect – he'd died within a few days of taking it, the blame being laid on a rare blood disease.

With him out of the way, Tokyo had then planned to wait for the perfect moment to storm the pub after closing and kill the reminder of the family in their sleep.

****

All this rushed through his mind as he watched Liz escort the drunk out of the pub and then spy on him through the curtains. He could see lines of anger pull her face this way and that.

Your next victim, cannibal? he thought, draining the last of his whiskey. "Another!" he snapped at the younger brother serving. *Jason? Yeah, that's right.* He looked at the lad and smiled. *I killed your brother, fuckhead.*

The drink was placed down on the bar, the money asked for.

When Liz pushed away from the window and walked towards the bar, Tokyo got ready to follow.

"Watch the bar a sec, Jay – I'm off to the loo," she said.

Tokyo caught her wink. When she shot by him, he got up and slopped out of the room behind her. He was careful to hang back and ducked into doorways and hidey-holes when she stopped. As soon as she started walking again, he was hot on her heel.

She led him to the back of the pub and walked through a door marked Staff Only.

"Fuck that!" Tokyo said, carefully opening the door and peeking around the corner. Liz disappeared out the fire exit at the end of a corridor. He rushed after her and followed her out into the night. He scrambled behind a bin and watched from the shadows. In the poor light, he could just about see her standing guard at the entrance to the alley.

What the hell is she doing? he thought, shifting into a more comfortable position.

Liz carefully peeped around the corner and saw the drunk pinball his way towards her. He was mumbling something, but she couldn't quite make out what.

A fool like him won't be missed! A nice treat for me and the family – it's been a while . . .

The man crashed through bins and almost went down, but a car kept him up as he fell against it. He laughed as he pushed himself off it and lurched forward. Now he was close enough for her to hear what he was saying.

"Fucking hotshot cunt thinks she can tell me wha—*HIC!*—what to do. I'll fucking show her." He bent over to pick up a bottle that was rolling towards the gutter. As he was doubled over retrieving it, he farted, which followed through.

The seat of his blue jeans faded to a watery brown colour. The stench floated through the air and assaulted Liz's nostrils, but she didn't bat an eyelid.

The drunk put his hand to his arse and felt the wet patch. "Fuck!" he said, sniffing his fingers. "Ah well, who cares." He burped again and walked towards the opening of the alley.

He didn't stand a chance against her fierce, ferocious strength.

She pulled the man into the alley, disarmed him, and threw him up against the opposite wall. His head struck the concrete, and he slid down it, leaving behind a bloody, slug-like trail.

"Fix me, will ya?" She stood half-in, half-out of the moonlight that slanted in through the alley's opening.

"N-n-no!" he cried.

She walked up to him and kicked him hard in the balls.

He instantly threw his guts up and pissed himself as he clutched his nuts.

She picked up the dropped bottle, which hadn't smashed, and held it before her. It had once held Beaumet Cuvée Brut. Liz put the top of the container to her nose and inhaled the fumes that had been left behind. "Must have been a bloody good year."

When she looked down, she noticed the drunkard was slowly pulling himself up the lane and out of harm's way.

Liz looked out the lane and saw the streets were dead.

Time for some fun. To let out some of that repressed family rage. Her face creased into a smile. "Where in the *fuck* do you think you're going?"

"N-n-no . . ." the guy continued to cry.

Liz stepped up behind him and grabbed his trousers with her free hand. In one violent movement, she ripped the garments from his body, exposing his shit-spattered anus and scrawny legs.

"You're fucking disgusting!" She turned the bottle around, knelt beside him, grabbed his sagging ball-bag and rammed the neck of the Beaumet up his arse.

He screamed, but not as loud as she'd hoped.

His puckered arsehole has been lubed by his crap.

She crushed his bollocks in her grip until they were nothing but mush as she fucked his arse. Standing, she breathed hard. When she noticed he was still alive, she got on her knees again and repeatedly smashed him about his head with the thick end of the bottle until it was nothing but a concaved mess.

Tokyo watched on, mortified, as Liz got her face close to the dashed-out brains and splintered bone, scooped it up and shoved it into her mouth. He put his hands to his ears to close out the awful sound of her smacking lips and sucky, chewing sounds.

Bile raced up his throat, burning it.

He crawled deeper behind the bin, fearing she would either see him or sense him with her wood-dwelling instincts that were buried within her.

Once she'd finished feeding, her face, hands and arms plastered in blood and dripping gore, the sexy, lath-like woman picked the man off the ground and threw him over her shoulder as though he was a rag dolly.

She then went back to the fire exit and slammed the door closed behind her. There was no trace to indicate anything had happened in the alley.

Sitting there, Tokyo found it hard to take control over his shivering body, but he did.

He didn't know how long he'd been there, but when a light flashed on from somewhere above, it startled him back to reality. From where he sat in a crumpled heap, Tokyo looked up – there was a glow coming from a second-floor window.

Something splashed against the glass.

"Oh, Jesus! What is she doing?" Tokyo crawled across the alley and pulled himself up with the aid of the ladder attached to the wall. He started to climb it, noticing it led onto a steel veranda that was opposite but looking down on the pub window that was lit up.

Tokyo tried to make as little noise as possible as he climbed the steel rungs to the top. His heart thumped against his chest. Sweat poured down his face, forming a liquid moustache, and dripped off the end of his chin.

I'm out of shape!

He huffed when he reached the top and pulled himself onto the balcony and into a shadowy corner.

"Oh. My. God," he muttered, looking through the window opposite. He put a hand to his mouth, aghast, as he watched Liz and her family crowd around the drunk she'd put on the dining room table.

The twin girls, who he'd thought were mere babies, were indeed grown women – teenagers, possibly – but he couldn't tell due to their hideous disfigurement: their heads were misshaped, with lumps and bumps at the back, and they had little hair.

Their mutant-like fingers dug into the drunk's ripped-apart belly and scooped out all the soft bits. They ladled blood into their greedy mouths with their huge, shovel-like hands.

"Nice, Nine-Ball?" Liz asked. "How about you, Billiard-Ball?"

The inbreds nodded.

"They're horrific," he whispered, continuing to watch on in morbid curiosity.

The man's entrails were yanked on, his tongue pulled free from his mouth. The twin who'd been referred to as Nine-Ball now had her hand up the man's back passage. Tokyo didn't know, or want to know, what she ripped out of him and put in her mouth.

Liz stepped out of the picture and back into it with a carving knife. "Who wants the pecker?!" she asked, smiling and flapping the man's limp penis with the blade's tip.

The girls started squabbling, Liz chuckled, and then someone else entered the room: a monstrously disfigured man who had to stoop so his head wouldn't drag along the ceiling.

"That can't be the nephew?" Tokyo blurted, slapping a hand over his mouth when he saw Liz step close to the window. She appeared to be looking straight at him, but he knew it was impossible.

Before she turned her back, Liz closed the curtains, blocking his view entirely.

His whole body trembled. He felt as though he was lucky to be alive.

This can't go on. I have to stop them. I was foolish to wait so long – why did I not listen to Sam and take them all when I had the chance?

The one positive to come out of this exclusive viewing of a cannibalistic feeding frenzy was that Tokyo now knew exactly what he was up against.

And I thought I'd be killing children. Fuck this, they all need to be wiped out.

He stood on shaking legs and stepped down the ladder's rungs one at a time. Once he was at the bottom, he rushed down the alley and onto the main road.

Tokyo didn't stop running until he made it to his front door, breathless, exhausted and terrified out of his mind. When he removed his front door key from his pocket and tried to slip it into the lock, he kept missing the snug slit due to his shaking hands.

"Come on, come on, for fuck's sake."

Unlocking the door, he rushed inside, slammed it closed and fell back against it. He wiped the beads of icy water from his forehead and puffed hard – his breathing came in ragged rips.

No time for resting, he thought, pushing himself off the door and making his way through the living room and down to the cellar. Once there, he went to his work bench and sought out the stuff he would need.

Tokyo removed a hammer and screwdriver from off the tool rack attached to the wall, along with a flashlight and saw. From there, he went to the wall opposite and dismounted his .410 bolt-action shotgun normally used for hunting wild rabbit. On a smaller bench beneath the gun was a tin of slug cartridges. He opened it and grabbed handfuls of them and stuffed them in all available pockets.

Finished, he grabbed a heavy-duty satchel and stuffed everything inside, including a half-empty bottle of whiskey he kept stashed under a floorboard marked with an *X*.

"I hope you aren't drinking down there? You'll have my broom across your backside if you are and I catch you!" his wife used to call down the cellar steps. Of course, she was only partly serious. "You know what the doctor told you, love."

Five years before his wife had left him due to his detective antics, Tokyo had suffered a mini stroke and had been told to lay off fatty foods, nicotine and booze. But when his son had gone missing, the stress of it and trying to find out what happened to him had brought it all back on – the drinking continued.

With the shotgun loaded, a slug of whiskey in his guts and a heart full of bloody murder and vengeance, Tokyo was ready to go back to the pub and finish what Sam and he had started so many years ago.

Tokyo took the cellar steps two at a time and headed out the front door. He was worried that if he stopped and thought about what he was about to do, then his nerve would fail him.

His jaw clicked as he clenched it. *Not a chance!*

The streets were deserted, which was a good thing. Before he'd exited the house, he'd slipped on his old high-visibility jacket, hardhat and duffle coat to disguise the shotgun on his back – if anyone should see him, they'd think he was on his way to work and wouldn't stop or think to question what he was up to.

Still, to be on the safe side, he took backstreets and lanes and stayed in the shadows where and when he could. In no time at all, he reached the Lamb and Flag. The pub was in complete darkness, as were the surrounding houses and businesses. There wasn't a soul on the street.

Tokyo made his way into the alley he'd been in earlier and walked up to the fire exit. Gently, he tried the bars. Locked.

He set his workbag down and drew out the work tools. He wedged the screwdriver into the door jamb where the lock was and started tapping it in deeper with the hammer. When it was in far enough, he pried it. Wood splintered around the bolt in the door, and, soon enough, it popped open with minimum effort and noise.

After replacing his tools, he went inside and closed the door at his back. Darkness enveloped him and panic lodged in his throat, but it was dispelled when his flashlight kicked in. He tried to slow his heartbeat and control his rapid, ragged breathing.

Tokyo felt he needed another shot of whiskey, but knew it was a bad idea. He had to keep his mind as clear and sharp as possible. He stood still for a few moments and shifted his torch around as he listened for any movement with pricked ears.

If they've had a good feast, they'll be sleeping soundly and won't hear me coming! he thought, moving forward at a slow pace and keeping vigilant.

He soon found himself in the bar area. Tokyo took his time, making sure to avoid the tables with glasses on them and the few chairs that blocked his path. When he got behind the bar, he spotted a knife block and drew the biggest blade. He then went through a door and found a staircase. He climbed to the second floor.

Once he was on the landing, he swept the upper floor with his torch and found another door. He went through it and found he was in the kitchen – his feet crunched as he walked about. When he looked with his light, he noticed he was treading in dried blood. His nostrils suddenly filled with the smell of iron.

Tokyo gulped down the bile in his throat.

His eyes glazed over.

"Jesus," he whispered, his torch beam falling on the drunk's remains on the kitchen table. There was nothing left but a husk. The eyeballs, nose, most of his cheeks, ears and lips were missing. His chest, like his stomach, was ripped open – there was nothing inside. In fact, when Tokyo peeked in, he could see the table through the gaping hole in the torso.

Small flies buzzed.

Stepping away, he aimed his light at the sink. In it was a pile of blood-spattered plates, utensils, pots and pans – even the kitchen units were plastered red.

More odours assaulted him.

"Can I smell shit and piss? Surely not!" he blurted.

Chunks of human flesh littered the floor, along with congealed pools of blood.

Shaking his head, Tokyo started towards a third door. Opening it, he saw it led into the living room.

There's got to be another set of stairs leading to the bedrooms, he surmised.

A floorboard creaked as he walked into the sitting room, which was rather sparse of furniture. No TV; just one sofa. A few baby toys lay scattered about the floor – a playpen stood erect in one of the corners.

There are no babies here . . .

Tokyo then found what he was looking for when he rounded a corner: stairs leading to a third floor. He went up them as fast as he could, not wanting to hang around much longer and take any chances.

He was faced with four doors at the top.

Ideally, he wanted to take out either the big fucker first, which he was convinced was the nephew, or Liz, the tribe leader.

Upon gently opening the first door, he was greeted by Jason. The sleeping lad was lying on his back with his legs dangling over the side of his bed. His sheets were in a knotted mess.

As Tokyo got closer, he could see the blood stains on the lad's face.

None of them are innocent. Just because he's a mere child, I can't let that stop me from taking him down. He must die.

Swiftly, Tokyo straddled the boy and clamped his free hand over the youngster's mouth. Tokyo was worried the lad would have impressive strength like his mother, but he didn't appear to. With his weight alone, Tokyo was able to keep Jason pinned to the bed as he slowly sawed through his neck with the knife.

He gargled and bucked.

Blood sprayed Tokyo's face.

When he felt a warm wetness spread beneath his arse, he knew Jason had soiled himself.

Jason stopped moving, allowing Tokyo to get off the dead boy. He didn't let what he'd done dawn on him, and moved back to the landing.

One down . . .

Tokyo headed back the way he'd come. He crept along the carpeted floor and gasped when he was forcefully shoved down the stairs.

He yelled as he rolled down them like tumbleweed, his legs smashing through the spindles that helped make up the banister's railing. When he hit the bottom and slid along the floor, he felt paralysed. The pain in his back and shoulders was beyond anything he had ever experienced, but he knew he had to get up, and fast.

From above, a light came on. This was followed by someone screaming and crying.

His vision was foggy, but he managed to see the huge blurred shape moving his way.

"*Fuck!*" Tokyo scrambled backwards on his arse, using his hands to help him. "No . . ."

The massive cannibal grabbed him and threw him against the playpen, which collapsed to the floor under Tokyo's weight. "Ugh!" he cried, feeling a rib pop.

He tried to scramble away again but was picked up like a rag doll and hurled across the living room. He crash-landed near a bunch of toys: cuddly bears, rattles and plastic keys – all covered in bloody fingerprints.

Tokyo crawled towards the kitchen.

If I can make it there . . .

His foot was grabbed and he was hauled into the kitchen – the drunkard's body was swiped off the table. Tokyo was scooped up and thrown down on it, which forced a violent coughing fit to ensue.

"*Jason!*" Tokyo heard a woman screaming, taking it for Liz.

Lazily, he opened his eyes and moved his head – the big cannibal had lumbered off towards the sink where a wicked-looking cleaver rested.

"*Argh,*" Tokyo wailed, rolling off the table and slamming against the floor.

The cannibal looked over his shoulder but didn't stop his journey towards the meat-chopping utensil.

Tokyo tried to slip the gun off his shoulder. He screamed in frustration when he couldn't quite get to it. "Come on, man."

The cannibal grabbed the cleaver, turned, raised it overhead and stalked towards Tokyo, who was still scrabbling on the floor with his shotgun. Frantically, he wrestled to get the strap over his head as the beastly man moved closer.

He heard the cleaver cut through the air, and then felt it slam into his shoulder.

Tokyo screamed, but he didn't allow it to stop him getting the gun free and into his arms. Before the cannibal could knock the gun to one side, Tokyo cocked the weapon and fired. The shell bit through his opponent's collarbone, propelling him backwards. This gave him a chance to reload and fire again.

The second cartridge drilled through the giant's chest and threw him onto the table.

Tokyo reloaded and fired once more. The slug smashed through the overgrown cannibal's forehead, killing him, before the shotgun was knocked out of Tokyo's hands. The gun slid under the fridge.

"Mother-*fucker*!" Liz screamed in his face, and then slashed her knife across the bridge of his nose and cheeks.

Tokyo fell to the floor and spied the dropped cleaver. Grabbing it, he sprung to his feet and went at her. "Fuck you, cunt!" he screamed.

Before he could reach her, a set of teeth clamped down on his left shoulder, and then his right, forcing him to drop his weapon and crash to the floor.

He felt his flesh being torn away in strips, his blood guzzled.

"Enough, girls. We don't want to kill him just yet."

Tokyo rolled onto his back and looked up at the hideous girls' faces looming over him – strings of bloody saliva clung to their drooping lower lips and chins, bringing to mind strawberry laces. Their teeth were broken and misshapen, and their eyes were mismatched in colour. Like Liz, they were naked – their sagging tits were covered in boils and blisters, which bubbled and oozed.

"Bite fingers off," the one drooled.

"Chomp cock," said the other.

Both girls giggled.

"This fucking bastard killed our Jason and Bear," Liz said, looking down at her dead nephew with tears in her eyes.

"I murdered that fucking brother of yours too," Tokyo yelled, spitting blood everywhere. "Do your worst."

Liz's face changed. "Onto the table with him, ladies," she said calmly.

"*Wait*!"

"It's too late for pleading, fucker."

He was once again slammed down on the table, his clothes ripped from him. Their talons raked at his skin, face and privates. "Don't you want to know about your parents?" he yelled, feeling he had one last card to play to try and get out of the situation.

"What about them?"

"Spare me and I'll tell you all."

Liz called the girls off with a wave of her hand. "Tell me how you know so much about us first."

Tokyo relayed all the information about his son and Sam, and how they had unearthed the dark secret.

"It's true – we do hail from a long line of cannibals."

"Why?" he choked out.

"Kill?"

"No. Why expose yourself by living out in the open? Some of you have genetic failure—"

"Because we've been able to survive much better this way. Long ago, your kind used to hunt my family down in the woods and kill them. Now, though, there's no stopping us." She smiled. "You were foolish to come here tonight. Even if you had killed us all, it would have still been a failure – we have family everywhere. Globally."

His mouth formed a perfect O. "So it's true…"

"What of my parents?" She put the cleaver to his face.

He licked his dry lips. "We killed them, Sam and I. Poison."

She laughed. "You did me a service – they were old, useless and in the way."

A flutter of hope swelled in his belly.

"Still, they were my blood and gave me this workplace . . . Have him, ladies."

"Oh Jesus, *no!*" he begged. "Let me go and I'll— *Argh!*" he screamed as one of the girls bit down and through his cock, ripping it and his testicles from his body.

The second girl tore his nipples off and sank her teeth into the side of his neck. Whereas the first girl's fingers had started to burrow into his arsehole, the second teen's digits worked their way into his mouth and yanked on his tongue, tearing it free and feasting on it.

Then there were fingers in his eyes and up his nose.

He prayed for death but the pain continued for a few more torturous minutes before everything slanted and turned black. The last thing he heard was Liz's laugh.

Jany-Jay Does a Duet

"**T**ime for the five o'clock rock out, with my mop out!" Jay said aloud, flicking his tongue whilst raising his fist and making the sign of the horns. "*Ooh*, yeah!" he continued, mimicking Randy "Macho Man" Savage as he eyed the ladies' toilet door.

With his other cleaning duties done, including the male toilets, this was his last port of call before clocking-off; the women's toilets were *always* his last job of the day, because it gave pupils/teachers time to leave the school. That way Jay could get on with his work in peace without having giggling girls pestering, asking for fags, flirting with him or making a general nuisance of themselves.

A smile flashed across his face as he slid his mop and bucket across the well-polished floor from the men's to the women's.

Horny sixth form girls are the best, man! he thought, hitting play on his Casio tape deck, his ears filling with Jailhouse Rock.

"Don't ever let them tell you CDs are better, ladies—they're for faggots and soft boys." He'd once told a group of tittering teen girls whilst mopping a hallway floor. "If you see a guy using tapes, you know he's a *real* man, baby, just like Elvis was."

This prompted Jay to wink at them and run his hand through his quiff whilst thrusting his hips, making the keys on his janitor belt shake, rattle and roll. "Love me tender, ladies!" he'd called after them, pointing and chuckling as the girls tittered and scurried down the corridor like rats up drainpipes.

As the rock 'n' roll pounded around inside his skull, Jay got on his tip-toes, snaked his hips, curled his upper lip and started singing into the haft of the mop handle as though it were a microphone.

"They threw a party in the jail . . ." Jay crooned, spinning on his heel, pressing his back to the door, and easing it open with the flat of his foot. ". . . The prison band began to wail . . ." Grabbing his balls, gently, he did a Michael Jackson jiggle of them and entered the toilets.

"Sweet. *Fuck!*"

He removed his headset and placed it around his neck, The King now singing to the veins and Adam's apple in Jay's throat, and looked at the mess before him. He spotted chewing gum stuck to the partitions, lipstick on the mirrors, toilet paper strewn across the floor, puddles of water, wrappers, empty cigarette boxes, cans and bottles, used tampons, blood up bins, snot down walls, graffiti . . .

"*What* is that smell? Has a fucking rat scurried up a piss-soaked cunt and died?" He slid his bucket inside and went back to his trolley to gather a few things he'd need: sweeping brush, black bag, various sprays, rags, and a dustpan. "Goin' to take me a fucking hour to sort that shithole out, man. Will ol' Jany-Jay here get extra? A slice of overtime pay? Will Jany-Jay fuck? Frugal *fucks*."

Sighing, Jay put his work tools down on the shelf above the sinks, brushing debris off it and onto the floor, and then grabbed his brush in readiness to sweep the floor. As he walked back towards the door, a piece of wall art grabbed his attention, making him grin.

The graffiti depicted a huge bleeding heart with an arrow slammed through it, complete with feathers and names etched inside the cartoon-sized organ.

"Janice luurvs Janitor JayMan and his shafty mop head! XXXX!!!" he read aloud.

Wet little bitches.

"Go on, show us your dick!" one of Janice's friends had asked him one afternoon, a few weeks back, when he'd gone in to clean. He'd caught them smoking and talking about boys.

"Maybe I will, if I can nick a smoke?"

"Shit, you won't tell on us will you, Jay?" one of the other girls asked, biting her nails and looking at her friends. "Mum will ground my arse 'til doomsday."

Always a fat one in the bunch.

"Depends if I get that fag or not, Jennifer."

"Uh-huh, the cig is for a glimpse of your sausage!" Carla smirked.

Jay smiled, "I think that'd be going too far, ladies. Watch this." Jay grabbed his mop, threw his head back, and placed the tip of the handle on his chin so that the whole thing was pointing towards the ceiling. He then snaked his hips as he balanced the cleaning implement.

The girls laughed, clapped, and encouraged him to sing as he did his party trick. Once he was done, he placed the mop to one side and started juggling bottles of cleaning fluid.

Carla screeched, "I bet you got all the moves in the sack, too."

Janice winked. "I wouldn't mind finding *that* out. Look, his dick is pushing against the front of his trousers!"

Jennifer choked on a laugh, and smoke blew out of her nostrils. "He's pretty happy to see us!"

"Right, out you go, ladies—a man has a job to do."

Shaking his head, Jay replaced his headset, looked down at the floor and started to sweep the litter from behind the sinks and bins before moving over to the six cubicles to sweep them out one at a time.

All the while Elvis continued to pound in his ears.

When he came to the third cubicle door, he noticed it was locked.

"Goddamn it! Not again." Jay rapped his knuckles against his legs. "They only do it to wind me up. Bitches."

He went back to the second cubicle, stood on the pan, and peered over the top of the partition to see down into the toilet with the locked door.

One of these days, I'm going to see one of them pissing, their knickers around their ankles.

A smile pulled across his lips.

By using the handle of his brush, he nudged the lock on the door to disengage it.

"*Ugh!*" he huffed, stepping in front of the door that had been locked.

With the third swept down, he moved on to do the fourth and then fifth. When he came to the final door, it too was locked from the inside.

"Girls, girls, girls . . . You really are asking for a spanking—" he thought he heard someone giggling from in there. "Hello?" he tapped on the door. "Housekeeping!" His smile widened. "I have some fresh towels for you. Would you like me to turn down your bed?"

Now, if there is a girl on the loo, Jay thought, *I might get in trouble,* but then he relaxed. He knew most of the children and they loved him. They wouldn't grass on him for being a little strange. Besides, he wasn't doing anything wrong. It wasn't like he was spying or wanking. Jay knew where to toe the line.

Flirting's harmless.

He'd never pinched a bum, wolf-whistled, or done anything else along those lines. He kept his hands to himself.

Jay tapped on the door again.

Got to be empty. I've never, ever seen a girl in here after school hours. Not in all the years I've been doing this job.

Don't Cry Daddy started playing on his Casio—the song had driven tears from him the very first time he'd heard it at his grandfather's funeral, almost fifteen years ago. Jay had been close to the man, who had been like a second father to him, and Jay had gained the love of Elvis from him.

"One of these days, I swear! I'll ring the little shits' necks. Bet you anything it's Janice who does this." He couldn't help but smile as he made his way into cubicle five to step on the pan to get his brush over the top of the partition to unlock the door.

Huh, maybe I'll find . . . His thoughts trailed off, his mouth swung open, and his eyes bugged . . . *Elvis* . . . . Sat on the toilet was Mr. Higgins, the gym instructor. His face ashen, his lips a blue/purple—in his left hand he clutched a pair of pink knickers, in the other, his small floppy cock. A fart squeaked from the cadaver.

Shock was replaced by amusement, and Jay started howling with laughter.

"Tut, tut, Mr. Higgins! What will Mrs. Higgins think? Well, she'll find out after I report this mess."

By using his brush, Jay repeated his trick and disengaged the lock.

After stepping down from the toilet, he went to the main door and locked it with his keys.

Let's have a bit of fun first . . . After all it's not every day I find Elvis dead on the porcelain!

"How about a duet, Mr. Higgins?"

Jay moved to the last door on the left, opened it inch by inch with a creak punctuating every move and stared at the body when it was in plain view.

Into the Ghetto replaced Don't Cry Daddy and Jay stopped the tape.

"You can be my Lisa Marie on this one, Donald," he said, going to the gym teacher and giving his limp leg a kick. A fresh laugh tore through Jay when he saw the man's green shorts and pants that had been thrown to one side. "Must have been eager to pump one out, big fella? I wonder if I can lug you around . . ."

Jay knew he'd be able to pick the bigger man up, as he was no slouch at six-two and two-hundred-twenty-two pounds. Before grabbing Donald and hoisting him up off the bog, Jay looked at the knickers and spied a name etched on the waistband.

"Priscilla. Priscilla Latch? The girls' gym teacher? You dirty *fuck*, Donald—she must be half your age. More, maybe!"

Thinking the whole thing will be embarrassing for the man's wife and his colleagues here at Pont-Y-Porth High School for girls, Jay couldn't help but laugh once more as he grabbed Donald and hugged him close to his chest.

"Are you ready, Don? We're going to have a wee dance and sing-song, son." Jay said, turning the man's head so he could look into Donald's dead white eyes.

A teeth-chattering chill seeped off Donald and found its way under Jay's clothes, but it didn't stop him from hitting play on his tape deck.

"Here we go. When I stop singing that'll be your queue to start. Got it? Also, try and put on your best Marie voice, son."

A surge of excitement coursed through Jay as he danced the body out into the toilet's main area and swept it around and around in circles as he sung his heart out. All the while the dead man's head bobbed and flopped on its fat plinth with its toes dragging along the tiles.

"Your turn!" Donald didn't sing, so Jay stopped moving and drew the headset off his head. "What's the matter? Frostbite? Rigor mortis got your mouth clamped shut? Some fucking fun you—"

"Kiss me, fat boy!" Donald yelled, his head slumping forward, issuing a snapping sound like a hundred icicles breaking at once.

Jay screamed, feeling hot piss shower down his left leg. "You . . . you're . . ."

"Dead?! Ha!" When Donald spoke, thick fog emanated from his mouth and nostrils—the temperature in the room plummeted. Jay shrieked when he saw the sinks, taps, pipes and floor cover with thick ice. The room resembled a meat locker.

"This . . . can't . . . Ugh!" he wheezed. The cold caught in his throat, squeezing his windpipe to the size of a pinprick. Jay felt his body begin to freeze—ice climbed his legs and found its way into his ball bag, hips, and guts. His organs grew frosty and laden—his heart slowed to a death-pace.

More pain exploded in his lower back as Donald's grip intensified, his nails digging into Jay's flesh.

Jay grew an icicle-beard within seconds, and heard his bones start to splinter like window panes.

"Lights out, Hound Dog!" Donald said.

"N—n—no—" Jay managed, his teeth clinking together and crumbling to frost particles.

The last thing Jay heard was his spine break and his ribcage collapse.

Mink

Stepping out of her shower, Tanya strolled bare-arsed into her adjoining master bedroom. The space was plush – the red shag matched the racy black and crimson bedding, along with the ruby-coloured drapes. The room didn't have a traditional overhead lighting fixture. Instead, there were sconces dotted around the room, four in total. There were no candles, just tiny bare bulbs that glowed cheerlessly and threw eerie shadows across the blood-red walls.

The deco had been her and Andrew's choice, which had matched their souls. Their passion, lust and desire.

Not love.

She had married him for his wealth and what he could give her. A marriage built on a stack of cash. Once she'd tired of him, she'd had him rubbed out by the very people that worked for him.

When Andrew died, she inherited his wealth along with everything he had owned: house, cars, foreign property. She didn't care for his business – that could go to rack and ruin. Tanya had all the money her heart desired and more.

Glancing at her bed as she slipped by, she noticed her jism-covered dildo lying among her tangled sheets. Next to it was a set of handcuffs, shredded stockings, whip, collar, paddle and anal douche. A smile played across her face. The night before had been filled with cocaine, champagne and rough sex, as two of her former husband's colleagues had worked over every orifice her body had to offer them.

Such a thing to do on the eve of my wedding anniversary!

A giggle escaped her.

Images flashed through her mind of how one of the big, brutish blokes had soaked her hard nipples in champagne and sucked them clean.

It had taken her all night to recover. For her arse to cool down from the beatings it had taken and for her legs to straighten.

A flash of excitement shot through her pussy and nestled in her stomach.

Sighing, she moved to her wardrobe.

Since his death, life has been grand! she thought, stroking the material of the evening gown she had hanging by a hanger on her wardrobe. It was silky-smooth, with a plunging neckline. A split raced up one side, which would reveal her left leg.

This cost Andrew a pretty penny. Five...No, six-thousand pounds.

Another pulse of pleasure shot through her lady garden. The thought of money got her engine running, especially if it was being spent on her.

Her bedroom was filled with expensive items her doting husband had plied her with. Her sugar daddy.

Dead daddy! She giggled, putting a finger in her mouth and lifting her right leg until her heel touched her buttock.

Looking down, she noticed the string of pearls he had bought her. She put them around her neck and fastened the clasp.

Her nipples stiffened.

How he liked to fuck me in these alone…

Tanya moulded her tiny tits, then lowered her right hand. It skimmed across her flat stomach and reached down further until her fingertips knotted with the lightly-coloured hairs that covered her near-bald twat.

She bit her lower lip as her fingers slid beneath her folds.

A creaking sound stopped her and brought her out of her trance-like state. Looking up, her eye instantly fell on her vanity mirror. In its reflection, she saw the mink coat.

The door to her walk-in-wardrobe had popped open…

A chill crept up her body.

Suddenly, all thoughts of sexual pleasure were gone. Her innards felt cold – the hairs on her arms and at the back of her neck stood on end.

The fur terrified her.

It was the one possession he had bought her that she could no longer stomach. When she'd first received it, she'd fallen in love with it. It had been the one thing she had always wanted.

A mink coat.

It had cost Andrew four-times the amount of the silky-smooth gown.

Before his death, everything had been fine with the coat. She'd looked like a million bucks in it, too. But after she'd planned and executed his assassination, the coat, as though it had its own mind, had turned against her.

Whenever she wore the fur, strange things happened, such as taking a tumble down the stairs, getting mugged outside a local theatre, outbursts of violence, deaths of loved ones, destruction to property.

Of course, the people around her put it down to bad luck – that every time something unusual occurred, she just happened to be wearing the coat. They told her she should stop overthinking things, and Andrew was not haunting her mink!

But no matter how much she tried to play it down, Tanya couldn't help but think the coat was haunted. Just like now, it watched her – it seemed to be everywhere.

Who's heard of a fur coat being possessed?! It's ridiculous. She tried to laugh, to smile, but the image of the coat in the glass had her scared stiff. A breath hitched in her throat – she couldn't rip her gaze away.

It taunted her. Not only by day, but at night, too – she even dreamed about the fucking thing!

Two weeks ago, it had tried to kill her.

Tanya had dreamt she'd been attending a posh do with Angelo, the man she was currently fucking (he was one of her late husband's employees, and also one of the two men she had been screwing last night. Whilst she was at this event, hobnobbing with society's finest, her fur had unleashed a ferocious attack.

Just like a Boa Constrictor, the coat had started to compress her. Ribs had cracked and splintered through her flesh. Her arms had snapped like dry twigs and her shoulders buckled and burst out her skin. Her screams of agony had brought forth three men who tried to rip the mink from her.

But their attempts had been futile – the coat made her fight them off. Tanya had hacked into them with knives that had lain close by on a table.

The black-and-white horror film inside her head had come to an end once the men had been sliced, diced and stripped of their flesh and she had been crushed to dust.

She'd awoken from the dream kicking and screaming – she'd reached out to the other side of the bed, forgetting that nobody occupied the space. After flicking the lights on, she'd found the coat hanging on the back of her chair in front of her vanity mirror.

Tanya had sworn she'd left it in the walk-in-wardrobe the previous week.

The memory cut a fresh chill down her back.

I'm glad I've got company for tonight...

Gingerly, she walked over to the open door, took one last look at the coat, and closed it.

Creepy fucking thing!

She turned and averted her eyes to the opera tickets lying on top of her handbag. A warm feeling spread through her. A smile returned to her face. "Angelo should be here at any moment," she uttered. "I best get a move on!"

Angelo, the man who had assassinated her husband, had been his number two, alongside another man known as Gerald, a six-and-a-half-foot beast of a man. He rippled with solid muscle, his body covered in scars from years of dog-fighting.

The door behind her creaked open once again, causing her to gasp. When Tanya turned, she saw her fur lying on the floor – it had slipped from its hanger.

"Shit!"

Hesitating for a moment, she finally walked over to the door, picked her coat up by her fingertips, and tossed it onto her bed.

"*Ugh!*" she gasped, mortified, as though she had just handled toxic waste. "That's it! As soon as Angelo gets here, I'm burning the fucking thing!"

Her mobile phone burst to life, causing her to yelp, scoff, and then laugh. Going to her bag, she pulled her phone out, saw it was Angelo calling, and answered.

"Hey, babe. You on your way? Ten minutes? Great, I'll be ready and waiting, you sexy beast!"

Ending the call, she put the phone back in her bag. She cautiously looked over her shoulder and spied the fur – it still lay where she'd flung it.

It's all part of the guilt process, that's all…But why the fucking fur, my favourite possession?

Think you just answered your own question, stupid!

"Fuck it!" she bellowed. Grabbing the jacket, Tanya stomped out of her room and lobbed the coat over the banister. It softly hit the marble floor below. Satisfied, she went back into her room and decided to start getting dressed.

It won't be long before Angelo gets here, she thought, looking at her clock on the bedside table. *Huh, I could always give the big boy a thrill!*

Her eyes fell on the stockings lying on the bed. *Nah, they're coated in love muck…*Going to her chest of drawers, she pulled the top one open and selected a pair of white stockings – the kind that reached the curve of her buttocks.

She sat and slipped them on, slowly. Tanya loved how her hands felt against her legs, as she rubbed them up and down in a lingering way with the soft fabric.

A tingle shot through her. She quivered.

Once the garments were on, she was pleased with herself. She didn't bother with a pair of knickers or a bra – she would go out in the stockings and pearls alone.

It wouldn't be the first time I've done such a thing! she thought, giggling.

After applying make-up, fluffing her hair and grabbing her ankle-length coat from her wardrobe, Tanya left her bedroom. As she went, she turned the lights off.

When she got to the top of the stairs, she looked down. The jacket was nowhere to be seen on the floor below.

"No…That can't be…" Her words trailed off. Her jaw swung loose. "But…I…"

The coat she had been holding fell from her arms as she tip-toed down the marble staircase. Her heels *clip-clip-clipped* as she went. The noise reverberated off the walls and sounded dark and intense.

A nest of ice-vipers nestled in the pit of her guts.

Halfway down the stairs, Tanya ducked this way and that, trying to see beyond the banister's spindles.

Where the fuck did that coat go? I knew it. I just fucking knew it was spooked. It's him – Andrew. It has to be. He's…he's…possessed it. Stay calm…There could be a logical explanation…

Her mind scrambled and went haywire when she saw a light below pop off, followed by a second and third – the lower level was now almost engulfed in darkness. A lamp on the table by the door was the only glow that remained.

Where the fuck is Angelo?

Her prayers were answered, she heard tyres crunch across the gravel outside her mansion.

Thank fuck!

"*Angelo!*" she yelled. "*Angelo!*"

With her back pressed against the wall, she hurried down the remaining steps and ripped the front door open. Her body was immediately drenched in the glow of Angelo's headlights.

"Help!" she yelled, but doubted he could hear her over the sound of his engine. *"Angelo!"*

The Mercedes became silent and its the headlights died.

"Hey babe, what the hell are you doing?!" Angelo asked, stepping out of his car. Everything from his expensive shoes to his greased-up hairdo screamed mobster.

"The coat – it's fucking with me!"

"What?!" he said, stepping over to her. The slight man, who spoke with a fake Italian accent, took her in his arms. "It's okay, I'm here. Let's take a look inside."

"No, it's loose in there…"

"It's a fucking *coat*, Tanya!"

"Have you got your gun?!"

"Always," he said, withdrawing it from its holster under his jacket. Cocking it, he entered the darkened house. "Who the fuck's here, huh?!"

"It's hardly going to talk to you. I told you there was something fucked up about that coat. It's Andrew. He's come back to finish me off. You know what night it is, don't you?"

"Huh?!"

"My fucking anniversary! He's waited…"

"Don't be so bloody stupid!" Angelo said, sneaking a glance at her small yet perfect tits. "You should cover up!"

"That's the least of my bloody worries! I tossed the coat over the banisters. I heard it hit the floor! Now it's *gone.*"

As they ventured deeper into the house they knocked the lights on.

"And you're positive you threw the coat down here?"

"Yes, I promise you!"

"Well, it's nowhere to be…" he said, clipping his words short.

"What is it now?!" she whispered.

"Didn't you hear that?"

She stood still in the darkness and pricked her ears. *"No!"*

"Who the fuck's in here?!" Angelo bellowed. "I'll shoot you where you fucking stand, you motherfucker. Do you know whose fucking girl you're messing with?!"

"Shh!" Tanya said.

"Shut up!" he told her.

"It's not a person, it's a *thing*…" Her words jammed in her throat, causing her to squeak.

"What?!" he snapped, turning to look at her.

Unable to talk, she pointed. In the distance, floating towards them, was the mink coat.

"No, it can't be!" Angelo said, raising his gun to fire, but his finger hesitated and hovered over the trigger.

"Shoot it!" Tanya screamed, crouching and burying her head in her lap. Her arms covered her head. "Please, kill it!" Parting her arms, she looked up at Angelo and then at the coat which glided closer. A whimper escaped her. "Angelo…"

Then, something about the mink caught her attention as it moved into the light.

"What the…!" Her jaw sagged, but she stayed on her haunches.

Into the light came a bald head, followed by a large, brutish pair of shoulders dressed in a well-tailored suit. The chiselled face fell shy of the glow as the person stopped in their tracks. The rest of their body was plunged in a silhouette with only sections of the face visible.

The jaw – what could be seen – looked strong.

Gloved hands held the coat at arm's length.

"Stop, or I'll shoot! Who are you?!" Angelo said, getting into a firing stance.

"Put the gun away, big man. You wouldn't want to blow your own toe off!"

"Gerald…" Angelo managed to say before four bullets ripped out of the darkness and drilled into his chest. His gun was tossed to the air. His body crashed against a wall, and as he slid down it, a thick trail of blood was left behind.

Angelo's eyes were wide with surprise. Blood trickled out of his mouth.

"Argh!" Tanya screamed, standing up. Turning, she tried to make a run for the open door, but she was too slow in her heels, allowing the giant of a man to catch her with ease.

He wrapped the mink around her throat and pulled it tight.

"Ugh!" she gasped as her air supply was cut off. Her fingers scrabbled at the material around her throat.

Gerald drew her close to his body so he could whisper down her ear. "Thought you could get away with it, didn't you, *whore?!*" he said, tugging on the coat harder. "You should have known Andrew wouldn't have let you, dead or alive. You killed my employer, you fucking *bitch!*"

"Urgh…" she screeched, causing him to loosen his hold. *"Huuggh…"* she gasped, drawing in a deep breath.

"How?!" she managed to say before the material was pulled taut once again.

"He had his suspicions. And when he did, he had you watched, by me. I found out that you were fucking Angelo behind his back. I gave him photographic proof, too. I have to say, you fuck like a high-class hooker, Tanya!"

"Please…I'll pay you whatever you want!" she said in a strangled, high-pitched whine. Tears streamed down her face. Piss ran down her legs and splashed on the marble floor. Some of it found its way into her high-heels.

"Nah, I'll have more fun in killing you. Besides, Andrew paid me to. He said, and I quote, 'If something happens to me, Gerald, I want you to wipe the cunts out!' I urged him to do it himself, but the man had no balls. He loved Angelo like a son. He also loved you – you both made him weak. But he knew I could do it."

She kicked her feet and thrashed her arms, as the remainder of air was taken from her body.

Not wanting her death to be quick, he loosened the coat once more, allowing her to draw breath.

"Pity, because I really did fancy screwing your brains out! Never mind –business before pleasure, that's what I always say!"

"No!" she gasped before the coat was pulled tight once again.

"You were his favourite possession, Tanya."

As her life ebbed away, she caught a glimpse of herself in the hallway mirror.

The mink, her once prized possession, looked ugly as it squeezed the life from her.

She had been right all along.

The mink coat was dangerous.

The last thing to cross her mind was Andrew laughing his arse off in victory, and then she heard the vicious snap of her neck.

Mr. Crusty and the Troll

Matthew swivelled in his desk chair, grabbed his mobile from off his bed, and proceeded to check Facebook. He was logged in under a fake name, Gareth Tomos, and spent the next few minutes flicking through his newsfeed and looking to see who was online.

"What do we have this evening, I wonder?" he whispered, noticing that some of his usual targets had updated their statuses with happy-fucking-clappy posts of good news, funny photos and memorable moments. He liked to piss all over these types of updates with nasty, childish comments, knowing he would upset the individuals they were aimed at. "Hmm… There's nothing much of interest *yet*, ladies and gentlemen. However, it is early."

Most of his victims blocked him; he then stalked them by creating numerous fake accounts and bombarding them with ruthless abuse, pornographic images, threats of violence and – if they were women/mothers – the rape and beheading of them and their children.

Matthew would tease those who didn't block or delete him on a smaller scale, so that he didn't scare them off. When he wasn't mercilessly cyber-bullying someone, he liked to play the good guy, often turning people against each other by making it seem as though *he* was the one being tormented.

It was fun and games and got him hot under the collar.

Some men had threatened to track him down and 'kick his fucking teeth down his throat', but they hadn't.

He smiled.

They *are even bigger keyboard warriors than me!* he thought, continuing to look at his phone.

His favourite type of individual to wind-up was someone who belonged to the indie scene: writer, publisher, editor, artist, musician, etc. They were easy quarry to get to through social media, as they craved new friendships to help build their public standing and presence.

And, because Matthew had many different interests across a wide spectrum of genres, he lulled creative types into a sense of false security by buying their products, sharing their posts, commenting positively and creating reviews on various websites.

This, in turn, showed him in a positive light, helping deflect whispers of him being an internet troll; a man who liked to aggravate and meddle in others' lives. He didn't just have fake Facebook and Twitter accounts, he had counterfeit ones for most online retailers, places where he could post snarky, mean-spirited reviews about books, CDs, paintings and other things associated with creative luvvies he was close to (but secretively despised) under a guise.

He loved and worshipped the wannabe.

But, knowing he couldn't be like them, Matthew ripped them down and helped destroy their artistic soul.

There were plenty of regular folk he liked to fuck with on a regular basis, such as people he'd gone to school with and former work colleagues.

Currently, however, he had two specific people on the go: a young female looking to be the next top model, and a guy trying to make it as a six-string player with a metal band. Both were contacts on his Gareth Tomos account, and were inactive at the moment.

"Where are my prey today?" he wondered, checking their pages. The last post from the would-be model had been a few hours ago. Before leaving her corner of Facebook, Matthew visited her photo albums and lazily clicked through them. His dick hardened when he got to her holiday snaps. "Such a beautiful creature. You could model for anyone!"

Not that he ever messaged her that.

He hated her because he knew he could never have her, that she wouldn't want a fat, ugly, unshaven, unkempt grease monkey like him. There had been plenty of women like her in school who had taken great delight in teasing him about his 'disgusting looks', 'ways' and 'hygiene'.

"Well, I've repaid *some* of those cunts!" he muttered, looking up at the news clippings on his wall. "My corner of pride." His eyes roamed the various headlines: "Internet Troll Takes Life". "Facebook Stalker Hounds Girl to Hang". "Twitter Troll Bullies Boy into Overdose".

The police couldn't catch him.

He hid behind codes and barriers that prevented him from being located. After pushing someone to their limit, Matthew would disappear online. Within minutes, he was someone new who lived on the other side of the world. He had the best PC equipment money could buy, thanks to the state benefits he received for being on the sick with epilepsy.

"Let's send her a message."

'Where are you? In the toilet throwing your dinner up so you can fit into your skinny jeans? It doesn't matter that you have a fat body and a saggy arse – you have great tits!'

He laughed. "She's going to block me soon, I know it. I can't believe I've lasted this long!"

When he'd first started talking to her, he'd been a saint, until she'd rejected him, even though he'd used fake pictures of good looking men. He'd started out slowly, telling her nasty things and saying he was only teasing.

She'd once been a chirpy person online, but, slowly, he was dimming her light. Her posts of recent were pessimistic.

"I'll break you yet, dear." Matthew put his phone to his lips and licked it. When he pulled away, he could smell his rotten, tobacco breath on the screen before him, prompting him to sniff the slug-like trail that was his saliva. "*Mmm*! I bet you'd like my warm tongue around your pussy, Jennifer!" he told the image.

He switched to the boy's account. He hadn't heard from him in days.

'You're going to end up with a fucking knife in your throat, pal!" had been the guitarist's last words to Matthew in Facebook Messenger. "I'll hunt you down, wait and see!'

Big words, Matthew had thought at the time, as he'd continued to needle the band member. *'You fucking suck! You couldn't play your way out of a wet paper bag!'* In reality, it was a lie. Matthew thought the boy played well and loathed him for it.

When there had been no response to Matthew's volley of abuse, he'd taken to Twitter and left multiple Tweets on his wall such as, *'You have shitty, lacklustre skills', 'Go hang yourself',* and *'You're a gay boy!'* Matthew had also insinuated he was a paedophile, sister-toucher and mother-fucker.

"Maybe Daniel *is* coming here to stick a blade in me!" Matthew said, chuckling whilst writing a message to his victim.

'Loser!'

Matthew casually threw his mobile onto the bed. "Let's wait and see if I get a reply from either of them."

He spun around in his chair to face his laptop, which was set up by the side of his PC and proceeded to scroll through the bogus Facebook account open on that device.

"There's nobody on this account to piss off any longer. Most of the good ones have blocked me. I'll have to hunt them down on my Tomos account!"

Matthew turned his attention to his PC and scanned his genuine Facebook, Twitter and multiple other social media sites.

"Yeah, it's all very quiet tonight. Never mind, it gives me a chance to chill."

He stamped his foot on the bedroom floor and yelled down to his mother. "Coffee! *Now*!" When there was no response, he stamped harder, using both feet like a toddler having a screaming fit in a supermarket. "Coffee! Now, bitch!"

When he heard the TV's volume being lowered downstairs, he smiled, knowing his mother had heard his demands.

She's getting sloppy in her old age, especially ever since Dad died! Still, what choice do I have? My whore of a sister is out tonight. A shame, because she's such a good, sexy skivvy is Beth—

"Coming, love!" his mother called up, breaking his chain of thought.

Moments later, there was a knock at his bedroom door.

"Your drink, baby," his mother said.

"Good. Leave it out there and fuck off! Next time, be quicker!"

"Sorry, baby. I…"

"Piss off, woman! I'm busy here in my Command Centre."

"Of course, dear. Let me know when you'd like your tea brought—"

"Go! Fuck off, *bitch*!" he screamed, grinning as he listened for the shuffle of her feet along the carpet. Satisfied she'd gone, he momentarily left his room and picked up his drink. "Now, where was I? Ah yes, chill time!" His eyes shifted to his PC.

He placed his mug on a coaster by the side of his computer and sat in his chair. Once comfortable, Matthew brought up a variety of porn sites he liked: Amputee Sluts, Pregnant Dogs Fuck, Abortion Porn Euro, Snuff UK, Strangled Angels and Bitches Beaten to a Pulp USA.

With all the sites open in separate windows, Matthew turned to his bed and stuffed his hand under his mattress, groping for the item he wanted. When his fingers closed around it, Matthew drew the article out and dangled it before him.

A sock. A baby sock he'd lovingly named Crusty. Matthew had come across the item of clothing years ago, in a box he'd found in his mother's bedroom. Within the cardboard container had been a ton of keepsakes from his baby days: a lock of hair, a scan photo, his hospital ID bracelets, his first toothbrush, a single sock and a few other bits and pieces.

"We've had a *lot* of good times, Mr. Crusty!" He grabbed the sock in both hands and stretched it. The cracking sound brought a smile to his face as dry, crumbling flakes of stale semen decorated his lap like a winter wonderland scene on a Christmas card.

The stale smell of cum assaulted his nose, but he welcomed it and breathed it deep. "*Mmm!*" he sighed. "Crispy fresh!"

His dirty, sweaty, trembling fingers fumbled with his belt before moving to the buttons on his jeans. Matthew stood, turned to make sure there was nobody going to barge into his Command Centre, and then pulled his underpants and denims down.

A sour, unwashed smell wafted up from his privates and lower body, causing him to giggle. With his jeans and underwear around his ankles, he put two fingers and a thumb to his micro penis and gave it a few gentle tugs.

"That's it, come out and play!"

Matthew's life had been made hell in school after the other lads had discovered he had a tiny dick, which, as it turned out, had been caused by a birth defect.

"Rolocock", they had tagged him. The nickname had stayed with him until he'd left education.

"*Fuckers!*" he mouthed, looking down at his shame. It was buried amongst a thick, smelly thatch of black hair that had dried chunks of come in it. His cheeks flushed.

"Come on, grow!"

Matthew continued to tease his prick until it was standing to its full, unimpressive height of three inches, and then slipped it inside Mr. Crusty and placed the tips of his fingers to his nose. "Smells like gone off milk." He placed his repulsive digits in his mouth and sucked on them, not caring about the dirt under his fingernails. "Delicious!"

The desk chair groaned when he flopped into it and reclined. Matthew put his bare feet up on his desk and slowly stroked his chode, his eyes catching sight of his overgrown toenails and the grime that lurked beneath them.

A stench like rotten cheese sailed towards him.

With an outstretched hand, he grabbed his sticky, smeg-encrusted PC mouse and guided the on-screen arrow to the window after his Facebook page. Clicking on it, he found himself on Abortion Porn Euro. Not bothering to search through the plethora of videos, Matthew picked the first one he came across and clicked on the icon to begin playback. The screen showed a nude woman, whose pregnancy was clearly obvious, lying on a bed in a simulated hospital room. Three naked, male doctors stood around her.

"Get it *out* of me, doctor!" she screamed.

Incisions were made in her distended belly – grabbing hands were thrust inside her.

Matthew started beating his cock at the sight of blood, and to the sound of screaming.

As one doctor tore the still form from her and tossed it against a wall, his aides masturbated until they came over her bleeding twat, tits, face and hair. The video ended abruptly, causing Matthew to switch to the next screen along: Amputee Sluts.

Limbless, gyrating women flooded his screen, spoiling him for choice. Some were being beaten; others were having their stumps licked, sucked and teased in various ways that would make a 'normal' person gag. Then there were the diseased amputees: jism was smeared on their withered, infected arms and legs that were covered in weeping boils and blisters, which were popped and sucked clean of semen and pus.

Some of the actors threw up, enticing the filthy women on-screen to lap at the multi-coloured sludge like the proverbial cat.

"Yeah, slow for daddy!" Matthew gasped, wanking as fast as he could. "Suck it up! Make sure that floor is clean for your daddy!" His eyes glassed over as his orgasm built.

Got to slow it down!

Matthew spent the next twenty minutes leisurely caressing his cock to a range of clips found on Snuff UK, Strangled Angels and Bitches Beaten to a Pulp USA. Seeing women punched, kicked and murdered got him going more than anything, even the trolling. It wasn't the sight of their helplessness, blood and screaming that excited him, it was the thought of him actually doing it to a female himself. He would often shout abuse and swear at the screen as he wanked angrily.

Deep down, though, he knew he didn't have the balls to do it. The only person he knew how to talk tough to was his mother. The realisation of this made his hard-on falter, but he managed to keep going. He knew he was a coward. It was nothing new to him.

Focus on the porn, Matthew!

He watched as two naked men beat and tortured a woman to death in a cheap hotel room. As one guy pummelled her with fists and kicks, his cohort raped her with a broom handle.

The violence seemed to go on forever, thrilling Matthew and making his cock ache and twitch for release.

"Not yet!" he said with gritted teeth, pulling his hand off his penis. He didn't want to lose his load over violence and snuff porn tonight. He moved to the last screen, which he knew would help him squirt his dirt: Pregnant Dogs Fuck.

There's just something about watching bitches with a belly full of pups getting screwed by their male owners, he thought. *It's pretty fucking hot when females fuck their pregnant dogs with strap-ons, mind!*

Matthew had done research into dog porn, finding that some bitches lost their litter if fucked too hard. He sometimes liked to imagine the pups dying as he played with himself. It added to the thrill.

But not now, because he was close to the vinegar strokes. There wasn't time. Before he knew it, his muck was spewing against the toes of Mr. Crusty. His body bucked, and the chair rattled and creaked as his twenty-stone frame flip-flopped like a virgin in the sack.

Spent, he relaxed into his chair, his feet falling from his desk. His knees knocked; his thighs quivered.

"Fuck! That was so good."

A jingle from his phone alerted him to a notification from Facebook.

"Ooh, wind-up time! The fun never ends around here."

He pulled Mr. Crusty from off his cock and rammed it back under the mattress. "I'll probably need you soon, pal!" he said, picking his phone up off the bed and activating Facebook.

Jennifer had responded to his messages.

'You're mean! But you're right, I really am fat! What do you think I should do?' :'(

'Fucking hang yourself, you fat, bastard pig!' he responded, smiling.

When there wasn't an instant reply, Matthew checked Daniel's page to see if there was a message from him. Nothing.

"Why ignore me? You could just block me, you fucking moron!"

'Are you out practicing with your pretend band?' Matthew messaged Daniel. He then replaced his phone on the bed and waited for a response from Jennifer.

"Shouldn't take…" A noise from outside derailed his train of thought. "What the hell was that?" Matthew got out of his chair and went to his window, which was ajar. On parting his curtains and peeking from behind the nets, his ball bag shrivelled. A nest of ice vipers slithered around inside his guts.

"No, *impossible!*"

Outside, parked across the street from his house, was a van. Written across its dented bodywork in stark white lettering were the words *Pitbull Guitar Amps Co.* There was someone sat behind the steering wheel. A second person stood smoking a cigarette under a streetlight by the side of the van.

Matthew pulled away from the curtains when both parties looked up at his window.

"Oh, *shit!*" he yelled, dropping to his knees. Matthew commando-crawled over to his light switch and flipped it. His room descended into darkness. "What the fuck am I going to do?"

A car door opened, then slammed shut.

He remained quiet, straining to hear what was being said.

"This the place?" he heard someone say.

In that moment, Matthew needed to piss. Badly.

"Yeah, it is!" a second person answered. "Let me finish my smoke before we take care of business."

"Shit, shit, *shit*!" Matthew spat, sweat breaking across his brow. "My phone! Maybe I can message him and tell him I was joking? Just teasing, that's all!"

"Want me to get the boys out of the back?" the first person asked.

"Better had, aye – they haven't come all this way to miss out, man!"

Not wasting any more time, Matthew got to his feet. *They won't be able to see me in here, not with the light off!* he reasoned, snatching his phone off the bed and opening Messenger. He noticed that Daniel had viewed his latest messages.

'*No need for violence. I'm sorry!*' he messaged. Daniel instantly 'saw' the message. '*Please. A misunderstanding, that's all!*' Again, his prey 'saw' the message.

'*What are you talking about, dude?*' Daniel replied.

Before he could reply, Matthew heard more voices outside. A knock at a door. "What the fuck!" He went to his window and peeked out, fearing he would be caught again. "*Ha*!" he bellowed, seeing the men from the van enter a house a few doors down from where they had parked.

What a tool I am! he thought, looking down at the small wet patch at the front of his jeans. A burn roasted his cheeks. *Fuck it. Not like anyone is going to know!*

His phone suddenly went crazy, alerting him to notifications.

"What's this?" He smiled, noticing Jennifer had put a morbid status on her page.

'*I can no longer fight the good fight. The darkness has consumed me. I'm off to be with my daddy in heaven!!!!*'

Matthew commented on her post. '*Go on, do it, fatty! One less tubby cow in the world to feed!*'

"Finally, after six months of taunting her!" he said, and read through the '*don't do it*' and '*we love you*' comments that piled in, along with insults and threats towards him. "*Ha*! Got to fucking love it. Bitch doesn't have it in her, I'm—"

A thunderous crashing sound from within the house startled him. His mother yelled incoherently from downstairs.

"That came from Beth's room…" he said, venturing out onto the landing. "Beth?" he called, going to her door and knocking on it. From within came the sound of smashing and struggling.

I thought Beth was out tonight! Shit, I could have got a look at her in the shower had I known! Her pussy is shaved and so smooth… he day-dreamed.

"Beth?!" he called again, rapping on her door.

"Uh-ugh!" Matthew heard her gasp when he put his ear to her door. He'd always loved his older sister. He'd fancied her from the moment he knew what his dick was used for, other than pissing through.

"I'm coming in! I hope you're decent!"

"What the hell is going on up there, Matthew?" his mother yelled.

His heart thundered as he opened Beth's door and pushed it wide. His jaw sagged. Beth hung by her neck from the light bulb fitting. A bedsheet had been used to choke her. A stool lay on its side by her feet. Piss trickled down her exposed legs and dripped off her toes. The urine formed a neat puddle on the floor.

The nightshirt she wore had ridden up her body, revealing her curvy figure and the undersides of her large breasts. Her face was purple, her tongue lolling. Beth's fingers were dug beneath the cloth around her throat – evidence that she had tried to free herself.

Scattered about the floor were smashed trinkets which appeared to have toppled off her chest of drawers, caused by her kicking legs as her life was slowly draining from her.

"Oh, my God!" Matthew's mother screamed at his back. "My baby! Help me cut her down!"

Matthew's eyes flicked to the illuminated screen of Beth's laptop, which was on her bed. He went to it, leaving his mother to scream and bawl. When he looked at the open Facebook page, it dawned on him that he wasn't the only one with a fake Facebook account.

His sister had been posting as Jennifer.

She'd always had a battle with her weight.

He wanted the world to open up and swallow him whole.

Matthew stood motionless, frozen in shock as he read the note he found on the bed explaining why Jennifer had done what she had, and why she felt the need to hide behind a glamorous identity.

I thought the fat shaming had stopped when I left school, but it continued in college. When I thought I'd found escape online, internet trolls were just as cruel. I'm no longer fit for this world. Forgive me. Signed, Jennifer.

Matthew let the note flutter to the floor.

Odd Owen and His Mobile Fortress

"Halloween," he moaned, parting his blinds and looking out into the street. The afternoon sky had turned from warm and cloudless into a brooding, bruised evening, reminding him of damaged fruit. The autumn trees, which looked skeletal with their gnarled and empty branches, seemed to loom over the street. They cast deep, menacing shadows, like the image of a masked killer hanging over a town on a forbidding movie poster.

At neighbouring houses, the glow from tea lights inside gutted pumpkins with creepy faces and evil eyes threw shades of colour across the street from behind the windows and porches on which they sat. The butchered fruit was a tell-tale sign for children that the occupants of the home wanted them to call. That tasty treats waited.

Crisp, orange-yellow leaves blew against his window, startling him. Owen removed his fingers from the blinds and pulled back. "Soon enough, there'll be little blighters out there – monsters of all ages and sizes! Well, they won't be welcome here, not this year." He crossed his arms.

Not that the children would call on Owen, or Odd Owen, as they liked to chant when they saw him walking in the street. Even before his wife had left, taking their children with her, the whole neighbourhood had found him weird.

"You want to stay away from that one, children," he'd overheard one of the teachers at the elementary school say. "He keeps bizarre science experiments locked in his basement!"

"What type of experiments, miss?" an overexcited girl had asked.

"Creepy, ghoulish ones," a boy had answered, making scary noises and sticking his stiff, crooked fingers in her face, causing her to shriek and hide behind her teacher's legs.

Owen had tutted, shook his head and moved on without saying a word.

The science aspect was true, as it was his forty-hours-a-week day job, but on the weekend and in his spare time, he was a have-a-go inventor. He was a creator of the weird and wonderful, but not of things that would eat little children or hack up the neighbour's cat, even though he was perceived that way.

In a nutshell, he'd been cast as the village idiot. Nobody got him, not even his own family.

The constant banging, thumping, drilling, screwing, welding, sawing and crazy ideas, as well as toasters that set fire to his wife's prized curtains, were only a part of the final straw that broke the camel's back. When the children asked for pets, he *made* them: robot cats, dogs, hamsters and a parrot. The hamsters ate the children's homework, the dogs attacked the postman, the cats defecated grease-covered nuts and bolts and the parrot had a nasty habit of spitting blue sparks of electricity, frying everything and anything in its path, including his wife's expensive shoes and handbags.

Putting down the robotic abominations hadn't been enough.

"You're not Thomas fucking *Edison*!" his wife, Cynthia, had screamed. "Stick to the day job, you dippy, daydreaming bastard."

"But one day I may invent something the world can use," he'd argued back. "I have to keep trying."

"Owen, you have a job – concentrate on that. You've already been warned by your boss that you're slacking!"

He'd tried to focus on it, God only knows how hard, but his mind was a constant twirling, swirling mass of ideas that needed to be put into action. His weekends became swallowed, his family and date nights lost, as he started a new project.

"What the *hell* have you done to your car, Owen?" Her face turned red, the veins in her neck protruding.

"It's a prototype," he'd answered in a blasé way. "Wait until the Hollywood stars and ageing rock 'n' rollers get a load of my Mobile Fortress. They'll be queuing up to throw their money at it."

"When you smile like that, you look like a mad scientist. It's scary, and I can't take this shit *any* longer – it's your barmy ways or me and the kids."

He hadn't heard her. He was too busy staring out the window, his eyes glazed over as he looked lovingly at his Ford Fiesta. It was still the same car underneath, but with a lot of modifications. All the glass and Perspex encasing the lights had been replaced with bullet-proof glass and enveloped in mesh wiring, the body reinforced, the tyres covered with sheets of metal, the passenger seat removed, the rear ones lowered and turned into a sleeping/bunking area. Blind curtains had been installed over the windows, the doors welded shut (except for the driver's), the petrol tank fitted with a metal lattice to stop it from being tampered with or pried open, a bull-bar complete with winch attached to the front and a bubble with a hatch built into the roof.

Also, a few additions had been made on the inside: ports to plug in his phone and laptop had been fitted (which ran off the car's upgraded battery, allowing for longer use), and a kettle, toaster and mini DVD player/TV had been put in.

"She's not quite there yet, but soon…" he'd responded, his words trailing off as he slipped further into his trance-like state.

"*Ugh!*" Cynthia screamed, picking up a few plates and smashing them on the floor. "You'll amount to nothing, mark my words."

"I'm off outside to work on her." Completely blanking her outburst, he walked away and trudged through the tiny particles of annihilated china.

"You act as though these stupid inventions are going to save the human race!"

The following day, Cynthia left him whilst he'd been in his boss' office, getting the sack for taking time off during a busy period.

"But I'm close to unveiling a revolutionary—"

"*Enough,* Owen!" his boss snapped, slamming his fists against his desk. "I'm sick of hearing about your crackpot schemes and dreams. Well, now you'll have enough time to work on your Lego-built ventures. Get *out.*"

It pretty much went through one ear and out the other. Owen wasn't concerned or upset, not even when he returned home to a note from his wife.

By the time you read this, it read, *the kids and I will be long gone. Don't try to find us. PS. I took half our savings. Bye!*

He let the note flutter to the floor as he walked out to his garage to work on his Mobile Fortress.

"You were only holding me back." His words were undecipherable grumbles. "Much like my job was."

Two weeks later his power, gas and water were cut off – a notice of eviction was placed through his letterbox. Owen didn't care one iota; he was through playing by the rules.

"I'm going to jump in my baby and live off the grid!"

A few days before they turned up to evict him, Owen sold everything he could and drained his bank accounts. The only possessions he kept were blankets, pillows, a scant amount of books, CDs and DVDs, some kitchen utensils and clothes. After transferring everything into his Mobile Fortress, he pulled off the drive and parked in the street's hammerhead.

He put his fingers back to the blinds and parted them. The street was still devoid of children. Looking over his shoulder, he saw it was just past seven by the clock mounted on the dashboard.

"A little early yet, I guess." He gazed out his window and spotted his old neighbour, Mr. Summers, who he'd never seen eye-to-eye with, especially after he'd fixed the man's mower, which had then malfunctioned and blown his shed up.

Their eyes met, neither man looking away.

"We all know you're fucking Cindy Stomers down in number thirty-three, Vik," Owen whispered, fogging the glass in front of him. Then he saw Ms. Dudley leave her house to take her dog for a walk. "And we know you poisoned your husband, *bitch*."

Out of the shadows jogged Mr. Griffin.

"Another one with a secret. And you lot think *I'm* odd? Mr. Griffin, the man who's been sucking off the tranny queen at the end of the street behind his husband's back. *Tut-tut*."

When his kettle came to a boil, he let the blinds go and turned to more pressing matters. On the front seat of his Mobile Fortress was his mug and open tool box; the panel under the dashboard on the passenger's side was pulled open.

"Now, let's get that wiring sorted once and for all." He lifted the kettle and poured the water over his tea bag. As it brewed, he took a screwdriver from his kit and set to work on trying to fix the electronics which were playing havoc with his laptop.

Maybe it's the connector I put on the computer's adaptor? he mused, his face lost amongst a tangle of wires and fuses.

Ten minutes later, frustrated and sweating, Owen gave up. He threw his tool back into the metal box, grabbed his mug, disposed of the teabag and drank. As he did so, he looked about with a smile on his face. Most of the interior's furnishings had been bought online, such as the cushions lining the sides of the bunk area – it reminded him of a layout found in a caravan's bedroom or lounge. The blinds, although cheap, kept the inside dark; if it weren't for the light fixtures he'd attached to either side of the roof, which gave off a cheery glow, he wouldn't be able to see anything.

Over the days he lived in his Mobile Fortress, Owen had developed additional touches: shelves, hidey-holes for keepsakes and new carpet.

When the weather comes, I'll give her a spray job and replace a couple of the panels, he thought, blowing on his already cold tea. *I should try and—*

Hard thumps to the back window broke his chain of thought. His forehead furrowed, his eyes narrowed. Pushing his glasses back up the bridge of his nose, Owen held his breath and remained still. His ears pricked.

Thump, thump, thump… Three more welts. This time it came from his left.

Sounds like something striking the bod—

The door handle rattled; the Fort shook gently on its chassis.

His heart rate increased. Sweat broke across his brow.

Don't be absurd, he thought. *It's safe in here.*

He raised a hand and slowly reached for the blinds on the rear right passenger window. Before he could part them, however, he heard a chorus of children's voices.

"Poke your head out, freak!" one yelled.

"Odd Owen, Odd Owen, Odd Owen!" bellowed a second.

"My dad says you best move this heap of shit, or he's going to do it for you!" blasted a third.

"You're not welcome here any longer, douchebag!" a fourth joined in.

Owen parted his blinds, yelled, and fell back against the console, knocking the radio on.

"Happy Halloween!" screamed a rock DJ. "Time for a bit of Alice Cooper on this, the most frightful night of the year, kids. Aaaaoooooowww!" he howled like a wolf.

Pressed against the glass had been a masked face depicting Frankenstein's monster; a ghostly one had floated behind it.

Pushing himself up into a sitting position, Owen moved to the rear of his vehicle and looked out the back window. Two children: one wearing a Gene Simmons Kiss mask, the other sporting werewolf fur.

"Little bastards! Get out of here, or I'll call the—"

Rotten eggs thundered and exploded against the window. "I've told you once, you're not welcome here. We're going to make your life a living misery until you piss off!" Gene Simmons told Owen.

"I'll do as I please," Owen argued, eyeing the children. Judging by their size, he guessed they were teenagers. Banging from the front of his car detracted his attention, but he didn't move from where he was. "You won't get—" He saw that Simmons and Werewolf were holding crowbars.

They mean to harm me?!

"Going to kick your fucking teeth in!" Werewolf said, showing off his mind-reading skills.

The Fortress rocked as it was hammered and shunted.

Over the shoulders of Simmons and Werewolf, Owen saw some of his ex-neighbours standing on their doorsteps; a few of them pointed and laughed.

Now that they were out of eggs, the flour came next, followed by toilet paper rolls.

The sound of metal on metal assaulted his ears; someone was trying to jimmy the driver's door.

"Stop that!" Owen let go of the blinds and snatched up the wrench from inside his toolbox. His eyes fell on the keys in the ignition.

Start her up – that'll scare the little fuckers off, he thought.

"Can you get a hand under there?" he heard one of the youths ask. "You can? Great. Stab his fucking tyres. This prick's getting it tonight."

"Best of luck, shitheads," Owen whispered, getting into the driver's seat and buckling up. Even though the tyres were covered by metal sheets, enough of a gap had been left so the vehicle could manoeuvre over speed bumps in the road. However, Owen had invested in durable rubber to fit to his wheels, which couldn't be easily punctured or ripped apart.

Lifting the blind on the driver's side window and securing it into place, Owen looked in the wing mirror. The wind had picked up and the sky had darkened further, but the shadows cast by the various lights helped him see what was going on.

In the whirlwind's eye of leaves and debris, Owen spotted little trick 'r treaters in their droves; most were being escorted by larger figures, who he guessed were older siblings or parents. Some of his ex-neighbours were screaming in mock, blood-curdling terror.

A brief smiled danced across his face before his wing mirror was smashed off – bits of wires poked from the plastic stump.

His mouth formed a perfect O. "You fuck—"

"Davey, *help*!" a youth screamed from behind.

Owen's gaze lifted to the rear-view mirror. Through a crack in the blinds, he saw a bigger child, more like a man, dressed as a zombie and attacking Simmons. More followed, until the four boys and the Mobile Fortress were enveloped.

"What. The. *Hell*?!" Owen said. His grip on the steering wheel became so ferocious, his knuckles turned white.

The groans and moans coming from around him were almost deafening.

He thought it was some kind of Halloween prank, until Simmons' blood suddenly squirted up the back window, followed by Werewolf's.

"Argh!" Their screams became shrieks.

Eyeballs were savagely ripped from sockets, tongues were wrenched from yanked-open mouths, and guts were pulled out in great big bleeding batches.

Owen started to whimper, and it took all his will not to piss his pants. His hand fumbled for the keys in the ignition, but a gathering of putrefied flesh pounding at his window caused him to jump out of his seat and into the back.

He wanted to lower the blind but was too scared to move. Gobs of decomposed skin clung to the glass from where it had pulled free from their fists and arms as they hammered away; the echoes thundered in his ears.

"What's going on?" His voice was barely audible over the drone of the dead. He brought his knees up to his chin and rocked back and forth.

"We interrupt this programme due to an important break in the news…" a broadcaster came over the radio, cutting off the rock DJ and his 'noise'. "…reports of roving gangs of thugs and looters within the city and surrounding areas are flooding in. Police have no idea how or why this is happening but are taking every measure possible to bring these spontaneous attacks under control, as local hospitals fill up. It's also been reported that the fire service has been stretched to its limits due to a number of blazes cutting destructive paths through the city. People are advised to stay indoors and not to open up for anyone, be it friend, family or neighbour…"

Over the sound of the radio, un-dead and their slurpy-sucky eating sounds, Owen picked up on a woman screaming for help. Forcefully, he moved from his frozen spot and peeped out the back.

A gasp caught in his throat when he saw a dozen or more rotting faces mashed against the glass – maggots rolled off their disintegrating heads. Beasties of all shapes, sizes and descriptions wormed out of their mouths and tumbled free from empty eye sockets.

Owen's gaze fell on one set of ravaged cheeks – through the cavity he could see the zombie's tongue was nothing more than a worn-down stump, its teeth bent, broken and brown. When it opened its mouth to snarl, a fat rat could be seen nesting inside, its equally plump tail dangling out of the zombie's wasted chops.

Hot, burning spew raced up his throat, forcing him to clamp a hand over his gob and swallow the lava-like liquid. Tears stung his eyes. He shook his head to ease the feeling of nausea, but out it came when he saw a female zombie rip through Simmons' jeans and tear the dead teen's bollocks off and ram them into her mouth.

Owen watched on, convulsing and draining his guts of liquid, as the balls popped like grapes in the seemingly robust jaw, spitting yellow-red fluids; it reminded him of a certain sweet bursting apart.

And then, for the first time, he noticed the dead's stench seeping through the open vents, encircling him and adding to his sickness.

When he finally had control over his flip-flopping guts, Owen peered over the shoulders of the crowd and saw the 'tranny queen' running in his direction.

"*Owen!*" she screamed. In one hand she held a dustbin lid; in the other, the handle of a broom. He watched as she fought, ducked, dipped, weaved, dived and rolled her way through the zombies until she was close enough for him to see her erect nipples poking through her top. Her jogging gear, complete with yoga trousers of psychedelic colours and sweat band, was plastered in dripping gore.

Even though the people in the street had all given him black looks and the cold shoulder, she, S*aman*tha, had been the only one to give him the time of day. In an odd way, he'd felt a connection with her. Just like Owen, she was an odd-one-out – a weird shaped block that didn't fit the standard slots.

A bit like the boy at the end of the street who can't stop wanking and shitting his trousers, he thought.

"Owen, please!" Samantha cried. "*Help!*"

"I could be the hero, this time…" His eyes fell on the wrench he'd dropped. "I can see the headlines now – 'Bonkers Bell Wannabe Bags Trans and Saves Planet Earth'." His hand enclosed around the tool with gusto. "I'm a-coming, you glorious he-she!"

Screaming like a banshee, Owen got to his feet, opened the turret and popped his body through it. "Come on! This side's pretty clear," he yelled over the groans and indicated the passenger's side.

"Argh-*uch*!" a zombie screeched as it scrambled up onto the roof and lunged at Owen.

He saw the attack coming in his peripheral vision. Turning, he swung the wrench like a golf club and smashed the monster's jaw clean off its hinges. He then swept it back the other way and caved the cadaver's skull in, killing it outright – blood, brain and bone matter spewed, flew and spun into the autumn night.

But he didn't stop there, as more of them scrambled up the Fortress.

"Eat it, bastards." He clubbed skull after skull – blood washed up his face and arms, and gelled his hair.

Samantha got closer to the vehicle and smashed in the faces of the dead with her dustbin lid, which was fast becoming crumpled.

"Give me your hand," he called down to her.

When she thrust her arm out into the air, he grabbed it and hoisted her up and out of danger. After they dropped inside, he quickly closed and sealed the hatch and turned to her. Samantha's hair was a windswept mess, partly covering her thin lips and flushed cheeks. She was breathing hard; his attention was drawn to her flat stomach and strong thighs.

A bulge developed in her crotch as she thanked him. "I guess you're my white knight, Owen," she panted, a giggle escaping her. "What happened here?"

"Why I'm living in a converted…?" he trailed off, realising she meant the horror around them. Heat burned his cheeks.

She smiled. "You can tell me that story later. Unlike the rest of the pricks around here, I don't tend to listen to the street's gossip." She winked.

He had the urge to go to her; to sweep her up in his arms and *take* her. To claim his prize.

The jackpot has been struck. Keerrching! No, I must be a gentleman about this. What would a real hero do?

"Get us the fuck out of here, that's what," he said, jumping into the driver's seat and starting the engine.

The Fortress kicked to life, the enhanced engine growling like a half-starved lion. He put the Ford into first gear and used the bull-bar to ram his way through the gathered pack of zombies at the front. He heard heads, limbs and guts squish, crunch and obliterate under his mighty wheels.

"What?" she asked.

With all the cheese he could muster after hitting play on the CD player, Owen answered, "Nothing, sugar. You just sit tight whilst Batman here gets us out of this shit and to safety."

Then the hatch popped open and a zombie fell inside.

"*Fuck*!" Owen got out of his seat, resealed the hatch and was about to deal with the zombie when he was stopped in his tracks by Samantha's actions. She whipped her trousers down and her 'cock' sprang to action. She grabbed it and rammed the black, twelve-inch strap-on through the eyeball of the naked male undead that was level with her privates.

Owen couldn't help but snatch a glance at her shaved pussy before she ripped her trousers back up.

"I—I thought—"

"I was a man, Owen? Everybody does. It's how Griffin wanted it – he didn't want people knowing he loved the fanny, and not the cock. It was a smokescreen," she said, smiling. "Now, get us the fuck out of here."

After dealing with the body, Owen drove down the street with Roy Orbison blasting from his speakers. Decomposed bodies fragmented into clouds of red mist as he smashed through the dead at great speed, stopping for nothing.

He had a race, planet and prime minister to save.

Not to mention my next smokin' hot wife, he thought, eyeing the luscious Samantha in the rear-view mirror.

A smirk slipped across his face as he fixed his gaze on the road again. *See, Cynthia – I* will *amount to something!*

Punk is Dead

She rounded the corner and found herself on her college's street. Dark, bruised and threatening clouds filled the early morning sky. With winter still lingering, it remained gloomy at seven o'clock in the morning – dawn wouldn't break for another hour or so.

Punk loved being out at this time, even though she rarely got to do it because her parents worried about her.

"You don't know what type of nutter, weirdo or pervert is walking the streets at such an hour, dear!" her dad would often say.

"Anyone could snatch you!" her mother would add.

They think I'm a baby! she thought, turning the volume up on her Walkman – the Dead Kennedys blasted out of her retro-style headphones. The cassette player was plastered in punk band stickers: Ramones,

Rancid, The Clash, Sex Pistols, The Stooges, Misfits and Raining Spears.

Wrapped around Punk's left hand was a Mirror Threat bandana – she also had one depicting the band The Damned tied around her skinny left thigh. Her right hand was gloved and her fishnet tights were ripped and laddered, exposing various tattoos on her calves and around her knees.

Unlaced Docs graced her feet. They were mismatched in colour and style: the right was covered in the Union Jack; the other, the Welsh flag. Even though it was chilly, Punk wore holey cut-offs with a lumberjack shirt wrapped around her waist. The Icons of Filth American football jersey she wore cut off below her A-cup-sized tits and exposed her flat stomach. Her denim jacket was missing a sleeve, the other intact and covered in patches of various punk bands, horror films and things that meant something to her.

Her lip, nose, eyebrow and bellybutton were pierced.

A small tattoo of *I Eat Pussy Like the Devil* could be seen etched along her collarbone.

Punk's long, loose purple, blue and green multi-coloured hair reached her arse cheeks and blew wild in the early morning wind – she never brushed it. Punk liked the just-got-out-of-bed look, which drove the boys crazy. Her lively shock made her jade-coloured eyes stand out against her soft, milky skin; this, combined with her four-ten, seven-stone stature, made her look like a small porcelain doll.

"China is what we should have called you!" her best friend Ryne once told her.

"Nah! We all know how much I love my punk music, which *isn't* dead!" had been her reply.

Punk had gone by the nickname for so long now that she couldn't remember her Christian name. Even her parents called her Punk.

She ran her fingers along the railings surrounding her college as she walked towards the entrance – her rings clattered against the steel. Then a blast of wind fluttered her loose jersey, briefly exposing the undersides of her tiny tits. Her nipples poked at the coarse, perforated fabric, causing her to throw her head back in ecstasy.

There's no denying it – a good blast of icy wind does it for me! she thought, clamping her teeth together and shivering.

When the breeze died down, she opened her eyes and looked straight ahead – there wasn't a soul about. Not even a car passed.

It won't be long until the tutors start arriving, she thought, glancing over at the college and seeing lights on inside. *The cleaners and caretakers are already here, poor bastards!*

Her stomach rumbled.

Coming out before breakfast was a bad idea. Yeah, but it's so peaceful! I can always go back and get something. No, not now, she thought, approaching the gates. *Why? It's not like I—*

The blare of a car horn and flickering headlights broke her chain of thought, and so she slipped her headphones off her ears. Before hitting Stop on the tape player, she heard the boys' loud jeers.

"Didn't realise it was Halloween, boys!" the prick behind the wheel yelled out his window at her.

Punk gave him the middle finger.

"*Woof!* A feisty fuck, aint she?!" Back Seat said.

"No tits, all attitude!" the guy sitting next to the driver blurted, causing them to laugh like loons.

Chocolate boys, she thought, placing her headphones around her neck. Punk knew them of old – they liked terrifying younger students. *Well, they ain't going to push me around. No way! They're all mouth and no drawers!* she thought, trying to steel herself. A laugh escaped her. "You pricks are pathetic! Why don't you pull up around the corner and help each other stroke your little dicks?!"

"Bet the cunt-whore would like that," Back Seat muttered, thinking she couldn't hear him.

"Yeah, the thought of it is probably wetting her fucking lettuce!" Co-Pilot harked.

"Shall we find out?!" Driver said. He killed the engine, which cut the headlights and CD player.

Oh, fuck! Don't blink, Punk, baby. They're just testing your mettle! She bent a knee and put her hands on her hips when she saw they were unmoving. *As suspected – all talk! There's not a working set of nuts between them. I hope…*

Punk gulped when the car doors opened. Driver, who wore a baseball hat, got out and leant against his ride. Back Seat and Co-Pilot joined him and grinned like a pair of repulsive Cheshire cats. Their fake tans looked hideous in the greying sky.

Fight or flight?

The three lads were strapping: each was close to or over six-foot tall and sported ripped, rock-hard bodies. They wore T-shirts that looked as though they belonged to their younger brothers, making their biceps stand out against the itty-bitty short sleeves.

I won't like them when they're angry…! Run home. Now! I knew I shouldn't have come out this early. Damn it. Never again. Never.

"Gonna rip your top off and suck on 'em pre-schooler tittes!" Co-Pilot said, giggling.

"How old are you, princess? Seventeen? Eighteen? You seem a bit old to be in college," Driver said.

"Surprised they allow her unorthodox way of dress!" Co-Pilot said.

"Unorthodox? Wow, big word – surprised your pea-sized brain could wrap itself around that one!" Punk retorted.

Back Seat laughed, provoking a nudge to his ribs from off Co-Pilot. "Hey! Shut up, dude!"

"Knock it off, the pair of you!" Driver said, pushing off his car and taking a step towards Punk.

She backed up until her minute arse pressed against the cool railings. *Should have brought my Mace!* "Guys, come on! There's no need for this!" *They'll have me for* their *breakfast! Maybe they haven't eaten?! Now is not the time to be joking!*

"You should have thought about that before you started abusing us, *bitch*!" Driver said. "Name-calling isn't nice!"

"She damaged my feelings," Co-Pilot said.

"Mine, too!" Back Seat piped.

"Look, I—" Without thinking, she turned and bolted like a horse from out of its stable. She pumped her arms and legs as hard and fast as possible. Behind her, she heard one of the boys yelling, possibly Driver.

"Get in the fucking car!"

Moments later, Punk heard the engine kick to life and roar. Rubber squealed. The boys yelled, whooped and shouted crude, abusive language at her over the sound of the growling vehicle.

She risked a glance over her shoulder and saw the car hurtling towards her.

Fuck! There's no way I can outrun them! she thought, looking ahead. When the woods came into sight, Punk aimed for the trees. Over the sound of her erratic breathing, she heard the car come to a hard, tyre-screaming halt. Seconds later, the doors opened and thumped shut. Soon after that, heavy footfalls trampled the foliage behind her.

Oh, fuck, fuck, fuck! her mind screamed. Punk braved another look over her shoulder – she couldn't see them, but could hear their scrambling approach. *I need to find somewhere to hide! If they catch me, they'll fucking destroy me.*

Her heart slammed against her ribs.

The boys reminded her of wild hunter-gatherers, as they screeched and made Native American sounds in their pursuit.

"Gonna fuck and kill ya out here, *bitch*!" one of them bellowed – his voice surrounded her. "Let the fucking crows peck at ya remains. Peck, peck, peck!" He then cawed like a demented bird.

"Nobody's going to find your naked carcass for weeks. Months, even!" another said.

Punk wanted to cry.

No, not just cry, but collapse to the ground and huddle into a ball and wail.

She wanted to shout at them, to tell them to fuck off and leave her alone, but she knew things had gone too far – a line had been crossed. *I doubt they'll hurt me! No, just rape my arse!*

There was no telling how far they would go, or if they were just joking around and trying to scare her.

She couldn't take the chance.

Punk *had* to get away.

Branches slapped at her legs, body and face as she charged past trees and through bushes, taking herself deeper into the woods. Punk stopped for a quick breather, noticing how the grey, early morning light couldn't penetrate the denseness of the green covering her.

Christ, how far have I come? Where am I? Where do I go? She scanned the surrounding area, and that was when she saw the old, familiar tree. A smile spread across her face. "Thank fuck!" she uttered, going to the huge oak and running her fingers over the carving found in its ancient bark.

The word *Punk* was inscribed in the wood.

The old hideout should be up ahead! If I can get there, I'll be safe.

Punk raced onwards.

She ducked low, thick branches, and hopped over snaking tree limbs, roots and stumps. It didn't matter how much noise she made, because she knew the ruckus they were making covered her getaway.

A few minutes later, Punk stopped for another rest. The boys couldn't be seen. Their jeering, yelling and whooping sounds were faint. *There's a good gap between us!* she thought, scrutinizing the trees around her. To the untrained eye, the den would not be spotted, but Punk was confident she could locate it.

"Come on, come on! I know you're—aha!" Punk rushed over to the construction, which bird watchers would have used years ago, and prayed the door was not barred by a fallen tree or that the structure was damaged in any way. When she was closer to the bunker, she could see it was intact.

"It's a chameleon!" she uttered.

It was barely visible against its backdrop: its wooden walls and roof were covered in bird shit and moss, and stained a green-brown thanks to the weather. The hole at the front, which would have been used to poke telescopes and binoculars out of, was covered over with a sheet of wood and nailed in place. A thick, khaki-coloured net rested over it, which was hidden beneath a scattering of leaves and foliage.

The forest had claimed the archaic-looking building decades ago.

Punk rushed to the door, which was ajar, and threw her weight against it. She crashed through it and sprawled across the soft floor – rats scurried and squeaked, making her jump immediately to her feet and slam the door closed. Punk collapsed against it and tried to slow her racing heart.

"Calm down, calm down!"

When her breathing became less erratic and the blood stopped pounding in her ears, she was able to hear her pursuers. They were much closer, and sounded annoyed. In total darkness, Punk held her breath and listened.

"Fuck sake! You dickheads lost her!" Driver said. "Nice one. *Fuck*!"

"The little cunt is fast, man – there was no way I could keep up!" Co-Pilot piped, wheezing.

"Fan out. Look for her. She can't have gone far," Driver said.

"What if she managed to get behind us? She could be back at college by now," Back Seat said.

"Nah, she's still out here. I can feel it," Driver said. "Now, spread out and look for her, *dicks*!"

Punk heard them thrash through the greenery, and it sounded as though they were moving away from her.

Thank God!

She wanted to cry with relief.

When their wading sounds faded, Punk thought she was in the clear. *They've overshot me! I knew this was a good idea.* Her smile widened when she heard their voices drift into the distance.

She released her breath and inhaled, sucking up the stench within the bunker. It smelt as though people had been using it as a public toilet: a heavy aroma of shit, piss and spew assaulted her nostrils, bringing tears to her eyes.

There was also a hint of dead animal in the air.

"*Fuck*! That's rank!" she uttered, covering her nose. "I'm glad I can't see anything." A titter escaped her. She shook her head and stood. Before putting her hand to the bunker door, she listened – nothing stirred outside.

I should get moving. They may think I've hidden somewhere and turn around to look for me. I need to get back!

Slowly, she opened the squeaky door and poked her head out. It appeared to have grown darker in the forest.

Impossible! Punk looked to her left and then right – the boys were gone. *I'm safe.* She then pulled the door completely open and stepped outside. She breathed in, filling her lungs with clean air.

"*Aargh*!" Punk screamed when a hand was placed against her chest from above.

Driver poked his head over the roof and looked down at her. "Peek-a-boo!" he yelled. His upside-down smile made him look sinister. "You're not coming out!" He shoved her backwards.

Punk sat on the floor, hard – a cry of pain escaped her. "You *bastard*!" she screamed, looking up at him. An image of a bat sprang to her mind.

He swung off the roof and called his mates. "I've found her! Over here!"

"Please, let me go!"

"Not a fucking chance."

She watched as he grasped the door handle, her attention on the padlock swinging there.

"This is your home for the day, sweet cheeks!" he said, slamming it closed.

"*No!*" she shrieked, getting to her feet and pounding on the solid entrance. "Let. Me. The. Fuck. Out!"

She heard him laugh and tell his mates what he'd done.

"We'll come back and fuck with her tonight!" one of them said.

"Yeah, bring a few beers up here and make a night of it. We can take turns screwing her!" another said.

"Man, I'm going to be dreaming about sucking on those titties all day!" Driver said.

"You bastards!" Punk continued to hammer on the door. "Free me, now!" Tears spilled down her face when she heard the padlock snap into place.

"Ha-ha!" the boys laughed in unison.

"Come back!" she shouted, hearing them walk away. "I can't see anything! Help! *Someone!*" Her energetic movements made her sweat, causing her body to overheat. That, combined with the smell and warmth within the bunker, made her feel dizzy. Her eyes rolled.

I need to sit down! she thought, slumping against the door and blacking out.

When she woke, Punk felt scared and rolled herself into a ball. She had no idea what time it was or how long she had been unconscious.

She shivered, her teeth chattering.

I need to get up and out of here! Punk looked about her, but couldn't see. *Is it morning or afternoon?* Not a hint of light or shadow dappled between the boards of the bunker. *We always used to joke about how dark it was in here...*

The memory of playing childhood games in the disused bird watchers' nest brought a brief smile to her face, but was soon consumed by the fear that coursed through her.

Try to stay calm. Someone might happen along. Her stomach rumbled. Her throat was sand dry. *They'll come back soon. And what if they don't? Good! I'll be glad. Will I...? I need to break out.*

Punk got to her hands and knees and crawled. When her fingers brushed what felt like piles of animal shit, she heaved and got to her feet. She managed to keep down what was in her stomach, before placing her hands to the boards and pushing.

It was useless. She was too weak to shove her way through the walls.

Punk sat back down. *I'm fucking melting in here!* she thought, letting her eyes close. *It must still be day – I can feel the sun's heat coming through the walls. Shitheads best come back!*

I should look for a weapon...

Punk couldn't move – her energy was zapped.

Thunderous banging and shouting alerted her to their presence, but didn't scare her – Punk had long awoken and had found a crawlspace towards the rear of the building.

She no longer felt dizzy or sweaty. The heat from the day had since burnt out and night had settled in, leaving the inside of the bunker cool.

Punk loved the night as much as the dead of morning – it was peaceful, allowing her to roam wild and free. However, tonight would not be quiet, but loud and filled with rapturous killing.

She crawled from her space and stood.

Earlier, she had been weak, causing her to panic – this was nothing new to Punk. Her fear had finally subsided, giving way to excitement. Of course, she had known this would happen once night had settled in. But still, she couldn't help but take on the emotions of the little girl trapped inside her; the one who yearned for her old life, friends and family. She was gone.

Punk is dead.

A smile grew across her face. The fearless one inside her was up and awake with the moon and other creatures of the night.

Her heart raced as her fingernails grew to jagged points, resembling shards of glass.

She slipped her headphones on and pressed Play on her Walkman. Her punk music wrapped her up in its colourful world as she continued to undergo her nightly change. Punk felt her body become Popeye-strong, without aid of spinach. A mist rolled over her eyes and her teeth elongated to needle points.

Her face lost its charm, becoming a horrific patchwork of pulsating veins.

She foamed at the mouth.

They won't want to fuck me now! Shame, because my pussy's dying for some cock! she thought, feeling her cunt snap its teeth together. *If only they'd let me have breakfast. One of the cleaners at college would have done. Still, suspicions were starting to mount, what with me having killed five workers there in the last six months.*

Punk couldn't help but return to the home of her education time and again – the place held many fond memories, even though the new Punk didn't approve of such wishy-washy sentiment.

Over the top of her music, Punk could hear their blood racing through their soon-to-be-punctured veins. Their dicks were hard in anticipation.

She licked her lips and patted her pussy. "You may get some yet, girl!"

They were eager.

The lock broke, and the door inched open, allowing moonlight to climb her legs, exposing her body and face.

"I'm not sure which is the palest: you boys or the moon!" She then barked with laughter.

"What the fuck?!" Driver exclaimed, pissing himself. His urine splashed leaves.

Co-Pilot and Back Seat ran.

"Leaving so soon, *boys*?!" she screeched, going for Driver and tearing his cock and balls off.

"*Eee-ugh*!" he squealed like a pig.

Her free hand slashed his throat open, drenching her in blood. As he fell to his knees, clutching his torn throat and destroyed fun zone, she devoured his privates and licked her lips. "A small meal!" She winked, pushing him aside and taking flight. "You can run, but you can't hide!" Punk screamed at the fleeing boys.

When she was overhead, she swooped down and clotheslined them to the ground. Punk trapped Co-Pilot beneath her and straddled him – her pussy went to work, chewing its way through his stomach.

In Punk's left talon, she grasped Back Seat's ankle.

"Please! Let me go – we were only joking. *Please*!"

Co-Pilot bucked. His blood shot up her body.

"Don't you want to suck on my tits?!" she growled, ripping her top off to expose her breasts. They were covered in pulsating, oozing boils. "Come on, handsome!"

"*Argh*!" he screamed, trying to kick her in the face with his free leg.

"Playtime is over!" She bit through his Achilles tendon and stripped the flesh from his calf in seconds. "*Mmm*! Finger-lickin' good!" Punk said. Strips of flesh dangled from her flapping mouth and trails of blood trickled down her chops. "How about some head?!"

She then impossibly dislocated her jaw and started to devour Back Seat like a boa constrictor would its meal.

"Oh God, it *burns*!" he screamed as he started to disappear down her throat feet first.

"Gulp, gulp, gulp!" She gagged as she consumed him inch by inch. The acids inside her dissolved him faster than any other comparable substance on the planet.

"*Ugh*!" Co-Pilot groaned, slipping into death.

"Why go out for breakfast, when you can have a foot-long beefcake for supper?!" she said, looking down at the dying Co-Pilot. Punk then ripped his face off and stuffed it into her mouth.

Scarab

Jason picked up the framed photo from his mantelpiece and looked at the happy snap beyond the plastic glass. Tears welled in his eyes and eventually dripped down his face and onto the false pane and cheap pine casing.

The picture was captured at a pleasing point in his life; a time almost forgotten—a period that was nothing more than a cheery, distant and warming glow found in the depths of his mind. The only time he could recall the happy moments from yesteryear was when he was sober and not crawling around inside a bottle of gin.

"I've been dry for thirty-two-days-and-a-half!" he uttered, tracing the frozen faces with his thumbs. "I should have kicked it, but I wasn't strong enough to stop…"

"It's always one *more fucking job with you, Jason!"* he often heard his ex-wife's voice say. *"The kids need a father who's going to be around to watch them grow up. To have a dad they can play with and take them to the park. What they don't need is a drunken, good-for-nothing thief!"*

"It kept you living your airs-and-graces lifestyle. You were quite happy to gobble my cock for a new handbag or a fistful of fifties!" he'd yell back. The whisky and mother's ruin and rum and brandy and beers made it all go away, but not for the last thirty-two-days-and-a-half. All the angry, slurred voices and the screams and tears of his children were there.

They were gin-clear.

Jason could see the pained expression on his children's faces whenever he and Tina argued in front of them—they rarely had glowing, teeth-exposing grins on their chops like they did in the photo he now held. He dragged the forming snots in his nose and throat and swallowed the jelly-like muck.

"Daddy's going to make things right, kids. *One* final job and I'm out. Done! That's a promise. No more." Jason wiped the tears from his eyes so he could see the images of his children with clarity. The palm trees in the background suggested the photo had been taken on one of their numerous family holidays.

When the bank, mulling and gun-running jobs were coming in thick and fast for Jason and his posse, he lived a lifestyle that rivalled Tony Montana's—the world was his. But a few stints in prison put paid to his activities, and soon he was a number-one target on the police's radar. He couldn't fart without a copper knocking his door.

This job's different, he thought, continuing to look at the photo. *It's fool-proof and worth over ten-million fat ones each! Enough cash to get me and the kids out of the country and away from this shit-hole for good...*

A plan to snatch his children during the raid was in place: a member of Jason's crew, Juice, was to go to Tina's house and take them by brute force, if necessary, but not deadly force. Once the kiddos were in his care, he was to drive to the airport and meet Jason and the rest of the outfit there, where they would board a plane to Hawaii.

The tickets were in place; so too was his crew and scheme. All Jason had to do was put the whole thing into gear and get the job done. Before he knew it, he would be drinking beer in the sun and enjoying his lolly with his children.

Nothing can go wrong... me and the boys have been through the arrangements a hundred fucking times. It's taken us two years to get to this point—no stone has been left unturned. Hopkins and Sons Jewellery won't know what's fucking hit it!

The small, family-owned, family-operated shop was a goldmine; a target waiting to be hit; a grape ready to be plucked from the vine. Hopkins and Sons was a little different than your ordinary jewellers, as it stocked the unusual—ancient artifacts and special items that should only be displayed in a museum—along with the usual: watches, necklaces, rings, and so forth.

It was a shop built for the rich, a place where they could splash their cash on rare items like the materialistic whores they were. It had been a splendid find by Jason, who had stumbled across the shop while doing honest work with a road crew a little over two years ago.

Whilst digging the road to lay new pipes and lines opposite the shop on the busy high street, Jason had spotted it; he'd watched as highfalutin wretches came and went with pound signs dancing in his vision. The sound of cashing tills rang in his ears and caused him to salivate.

On his lunch break that day, Jason had meandered over to the shop and nosed outside like a flunky—he'd already had it planted in his mind that he was going to knock the joint over, so he didn't want to go inside and show his face. Even though he knew it would be a long time before he hit the place.

The golden Lynx-engraved tiaras looked as though they hailed from darkest Africa, and had him rubbing his whiskery chin with excitement. The need to steal had him shaking, much like the horn makes a pervert tremble with the need to climax. Not only were there tiaras on display, but rings from Congo, diamonds from Peru, necklaces from Serbia, pearls from Persia, prehistoric Welsh love spoons studded with twinkling gems, and a whole host of other treasures.

Every day for the following six months Jason visited the shop, but only stepped inside once, when temptation got the better of him. Security was at a minimum: one fat guard leaning on his baton and CS Spray and three cameras dotted around the shop. When he told the elderly man behind the counter he was looking for a special ring for his fiancée, Jason was led right to the vaults below.

Underneath the shop, in the warren-like chambers, Jason found there to be another lazy guard and four more cameras. He also saw some rare items, such as a scarab belonging to an entombed mummy god from ancient Egypt.

"That, my boy, is one of the rarest, most expensive items on the planet! It is owned and stored here by a descendent of the sun god Ra... In ancient Egyptian religion, the sun god Ra was seen to roll across the sky

each day, transforming bodies and souls. Beetles of the <u>Scarabaeidae</u> family dung beetle rolled their dung into balls as a source of food and an offspring chamber in which to lay their eggs; when the larvae hatched it was immediately surrounded by food. For these reasons the scarab was seen as a symbol of this heavenly cycle and of the idea of rebirth or regeneration. The Egyptian god Khepri, Ra as the rising sun, was often depicted as a scarab beetle or as a scarab beetle-headed man. The ancient Egyptians believed that Khepri renewed the sun every day before rolling it above the horizon, and then carried it through the other world after sunset, only to renew it the next day. A golden scarab of Nefertiti was discovered in the Uluburun wreck…" Old git Hopkins had informed him, but Jason had mostly tuned out after the words 'rare' and 'expensive'.

Funny, it doesn't look like much! he'd thought at the time. *Still, if it's as rare as the old man says…* The drool returned to his chin.

The pound signs again jumped up and down in his vision.

Before the discovery of the jewellers, Jason had been clean for almost three years after spending six behind bars for armed robbery; he should have served ten-to-twelve, but his sentence was cut for giving up the loot and keeping his nose clean whilst inside.

He never gave his gang members away, and felt no resentment over the course of his porridge for them not serving time. He'd told the people of the high court that he'd acted alone and took full responsibility, even though witnesses had informed the police that there were indeed five involved in the heist.

Once released, Jason had made a promise to go straight, especially after finding Tina had left him and taken the children to live in the city. He cleaned his act up and got a job with the council, becoming a highway maintenance assistant.

As hard as he tried, Jason couldn't quite conquer the demons. And as soon as he'd stumbled across the Hopkins' goldmine, he was quick to cave. The old lusting for fortune returned.

Within weeks Jason had reassembled his crew—most of whom were still working small jobs, whilst others had gone straight and were begging for the opportunity to break the law in a huge, bank-account-busting way. When Jason went a knockin', they rolled up to go a rockin'.

****

He replaced the photo and dried his eyes.

I can't meet the guys with tears running down my cheeks like an old dear! He sniffed, snorted, and shook his head until the girlie, wimpy thoughts and ideas were banished from his hardened criminal mind. Jason looked into the mirror hanging over the mantelpiece. *How in the hell did I ever get a job in the first place?* he wondered. His head was shaved bald, and jailbird ink decorated his left cheek and the underside of his right eyelid. He also had a scar running the length of his jawline to the top of his shoulder, which had been inflicted upon him with a bottle during a fight in a nightclub when he was nineteen.

Almost twenty-five years ago to the day!

He could still recall the bouncers who pried him off the lad who had struck him with the glass. If Jason hadn't been stopped from pummelling the lad, he would have killed him.

"Fucking bouncers..." he uttered, running his fingertips down the purpley-pink tramline. The rest of his six-foot-four, nineteen-stone frame fared the same: scars from knife attacks, bites and dents all over from punches and kicks, not to mention the grotty ink comprising flaming ace cards and naked women.

He was a product of his business and the underworld he'd grown up in, which in turn had stemmed from Jason being a victim of his youth—a casualty to the anarchy that had stormed within his guts throughout his teenage years.

"Ah well, fuck it! I was never destined to be the next brains of fucking Britain," he told his reflection. "I'm destined to be fucking rich. To have all the wonga in the world and to be able to spoil my children and give them the life I never had."

Jason pulled the cuff of his black jumper back to check his watch and noticed it was almost midday. "Time's kicking on!" He'd arranged to meet the gang at an abandoned airstrip outside the city by one o'clock. Once gathered, they would go through the plan a final time before putting it into action.

Before heading out the door, Jason checked his gear, which was located in a bag by his side: balaclava, flashlight, sawn-off shotgun, tape, rope, explosives, ammo, passport, spare clothes, and a few other bits and pieces.

He zipped the sports bag up, flung it over his shoulder, and headed out the door.

****

At precisely five-to-one, Jason was at the meet zone. Big Bobby Briggs, explosives expert and getaway driver, was leaning against his Transit van smoking a fag. He kindly informed Jason that the others were in the back, ready to rock-and-roll.

The 'Big' part of Bobby's name was a slight faux-pas on one of the other gang members' behalf. He'd been told Bobby was a giant of a man when enlisting a fresh face into the team. When Bobby turned up for his 'interview', Jason had told him that he was not applying for a job as a Christmas elf. Bobby had seen the funny side and was called Big Bob from that moment on.

Jason entered the back of the van and greeted his boys—it had been a while. There was Juice: all-round scout, weapons merchant and safe-cracker. His job would be to get Jason's children to the airport. A car was awaiting him across the street from the jewellers.

Harry 'Wires' Peterson was the man to knock out electrics. He would be taking care of the cameras and whatnot within Hopkins from the safety of the sewer system, which he possessed the blueprints to. Before Jason stepped foot out of the van, Wires would be sent under the street to kill everything before returning, enabling the gang to simply march into the shop.

Bosco, hard man of the crew, was not much of a thief but was a cracking streetfighter who'd rolled with Jason and his team for years. His body and fists had come in handy many a time when they'd been looking to make a quick buck. He would be Jason's support on the inside, along with Wires, while Bobby waited in the van.

After greeting his lads, Jason told Bobby to get behind the wheel and wait for his command. Jason laid out photos, plans and blueprints on the van floor for them all to see.

"Bosco, as soon as we get inside make sure you take all the guards down. Without panic buttons, cameras, and silent alarms to worry about, we should be fine. Once they're taken care of, and we have the keys to the vault, I'll take Hopkins down there and clean the place out. The scarab is the most important piece! Do we all know what we're doing?" The crew nodded and murmured amongst themselves. "Good. I don't want fuck-ups. We pull this off, we're set for life. Bobby, get this piece of shit rolling!"

****

By twenty-to-three, the Transit was parked opposite the Hopkins and Sons jewellery store. The street was bustling with shoppers, which was perfect—the throng of people would provide the perfect cover. Jason and his boys would be lost faces in a sea of consumers.

"Right, Wires, off you go, there's a good lad! We're slightly behind schedule, so don't go pissing about down there, playing with the rats. Get your job done and your arse back here pronto. Capiche?"

The bespectacled fella nodded, grabbed his bag, and exited the van without a word.

Jason poked his head between the driver and passenger seats and watched as Wires jogged across the road before slipping down an alley. He looked at his watch and gave his man thirty minutes, even though it had only taken between eighteen and twenty-two on their trial runs.

He turned back to his boys and looked at Juice. "Okay, Juicy. Your turn!"

"I'm ready, boss man."

"Come here," Jason said, leaning between the front seats again. "See that Ford Fiesta over there?"

"The black one?"

"That's it. Here's the keys." He placed them in Juice's hand. "Take good care of my children, and make sure you get them to the airport in one piece. Got it?"

"Of course, boss. You can trust me. We're like brothers."

"I know," Jason said, throwing his arms around the man and pulling him close to his chest. "When this is over, we're going to be stinking rich!" The others cheered. "Now, off you go."

Just like he'd done with Wires, Jason watched his man through the window before sitting beside Bosco. He looked at his watch—eight minutes had passed. A tightness knotted Jason's guts as he listened to the seconds thunder down. *Not much longer,* he thought. He always got tense before a raid.

Jason closed his eyes and willed his stomach to stop flip-flopping. Bosco and Bobby were talking, but he couldn't hear what they were saying. Everything seemed muffled, distorted almost.

"Looks like he's on his way back, boss!" Bosco said, giving Jason's arm a tap.

Jason opened his eyes and stood. He saw Wires running across the street. "Open the doors for him, Bos." The muscleman did as instructed, allowing Wires entry to the van. He jumped in. "Everything run smooth?"

"Yeah…" Wires gasped. "Fucking simple! Nobody suspected a thing."

"Right, let's fucking roll!" Jason said, removing his balaclava from the holdall and placing it on his head, so that it looked like a woolly hat. He zipped the bag back up and put it over his shoulder. The others did the same.

Jason moved across the street with Bosco breathing down his neck. When he looked over his shoulder, he saw Wires was a few steps behind. In the van, Bobby nodded at him. Jason returned it.

Nobody seemed to notice the darkly-dressed, slightly conspicuous men. People were too busy rushing around; shoppers mixed with business types, who were eating on the go.

Just after they entered the jewellers, they dropped their balaclavas and removed their sawn-offs from their bags.

"Everybody get down on the fucking ground! *Now!*" Jason yelled, firing a warning shot into the ceiling. Glass and plaster exploded and cascaded down around him. Customers yelled and screamed. Before anyone could escape, Wires had the main door locked, the blinds drawn, with Bosco manhandling the guard on the top floor. When Bosco had the man to ground and cuffed, he went and sought out the others.

****

Within ten minutes, Jason and his boys had everything under control: all the guards were on the floor, cuffed and rendered useless, with the customers lined up against the window. Bosco and Wires had their guns on them.

"Anyone fucking cracks a fart, let alone moves, gets a cunting round to the back of their skull!" Bosco said. He had one sole foot placed on top of the guard at his feet. The women wept and grizzled, but the men tried to look tough by keeping their shit together.

"Now, Mr. Hopkins," Jason said, walking around the counter and grabbing the old, frail-looking man by the collars of his jacket and yanking him close to his face. "This nastiness can be over and done with in the next few minutes, if you'd be so kind to give us what we want!"

"Yea… Yeah, anything! Just don't hurt anyone…"

"Give me the keys to your vaults downstairs!" Hopkins shot his son a nervous glance, who shook his head in return. Sweat broke across the old man's forehead. "Are you telling me no?" Jason asked, stuffing the barrel of his sawn-off under the father's chin. "I'll blow your fucking brains out all over your fucking ceiling, cunt!"

"Nothing from below can be taken…" the son said.

Jason looked at him. "Oh, is that so?"

The boy nodded. He couldn't have been much older than thirty.

"It's true, sir," the father said. "Many sacred items. They can't be tampered with. Please, take everything from up here!"

"That's very kind of you, but I want what's in your basement. The rare, priceless stuff. Now, give me the *fucking* keys… I won't ask again."

"I… I can't…" Hopkins said.

Jason pushed the old man away from him and cracked him across the bridge of his nose with his sawn-off. Bone cracked; blood squirted up Jason's balaclava and splashed across one of the glass display cabinets.

"*Now*, motherfucker!"

"Dad!"

"Back the fuck off, junior!" Jason said, levelling his gun at the younger man's chest.

"Here, take the keys!" He removed them from around his neck and tossed them at Jason.

"Thanks." Jason snatched the keys from out of the air and grabbed Hopkins. "Come on, son. You're coming with me. Boys, keep an eye on the lad."

"Will do, boss," Wires said.

"*Up*!" Jason told the old man, helping him to his feet by yanking him unceremoniously up off the floor. He then pushed him towards the entry leading to the back room, where Jason knew there was a set of steps leading to the vaults. "Move!" he bellowed, giving Hopkins another push.

The man rushed forward, tripped, and fell headlong down the stairs. He yelped and screamed as he tumbled with a crash. When his body hit the wall at the bottom, Jason laughed, especially as he could see the man had not seriously hurt himself—he was still moving.

Jason casually walked down the steps and clutched Hopkins by his jacket. He then dragged him along the floor behind him. When he got to the room with the vault he was looking for, he forced Hopkins to open the door. Once inside, Jason demanded the vault be opened, much to Hopkins' protests.

Upstairs, he could hear his boys clearing the glass cabinets of their goodies. A smile stretched across his face.

"I beg you, don't take these possessions!" Hopkins pleaded.

Jason didn't have time for this. He had a schedule to keep and a plane to catch. He snatched the keys out of the man's hand, levelled his sawn-off, and pulled both triggers. But only one barrel roared with gunfire.

Because of the shortness of range, the cartridge ploughed through the man's chest, and the ferocity of impact took Hopkins off his feet and propelled him backwards. His back hit the vault, and he slid down, leaving behind a bloody, slug-like trail. The spray of ball bearings peppered the walls and floor and burst certain objects within the room, such as framed photos and glassware. A thick, cloying smoke filled with the stench of gun oil permeated the air.

Jason coughed and looked at Hopkins. The man's mouth was flapping like he was a fish out of water. Blood trails snaked down either side of his mouth; bubbles of crimson burst as he tried to speak. Jason was shocked the man was still breathing, because Hopkins had a crater the size of a fist in his chest.

"Get out of my fucking way!" Jason raged, grabbing Hopkins' ankles and dragging him to one side.

It took Jason a little longer to gain access to the vault because he had to sort through the keys until he found the ones he needed to 'open sesame'. Once he gained access, he drained the secure safes and dumped everything into his bag.

Before leaving the room, he removed the precious scarab and pocketed it. He then made his way upstairs, reloading his sawn-off as he went. He thought he might start feeling guilty about blowing the old cunt away, but no. *It was rather pleasing, actually!* It was the first time he had killed anyone, even though he had been offered hits for jobs before. *I've hurt enough people in my time, so who knows—one or two of them may have died on a hospital gurney somewhere.*

He shrugged and continued walking. When he got upstairs, he turned right and walked the length of the corridor until he was back in the main room. Wires was standing over a woman with a bleeding mouth.

"She was giving cheek, so I shut her the fuck up!"

"Fair enough," Jason said. "Have you two cleaned everything out?"

"Yeah," Bosco and Wires said in unison.

"Where's my *father*?!" Hopkins Jr. asked.

"Dead, *motherfucker*. Just like you will be if you don't get down on your hands and fucking knees, cunt!" Jason spat. "Boys, get the door."

He heard the locks clack. Outside, Bobby pulled up, the tyres of the Transit screeching to a halt. Slowly, Jason backed out the door, keeping his gun trained on Hopkins' son, who was crying. When he got to the threshold, he noticed Bosco and Wires were holding the door for him.

When he stepped outside, the floor started to shake violently—car alarms blared, people ran off screaming and crying while others took cover in doorways, bus-shelters, and under parked cars. The concrete in the road split and widened by a good forty feet, revealing a blinding array of red and orange.

Jason watched as people fell into holes and crevices that were starting to appear—mothers, children, business people, the homeless. Mass hysteria kicked in as herds of people began stampeding. Buildings around them vibrated with such force that they collapsed into clouds of thick white dust and twisted metal.

Water pipes burst.

Telegraph poles snapped their wires—the live cables skipped across the pavements and roads like snakes from a sci-fi novel. People were either scorched, electrocuted, or blown off their feet as the downed lines cut destructive paths through the mobs.

The air filled with a dense smoke. From behind, Jason heard the customers inside the jewellery store screaming. Some of them fled, seemingly no longer caring if Jason and his gang shot them down.

"What the *fuck*?!" Bobby screamed out the driver's side window. They were his last words, as the ground beneath the van burst apart and devoured the Transit.

"*Jesus*! Get back!" Jason told Bosco and Wires. Before heeding his own advice, he braved a look into the cavern. At the bottom of the ravine was a lake of molten lava. He watched as Bobby screamed his way down and plunged into the red-hot river. "This can't be happening…" he muttered.

"Oh, but I'm afraid it is, sir!" Young Hopkins said. Jason turned to see a huge grin on the man's face. "We're all going to hell," he bellowed.

"What the fuck is happening?" Bosco raged.

"We told you not to take artifacts from downstairs. They belong to the ever-powerful gods from worlds long forgotten."

"Fuck you!" Jason screamed, lowering his gun and firing both barrels into Hopkins Jr.'s chest. The impact threw him through a glass case.

"What the hell did you do that for, boss?!" Wires said. "He was the only one who knows what's going on here."

"You don't believe in all that mumbo-fucking-jumbo, do you? What we have here is an earthquake, gentlemen. As soon as it blows over, we're out of here!"

"Try telling that to Bob…" Wires muttered.

"Do you want to fucking join him down that hole?!" Jason raised his voice to be heard over the screaming, charging people and blaring alarms. The gang had the entry to the shop completely blocked, as they stood huddled in the doorway.

"Like something out of a Spielberg film!" Bosco muttered.

All around them, concrete, mucky water, and earth were tossed into the air. Smoke belched out of storm drains. Jason could hear sirens somewhere in the distance. *We need to make a move. The last thing we need is the boys in fucking blue turning up.*

"Not like the UK to get an earthquake, especially one of this magnitude," Wires thought aloud as the ground stopped shaking.

"See," Jason said. "Right, let's get—"

"What in all that's holy?!" Bosco yelled. "Look!" He pointed. "Over there! Are they what I think they are… No, surely not!"

Jason poked his head around the doorway to see what Bosco was pointing at. All the people in the street had stopped and were standing around, perhaps discussing the event and helping each other.

But they should have continued running.

In the near distance, not too far from the section of road Jason and his maintenance crew had been digging up a few years back, arms and heads started emerging from the ground. The limbs appeared to be rotten, the faces missing chunks of flesh.

"No. Fucking. *Way*!" Jason screamed.

"It's whatever you took from downstairs. Maybe if you put it back, we can reverse this?" Bosco suggested.

Before Jason could answer, his attention was drawn back to the streets—the crowds were now running and screaming once more, as more limbs and heads pushed up from the ground, followed by decayed bodies. This new threat pounced upon the terrified populace and ripped the flesh from their bodies and drank their blood.

Jason witnessed one woman getting flanked by what could only be described as the walking dead. They pinned her to the floor and ripped her blouse open and tore her skirt from her body. The dead clawed her torso open and snacked on her innards, then chewed through her naked tits and face.

Children were easily picked off, as their parents left them behind to run for the hills. Soon, the avenue was overrun by the rotten, groaning dead; their stench wafted down the street.

"*Inside*!" Jason screamed. They backtracked and slammed the door behind them. Wires was quick to engage the locks.

"What's going on out there?!" a nervous teenage girl asked.

"You fucks are responsible for this!" a suited and booted man snapped.

"Fuck you!" Jason bit back, stepping up to the man and upper-cutting him. The blow sent the scrawny businessman to his arse.

"Calm down," the teen said. "Arguing and fighting amongst ourselves isn't going to help."

A scream and hard thump from behind caused them all to turn. A young man was pressed up against the shop's window by three undead fucks. His throat was chewed out, sending blood geysering across the glass. As the dying man bucked, his weight thumped against the window, causing spiderweb cracks to develop. The undead left behind bits of their own flaky, bloody skin as they dragged their prey to the floor and out of Jason's view.

"We have to get the fuck out of here," Wires said.

"Stop getting hysterical, man," Bosco told him.

"Maybe you should try replacing what you took?" the teen offered, raising her voice. Some of the undead had now gathered their emaciated frames at the door to beat their fists against its glass. One of them only had half a tongue. It rubbed its stump of an organ against the window.

Jason looked away as cherry-coloured clots dropped off the creatures' faces, arms, and hands and glued to the glass. His guts somersaulted. "*Jesus*!" he muttered.

The shop's main window started to crack further, causing the blonde teen to whimper and shriek as particles of glass fell away.

"We need to get downstairs," Bosco said. "We'll be safe behind the thick doors down there."

"But we'll be trapped!" the suit said, getting up off his arse.

"I don't hear *your* suggestions," Wires said, jumping to Bosco's defence and getting between the men.

Probably worried Bos will level the cunt into an early grave, Jason thought.

"Let's keep calm, okay? What about up?" Wires suggested. "Boss, when you were casing the joint, did you happen to notice if there was a second floor or attic?"

Jason shook his head, unable to take his eyes off the main window; the cracks were getting bigger as more undead bodies piled in behind their comrades. Splits raced up, down, vertical and horizontal. The centre of the pane resembled a huge spider web; the sound of splintering glass became deafening, rising above the noise caused by the few undead hammering at the door.

"We need to head down!" Jason said. "There is no upper level." His eyes flicked back to the door; it was rattling in its jamb. The lock shook as flocks of the undead engulfed the outside. In the background, Jason could see more vehicles and people being lost to the cracks in the ground.

The world was ending.

Maybe there's a chance I can fix this!

"Come on, move!" Jason yelled, pushing the girl onwards. Wires and Bosco followed behind. As they headed through the door leading to the back, the businessman screamed. Jason looked back and saw hands reaching up through the floor, grabbing the businessman around his ankles—the dirty, chipped and broken nails of the dozen or so hands were raking the man's flesh.

When he fell, Jason made to go back for him, but was stopped by Bosco and Wires.

"He's a goner!" Bosco said. "Let's keep moving."

Jason's eyes fixed onto the businessman's face; the sheer terror that was etched on it was the stuff of nightmares. Dirty digits were forced into the man's mouth and relieved him of his tongue, which stretched until its cord snapped. Blood pooled from his mouth. More hands came through the floor. Their roaming fingers stabbed through his eyeballs, whilst other talons grabbed, slashed, yanked and ripped. Before Jason turned away, he saw the man's privates being torn free; the bollocks and cock were pulled through the floor.

Probably being stuffed into a hungry, greedy and waiting mouth! Jason shivered at the thought. From below, he thought he heard the slurping and smacking of chops. Another shiver cut down his back.

The window and door exploded simultaneously. The undead flopped through the shattered glass and shredded their taut yet weak flesh on the jagged shards left in the frame. Blood pumped and squirted across the floor, which now resembled the inside of an abattoir.

"Shift your bloody arse!" Wires grabbed Jason and pulled him down the corridor. Whilst being dragged by his scruff, Jason watched as the army of darkness flooded the shop and meandered, stumbled, shuffled, and pin-balled in his direction.

They groaned, snarled and snapped their decayed teeth together in a lust-hungry way. The horde bottle-necked their way into the corridor and staggered after Jason, who was wrenched down the stairs to the vault area.

He shoved Wires' hand off him. "It's okay, I'm cool now! Turn right and head through the door. We'll be able to lock that motherfucker."

When they reached the bottom of the stairs, Jason heard thuds from behind, which sounded like bowling balls being tossed down the steps after him. He glanced over his shoulder and saw the first few undead had literally launched themselves after him.

They can't take the steps, but it won't stop them!

Bones broke, necks snapped, shoulders were jerked from sockets and legs were twisted into various unnatural positions.

But still the undead came.

Their groans intensified which, in turn, breathed forth a rotten, wet earth stench that caused Jason to gag. The putrid, skinless faces on some he'd seen pushed against the windows upstairs had had maggots and beasties scurrying around inside their mouths and skulls.

The images would stay with him until his dying day.

When Jason and the others got through the door leading into the vaults and the rooms beyond, they closed and locked it behind them with just seconds to spare. Soon, rotten dead fists began pounding at it, to no avail.

"It'll take a tank to get through that!" Bosco said. "We're safe for the time being."

"But we're trapped down here—what do we do?" the teen asked.

"I have explosives in my bag. Enough to blow a hole in a wall down here," Jason said. "I'm sure I can get us out of here, don't worry. Let's take five, regroup, and plan our next move. If the streets are crawling with those things, then maybe going out there isn't such a hot idea!"

"But we can't sit here, either," Wires said. "We have no food or water."

"Fucking chill, *princess*!" Bosco winked. "We can go a few hours without either of those. Besides, I have some snacks and a few cold drinks in my bag. I don't go anywhere without a small ration of refreshments."

The hammering on the door reverberated around the vault-like corridor/room they stood in. Either side of them were various rooms filled with numerous treasures.

"You could have taken all this, too!" Wires told Jason.

"Nah, the scarab is *priceless*."

"Put it back!" the girl snapped.

"Maybe you should put a fucking sock in it, or I'll ram my fist into your mouth," Bosco threatened.

She crossed her arms and poked her tongue out at him. Jason couldn't help but smile. Her attitude matched her jumper, which had a big anarchy symbol on it—the sign was made to look as though it had been painted on, as the dye had a running look to it. On her feet, he could see she was wearing Doc Martins—*Beetle Crushers is what Mum used to call them.*

"Putting it back might not be such a bad idea. With the score we've got, we can still piss off out of the country and never look back," Jason informed his gang.

"*Dude*! Wake up! The world has gone to tits. Money is no good, especially if you can't rectify your mistake."

Jason poked his head into the room he had cold-bloodedly mown Hopkins down in. The man lay in a lake of coagulated blood, his face ashen. *At least he ain't up and walking the fuck around like something out of Living Dead at the Manchester Morgue!*

A rumble underfoot caused him to snap his head downwards. Jason half expected to see the ground cracking beneath his feet, but the hard, marble floor was intact. "What the hell was that?!" he asked.

"I can't see them coming through this floor," Wires said. "It's blast-proof."

The earth below shook and groaned again, but the marble remained solid. A collectively held breath was released. The three men placed their bags on the floor and looked around. Jason went to the last room on the left and entered. He made his way to the corner and tapped on the wall.

What is beyond them? How far down are we? If we blast and let a fuck ton of dirt in, it may bury us alive! And if it doesn't, it could take us months to dig our way out. We'd never survive... Fuck!

"These walls are probably the weakest, guys!" Jason yelled, giving the brickwork a few more taps. "Some explosives by here and... *Boom*!" he muttered to himself.

Jason set his bag down and removed enough C4 to level a handful of walls. He also took out extra shotgun ammo and reloaded his sawn-off. He placed his gun by his side and rigged the explosives to the detonator.

We might need a quick getaway!

Jason walked back to where the others were.

"Are you replacing that stone or not?" The girl glared, crossing her arms once more and shooting him an unimpressed look.

Full of sass, ain't ya?! he thought. "Yes, I'm going to replace it." He dug the scarab from his pocket and showed her. "Here it—"

She snatched it from his hand before he could finish his sentence and ran into the room containing the body of Hopkins.

"*Hey*!" he yelled, watching her go.

"Which drawer did you pilfer it from?" She stood in the jelly-like blood, her back to the vaults.

"If you give me a—" Again his words were cut short, as the floor started to groan and protest once more. "Shit..."

"I'm not liking *that* noise one bit, guys!" Wires admitted. "Sounds like girders are being twisted."

They stood and listened as the sound continued. Soon the floor did start to crack, but not like it had outside. Splits developed, but the ground didn't part like the red sea. As the marble broke, particles were tossed into the air along with a thick, cement-like dust.

"We need to go! This place isn't going to be safe for much longer," Jason said. "Replace the stone. Top drawer."

He watched as the teen ripped the right compartment open and dropped the stone inside. She let out an "*Oops*" as she did so.

"What?"

"I broke it!"

More cracking. Only this time it wasn't the floor; it was the wall in front of the girl. Jason could only watch as she stood frozen to the spot, her body trembling.

"What… what's happening?!"

"Get out of there!" Jason screamed, but it was too late. Mummified arms smashed through the wall and grabbed her shoulders. The huge arms pulled, ripping the youngest in two like a piece of paper. Her guts and innards smashed against the floor, causing a crimson explosion. Her head popped off her shoulders and into the air like a bottle cap.

Then the mass pushed through the wall. Bricks, plaster and dust flew everywhere; the powder from the stonework was that thick, Jason felt as though he was lost in fog.

Through the clouds he could see jade-coloured emeralds glowing, which were the mummy's eyes. Its bandages were an ancient yellow, all tattered and moth-eaten.

Only its piercing eyes could be seen—bandages covered everything else. The thing's massive frame appeared to ripple with muscle beneath its wrap. Bricks disintegrated under its footing.

Behind it, more of the undead spewed from the shattered wall.

"Oh, fuck!" Wires screamed as he fled the room and ran down the corridor.

Jason raised his gun and fired both barrels. The shells drilled into the eight-foot mummy's chest but did nothing but disturb dust and singe bandage. However, the ball-bearing spray tore through some of the undead, sending a couple to ground.

Flesh and gore splashed the walls.

"Run!" Jason yelled, and turned to bolt out the door. As he ran past Bosco, he could see the man was taking aim with his shotgun. "There's no point!"

"Die, bastards!" Bosco screamed. His sawn-off roared.

Jason left him to it and rushed down the corridor to his detonator. When he got there, he saw Wires had it in his hands. "Get back, you're too close! I've set the lot—" Jason was blown off his feet and sent back along the corridor. As he floated through the air, he saw Wires turn into a liquid cloud of red nothingness.

When he hit the deck, he heard Bosco scream from behind, which carried over the horrendous sound of the walls and ceiling caving in. Bosco's cries were followed by that of wet, sloppy sounds.

Jason couldn't think about it.

He pushed off the floor with his palms and stood on shaking legs. He detected a faint ringing in his ears. He tried to walk towards the mound of earth before him. Above, daylight could be seen peeking through.

I'm saved! He stumbled forward, unaware of how close behind the mummy was.

He looked over his shoulder and screamed. His legs tangled and he was sent backwards. He landed on the earth with a hard smack. The bricks and jagged slabs of concrete hidden in the dirt dug into him. He pushed his heels into the soil and boosted himself up until his fingers were through the gap.

"Just a few more inches…" he grunted, and then he was being pulled. "*No!*" Jason looked down to see the undead were clutching his ankles and lethargically yanking on his legs. He stabbed his fingers into the dirt and tried to stop himself from sliding.

Below, the mummy waited.

Jason felt hot piss shoot down his leg. He clenched his anus.

"*Please…* You have it back… We didn't mean to!"

His grip on the earth weakened and he started to slide towards his demise.

All he could do was buck his body and try to kick out with his legs, but more of the undead had gathered and were reaching up for his legs. Dirty hands and fingers clawed his shins, calves and thighs, causing him to pull his fingers out of the dirt and grab his hurt. He lost his grip.

When he hit the floor they huddled around him.

Manic laughter escaped him as hands punched through his stomach. His guts were torn free and devoured, his face was clawed to ribbons, and an eyeball was plucked out.

The mummy stood over him and looked down. "I am Ra, the ever powerful sun god!" he roared

"Fu… Fuc… Fuck *you*!" Jason managed with his final breath.

Sisters of Solicited

*"We walk right past each other, every single day.
Like cold machines, we're marching on and on and..."* –Alice Cooper

"Unsolicited," Wendy uttered. The word was ugly, heavy, when spoken aloud. It was cheerless, with sharp edges, like the world had become.

Her grip on the steering wheel intensified.

It sounds like it means someone who isn't represented by a solicitor, she thought. *Fucking snowflakes.* A smile pulled across her face as she peered out the van's tinted windshield; its engine idled in readiness.

"It's on the snowflakes' crest, you know, Wends," Capri chirped as though reading her friend's mind.

"The snowflakes?"

"Uh-huh."

"Aye, I know. It's also in their fucking mantra, too." Wendy stared out the window with intent. "What time do these dried-up old fucks meet? It's now ten-past two."

"Two. Let's just hope for their sake they're getting the sticks surgically removed from their arses."

"They're as tardy as they are wretched."

"Not that it'll matter soon!"

Wendy turned and looked at Capri. "True."

Capri, like Wendy, had worked in the modelling industry (twenty years of service between them) before the world went to shit and turned itself into a cold, mindless utopia of robotic madness.

The spiral started off slow between 2010 and 2018. Stories about sex scandals and rape hit the news and were splashed across the papers' headlines; celebrities and the ilk—directors, sports doctors, authors, musicians, footballers, studio executives, actors—were named, shamed, and sent to prison

It had been triggered by the 'unsolicited dick pics' and *#MeToo* movements, which gained traction fast. The government clamped down with immediate effect.

But then *everyone* seemed to have a tale to tell regarding rape and molestation that spanned ten years or more.

It was hard to know who was lying.

Many jumped on the bandwagon.

Careers and reputations were left in smouldering ashes.

A lot of innocent men got their arses fucked in jail! Wendy thought.

Of course, the ones who deserved it got what they so richly deserved. Wendy believed this, and so did her Sisters of Solicited. They were all for the empowerment and equality of women. Wendy wanted her sisters, globally speaking, to have the same opportunity, pay, and standard of work conditions and respect (to a rational degree) as their male counterparts.

For a while, it worked. And, had it not been for the liars and the oh-so-easily offended who saw an opportunity to ram their views down everybody's throats, it would have continued to do so.

The women who'd fought for fairness, building on what the Suffragettes and countless other female organisations had done over the years, slotted into place.

The world *was* changing.

Men and women of an old-fashioned way altered their behaviour, practices and thinking. Workplaces, and indeed the streets, became safer – a no-nonsense tolerance towards lewd and unfitting behaviour was introduced.

However, the power went to some people's heads through their victories. And the more ground they took, the more they wanted.

High horses were mounted.

Snobbery shot down the nostrils of the well-to-do and arrogant.

This rational, disciplined, and proper way individuals started conforming to was pushed that bit further to the brink of psychosis, when activists wanted the good ship Morals to be battened down further.

They saw to the banning of lap dancing joints, strips clubs, prostitution, modelling, escorting and any other form of 'degradation' of the human form where it was exploited for money.

A public outcry erupted.

Women and men lost good-paying jobs, and, in turn, their houses and families.

Their complaining and ranting was shut down, closed off.

The government stepped in and supported the maniacal do-gooders. Why wouldn't they? They were supporting the people to suppress the people. It was a win-win situation. No more money wasted on 'eyes in the skies', Big Brother, subliminal messages, phone, radio and internet tapping; the snowflakes were doing it for them.

Instead, the extra money was used to build walls and put extra teams of police, who ruled with iron fists and cattle prod, on the streets.

People were kept in line, too scared to look at each other, let alone offer a smile or greeting. They became cold machines.

And if that wasn't bad enough, the lunacy went a step further.

No wolf-whistling.

No lewd jokes.

No banter.

No comments or anything of the sort.

Short skirts, heels and any other form of sexy clothing and underwear were also outlawed.

Flirting became a capital crime with a *stiff* punishment: men were castrated, women bunged.

All derogative music, film, books, words from the dictionary, porn, art and images were banned. Removed. Burned.

Creativity no longer existed.

The freethinker was hobbled.

Wendy watched the world implode on TV.

"The world's gone PC mad! You're nothing but a bunch of prudish crybabies!" argued one lady on a panel show of men and women ranging from the far left and right parties, to those who sat on the fence and everything in between.

"I guess any and all types of behaviour goes after Auschwitz, eh?!" a man yelled back.

The snowflakes thought they'd won.

The masses were cowed, held in place and laying dormant with the fight burnt out of them.

It seemed only Wendy and her friends could see what was happening. How the downfall of society was occurring. The human race was speeding towards its impending annihilation on a tidal wave of over-the-top principles and foolishness.

When Wendy lost her glam modelling/stripping/posing career, along with Capri and a dozen other girls, they stuck together through thick and thin, forming an underground society by the name of Sisters of Solicited, or SS for short, which resembled lightning strikes on their crest.

It was yes to fun.

Yes to acting wild.

Yes to being their *own* woman.

Yes to fighting back.

Yes to male attention.

And yes to everything else they'd been stripped of.

They weren't just sisters doing it for themselves, but for all women, men and growing children.

It was time to take back some of the control.

Funny, she thought, *how they've taken away the very thing they were fighting for: to give women a voice. They said we could be anything we wanted to be—but within reason, of course.*

"It's not just *their* fault, Wendy," Capri said, again reading her friend's thoughts.

"Never said it was, Sister."
Both women laughed.

After forming their secret group on the agreement of striking back with force and not just sitting around on their hands talking issues through, they found themselves a clubhouse, a place where they could sharpen their knives, strategise, and organise.

The first target on the list was the Houses of Parliament. The Sisters wanted to try and take out as many thick-headed, power-hungry pricks as they could in one hit. Cut off the monster's head, so to speak. With them gone, the reins of power would be left flapping in the wind like cow's ears.

Rules and regulations would fold.

It would give someone the chance to step in and take over. A person who wanted to revert to how it was before the crazy train smashed through its final stop and hurtled towards hell.

Or so they hoped.

Wendy, along with her women, trained to use various weapons and learned bomb-making skills from within the shadows. As luck would have it, there was still a black market, a fence in the system, for certain people to acquire specific goods, which went unmonitored.

Thanks to the money they'd saved whilst working, the Sisters managed to lay their hands on all kinds of hard merchandise: machine guns, handguns, shotguns, grenades, sniper rifles. They built themselves a well-stocked arsenal that rivalled Arnie.

It was surprisingly easy for them to pull off the attack on the Houses of Parliament. Over three hundred were reported to have lost their lives in the blast the Sisters detonated.

It wasn't just politicians and the like killed, but people who'd been close to the building at the time. Tumbling rubble crushed skulls and snapped necks; shrapnel tore out eyes and ripped flesh and veins open.

The streets ran red with liquefied bodies.

Guts, innards, and body parts bobbed along the crimson waters.

A stench of charred remains clung to the air, and a number of neighbouring structures were left scorched, blackened.

Screaming was heard for miles around.

The swift, brutal assault was carried out after a month of planning. No stone was left unturned. They were to go through the sewers and plant enough explosives to cripple the building twice over.

Kegs of gunpowder, sticks of dynamite, cans of fuel, and grenades were planted over the course of a week.

Wendy thought for sure they would be found out, that a sweep of the sewers would expose their trap.

But it never happened.

The powerful had become comfortable in the knowledge that they were safe. Untouchable. That their war machine had crushed everything in its path and that their people were in full support. They had been seen as 'doing something'.

How gullible one becomes on a pedestal of power.

Did they honestly think their ivory tower was impenetrable? They were wrong.

On the day of the attack, Wendy and her crew were gifted with an upheaval that broke out on the streets outside the Houses of Parliament: snowflakes clashed with protesters, involving a large amount of armed and mounted police.

Tear gas was deployed.

Water cannons were sent in.

Beatings were vicious, tenfold. Hospitals filled up and ran over.

The perfect distraction.

And even though Wendy thought some of their own would be killed in the strike, she knew it had to be carried out.

It was all in the name of liberty.

There was a lot at stake. Not just for her and their few, but for the generations to come.

That was if things got that far, she thought. *And the way it was going...*

As the riot raged on, Wendy and two of her Sisters went beneath the city and carried out their plot by running a lengthy fuse from their mountain of explosives. When Wendy set it alight, they ran out of the sewers, collected the rest of their gang, and hightailed it out of the city.

The blast was seen from two miles away.

A mushroom cloud consisting of human remains, blood, guts, dust and debris ascended into the sky and spread, dotting out the sun for the briefest, blackest of moments.

Afterwards, Wendy and her Sisters sent a message via video link to those still left standing in office.

They wore Guy Fawkes masks.

"No longer will we sit back and watch as you and the many destroy mankind with your child-like feelings and musings. There will be random attacks on you and your like until you have either backed down or reverted..."

Wendy's message had stretched several minutes, demanding change.

She'd given them a month.

"If there's no revolution by then, consider your death warrants signed!"

Not the slightest of difference came.

When a new leader was placed in charge, their extensive communication was returned: "*We will not be bullied into indecency and a Neanderthal way of living by scare tactics and cowardly assault. We will stand defiant in its face. You are nothing but common thugs, Nazi sympathisers and terrorists of the worst kind...*"

They went on.

And on.

The Sisters had taken great pleasure from the rant in their hangout.

"The guy sounds like he needs to find his fucking sack!" Candy blurted, causing the other women to laugh.

"What type of faggot-arse fella speaks in such a way?" Pip wanted to know.

"A she-male!" another Sister chirped, bringing a fresh roar of laughter to the room.

"Okay, ladies – that's enough. We need to get down to action."

"That's what my husband used to say!" Pip confessed.

More laughter.

Wendy chuckled. "Yeah, back when *fucking* wasn't a crime."

"We should have seen it *coming* when they took our dildos away," Capri said. "Bunch of fucking wankers."

"They took everything away. Can't remember the last time a fella grabbed my arse."

"Ladies, ladies, please! We must start planning our missions."

"I say we hit the Welsh Assembly next," Pip suggested.

"And take out our new president over in London," Capri said.

"Yes," Wendy confirmed. "Also, in a few weeks' time, there's a meeting of minds in Scotland."

"The one with the world leaders?" Candy asked.

Wendy nodded. "That will take some planning. In the meantime, let's hit the Welsh Assembly and go from there. We should be able to take them out with ease."

For the next six months the Sisters lay dormant.

They recruited ex-lawyers, nurses, doctors, scientists, page three girls, dancers, firefighters, soldiers, and more. They also planned, modified, and restructured, bought vehicles and tactical clothing and constructed a large assault course within their base (which was an old aircraft hangar).

When the media thought Wendy and her Sisters were never going to act again after such a lengthy period of time, they started whipping up stories in their tabloids: *Terrorist Captured, Tortured and Executed at Tower of London! Houses of Parliament Bombers Cleared Out!*

This riled some of the women.

It ignited Wendy. "Let it stoke your fire for war, ladies, but don't let it blind you. This is what we wanted. It will make them drop their guard."

Quiet murmurs of "yes" and "she's right" rippled through her troops.

Heads nodded, guns were cocked, and knives were drawn; teeth-exposing smiles gleamed in steel.

As the Welsh politicians and leaders gathered at their place of work on a sunny June morning—exactly eight months after the annihilation of the Houses of Parliament—ten large four-by-fours screeched to a halt at the curb, kicking up dust and gravel.

Supporters who had congregated outside the important, immaculate building displayed placards adorned with slogans of support: "We're all with you!", "United in terror", and Wendy's favourite, "Snowflakes not Sinners!"

The blackened windows to the jeeps rolled down and out popped a dozen or so machine guns. Uzis and AK-47s, mostly.

Sisters popped out of sunroofs.

Others got out.

Hand grenades were tossed.

Bullets rattled off in the hundreds.

Empty casings spat, spinning into the air before cashing into a heap of spent brass.

Bodies were riddled and ripped apart.

Blood jettisoned.

Screaming blared over the clatter of automatic firepower.

"Cease fire!" Wendy called, who was one of the ladies poking out of a sunroof.

"*Ooh*, fuck!" someone screamed.

Wendy turned her head and saw Capri slumped against her jeep. She had a hand between her legs. "Are you hit?"

"N-n-no," she panted. "The damn thing gave me an orgasm!"

"Fuck sake. Hit the tape, will you."

Capri nodded and ducked into her jeep. Wendy's modified voice boomed from the speakers mounted on the vehicle.

"You think we'd back down? The Sisters of Solicited will crush the snowflakes, their leaders, and supporters. If your ignorance continues, we will be forced to roll over you like a tidal wave – we will stop at nothing. As

long as we have fight in our bodies, we will press on until the last of us is standing…"

The message continued to play as the jeeps rolled away.

Many of the perforated crawled and clawed themselves from the carnage.

Many lay dead.

Only a few politicians had been wiped out in the attack, but it didn't matter – the message had been sent.

At the time of the Welsh Assembly ambush, some four hundred miles away, another section of Wendy's organisation was dealing white-hot justice in the form of an assassination from a rooftop overlooking the world leaders' meeting in Scotland.

They thought they were secure.

But, just like the slaughter in Cardiff, this assault also had people on the inside who'd paid the guards off and replaced the bullet-proof windows with regular glass.

When the sniper rifle slugs started flying, *nobody* was safe inside the building.

The US president was the first to go.

"He's nothing but a jumped-up, half-witted celebrity with a bad complexion!" Wendy had stated.

He was followed into the afterlife by the French and German leaders, who some had said were nothing other than androids or cyborgs or some shit.

"I guess I can confirm that," Carpi said as she loaded another round into the high-velocity gun and watched the aforementioned presidents frazzle, fire and spit blue sparks.

She put three more rounds into each.

"Got to make sure." She raised her fist and yelled, "Liberty!" The wind flapped her unbuttoned, camouflaged shirt, exposing her *Tank Girl* t-shirt underneath.

As she put her eye to the scope once more, she snapped her bubblegum. "Come to mama, babies."

A bullet barrel-rolled out of her gun's muzzle, smashing through the face of another country's front-person, spreading their brains all over a wall.

"You say something, C?" Abigail called over. She wore her hat back to front – a fat cigar jutted from her mouth.

"Nah—*woah*! Did you see that fucker's head come apart?"

"*Help*!" one of the leaders screamed from inside the room that was quickly starting to resemble an abattoir. He banged on the door, but it was futile. They'd been locked in by the Sisters' insiders.

"You want that fucker banging to get out?" Abigail called over, rolling her cigar from one side of her mouth to the other.

"Bet you thirty quid I can shoot the toupee off his head without killing him?!" Capri said, turning to look at her comrade. "What you say, sugar tits?"

"Thirty quid plus a rug-munching and you're on."

Capri's bullet went wide, taking a chunk of the fat man's ear.

"Ugh-*argh*!" he squealed like a pig with a slashed throat, his hands going to his boo-boo.

"Ah, *fuck*!" Capri slapped her fingerless-glove-covered hand to the side of her rifle. She loaded another round but was too slow: Abigail's bullet tore through the back of the man's head, spraying the door with blood, bone, and gore.

"Would you like to face-fuck me here, my place, yours or the hangout?" Abigail smiled as she stood, her hands going to her belt buckle and zipper.

"How about I buy us some beers out of the thirty and take you back to mine later tonight?"

"Deal."

Shortly after this attack and the one in Cardiff, the establishment found itself chopped off at the knees, with the world's most powerful, prestigious leaders dead.

Allied countries distanced themselves.

Soon, they turned their backs on the imps and strove for a fairer ground for the common people.

The tide had indeed turned, thanks to Wendy's efforts.

When photos of the android leaders hit headlines on a global scale, the snowflakes lost a monumental amount of support, exposing the few that stood between Wendy and her victory, as they tried to get the Man back on board.

"We will help protect you!" had been the snowflakes' bargaining chip.

"They have superior members of the police, Army and many others of influential power in their pockets," was the reply, but it wasn't spelled out in such a pretty way.

A couple of weeks after arriving home from their successful mission in Scotland, Capri and Abigail were pleased with the news Wendy had to share with them and the rest of the Sisters.

"I received word this morning that the government want us to back down. That—"

"How did they find out about us?" Pip wanted to know.

"They have no idea who they are dealing with. The message was sent via a dark channel in hopes it would reach our ears. And it has. They're calling for peace, and are happy to agree to any demands we may have."

"Why do I feel like there's a 'but' coming?" Capri said.

"There is. However, it's a good one. Something you ladies will love." A smile spread across Wendy's face.

"Didn't take much to get them to back down!" Abigail said.

"Only a few dead world leaders and a truck full of dead politicians," chirped Candy, winking.

"They're scared. Not only have they lost the support of allied countries, but also political ground, finance and, since Brexit, trade deals and everything else that comes along with it. Britain is in turmoil, with no great dominant force to take control. Until someone does, the UK is a lost cause. We've hit them where it hurts, ladies."

"Going back to accounting after this is going to be some challenge!" Abigail said.

Others laughed.

"What's the 'but'?" Candy asked, pushing aside her pink-coloured dreads which were blocking her field of vision.

"There's a large group of snowflakes standing in the way of the government being able to change the course of their thinking. They want us to remove them."

"Who are 'they'?" Candy asked.

"An all-female activist group. They were among some of the first to trigger this whole fucking war," Wendy said. "They got what they wanted and pushed for more, doing tons more harm than good."

"Yeah!" the Sisters said in unison.

"How do we take them?"

"Through the government. I have a place, date, and time."

"And if we do this?" Capri spoke.

"Then we get what we want, within reason. They're willing to take on our changes, or 'demands', as they call them, and work them into a new way of living. One that fits all. Of course, we get to say whether we like it or not."

"And if we don't?" Capri wanted to know.

"Then we continue the war!"

The Sisters raised their hands and yelled in agreement.

"So, do we take them up on their offer? All those in favour, let me hear you!"

The entire hangar erupted in yells, whoops, and cheers.

Two days later, Wendy replied to the deal, which was sent back through the underground channel.

Her message was simple: *"We accept."*

A response came containing the required information and instructions Wendy would need to complete her task. Within, she found a note scribbled on a piece of paper:

Once a month, the bigwigs of this outfit put in an appearance to discuss matters at hand. It is the only time they are all in one place, giving you the opportunity to kill them in one. With them gone, we will be free to negotiate.

Over the next few weeks leading up to what they hoped would be their final mission, Wendy pushed the girls hard during training and went over their plan until everybody knew it inside out, back to front, and upside down.

At exactly one-thirty pm, Wendy and her crew pulled up outside their targets' HQ. The building looked rundown, disused. A couple of the windows were bricked-up and the large double-doors were weather-worn and tired-looking. Slate was missing from the roof and birds were nesting in the chimneys.

The joint looked beat up. Abused.

Graffiti coloured most of the walls and pavement.

Of course, Wendy knew it was the perfect ruse to avoid unwanted attention.

"Hey, look at that," Capri said, pointing out a massive, multi-coloured dick and balls. Underneath the cartoon-sized prick were the words *Home of the Anti-Cock and Ball-Busting Brigade.*

"Ha! Love it. These camel-toe-sucking bitches won't know what's hit 'em in their pompous morals by the time we're finished."

The streets were dead.

Nobody came or went.

"Almost two-thirty now…" Wendy muttered.

Both ladies were decked out in black clothing, with balaclavas in place to pull down over their faces when the time was right.

"We should have blown the place up, dude. It would have been easier, and safer. I don't like this at all."

"Relax. We have Sisters all around us if the brown sticky stuff should hit the fan. Besides, this way sends a stern message." Wendy looked over at her bleached-blonde friend and saw that her knee was bobbing and her jaw was working a piece of gum overtime. "Chill, yeah? You don't think I'd let anything happen to my ladies, do you?"

"Nah, course not. But there are some right sneaky fucks out there."

"Not as sly as us, babe." Wendy winked, patting her friend's knee.

Twenty minutes later, the scratched, in-need-of-a-paint-job doors to the building swung outwards and the first of the young women appeared.

They didn't seem nervous or panicked, as they spoke and laughed among themselves.

More women piled out and into the streets.

"Capri, unleash the Jets. Let's give these bitches something to really fucking scream about. Take away our rights, will they? Not if we've got something to say about it."

"You got it, *amigo*." Capri opened her door and got out.

Wendy's hands tightened on the steering wheel as she eyed the women in detail. Some wore pins and button badges that showed their support for hard feminism. Others held placards demanding respect among men and women.

"It ends here." Wendy got out of the van, grabbed her AK-47, and made her way around to Capri, who was unlocking the door to the trailer attached to their vehicle.

"They sound wild in there, Wendy. Starving them and shooting 'em full of drugs has done the trick."

"When you throw the door, make sure you get out of the way."

Capri nodded.

Wendy turned to the other vans and signalled the drivers and passengers into action.

"We're good to go," Capri said, feeling the door of the trailer being pushed from the other side. "I'm not going to be able to hold them much longer."

"One second." Wendy checked to make sure the other Sisters were in place. They were. She raised her hand and brought it down. "*Now!*"

Capri ran from the door and jumped behind Wendy, who fired her gun into the air.

The trailer gate burst open, slamming against the box itself as six black horses stampeded out. They snorted, brayed and whinnied, nostrils flaring. Their shoed hooves made a thunderous racket as they crashed down the street towards the female congregation.

More horses shot past Wendy and Capri.

Screams filled the streets, followed by that of bones snapping and bodies twisting, overpowering the sounds created by the beasts themselves.

Wendy waved her hand. "Move in," she ordered, brandishing her machine gun. She strolled down the road with Capri by her side and a small army of Sisters at her back. "Club the wounded to death. Spare nobody."

By the time Wendy and her crew reached the trampled women, the horses were long gone.

"P-p-please!" one of the women begged, holding a bloodied hand out to Wendy.

Capri stepped in and staved her head in with the butt of her shotgun. "Fuck you!"

Wendy spat, her phlegm spattering the woman's smashed-in skull. "Told you there was nothing to worry about," she said, casting her eyes over the dead, dying and crawling before her.

In the distance, the sound of heavy helicopter blades split the afternoon air asunder. Out of the dark clouds chugged a gunship, its side door open. A robust, fifty-calibre machine gun mounted there was trained on Wendy.

Before she had time to think, formidable bullets ripped into the concrete around them like a meteor shower on steroids.

"Run!" Wendy raged, throwing herself under a nearby car.

"It's a fucking double—" was all Capri managed to say before being riddled with bullets. Her arm was torn off, her face chewed up. Squibs of blood splashed in all directions.

All around Wendy, Sisters hit the deck.

Fuckers are trying to kill two birds with one— Her thought derailed as the chopper fragmented into twisted, burning chunks that rained down to earth. The stench of cordite filled her nostrils.

"Wendy? Wendy?!" she heard a Sister call.

"Candy?" Wendy rolled from beneath her car and clapped her eyes on the pint-sized lady with pink hair, who held a smoking bazooka. "Ain't you a sight for sore eyes!"

"You got it, sugar tits."

"Gather the girls. We need to hit the bricks back to base."

"What do we do now?" Candy asked.

"Now we crush the bushwhacking fucks into the ground!"

Back at HQ, Abigail was screaming and panting as the throes of a fifth and final orgasm washed over her. She placed her hands to the back of Candy's head and kept her face buried between her legs, the woman's tongue lashing her sensitive bead hidden within the holy hood of her pussy, her thighs wet and sticky.

"Oh, God—don't stop—C-Candy!" Abigail panted, slapping Candy's arse whilst imagining it was Capri munching away at her shaven kingdom. But then she felt bad. *Candy was good enough to uphold—Jesus, this girl has a mean tongue!* And then reality kicked in. *This could be my last fuck ever. We'll be at war tomorrow—boo-yaa!—and I might not make it back.* The thought galvanised her, making her last bout of pleasure that little better.

And then an alarm blared within their hideout—it was the ten-minute warning.

Candy pulled away. "Our night went fast," she said, looking at her watch. It was almost six a.m. "We need to get our arse over to the war room, Abi. It's time to rock and roll, babe."

Both women got off the bed, kissed, fondled each other and hugged. "When we finish the bastards off and get back here, it's my turn to do you," Abigail said with a wink, throwing a tee on and grabbing her boots and gear.

Candy did the same, slipping a stick of gum in her mouth. "Fucking-A. I can't wait to kill me some more government fucks, Sister."

As they walked out of the bedroom, they high-fived, laughed and headed towards the hideout's war room, where all Sisters were to report ahead of the day's mission.

"Ready, ladies?" Wendy asked, rallying her troops. She was met by choruses of enthusiastic yeses. "Then let's roll, Sisters!" Wendy raised her fist, opened the door to the hangar, and jumped behind the wheel of her four-by-four. It was time to take out the rest of those who stood between them and liberty.

Sticky Buttons

The year is 2080—the not so distant future—and Chinatown is a prison. One hundred years ago, between 1980 and 1990, hardcore arcade gamers, cinemagoers, TV freaks and comic book nerds took over the large oriental area and turned it into a no-go zone. The streets became violent, corrupt and the powers that be lost control. The innocent were evacuated, a bomb to be dropped, but the plan was seen as too *rad*, and so a large wall and river were constructed around the city; the waters were filled with sharks and patrolled by the government's secret police, who had more artillery than *Rambo*.

There is no escape from Chinatown—not that they want it, as they are content living out their sadistic, perverse fantasies of being their favourite character from their beloved games, movies and shows from a decade long extinct (but not in Chinatown, for it's *always* the 80s).

The streets are teeming with the likes of Snake Plisskin, Jack Burton, the Mad Gear Gang, Wing Gong hoods, thugs from *Class of 1984*, men and women who think they're Alex Foley, Tank Girl, Judge Dredd, Frank Castle, OCP cops, Officer Murphy and cybernetic robots, Rick Deckard, the A-Team, WWF superstars, Lt. Marion "Cobra" Cobretti… The list is inexhaustible.

Not a day goes by that doesn't see someone get body-slammed through a table or vaporised by a proton gun, and eruptions of all-out gang warfare are commonplace. Two days ago, Teenage Mutant Ninja Turtles wannabes were seen doing the knuckle dance with a roving pack of Romero-style zombies (Shuffles, they're called here).

However, there are those who dedicate their time in keeping the violent ones off the street, the vampires at bay during near-dark and the drugs from children.

Enter the Sticky Buttons, a trio of friends who fight for truth, justice and the American Chinatown way…

Chang (Hagger) Sing, AKA Martin Sprocket from 36 Hong Kong Avenue, thought he was Chinese *and* Mike Hagger, the 1989 digital professional wrestler-turned-mayor from the smash-hit arcade beat-'em-up *Final Fight*. Chang, the most delusional of Chinatown's residents, also had it in his head that his daughter, Jessica, was being held captive within the city, and so he spent his time searching for her.

At current, Chang was on the floor—like the other Sticky Buttons—surrounded by thugs with wild, multi-coloured hair of various styles. The hoods wore neon-coloured shades and nifty pump trainers, knee-length boots and rollerblades. Their ankle-length, graffiti-covered leather jackets matched, and their hole-ridden jeans exposed corresponding tattoos and scars.

They snapped gum as they pummelled Chang and bashed his Buttons with chains, fists, kicks and anything else that came to hand whilst the rest of their mob listened to tunes on tape decks and blasted ace hair metal on boomboxes in the background.

"Get to the *chopper*!" Chang heard someone scream as they ran past the danger zone. When he looked through his splayed fingers, his large hands covering his head and face to stop the thugs from staving his skull in, he saw an alien whiz by—it was in hot pursuit of a musclebound man with a machine gun.

And then he heard Wang (Cody) Chi, AKA Brit Jennings, his Button brother and *Final Fight* amigo, cry out as he took a skateboard to the back of his head. Chang saw the multi-coloured wheels that once belonged to the foot vehicle spin off in different directions before crashing down around him.

Some of Wang's teeth skipped along the floor, mixing with blood and gravel. He went to ground and got swamped.

"*Argh*!" Chang roared, grabbing a stomping leg. He twisted it. Bone snapped. The knee burst.

"Holy *fuck*!" the scumbag cried, hitting the deck. He held his hurt. The skin around the joint was split. Bone jutted and glistened red.

This left Chang's ribs exposed, and a flurry of boots blasted into him. He retreated into a ball with his hands over his head and gritted his teeth. "Fuckers!"

"*Ugg*! Chang, *help*!" screamed Eddie (Guy) Lee, AKA Simon Clunkworthy, the third and final member of the Buttons and *Final Fight* fanatic. He'd been set on by a thug with a baseball bat—his flame-orange Ninjutsu suit was soaked red. He held a bloodied hand out towards Chang before taking a broken bottle to the left pectoral muscle.

Eddie collapsed forward, unmoving.

What the hell was I thinking? We're not crimefighting heroes! We should have just stuck to dressing up like Mike, Cody and Guy, and not—

A stomp to the head brought him back to his dire situation.

He swallowed his fury.

A fire burned in his belly.

Chang was wrong, and he knew it—he and his Sticky Buttons were totally bitchin', man. They were hard-arses. And these goons, these Mad Gear thugs mixed with Wing Gong enforcers and Lords of Death hoodlums, were going down once and for all.

It was time to take Chinatown back.

"*Rrragh!*" Chang roared, pushing himself up to his knees and shoving aside the three thugs surrounding him. One, with a Mohawk, crashed through a load of bins and cracked his chops on the pavement. Teeth and blood poured out of his mouth and into his cupped hand.

Chang did his spinning chariot move, taking out the two thugs who came at him with bats and chains.

A woman with pink hair jumped on his back, and he grabbed her by the ears, ripping her over his huge shoulder and slamming her against the floor. Her braless tits jiggled, her nipples stiff and poking at the thin fabric covering them.

"Roxie," he uttered. He stamped his size sixteen foot down on her throat, crushing her windpipe. A puddle of piss spread beneath her.

"It's cool, dude. It's cool!" The thugs listening to their gnarly tunes cleared out, taking their wounded with them.

"You fucks are *dead*!" one goon slurred back, holding his mouth together.

Chang wanted to give chase, but his Buttons needed him. He watched as the thugs tore up the street and disappeared. The fog-filled, neon-drenched streets were alive with house and car alarms, screams of murder and rape, howling dogs, gunshots and general danger.

The rage burned out of Chang. His barrel-like chest, which he'd worked on at the gym for years, heaved. His breaths came in ragged rips.

"These nightly dust-ups will be the end of me," he muttered, turning to help Wang up off the floor. "How's the head, big man?"

"I see birds dancing around it."

"We need to get you to the hos—"

"Nah, I'll be fine, Chang. It's just a scratch."

They went to Eddie, grabbed an arm each and hauled him off the floor.

Fragments of glass dropped off him, and Chang yanked the bottleneck out of his friend's chest.

"Shit!" Eddie winced, sucking in a sharp breath through gritted teeth. "Fuckers. We need to get patched up and back on the streets."

"I don't think we're in any fit state to keep going tonight, guys—we've taken a lickin'."

"Yeah, and we're still tickin'!" Wang interjected.

"Come on, let's get back to the clubhouse first. Maybe we can gather up Cobra, Rocky and a couple of other hard-arses to help us fight the good fight tonight," Chang suggested. Eddie and Wang nodded. "I just know we'll find Jessica soon…"

Trigger Man

I've got it carved in my forehead "Slave To My Sin"/ Too violent for the brotherhood to ever take me in! – Alice Cooper

Have you ever seen a baby burn? Their innocent, snow-like skin peels off and drifts like a satanic blizzard. And, if you're lucky enough to be standing close by when it happens, as I was, then you will smell their fresh newborn scent interlace with the stench of smoke and charred flesh; you'll see their fine hair float away within the thin trails of black smoke.

"I managed to walk into the hospital and onto the baby ward with a couple of skilful lies and a silver tongue. I had my face partly covered, but not enough to raise suspicion among staff, patients and new parents. And it wasn't just one baby I burned alive, but the whole wing. I didn't use any fancy grenades or bombs that were built from various parts bought off the darkest corners of the internet. No. I used good old-fashioned diesel – I poured litres of the stuff into beer bottles and stuffed rags down the necks. Molotov Cocktails, I believe they're called? I'm not too sure. All I do know is that they worked a treat.

"It really was like being caught in some sort of sombre snowstorm: the thick black flakes of skin encircled me as if I was caught in the eye of a tornado.

"The papers called the crime 'heinous', and the person responsible a 'sick, unhinged coward'. It made me smile. They think I'm a monster, but I am not – I am a dealer of punishment who serves a greater God. A master. And, just like my Allah brethren, I correct the infidel and help them see the error of their ways. Soon, there will be a lot more like me, for they too will see the higher plane – a pedestal, if you will – that awaits warriors such as myself. Already, there are many the world over fighting a similar cause so we can go home to our Father; our Lord, Master and Saviour."

He reached out and stopped the Dictaphone. He then briefly looked himself in the eye in the bathroom mirror before starting to fill the sink with water. Once it was at the required level and heat, he washed his face and body. After he dried himself, he started the recorder again.

"After I killed the babies, I lay low for a few days – the police were out scouring the streets in force. They had the CCTV footage of me at the hospital, but I couldn't be recognised. They were grasping at straws. Why? Because I'm faceless and nameless – I have no friends and all my immediate family are dead. For the first half of my life, I was a good boy and conformed, meaning I had no criminal record. When I decided to take up arms in the name of my saviour after he came to me in a vision, I went off the radar and destroyed all records of my existence.

"There really is no catching me.

"A few months after the hospital, I struck four times in a single week. These crimes were on a smaller scale, but, nevertheless, they were integral to the fear and lessons I wanted to spread to help seal my place by my God's side in his pleasure kingdom.

"The first of these crimes was an inside job. On April 3rd I helped twenty-seven convicts escape a local high-security prison, who went on to cause mayhem and destruction within the city. Some of these individuals were rapists and paedophiles who were escorted to schools and feminist groups, where they could carry out more hate crimes against the infidels of this country.

"Two days after this, with many criminals still running large and slaughtering people on the streets, I went on a knifing spree. I randomly hacked, slashed and stabbed twelve people to death, whilst wounding a further six. Among the dead were three children, one priest, one homosexual (sick *fuck*!), two homeless women (scrounging *cunts*!), three toddlers and their mothers, and two everyday teenaged fucking hippies who tried to prevent me from killing others.

"I slit the toddlers' throats after I smashed their mothers' heads in with a brick. The children bled out like stuck pigs, their wee tongues bobbing as they screeched and cried. When I was done there, I went to the nearest park and planted a few nail bombs behind trees, in bins and out of sight.

"I couldn't resist hanging around to see the results.

"Eyeballs and flesh were torn from the faces of parents, children and people out jogging and walking their dogs. A German shepherd managed to get itself engulfed in a serious blast, pinning it to a tree. Its mouth had hung open, its tongue lolling – blood had poured and pumped out of it. The fucking thing managed to last a few minutes before succumbing. I'm sure its pitiful howls will haunt the survivors' dreams for years to come.

"Yes, it is pride you can hear in my voice. After all, I am a soldier fighting a good fight.

"After the explosions in the park, I moved on to a homeless centre and planted another, larger bomb under the floorboards. The detonation was so strong, it crippled the buildings either side of it, killing forty-three people and wounding a further seven. Out of the seven, five were critical.

"A few days after my spate of bombings, the newspapers dubbed me 'Trigger Man'. However, the name had a second meaning behind it, which was explained in the article below the 'Trigger Man' headline: '*We have a person who seems to be killing at random – who hasn't spoken out about motive. Is he doing this in the name of religion, ISIS, or another terrorist group? If you are reading this, 'Trigger Man', then please tell us what triggers or drives you to carry out such vile hatred against your fellow man?*'"

He stopped talking and clicked the off button on the tape recorder once again. Turning, he looked at the clock on the wall beside the bathroom door. It was close to seven PM.

Time to start getting ready, he thought. *It won't take me long to finish my recording. As soon as I'm done, I need to be out the door.* A smile stretched across his face. He couldn't wait to be in the lap of the pleasure kingdom. *Virginal pussy and drink – what more could a guy ask for?*

Clearing his mind, he exited the bathroom and went to his bedroom. Displayed on the bed was a mini arsenal: a vest strapped with explosives, two Browning handguns, a combat knife, three hand grenades, a garrotte, map, compass and the keys to a rented Transit van that was parked outside his house.

He went to the wardrobe and removed a pair of combat trousers and slipped them on. He then took a plain black t-shirt off a hanger and put it on before going to the chest of drawers and grabbing a pair of socks. Once he was dressed, he put two belts with holsters on them around his waist and slipped the guns into them. There was also a sheath for his knife, which he slid it into.

He then put the garrotte, compass, map and van keys into the various pockets on his cargo trousers. Picking up the vest, he carried it into the bathroom with him and laid it gently onto the floor. Happy it was safe and sound, he turned back to the mirror and started recording again.

"After my four-crime spree the week beginning April 13th, I again kept low for a couple of months. However, all around me, my brothers and sisters carried out attacks of 'terrorism' here, there and globally, so I didn't feel too guilty about resting on my laurels.

"When it was safe for me to raise my head once more, I again went on a rampage. On June 22nd, let it be known that it was I who disabled a string of fire and police stations, along with orchestrating the assassination on the local mayor and mayoress. And yes, it was I who detonated the blast at the world leaders meeting on June 24th, which ended the life of the head of Germany, the USA, France and Britain.

Of course, I didn't act alone on that one: I had people on the inside. Not all officials who walk among you are trustworthy. Next time you see a politician on the TV or a cop on the street, just think: they could be a part of what's going on . . .

"After my destruction of the world leaders, which was my eighth act, I went on to bomb four more buildings on the 2nd of July: UWIC University, George Thomas Hospital for the elderly and infirm of mind, four national banks – which cost the country millions – and Scotland Yard. As you're aware, countless died.

"And now for my fourteenth and final act, date July 23rd: my master has ordered me to strike a local mosque and a Muslim haven next door. This will be in the name of white power, and it is my hope to turn fellow man against man, woman against woman . . .

"I have seen the afterlife; wine, women and song aplenty await me after my missions here, in this life, have been done. I know this for my master has told me. He has reached out to me on more than one occasion. The first time he came to me, he showed me what I had to do to achieve my place in his holy kingdom. After that, he entrusted me with a certain amount of assignments.

"'Only after your fourteenth act has been committed may you come home, child', he'd said, showing me a glimpse into the land of paradise and promise he controls.

"I'm looking forward to going home. I'm weary, but I know in my heart I have fought a good fight. I have purified myself by bathing in the blood, pain and misery of my Lord's enemies – the sins of the world. My actions will earn me an eternity of happiness – I'll be a hero, a martyr, to my people and the other followers of my Lord.

"My name is Joshua Crossman, I'm twenty-five and I am a Satanist. My master is Lucifer, and he is expecting me at his domain today, so he can bestow on me his gifts. Some will say I have been brainwashed, but to this I say you are the ones who are programmed. You've been drilled like sheep by the ones who hold the power over you.

"I must now stop recording and go fulfil my fortune. You will read about me in the newspapers tomorrow, and gasp in awe at how brave I have been in taking the battle to you. How I've made you cringe in my shadows the last few months. You should be scared, for your time is coming to an end, and after my final mission today, the streets will run with rivers of blood as your neighbours start attacking each other.

"It's so sad how you, the traitors, can't see that you are losing the divine war; that day by day you lose people and ground. It's rather pleasing how fast we're pushing you back into a corner. Soon, we will have full control. I will not see it in my lifetime, as my calling is on the wall, but the soldiers that follow behind me will. It reassures me that my efforts will free them up to walk the Earth freely – that I, and the others, will have rid the place of you, infidel.

"You're not just non-believers and traitors, but scum; unholy, base-of-the-chain bottom feeders. I spit on you! I am the Trigger Man, and in the name of Lucifer, I condemn you all to *death*!" he yelled, knocking the tape recorder off and removing the small tape, which he placed inside an envelope marked with the Daily Mail's address on it. Along with the tape, he placed a scrapbook in the envelope that contained all his newspaper clippings – his heart swelled with pride.

The shitty newspaper should get it by this evening, he thought, picking up his vest and slipping into it. Once it was on, he pulled the straps tight, which secured it to his body like a second skin. He eyed himself in the mirror and smiled. *I'm coming home, Lord.*

He trudged downstairs, put his jacket on, headed out the front door and got into his rental van.

Thirty minutes later, he parked across from his intended target. He watched as Muslims came and went. Joshua hated that he had to act against his brethren, but knew it had to be done.

In the days leading up to this attack, he had read *Mein Kampf* daily. Even though it didn't relate, it kept his hatred fed. *I'm the devil's little solider. I'm the devil's little tool,* he'd thought, recalling lyrics but not remembering the artist or song.

When a swell of people turned up at the mosque to pray, Joshua steadied himself. On the passenger seat was a house brick. Grabbing it, he started the engine, making sure the handbrake was still engaged, and put the stone on top of the accelerator.

Before he got out, he looked over the seats and saw all the explosives.

He smiled and dug the detonator out of the glove compartment.

He opened the driver's door, got out and leaned back in. In one quick movement, he disengaged the handbrake and jumped out of the way. The van cut across the street and smashed through the wall of the mosque. The vehicle's petrol tank cracked, spewing diesel everywhere.

People started to panic, run and scream.

Others stood and watched in stunned silence.

Joshua drew his pistols, detonated the van and started to walk across the road. Chunks of flesh rained down on him from victims who had been standing close to the danger zone, and body parts smashed to the ground around him.

When he heard screaming, he turned to see people, who were on fire, run out of the mosque.

Don't shoot them. Let them burn, the voice inside his head said. It was his master. *Now, chant what I told you to!*

"We don't want you fucks here! Go home – I kill in the name of white people. This is our revenge!"

Joshua stormed into the building opposite the crumbling mosque and opened up with his Brownings. He shot, killed and wounded multiple men, women and children before his guns ran dry. When they did, he activated the bombs on his vest, prayed to his Lord and blew himself to bits, along with everyone else inside the building.

The searing heat forced his lazy eyes open. Everything was a blur.

"Where—where am I?" Joshua coughed, raising his hands to his face to rub his eyes. *I have arms and a body*?! he thought, lifting his head and shaking the fog from his vision. "I'm whole!" he yelled, ignoring his surroundings. "I knew my master wouldn't fail me."

The thunderous sound of crashing waves caused him to turn his head. His jaw hung loose and his mouth formed a perfect O shape. In the near distance, a sea of hot lava stretched out as far as the eye could see. Within it, people writhed, their mouths twisted into screams. All around him, the cave-like walls seemed to yell and cry.

If it weren't for the light cast by the ocean of fire, Joshua would have been sat in darkness.

He turned his head, his torso following, and looked over the other shoulder. Lines of people were herded towards the waters and pushed in, much like how pirates forced hostages to walk the plank. The men, women and children couldn't turn and flee because they were guarded by what could only be described as spectres: their black bodies see-through, their red eyes piercing. They held in their hands pitchforks.

Where is the wine, women and song? he thought. *The merriment? The epitome of pleasure? All I see is death and cries of pain!* He wanted to sob. His bladder suddenly felt full.

There was a *poof* and an explosion of smoke, much like when a magician disappears. Joshua screamed and turned to face the large figure standing over him. The man, of middle-age, was well-dressed: he wore a pinstriped suit, matching tie and shoes so well polished that Joshua could see his reflection.

"Thanks for obeying your master, Joshua," the man said, a smile playing across his face.

"Who—who are you?!"

"Why, don't you recognise me?"

Joshua shook his head.

"I haven't changed since the day you sold me your soul and came to work for me."

"You—you are my Lord? Luci—"

"Tut, tut," the man said, wagging his index finger. "Let's not play these games. You know very well who I am."

"*Master!*" Joshua said, getting to his hands and knees and kissing the ground at the man's feet. "Oh, thank you for letting me serve you and for bringing me here, to your domain. I await my rewards," he grovelled.

The man laughed. "Oh, you will be treated, alright."

Joshua looked up at his Saviour. "Why is there so much pain in your pleasure kingdom, oh Dark Lord?"

The smile turned into a shit-eating grin. "Because there's only hurt here, boy," he said, pointing his talon at Joshua.

"But . . . you promised to fulfil my fantasies and dreams. You said I would want for nothing!"

"You didn't honestly believe that croc of shit, did you? Like you've been doing, I prey on the weak and feeble – I enlist the likes of you into my army of the night on promises I have no intention of fulfilling."

"Oh!" Joshua gasped. "You mean I've killed—slaughtered the innocent for . . . nothing?"

"Not entirely for nothing. You've damned your soul, and I need as many as I can to keep the hatred above ground fed. For when I have enough, I'll be able to rise and claim Earth for myself, taking my army with me to trigger Armageddon."

"Jesus, what have I done?"

The man laughed, a pitchfork appearing in his hand from nowhere.

"No!" Joshua turned on his knees to scramble away but could only yell and cry when he felt the prongs of the fork punch through the softness of his anus.

He was then lifted off the ground and thrust towards the fire like a marshmallow.

"Not in there, please. I beg you, Master!"

"I'm glad you got the 'Master' part right, because you are going to be my slave for a long time. Now for your punishment, Joshua – I mean, prize!" The man laughed and walked towards a prison cell that was dug into the walls.

When the gate opened, Joshua was thrust towards it. Inside, he saw the countless faces of the people he had killed – they held in their hands various clubbing instruments, such as baseball bats, golf clubs and hammers.

Some wore strap-ons.

"You're going to get beaten and fucked for all eternity. Isn't that one of your fantasies, you dirty boy?" the man said, removing Joshua from his fork and throwing him inside.

"*No*!" Joshua screamed. "Oh, Jesus!"

The cell door slammed shut, trapping him inside with his tormentors. When the mob engulfed him, he held onto the bars so they couldn't drag him off into the darkness and have their fun.

But it was futile.

And as his fingers let go one by one, with his newfound friends whispering sweet nothings of pain and a bleeding arsehole down his ear, Joshua cried, shit and pissed himself.

The last thing he saw before he was dragged off was the face of his master.

"Welcome home, my faithful little soldier…"

Where the Crow Flies

"**T**am, that's—*ooh*—don't stop," Brian gasped, his fingers digging into the chair's soft armrests. His naked arse caused the leather to squeak as he writhed in the seat. "You could suck a golf ball through a garden hose, babe."

Thirty-six and I'm stuck serving cheese-covered patties and fries to snot-nosed teens and obnoxious adults. And if that's not embarrassing enough, Tamra Crow thought, *I have to do it on fucking rollerblades. What type of grown woman wears skates to work?*

"*Ouch!* Little less teeth, sexy. You know I don't like biting. Fuck yeah, that's the ticket right there. Work for your promotion."

Roller-Burger was meant to be a steppingstone to something bigger. Fame and fortune were meant to be waiting for me as I left California, not grease and perverted bosses.

Tamra sank her teeth into Brian's thick, larger-than-expected prick, and smiled. She suppressed a laugh when he sucked air into his mouth and wriggled like a virgin.

"Jesus, woman, do you want to make supervisor or not? Because you can't even take simple cock-sucking instructions!"

She removed her mouth from around his pulsating bell-end and sat upright. Strings of saliva mixed with pre-come clung to her lips. She fluttered her eyes. "Sorry, Brian, I guess I got carried away when I felt your balls throb against my chin." Tamra bit her lower lip, raised her arms up, and shrugged. "It won't happen again, promise. Okay? And you know how well I can take dick-swallowing orders," she said, winking. A child-like giggle escaped her.

God, he's a fucking moron.

His eyes were narrowed and transfixed on her face, his lips pulled back and exposing teeth. "You hurt little Brian, Tam, which isn't the first occasion. You drew blood the last time, remember?"

I sure do, Mr Boss Man. I almost had me a bell-end breakfast. Would have been a small meal, mind.

"Maybe this will help." Tamra put her hands to the thin straps of her tank top, which was emblazoned with the company's logo and a lady on skates wearing a frilly apron and pink dress, and lowered them. Her pert, braless tits fell out. Her neon pink nipples stood erect.

His mouth formed a perfect O. It was the first time he'd been allowed to see her knockers.

Tamra cupped his warm, hairless balls and massaged them. "If you're good to me, then I will be the same to you, Brian. You'd like me as your second-in-command, right? Think of all the things I could do for you…" She licked her lips and laughed. "Oh, God."

With her free hand she placed her index finger on top of his sticky dick and made circular movements. "Well?"

He tried to speak, but couldn't. His body convulsed.

"*Hmm*?" she pushed, biting her lip and smiling at the way his mouth moved and twitched. A drop of sweat dripped off his nose and clung to the perspiration moustache he wore.

Brian nodded. "*Yes*!" he gasped.

"Yes what, sir? You want me as your *personal* assistant? Someone you can call on at any time of day to help relieve the...*stress*. It's *hard* at the top, I bet."

"I really, really—oh, God, Tam." His knuckles turned white and his nails tore into the armrests' soft padding. Stuffing was exposed. "D-don't stop, please." His breathing came in ragged rips and his neck clicked when he threw his head back. The veins there protruded; his nostrils flared.

She heard his teeth grind.

Fair play, he's lasting longer than the usual two minutes.

"Would you like me to continue sucking it, boss? Swallow your load, shall I?"

"I th-thought you didn't do that, Tam?"

"I'm willing to make an exception for you, sir, but on one condition, mind you."

"*Anything*!"

"I want you to fire Tracy today, and promote me, got it? If you do, all the pleasure you can imagine will be yours."

Brian's head darted forward, his cheeks flushed. His voice was a whisper. "Yes, you got it. Consider her gone. I'll even make sure you're paid a supervisor's salary starting now." His hands shot out, grabbing Tamra by her pigtails, pulling her mouth towards his flexing dick.

She gasped. "You really are a—*ugh*!" she gagged as his hard-on was forced down her throat.

Tamra took every inch like a professional. *I could swallow rapiers for fun,* she thought, taking her mind off the duty at hand as salty liquid infiltrated her mouth, bringing a tear to her eye.

Tamra had started at Roller-Burger five years ago as a waitress and had only endured blowing Brian for the past twelve months, after he became manager. When she'd first clapped eyes on the geeky, weedy-looking twenty-something-year-old, who was engaged to a woman that looked as though she could consume the burger joint in one half-arse inhale, she knew there was hope for her.

I'll ride him to the top, so to speak, she thought.

Tamra wasted no time in getting under his skin, having taken him to one side for a chat.

"Anything you need, Brian, I'm your girl," she informed him with a coy smile, her one hand twirling a pigtail, the other inching her skirt up her thigh to expose her virginal white knickers with a love heart on the front.

He was a stumbling, bumbling mess from that moment onwards. His glasses steamed up and his cheeks coloured.

"Oh, my…"

A bulge developed in his trousers.

"Ooh, is that for me?" She winked, gasping with comedic horror as a stain blighted his blue-coloured company slacks with Roller-Burger stitched across the front of the pockets.

"I—I—oh, God! Don't tell anyone—"

Tamra put her arm around the squat, podgy man who sprouted small, yet prominent, man titties. "Our secret. Pinkie promise." She offered him her little finger, which he hooked around his and smiled.

"Deal. We're going to have fun, Tamra."

The statement caught her off-guard. She'd thought Brian a shy, retiring type – someone to manipulate to get what she wanted. But he proved her wrong. A shiver glided down her back at the way he looked at her from over the top of his glasses. The tables had been turned on her so fast that Tamra didn't know her anal cavity from her pussy hole.

"And if you do tell anyone about what happened here, I'll fire your bony arse and make sure you never work in the restaurant business ever again. Hell, you'll never work in Florida!"

"I told you I—"

He was quick to take advantage. Had he known she was playing him? "I'll want you here tonight, like every night moving forward, plus weekends."

"But I'm not a super—"

"You want to learn though, right? Isn't that what your dick-teasing charade was all about?" He leaned in close. "Do you think I'm a fool?"

She shook her head, almost crying. "Can we forget—"

"Uh-uh, princess. You started this, now I plan to break you, or mould you into my best troop."

The bulge was back.

Tamra gawked as he undid his belt and lowered his fly.

"Here's your first assignment. Let's see if you can suck the purple out of this…"

From there it got worse for Tamra: long, late shifts; blowjobs and hand jobs; inappropriate looks; banter and feel-ups (which went undetected by the other staff members and Tracy, the current acting supervisor).

All Tamra had been missing was a collar and lead.

She'd become a lapdog, answering Brian's every beck and call.

When she thought about quitting, walking, but realised she had no money and nowhere to go—her only family lived in Sacramento and they wanted nothing to do with her for running away.

I was chasing a dream. I wanted to be a singer—to amass enough fame and fortune to travel the world, she thought. *I'll never see Rio, London or the Sydney Opera House...*

Her dreams, hopes and ambition wilted with her motivation.

"You'll make supervisor one day, promise," Brian told her.

But Tamra saw that as a carrot dangling before her. Still, it was enough to keep her there and compliant.

"And the big money'll come with it. I'll make you comfortable, you'll see—just as long as you keep up the good work."

The accompanying wink made her cringe.

"Oh, I'm c-c-coming!" Brian whimpered, his legs shaking. He placed his hands on the back of Tamra's head, interlaced his fingers, and thrust into her mouth hard, deep and fast.

His pumping increased in speed, his foreskin and bell-end catching on her teeth, but he didn't seem to care.

Hot come pelted the back of her throat.

"Don't you dare pull away," he snarled from behind clenched teeth.

Tamra locked her lips around the twitching organ, ensuring she captured every drop of jism that seemed never-ending in its mad, rushing, spurting pursuit.

When his dick shrivelled, Tamra pulled away and turned her face from him. Swallowing, she poked her tongue out and scrunched her eyes closed. The ejaculate tasted like last night's Chinese or pizza takeaway.

She coughed, gagged and fought the rising sick back down her throat.

"Do *not* spit or throw up, woman. You hear me? All deals are off if you do."

Turning to face him, Tamra opened her mouth to show she'd drunk his load. "See?" She wiped the stray muck from her chin and sides of her mouth. "I'm a good girl."

Her insides seemed to wither.

"Now, don't you think you should straighten yourself up and get out there? People need serving."

"Yes, of course, Brian. What about—"

"Yeah, yeah, we'll get it sorted. Just—*please*. It's busy, and you've been back here twenty minutes or so messing about."

She felt her mouth sag. Tamra wanted to smack him, to punch his fat, pimply nose and spread it across his face like a squashed tomato.

"Don't just stand there agog, get a move on." He glanced at the monitors behind his desk and saw more people entering his already crowded shop. "Quick, get out there, Tamra."

"Give me a chance, will you?" she snapped, picking her five-five frame up off the floor and drawing her multi-coloured pop socks up her legs to above the knees. When she was done, she raised her top and affixed her nametag before grabbing her tape deck and clasping it to her apron string. With the music box in place, she put the headphones on her head and made for the office door, not hearing the panicked words Brian spewed at her back as A-Ha played "Take On Me" down her ears.

"Better sort my fucking promotion out, dude," she muttered under her breath, "or I'll bite it off next time. Sick of being your mat." Tamra put her hand to the door handle, depressed it, and gave Brian a fleeting look over her shoulder.

She gasped upon seeing her naked, sweaty boss rush towards her and throw his weight against the door, trapping fingers that had hooked around it and latched on to the jamb.

"Fuck off, or I'm calling the police!" Brian yelled. "Tam, help me close this thing."

Tamra removed her headset. "What?"

"Help me, for fuck sake. Come on."

Slowly, Brian was pushed backwards, his shoeless feet slipping on the wood flooring. "Shit, I can't get purchase."

She backed away until her arse connected with Brian's desk, rocking it. A pot holding a dozen or more pencils and pens toppled, causing the contents to roll and clatter to the floor.

"What's going on?" Tamra squatted, retrieved a spilled ballpoint, and held it up like a dagger.

More fingers appeared around the ever-growing gap in the doorframe.

Filth and blood-encrusted digits snaked their way around the door and gained purchase, enabling the owners to shunt with better leverage.

"I. Can't. Hold. Them—"

Groans and moans filled Tamra's ears, drowning out the music that was seeping from the headphones. She looked around and saw on the grainy CCTV monitors that the restaurant had become overrun with people who were attacking the staff and customers alike.

Tables were destroyed.

The front windows crumpled in a shower of glass.

"Holy hell…"

"*Help*!" Brian screamed like a little girl.

When Tamra turned, she noticed a hand had latched onto Brian's privates and were tugging at them, pulling him close to the jamb.

She leapt to action, slashing with the ball-point at the meathook violating her boss.

Flesh ripped.

Blood sprayed.

When the fingers clutching Brian disengaged, Tamra turned her attention to other intruding appendages until they were able to shut and bolt the office door.

"Thank. God." He collapsed against it, spent.

"The *fuck*, man?"

"I-I don't know," Brian wheezed. "I just happened to look at the monitors and saw the violence—" His mouth hung open, his eyes focused on something over Tamra's shoulder.

"What is it?" She turned. "*What*?"

"They're *eating* people."

"You're mistaken." Tamra stepped closer to the mini TVs and bent down for a better look. "No, this can't be happening."

On the grainy screens, Tamra witnessed teenagers being pinned to tables by men and women who proceeded to tear lumps out of their targets' necks, faces, arms, legs and any other portion of flesh that was on display.

Blood splattered across the monitors, blocking her view.

Two went blank.

The pounding, clawing, groaning and snarling at the office door intensified.

"The phone," Brian blurted. "Come here and press your weight against the door, Tam. Quick."

"Are you serious? I'm a hundred and twenty-five soaking wet. I'll never keep it closed if the lock goes. Who do you want to call? I'll do it."

"Sheila."

"Your *wife*?" She shook her head. "Wouldn't the police or National Guard be a better shout?"

"I need—*argh*!" Piss trickled down Brian's thigh as the wooden door developed a split. A sliver of light seeped through. "We have to do something, fast."

Tamra snatched up the phone and heard nothing but dead air. She repeatedly tapped the pips, hoping it would do something.

Static hissed at her.

"Bollocks." She hammered the phone with the receiver until the plastic obliterated.

"What are you doing? That was our only—"

"Lines are down." Tamra began searching the office for anything that could be used as a weapon, but only spotted an umbrella. "Don't you have anything in here that we can use to defend ourselves with?"

"Check the toilet. I'm sure the workman who was here last week left a few tools behind."

The door creaked again, spitting wood shavings and opening the split further. Fingers tried squeezing through, breaking nails and shredding skin around the filthy digits.

"*Hurry*!" Tamra heard Brian scream from the other room. "It's not going to hold much longer."

Around the back of the toilet bowl, beneath the septic tank, Tamra found a hammer, wrench and screwdriver. Gathering them up, she ran back into the office and placed her newfound treasures on the table, which she shoved towards Brian.

"Good idea, Tam." When the table was close enough, Brian stepped from the door and helped Tamra get the desk tight against the sole entrance. "That should hold them, but not forever."

"We could place the filing cabinet behind the desk?"

"Yep, let's do it."

Once the cabinet was situated, the pair sat on the floor for a breather.

"Have you got food and water in here?"

Brian shook his head. "Nothing."

"We can't stay here, then."

"What do you suggest?"

"Getting outside, onto the Tampa strip, and finding help."

"No way! I'm not going out there."

"What? Why not?"

"If those crazies are in my restaurant, then you can bet your sweet ass they are on the streets."

"You don't know that, Brian."

"The police will have this shit under control soon, you'll see."

"And you're happy enough to sit here and wait for that to happen? This thing could be bigger than—"

"Look, I'm the boss." He sat bolt upright, jabbing a finger towards her face. "And I say we wait. Got it?"

She stared at his red, sweaty face.

What am I going to do? Arguing could cost me my—

The door caved in.

Men, women and children spewed through the opening. They looked sick, diseased, and some were nothing more than shambling, rotted corpses. Eyeballs dangled from sockets and strips of flesh flapped from torn faces and bodies. Jaws were nonexistent, and tongues were holding by threads.

Some of them had knives and other sharp implements jutting from their torsos and limbs.

The stench was horrendous; their noise, unbearable.

"*Argh*!" Brian yelled as the first wave of sick engulfed him. His screams turned to wet, strangled sounds.

"Fuck," Tamra muttered, bouncing to her feet and grabbing the tools.

Before she could retreat to the toilet and engage the lock, a disease-stricken man dressed as a vicar lurched towards her. His clergy collar was ripped and bloody, much like his black shirt, trousers and purple gown. The tears in his clothes exposed discoloured, ruptured skin and protruding, sickly veins that ran black. A chunk of his left cheek was missing, revealing his teeth and tongue. He swiped his hand at her face, his bent, broken fingers missing Tamra by inches.

"Stay back, man," she warned, swinging the hammer.

The huge bite mark on his forehead wept yellow-pearl-coloured liquid. His nose and right ear were missing.

Tamra gagged.

He came at her again with snapping teeth. His hand raked her hair.

"Bastard!" She clenched her jaw and pulled her lips back. Tamra brought the hammer down on the man's head with all her might, staving it in. His eyeball popped from the socket as he collapsed to the floor. He twitched a couple of times before lying still. A pool of blood fanned out beneath him.

Got to make it to the toilet.

Turning to run, Tamra was pulled to the floor by her long red hair.

She had time to yelp before a teenaged boy fell on her, ripping her top clean off and trying to bite her nipple.

Shifting her weight, Tamra dislodged the youngster. With the advantage gained, she jammed the screwdriver into the lad's ear, killing him outright. However, there was no time to retrieve the tool, as the main pack was finished with Brian and had turned their attention to her.

"Oh God, oh God, oh God—" Her heart beat so fast that she thought it was going to explode or shut down. Tamra scrabbled backwards on her bum towards the office toilet.

A legless woman crawled after Tamra, her spine trailing behind.

"Get away!" Tamra kicked out with a skated foot, smashing it through the woman's decayed face.

Another woman fell close to Tamra's feet, followed by a man.

Before they could grab her, she was through the toilet door, locking it at her back.

Her chest heaved and her shoulders hiccupped.

Tears spilt down her cheeks.

A scream lodged in her throat.

Tamra's eyes fell on the small, not-much-bigger-than-a-dog-flap window, and she went to it. Not wanting to waste time trying to open it, she put the hammer through it, stood on the pan, and ducked her head outside.

The sun had started setting over Old Tampa Bay. The streets appeared quiet.

Maybe it is only happening here, at Roller-Burger.

Pulling her head back through the window, she eyed the gap again, knowing she could squeeze through at a push.

How on earth do I get myself into such scrapes? You know what Grammy would say if she were here: 'Where the Crow flies, trouble follows.'

"She sure got that shit right."

Tamra tucked the hammer and wrench into her apron's string and proceeded to try and shove her petite frame through the diminutive gap. Shards of glass picked at her skin, hair and socks, but didn't deter her.

Almost...

Tamra failed to hear the bathroom door fold, the lock break, and screamed when a hand enclosed her ankle – nails raked her calf.

"*Argh!*" Crying, she thrust with all her might and popped out the window. Her tape deck ripped from her body, the headphones remaining on her head.

As she ran, her tits bounced, but modesty was the last thing she cared about.

"Help! Help me, please! Someone, *anyone*! Help!"

She skated through the streets and saw couples out walking in the warm evening, others strolling their dogs along the beach, and some playing Frisbee.

"Nice rack, lady," someone called.

"Whoa, mamma," said another.

"Wouldn't mind sucking on 'em bongos," the first person admitted.

"Call the fucking—"

Screams erupted from behind her.

Tamra craned her head around and spotted the sick lurching out of Roller-Burger's front windows. A lone crow flew over the restaurant. Among the horde were Tracy and Brian – their uniforms were shredded and saturated with blood. She was missing a skate; he, his privates.

Tamra could only watch as the crazies started tearing up families, men, women, children and dogs. Tables were overturned, chairs sent flying.

Go! she thought. *Skate as fast as your legs can.*

Up ahead was Coconuts—a bar where she spent most weekends getting drunk and playing pool—which seemed quiet. *If I can make it there...*

Within touching distance of Coconuts, Tamra, who was now weak and tired, failed to spot the sick young girl shamble out of the shadows and blindside her.

The collision was strong enough to knock Tamra off-kilter.

Her skated feet went in opposite directions, taking her to the ground along with the teen, who fell on her and savagely bit off Tamra's right nipple.

Dizziness set in. Vomit rushed up her throat and out her mouth, splashing the teenager's face. Before Tamra could react further, another body collapsed onto her. More pain shot through her chest as her left breast was ripped away.

She refused to roll over and die.

Tamra punched the heel of her palm into the nose of the youngster, splintering the bone, which penetrated her brain. The child slumped down, dead.

With a grunt, she rolled the girl off her, escaped the clutches of the other, and got to her feet.

Bent over, with blood spilling down her, Tamra skated towards her favourite bar with all the strength she could muster. She held her hands out in front of her.

"Help. Please…"

She slowed to a complete stop. Her body swayed and she fell into the bushes surrounding Coconuts. She convulsed like an epileptic sufferer, coughed blood and stopped breathing after a few tortuous moments.

Ten minutes later and Tamra was back on her feet, pain free. She was hungry. Her guts grumbled, and so she continued towards Coconuts.

A big man wearing a Hawaiian shirt came into view. Her mouth opened, emitting a snarl. When she was close enough, she jumped onto his back and snapped her teeth towards his exposed neck.

Lunch was served.

Worldwide Terrors

By Professional Explorer David Owain Bear-Trap Hughes IV

Hello, my aspiring, death-defying explorers! Bear-Trap here, and I have a handful of terrifying tales to tell you. Each narrative is a hundred words in length and is as true as the day is long. My jungle trekking days may long be behind me, packed away with my blunderbuss, maps and binoculars, but I'm still in the loop, and the stories you are about to embark upon are accounts told to me by survivors and witnesses. Each drabble contains the whereabouts of every Universal Monster after their escape from the studios during the great fire which freed them upon us...

A Murky Swamp in Congo, Africa

The two men sat on opposite ends of the boat, backs to each other, their fishing rods cast in the murky waters before them. They'd come in search of the legendary twenty-foot fish nicknamed Codzilla.

"Got a pull, Jason!" one man said, grabbing his rod.

The strain was great.

Out of the exploding water came a fish-like man, complete with gills, webbed fingers and green, scaly skin. It shrieked, pulling the fisherman's hook from its mouth.

"*Argh!*" Jason backed off, watching in horror as his friend was hauled from the boat and dragged to the depths below him.

Bubbles erupted...

A Steamy Shower Room in Stuttgart, Germany

The eleven members of the female hockey team Courageous Cougars entered the changing rooms whooping, applauding, high-fiving and stripping: they were champions again. Their cheering faded when they realised the showers were running—coach nowhere to be seen—and the body of a man formed via the rising steam.

The girls gasped, for the room *was* empty.

A groan filled the space. "Soap each other!" the Invisible Man demanded, grabbing his hard-on, bringing the girls' attention to his short dick.

They laughed and pointed, and when the steam cleared, he was gone.

The door to the changing room slammed shut.

A Musky Theatre in Paris, France

V ictoria hadn't wanted to play the part of Christine Daaé in Tony's armature play of *The Phantom of the Opera*. And she especially didn't want to do rehearsals at the dilapidated theatre.

"I'm a model, not an actress, Tony!" she pleaded.

"Darling, you'll be fabulous! Where's Jean, our Phantom?" Tony called from the stalls.

"*Christine*!" someone yelled.

Victoria and Tony looked, spotting a man in black slide down the curtain and land on the stage. He held Jean's head.

"Finally, I'll have my queen!" he roared, grabbing Victoria, slinging her over his shoulder and taking her to the sewers below.

A Bell-Tower in London, England

H e staggered towards home—the whisky he'd consumed swished around inside his head. He ripped a piece of paper from off his door. "What's this?" he muttered, belching. Focusing his eyes, he read aloud: "Notice of eviction." His body swayed.

"Sorry, Quasi. I don't mean to give you the hump and shunt, but you're four months behind on your rent, mate."

"B—but! I lost my job at the freak show and—"

"Away, you fucking question mark. Before I set the dogs on ya!"

Quasi let the paper flutter from his hand as he stumbled off into the distance.

A Dog Pound in Hanoi, Vietnam

He played a melancholic tune on his harmonica and took to raking the drinking bowl along the bars to the cage he'd awoken in. A dog collar wrapped his neck; the tag read Bubbles.

"If ever there was a case of mistaken identity, this is it," he sang. The canines around him howled and whined as he drawled. "Don't worry, fellas – I'll spring us! We won't be *anyone's* dog meat." He looked up at the darkening skies and felt a change.

A full moon appeared.

His body expanded, sprouting hair and talons. The bars buckled and exploded.

Free, he howled.

A Beach in Florida, USA

"Loosen your bolts, Frank!" The Count said. He wore aviators and Speedos; his emaciated body soaked up the rays. Turning, he looked at his monstrous friend, who hadn't even removed his boots.

"You know I get sand in my stitches," Frank pouted, twiddling with a button on his jacket.

"Would you rather be at the studio, or here, perving on your wife?" He peered over the tops of his shades.

"Which one of you sexy boys is going to oil me?" she asked, removing her bra to reveal scar-covered tits.

"If I had blood in me, I'd take your virginity!"

A Billionaires' Black Marketplace in Rome, Italy

Rocking woke him. "Can't a guy get five minutes peace?! What—*ugh*!" A vicious thud threw him from side to side.

He heard a muffled voice.

"This beautiful artefact was retrieved from a pyramid in Egypt…Who'll give me ten million?"

The fuck…?! He pushed the heavy lid from his casket.

The crowd before him gasped and screamed. Most fled, but tourists with cameras stayed when he stepped into the sun. His eight-foot-ten, four-hundred pound mass made the ground quake. His yellowed bandages flapped. "Who dares wake the great Mummy Ali?" he roared, twisting off the head of the person closest.

Top Bunk

Toby stared up at the underside of the mattress, his nightlight illuminating it. The top bunk was only ever used for sleepovers.

"Have you been scratching yourself in your sleep again, son?" his dad asked.

"No. The burned boy did it. He lives in my bed."

Dad laughed at his childishness.

The springs above creaked.

Toby clutched his teddy bear and closed his eyes.

"Toby…" the scratchy voice called.

"No!" He looked, seeing the upside-down, chargrilled face of the boy above, his charcoaled hand reaching, his gnarled fingers searching.

"I'll take your soul to be a little boy again, Toby…"

The Restaurant:

Kick-Ass Kate the Waitress

Kate stood before the mirror, huffing. The morning had been testing, starting with her realising she'd put her knickers on back to front. Then, the first customer had left without their wheelchair, followed by a man who'd been grabby.

She looked at the scratches on her arm.

"*Bastard*!" She winced, swabbing them.

Nausea washed over her, taking with it her rage – blood trickled out of her nose, and vomit rushed out of her mouth. The cramps in her stomach were unrelenting, bringing with it an unslakable thirst for flesh.

She shambled out of the toilets, screeching, in search of prey…

Luscious Lucie the Kitchen Cleaner

"Lucie was scrubbing gunk off the kitchen floor when the screaming began.

"The *fuck*?!" Throwing her rag aside, she got up, walking into the restaurant to find Kate, her life-long friend and tequila-slamming partner, ripping the tongue out of a customer.

Squelching, slurping, chewing sounds ensued.

Blood jettisoned, catching in the rotating ceiling fan, which spread it like fertilizer.

"*Kate*!" Lucie yanked her friend off the man. "What the—*argh*?!"

Teeth clamped down on the fleshy part in between Lucie's thumb and forefinger, and she retreated. Within seconds, she was vomiting. Stomach cramps crippled her. The change took her over…

Charismatic Chris the Barman

Chris approached the restaurant, ready to start his shift with a song in his heart and a spring in his step, for he'd spent the previous evening with an energetic cougar.

The smile slipped from his face when he saw blood splash up the windows.

People fled the building screaming.

Chris put his hands up, ever the diplomat, to try and calm the stampeding crowd.

"Remain—*ugh!*"

Shoved off-kilter, Chris' legs tangled and he crashed over an outside table. Before he could stand, a weight descended on his back, and two sets of teeth worked at his neck and shoulder…

Annihilation

Luscious Lucie, Kick-Ass Kate, Charismatic Chris and Tongueless Customer, along with a forming horde of nameless, drooling, bleeding people, shuffled onto the retail park.

They parted ways, attacking, devouring and spreading their infection to everyone and everything in their path.

The police were called in, swiftly supported by the National Guard, as the situation spiralled out of control.

Hospitals filled up.

The dead started outweighing the living, and the minuscule amount of survivors formed camps, drawing lines in the sand and protecting what was theirs with extreme measures.

It was the end of the world— civilisation—as we knew it…

Worldwide Terrors II

By Professional Explorer David Owain Bear-Trap Hughes IV

Hello, and welcome back, my risk-taking, monster-dodging explorers! Bear-Trap here, with another batch of mind-shattering tales; and, just like the last lot, each narrative is a hundred words in length and is as true as the day is long. Now, my globe-trotting, sea-conquering and desert days are long gone, packed away with my compass and nautical gear, but I'm still in the loop, and the following stories are accounts told to me by survivors and witnesses. These drabbles contain the whereabouts of infamous monsters such as zombies, Jekyll and Hyde, Dorian Grey, the Headless Horseman, Cerberus, Yeti, and the Kraken.

A Random Street in Helsinki, Finland

The children rejoiced, for there was no school – the intense, snowy weather had brought the heating system to a standstill.

The aged complained of it being the fiercest winter they'd ever experienced.

However, it didn't stop the young, who wore impenetrable clothes. They slid their sleds, played in the drifts and built snowmen.

When the white, ten-foot-eight, six-hundred-pound mass of standing ape appeared, they froze. Yet, it was friendly—foxing them. It tossed snowballs, lightly—until the children retaliated, catching the abominable beast in its maw. It then hurled the hard-compacted balls of white with speed and force.

Heads rolled.

A Doorway in Toronto, Canada

Kristen Green, the kinky kiss-o-gram queen, stood before her customer's front door freshening her lippy. Finished, she plucked the photo of her favourite author from her cleavage and kissed it.

Happy, she replaced the image and looked down at herself. She wore a body-hugging Basque, fishnets, high-heels, rabbit ears and a fluffy tail.

She knocked on the door, pleased with how sexy she looked.

Locks disengaged.

She started singing.

The door opened.

She screamed as a zombie wearing a birthday hat lurched towards her. It clamped its teeth around her throat, ripping her voice-box out.

She fled the scene, croaking.

An Underground Race Course in Melbourne, Australia

The shady-looking punters were eager for the next race to start, their betting slips grasped tightly—did anyone but the house *ever* win?

Down on the track, fresh racers loaded into the starting gates, the course cleared of headless bodies.

A bell rang.

"And they're away!" a man yelled over the Tannoy.

The brightly dressed jockeys thundered down the track on their horses and looked behind as they went.

The crowd held its breath.

A second bell dinged, and the Headless Horseman was released, his sabre drawn.

Would a jockey finish, or would the soldier of yesteryear decapitate them too?

A School in Glasgow, Scotland

Mr Jekyll walked into his newly appointed class and sighed, for the children were unruly. They threw paper airplanes, clambered over their desks, drew on the walls and used the Bunsen burners like toys. When he tried to settle them, they laughed at him, and so he gave them detention.

Mr Hyde growled as he swaggered into the classroom detaining the misbehaving students. They immediately settled when they saw the demented appearance on his face, but there was one loudmouthed lad who thought he was above the law . . . until Hyde ripped his arms off to make an example of him.

A Tourist Attraction in Tenby, Wales

He brought the crowd to a halt in front of an open cave. Nearby, waves crashed against the rocks and beach.

"This, ladies and gentlemen, *was* the home of the infamous Bartholomew 'Black Bart' Roberts, the most successful pirate of the golden age . . ."

"Typical Welshman," someone said.

The others tittered.

A woman screamed, pointing. "*Look*!"

Out of the water burst a gigantic squid, a skeleton dressed in raggedy buccaneer garb riding it with sword and pistol drawn. It fired on the crowd, wounding and killing, as the Kraken swiped with its tentacles, crushing and hurling people into the raging seas . . .

In A Queue Outside A Sex Club in Prague, Czech Republic

The well-groomed, Adonis-like man stood in line surrounded by people wearing S&M gear. It titillated him. *I wonder if any of these studs would like to see my painting,* he thought.

"*Next!*" a burly bouncer called. "Invite. Name?"

The man held his invitation out. "Dorian Grey."

"It says *Christian* Grey on—"

"*Pft*! I'm a finer shade of grey!" He winked. "The invite was meant for me, I'm sure, and I'm told this is the place to party. Step aside, my good man."

"Look, *pal*, if you're not on—"

Dorian stabbed the man twice, pushed him aside, and entered.

A Safe House in Spain, Barcelona

He wasn't just a wanted man but rather a dead one walking, and had spent most of his time in hiding since completing his labours. The years hadn't been kind. He'd developed a beer gut, bitch tits and a bald spot. His muscles sagged, his looks gone.

His doorbell rang.

"Finally, the dog walker!" He opened the door. His jaw dropped.

Before him stood Medusa, her hair hissing and spitting. On a chain, sitting by her side, was Cerberus.

"It's been a while, Hercules. Ready for your thirteenth task? The odds say you won't beat us this time. Feeling strong?"

Virtual Reality

Danny's hands ripped at the bright birthday paper like a zombie at flesh.

"Hell yeah, King Kong." His pre-pubescent voice cracked.

He lifted the flap to his VR system, slid the game in and hit play. His TV exploded to life with colour and sound. A gorilla roared, beating its chest.

"This is going to be killer."

The television turned off, the game console's door flew open, and the game was spat out, hitting Danny in the face. The boy's eyes widened when a huge, flaming barrel squeezed out of his system and hurtled towards him.

"Fuck. This is…"

Virtual Reality Games Inc.

"Not happening," the CEO of Virtual Reality Games Inc., Dennis Chambers, said, addressing the press who'd gathered outside his building alongside an angry mob of parents. "Our games are not—I repeat, are *not*—killing children."

"Then how do you explain what's been happening?" a journalist pressed.

Dennis held his hands up. "All—"

"Oh, God!" a female from the crowd yelled. "Look! On the building." Screams erupted from the crowd. A stampede ensued.

Dennis turned to see enormous monsters and animals scaling his office block, causing destruction. Huge moths and bats circled overhead; one swooped for Dennis.

"Shit. We're…"

Game Over

"All fucked!" Carol Oats screamed. "I'm getting out while I can." The always serene anchorwoman rose from her seat but leaned back to the camera. "I suggest you do the same, people."

Outside, Carol froze: massive praying mantises, tarantulas and ants roamed the streets, killing and devouring people. Buildings lay in rumpled, smoking piles. Her city was ruined, much like others in the world thanks to VRG Inc.

"Get to the c—"

A colossal stinger punched through her, hoisting Carol off the floor and into the scorpion's pincers. She was pulled apart, dying before her guts hit the pavement.

Dancing

"Girls, stop arguing and biting each other!"

"Bitch drew blood, Dougie."

"I don't care. Get on that *fucking*

stage, Dallas." The fat boss snapped his fingers. "Time's money."

Dallas stumbled through the beaded entryway, collapsing against the runway's pole. She felt sick, but managed to gyrate her semi-naked body. Music played.

"Over here, baby!" a guy called, waving a fistful of singles.

She sauntered towards him, hair covering her face.

"Get 'em titties—"

She flew at him with vacant eyes, mouth open. Her teeth latched onto his throat, and she ripped his jugular apart, drinking the hot, squirting blood.

Cut Down to Size

Patrick rolled the cutter from his garage and eyed his overgrown lawn.

"We'll sort it, baby," he said, stroking his lawnmower.

Plugging his Flymo in, Patrick began.

Over the noise, Patrick thought he heard screaming, much like the last time he'd been mowing. Dismissing it, he carried on until he was done and holding a beer.

Whilst admiring his handiwork, the blades of grass started rumbling and moving together like chainsaw teeth. Patrick screamed as his feet burst into clouds of liquid, and he slowly sank into the ground as though he was being fed into a waste disposal unit.

About Your Author

David Owain Hughes is a horror freak! He grew up on ninja, pirate and horror movies from the age of five, which helped rapidly instil in him a vivid imagination. When he grows up, he wishes to be a serial killer with a part-time job in women's lingerie…He's had multiple short stories published in various online magazines and anthologies, along with articles, reviews and interviews. He's written for This Is Horror, Blood Magazine, and Horror Geeks Magazine. He's the author of the popular novels "Walled In" (2014), "Wind-Up Toy" (2016), "Man-Eating Fucks" (2016), and "The Rack & Cue" (2017) along with his short story collections "White Walls and Straitjackets" (2015) and "Choice Cuts" (2015). He's also written three novellas – "Granville" (2016), "Wind-Up Toy: Broken Plaything & Chaos Rising" (2016).

www.hellboundbookspublishing.com/authorpage_hughes.html

www.facebook.com/DOHughesAuthor/?ref=hl

http://david-owain-hughes.wix.com/horrorwriter

twitter.com/DOHUGHES32

Other HellBound Books Titles
Available at: www.hellboundbookspublishing.com

Puckered

Percy is kinky.
Percy is perverted.
Percy is a loner.
Percy is sneaky…

…But most of all, Percy wants to be left alone.

Whether it be a nagging mother or something from his past, it feels like he is always trying to escape something. Will he be able to find his own peace, or will the real world catch up to him?

There will be blood.
There will be s**t.
There will be unusual sexual kinks.
But most of all, there will be murder…

Psychological Breakdown

By
David Owain Hughes

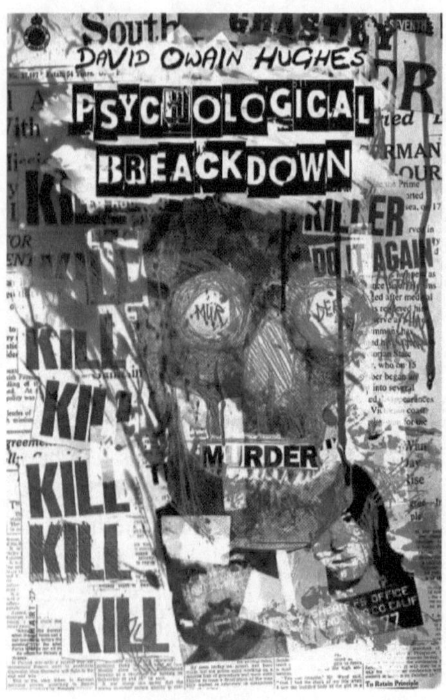

Within this tome lies eighteen tales of mind-bending terror, as Hughes delves into the human psyche and dishes out stories of what becomes of the broken minded, spirited and downright irked.

Part these blood-drenched pages at your own peril, for you will find diseased minds geared towards revenge and bloody chaos, with a few twists, turns and surprises thrown in for good, fucked-up measures.

Keep the lights on!

Man Eating F*cks

A dark, incredibly entertaining excursion into the delightfully twisted imagination of David Owain Hughes....

An average teenage girl and her father find themselves caught up in a brutal nightmare at their local recreational centre, when an age-old enemy comes stumbling out of the woods to crash a heavy-metal gig; a gig that has all the promises of being killer. This is one blood-soaked gig you won't want to miss!

Praise for Man-Eating F*cks from Ty Schwamberger (author of The Fields, Deep Dark Woods & The Death of a Horror Writer.)   "Man Eating F*cks is old school horror, but with a new, blood-soaked twist! David Owain Hughes effectively creates enjoyable and lethal characters in this tale that is sure to keep you up at night. This is the type of tale that you need to read with a light on…I'm serious. You better put your seatbelt on 'cause you're in for one helluva ride. Look out, Hughes might very well be headed to the major leagues after this twisted tale! Highly recommended!"

<u>**Man Eating F**kers**</u>

The eagerly awaited sequel to Hughes' critically acclaimed *Man Eating Fks...***

Two years on from her nightmarish descent into the woods, Storm is piecing her life back together, but trouble is forming...

A new threat is rising - one that promises to grip, shake and spin Storm's world out of control. But that's not all, as a 'friend' and sympathizer also poses a risk from the shadows, combined with a face from the past...

With the cannibals lurking in the background, waiting for an opportunity to deal white-hot vengeance, can father and daughter survive?

**** Features a bonus, previously unpublished short story by David Owain Hughes****

Cold Cocked

Another exemplary bizarro novella from the great and incredibly disturbed minds behind 'Puckered'!

Betty is sexy.
Betty is scarred.
Betty is an outsider.
Betty is a genius…

…But most of all, Betty wants recognition.

Whether it be a controlling mother or ghosts from her past, it feels like she is always trying to please someone. Will she be able to find her own peace, or will the real world catch up to her?

There will be blood.
There will be j**z.
There will be unusual sexual releases.

But most of all, there will be murder…

Schlock! Horror!

An anthology of short stories based upon/inspired by and in loving homage to all of those great gorefest movies and books of the 1980's (not necessarily base in that era, although some do ride that wave of nostalgia!), the golden age when horror well and truly came kicking, screaming and spraying blood, gore & body parts out from the shadows...

It was the decade that brought us everything in the cinema and on VHS from the Italian 'nasties' to *Elm Street, The Lost Boys, Hellraiser, The Thing, Day of the Dead, Reanimator, Return of the Living Dead, My Bloody Valentine, Henry: Portrait of a Serial Killer, Cannibal Holocaust*....and superlative directors such as David Cronenburg, John Waters, Roger Corman and - of course - Clive Barker.

All of this was, naturally, reflected in the books we devoured - Guy N Smith, Clive Barker's *Books of Blood*, James Herbert, Jack Ketchum, Gary Brandner and Richard Laymon, to name but a mere handful.

This exemplary 80's themed/inspired tales of terror has been adjudicated and compiled by one Mr. **Bret McCormick**, himself a writer, producer and director of many a schlock classic, including *Bio-Tech Warrior, Time Tracers, The Abomination, Ozone: The Attack of the Redneck Mutants* and the inimitable *Repligator*.

Shopping List 2: Another Horror Anthology

Once again, HellBound Books brings you an outstanding collection of horror, dark, slippery things, and supernatural terror - all from the very best up and coming minds in the genre.

We have given each and every one of our authors the opportunity to have their shopping lists read by you, the most wonderful reading public, and have the darkest corners of their creative psyche laid bare for all to see...

In all, 21 stories to chill the soul, tingle the spine and keep you awake in the cold, murky hours of the night from: Erin Lee, The Truth Artist, John Barackman, Serena Daniels, M.R. Wallace, Isobel Blackthorn, Alex Laybourne, Jason J. Nugent, Josh Darling, Jovan Jones, Nick Swain, Douglas Ford, Craig Bullock, Craig Bullock, Jeff C. Stevenson, PC3, David F Gray, Sergio Palumbo, Donna Maria McCarthy, David Clark & Megan E. Morales

David Owain Hughes

**A HellBound Books LLC
Publication**

http://www.hellboundbookspublishing.com

Printed in the United States of America

www.ingramcontent.com/pod-product-compliance
Lightning Source LLC
Chambersburg PA
CBHW030552170726
48283CB00002B/295